I0762293

THE

DARKNESS

WITHIN

THOMAS RAI

The Darkness Within

Published by Sora Press

Cover & Interior Design by Sora Press

Cover Image by Aleshyn Andrei/Shutterstock.com

This book is a work of fiction. Names, characters, businesses, organisations, places, events and incidents either are the product of the author's imagination or are used fictitiously. Any resemblance to actual persons, living or dead, events, or locales is entirely coincidental.

ISBN:

978-1-9161171-2-9

First Edition: 2019

10 9 8 7 6 5 4 3 2 1

CONTENTS

PROLOGUE

27th Hour of the 18th Day of the 14th Month
IY (Imperial Year) 101

This will probably be my last entry in this diary, being of my own mind and consciousness. Soon it will be the day I have been training for. It's been over 40 cycles since I started training. As expected, the council will be there, during the rite of Tasir.

Carila asked me whether I was frightened. I said no, lying to myself as usual, I'm afraid, make that terrified. Everything changes now, no longer myself, but one of the most influential people in the empire, except for his excellence.

All our people will hear my words, from the Winter Castle in Ajinar to the Coast of the Sea of Silence at Whitefall, and that is just here, off-world there will be more, billions more. Carila told me that over 800 billion would hear my address to parliament and the Emperor. Numarii would be proud, wouldn't she?

I mean, I have been trained well, haven't I? Am I afraid of what this means for me, of course; my life as I know it, is over.
They believe in me, which is good for me I suppose. But it's so different here, I feel lost and out of place, sometimes my thoughts bring me down, back to those dark places, but there are things that remind me of home, and that lightens my spirits. They have assigned Rako Alik as my aide, temporarily until the ceremony is complete. I must thank the Reverend Mother for sending him. His innocence will allow me to see this differently

than I would normally. Being quite the cynic has gotten me into trouble before. If they made the pages in this diary public, it would be a story to end all stories.

These 40 years have been tough, but I've been preparing for this. The tests, the psychological tests, the emotional tests, some of which I would want to forget. The etiquette, everything. I've read so many reports, historical documents, lessons in strategy and codes of practice. I feel like a walking book of Imperial law. Hopefully, everything they taught me will be useful.

I mean, these voices, all 47 of them. Previous Codex, keepers of the rules, and attaché to the emperor whoever that might be. His excellence hasn't been well for a while. Since losing his Highness Prince Vsalnes in the accident at Kalas. I hope his strength returns and I can be of use to him.

Maybe for the first time in over 100 generations, an empress will rule our empire. Not since the early days of the empire has such an event occurred, and I welcome it, a change occasionally is good. Some others argue this point why do they do such disloyal things. Whoever rules the empire is divine, and we are not to judge. But his highness has made no proclamation about his heir. Either of his remaining children would hopefully follow their fathers' example.

As usual I digress if my emotions and thoughts can be this erratic now. Then 47 sets of emotions and thoughts shall be tough to control at first. Even when we first tried sharing the emotions of just a few of the group, there was trouble for some. I pulled through it, didn't I?. I'm sure Numarii would have been better at this, she's the one who should be here. It was never my choice.

I must pull through it; there has never been a break in the position. I will not disgrace over 35,000 years of our history and trust by the people and the emperor by failing to do my duty.

As I have said, a thousand times before, in the 40 years in the cloisters. "I by a solemn vow, swear to uphold the duty of Commissioner of the Codex. To serve and protect the interest of the empire, in all manners. To protect the empire from tyranny and guard the future of our people."

Father would be proud of me. Mother hasn't spoken about him since his passing, saying it would interfere with my status. But, maybe I need this, some closure, not knowing what happened fully, I need time to grieve, it might ease my mind, maybe not, it might send me spiralling into the darkness Numarii mentioned before the end, Only time will tell whether I'm ready to do this...

I'm lucky to have had Carila here with me, she always calms me down. I don't know why she puts up with my temper, she's always been here for me, no matter what happens. Even when I've been angry, she always listens, I don't know what I would have done without her.

Had a surprise during the gala, Master Baelin was here, I mean he's here on Prim. I didn't expect to see him. It was the surprise I needed. A familiar sight, some reassurance. He always had a way of calming me down, that's probably because he listens I've not seen him in many cycles, not since father's death. The Council of Twelve have requested to see me, brings back old memories, I don't want to remember about that time in my life, not again, but I cannot turn down the council, it would ruin the family, I won't let that happen.

Wish me luck..

-Reira -

CHAPTER 1

Ateki Province
Aaelonia IV
18th Hour of the 23rd Day of the 7th Month
IY (Imperial Year) 101

It was the late afternoon; the shadows were elongated versions of themselves, growing longer as the afternoon gradually turned into evening. Along the black sand dunes of Ateki, a figure scrambled across an immense dune, it's feet sinking slightly into the hot sand, breathless it ran down a huge dune, before turning and looking over its shoulder for an instant then turning back and struggling up the next dune, onto a rugged stone outcrop.

Making its way towards the red glow of the setting sun, haze emanating from the sand in the heat. Quickly the figure dived and was motionless for a moment before it turned around. Before huddling in the shadows which were gradually growing in this late hour.

The figures breath slowed from a rapid succession of breaths to a more conservative one. The sound of its breathing masked by the howling winds whipping across the dunes. It raised an arm to its masked face and slowly pulled the mask away. Releasing air gradually from the automated breathing apparatus.

Beneath the outer mask, it revealed a set of bright amber eyes. A small amount of almost porcelain perfect white skin peeked out from under the mask. The rest of the head still covered by a red silk-like material draped over the head. A wisp of her silvery grey hair had found its way from under the headscarf. She flung the mask over her shoulder. Her athletic body covered in a figure-hugging grey woven bodysuit. Stained with a dark blue substance, finally the second internal mask was removed, this mask less intricate than the first, it was semitransparent, acting a more of a face guard than for protection.

Finally, the figure could breathe naturally. She was young, tall, her nose small, and elegant. Her expression was blank, but her eyes contained a look of pain and anguish. She raised her other arm and clutched in her hand was a small blade. It was covered in both a white and a dark blue, almost black substance, with her free hand she wiped a small fraction of the substance away. Revealing a dark red multiple striped tattoo around her wrist. She again tried to wipe the substance away before she winced, the pain overwhelming her senses, unable to hide the pain.

"Forgot about that..." she hissed, dropping the blade onto the rocky surface, with a clatter. Her hand quickly rushing to her right side. Grabbing hold on her body, pressing hard into the area before releasing again, Her clothing clinging to her body, she dabbed the area with her hand and looked at her fingers. A pearly white substance covered her fingers.

"I knew you got me this time, deeper than I expected though..." she thought as the pain coursed through her body, her brow drawing beads of sweat.

She turned and pulled a small vial from her belt. It suspended the small vial from an intricate silver canister, her nimble fingers flicked the canister over and pressed a small red button. A syringe quickly descended, glistening in the light. With the flick of the wrist she inserted the vial into the canister. Then pulled the canister closer to the now bleeding wound on her side before plunging the needle into the wound. With a hiss the contents of the vial emptied into the wound, the let go of the canister, dropping it onto the sand.

She grimaced in pain as the contents got to work. The chemical working its way through her veins as it traveled across her body. She convulsed, the convulsions becoming progressively worse as the contents surged throughout her body. The convulsions came to a head as she violently convulsed on the sand before gradually subsiding.

"Reira, why do you do this to yourself" she cursed. Biting down on her lip, causing it to bleed. Her eyes rolled back so only the whites of her eyes could be seen before blacking out.

It was now night; they plunged the desert into a cold darkness, a faint mist rolled out of the canyons before being swept away by the winds.

The rocky outcrop disappeared. replaced by a shifting dune, darkness had fallen and the light of the moon shone across the black sand. The severe winds were gone, silence permeated the air, finally the Ateki desert was at peace. The rising sun in a few hours would stir the winds again, bringing chaos back to the dunes.

A hand bursting through its depths ended the stillness in the dunes, fist clenched. Followed by the rest of her body, she panted, her breathing deep and laboured,

"I mean First the Xanti wanted to kill me, then a sandstorm to deal with, but now the sand wants to suffocate me as well..." she hissed, as she struggled to release herself from the sands grasp. It laboured her breathing, it was rough and shallow.

She slowly pulled herself out of the sand, struggling as the sand gave way as she tried to lift herself out of its grasp. She released herself before digging her hand back into its depths. Pulling out both of the face masks, the knife, and a small pouch, the sand pouring off them slowly.

In the moonlight, she opened the small leather pouch. Inside an orb of dark blue glistened, breaking the darkness within the pouch, it almost glowed before she closed the pouch again, keeping the orb away from potential predators.

She staggered to her feet, which sank slowly into the desert sand. Before carefully making her way down the dune. Occasionally looking over her shoulder she descended the dune. Leaving footprints in the dark sand behind her. Wincing slightly as the wound on her side hadn't completely healed. She shifted her weight onto her right side to ease her pain. The winds quickly eroding the footprints within moments of them being created.

"Time to go...", she reassured herself, as she descended a dune, her feet sinking into the sand.

As she traveled down the dune, the wind picked up. Causing small sand devils to appear for a few seconds before dissipating, She looked into the distance. The lights of a city could be seen glistening like a precious stone hiding amongst the sand. She looked up, dark storm clouds were making their way towards the city. It wouldn't be long before the rains would begin.

"I better get back before the rains begin, 'goddess give me strength'" she murmured to herself.

"Home..." she whispered looking into the distance. She paused, her breathing slowed, she tilted her head slightly. Seeming to listen to the wind, occasionally catching a rhythmic thud carried on the wind.

She began the decent down the massive dune, the sand sinking and shifting beneath her weight, each time she moved the pressure applied to her injury caused her to wince.

After hours of walking through the dunes towards home she stumbled, sending her spiralling down a dune, as she tumbled she struck a rock partially hidden in the sand. The impact knocking her out, blood poured from a small wound on her head, her breathing was shallow.

She did not move. The hours passed - the occasional desert mammal scurried up towards her. Sniffed around before scurrying back into hiding. The Hawks circled in the sky, cawing at each other. Discussing the eventual demise of the figure below them.

The sun beat down on her. Her energy levels were so low that even shielding herself from the sun was too much of a strain. The faint breeze stirred up the sand, blasting it into Reira's face. The sand so sharp and coarse that it caused to bleed. The blood running down her cheek before falling into the sand.

She shocked herself as she awoke from the impact, her mouth dry from the heat, she opened her eyes, realising she was lying on the sand with her face turned to the side, she could faintly see the rock that had knocked her out. She struggled to move, her energy levels were already low, and this accident had taken what energy reserves she had, the immense heat sapped any remaining energy.

"Perhaps, this is the end..." she whispered, her voice trailing off at the end.

"Shame, if this is the way I go, ...I had so much more to offer..." she grunted as she turned herself over, now her face looked straight up, her eyes closed slowly as she passed into unconsciousness.

CHAPTER 2

A Day Earlier, Across the Desert

Temple of the Enlightened Flame
Ateki Province
Aaelonia IV

A myriad of golden beads jangled to the rhythm of a mounting beat.

A young man stood in the darkness, he stood shaking rhythmically. Multiple chains of beads were attached to a sceptre, with every occasional beat of the drums he shook it. The beads clashing together with every movement. The air was thick with incense, every shake of the sceptre, causing the incense to swirl before mixing again with the dusty air of the temple.

He stood looking at an enormous fire pit. The wood within the pit, crackling and occasionally spitting, sending small embers floating into the air. The flames illuminated his light blue eyes. The skin on his face seemed to gleam like bronze. A white satin line that was smeared down both of his cheeks broke this bronze gleam. From his eyes to his jawline. His dark red robes, seemed almost black in the darkness. Only the occasional flare of the fire revealed their true colour. Before sending them quickly back into the darkness

The rest of the Temple hall was unlit, only the rising flames cast light onto its walls. Occasionally revealing intricately engraved scripture. Eight large drums stood in semi-darkness;

their drummers cast completely into the darkness. The beat of the drums seemed to dance between bass filled and a lighter more melodic cadence. The smokey haze of burnt incense drifted across the space between the floors of the temple. Its scent delicate and addictive.

The figure walked around the fire. The temple hall, was an impressive sight, a massive structure. With magnificent views out of its windows on the higher levels. Views of the city below were breathtaking. Especially at night, with the sky clear a brilliant view of the stars could be seen.

The temple was a masterpiece of construction. Minimalist but conveying a singular message "From the Flame Everything Comes, and everything shall return." It was decorated with statues of the twin goddesses of life and death and their three triplet children. The walls were decorated with inscriptions of key text from scripture. Carefully placed alcoves allowed to someone to sit inside the alcove and meditate. The alcoves were dark, the fire casting enough light into them.

One solemn figure dressed in a long white dress appeared out of the darkness. She stood in the light which shone onto the mezzanine. Her face half painted white, and half painted black. The flames flaring up enough that her completely white eyes could be seen. She seemed to whispering speaking. The crackle of the fire and the changing beat of the drums drowning out any chance of hearing what she was saying.

The beat stopped as he raised his hands into the air. Punching the air above him, the drummers relaxed their arms and put down their batons. The figure eventually sighed.

He turned away from the fire pit, into the darkness, "Nidiri..." he lamented, his voice breaking as he spoke.

"May the goddess find it in her ways to bring you back to us..." he rasped.

He tried to hide the emotions from his face, his face etched with sadness, he tried to hide this by shaking his head trying to clear head. His shoulders dropped to his sides, in defeat, he would not take this, he clenched his fist before he sighed again, turning back towards the flames that were rising eight feet into the air.

His expression changing from sombre to powerful and commanding.

"Now this time" he declared, his voice echoing across the hall before dissipating into the darkness.

"I want the sound of these drums to be heard all the way across the empire, even to Prim, maybe then the goddess will be able to bring our beloved Sister back to the temple safe..." he preached. The power and conviction in his voice, rallying the drummers.

Each of the drummers picked up their batons. Looking at each other from their position on the mezzanine. Then turning to look at the figure again.

"Your Eminence" one drummer spoke. breaking the silence that permeated the great hall.

"We want to perform the rite of the returning warrior, hopefully, this will guide our Sister home..." he gushed, his enthusiasm making the other drummers snigger.

"So be it..." the figure announced. His voice becoming booming and echoing throughout the darkness of the Temple.

"I, Zamir. High Priest of the Order of Ehji-Ha. Wish to offer the rite of the Returning Warrior to our Sister, Nidiri Reira Abrasar. May the Goddesses Idara and Ishara (Goddesses of Life and Death). Find it within their means to help her return home." He implored, as he spoke a ring of green fire littered with arcane symbols encircled where he stood, appearing out of nowhere.

As he finished, the drums began beating. with even more emotion than before. He quietly mumbled an incantation as the beat travelled out of the Temple throughout the surrounding city., cascading off the walls of the surrounding buildings.

A young man walking through the partially lit street stopped in his tracks. Listened to the pounding of the drums for a few seconds. Then looked into the sky and whispered:

"In her name, Bring them home." He commanded as he placed his index, and middles fingers of both hands on his forehead. Then gestured them towards the sky. Before continuing to walk down the empty street before disappearing into a dimly lit bar.

Inside a small building, a baker was busy working with dough. Kneading it with his large hands, making easy work of kneading the dough. The kitchen was lit by the fire of the bread oven. The sound of the drums reached the bakery echoing throughout its walls. The baker immediately stopped what he was doing. He placed the dough down on the work surface before reaching across the table. grabbing a small pinch of what looked like a dark blue flour and flung it over his right shoulder.

"In her name, bring them home" he bellowed, before

kneading the dough again.

Throughout the small town, people who heard the beat of the drums stopped what they were doing. Performing their own small religious or traditional gesture before reciting.

"In her name, bring them home." Before continuing with their own lives, the winding streets of the town lead up to the Temple. The temple gate walls casting shadows across the buildings on the other side of the wall.

* * *

A day earlier.

8th Hour of the 21st Day of the 7th Month
IY (Imperial Year) 101

The shadows in the desert had almost disappeared. Making this place even more desolate. The eastern desert of Ateki was vast, it spread out for thousands of miles in almost all directions. Life in this environment was difficult and sparse. Most life could be found in the canyons and ravines, which were a few days travel from the closest outpost.

Huge Atarian Hawks soared high in the sky to find their next meal. Reira looked up, raising her hand to shield her eyes. Watching the hawks circling a recent kill, or death of a desert inhabitant. Life out in the desert was hard. Almost impossible. There was sparse vegetation, which had adapted to the desert environment.

Subterranean water that occasionally bubbled up to the

surface from the vast network of underground streams which crisscrossed the planet, but didn't last for very long. Sometimes drying the instant is settled on the surface. Fierce winds made life even harder, the winds would whip the sand and cause immense sand storms, the summer storms would even plunge the outposts into total darkness. The shifting sand showed the cracked and lifeless soil below before being recovered by the winds. Life here on Ateki was hard, a miracle in anyone's mind.

A trail of huge footprints danced across the sand, followed by a smaller set of identical tracks.

Reira lay on the sand at the top of a dune, downwind, watching and waiting. Moments later they appeared across a dune, like a mirage. Their white coats reflecting the 140-degree midday heat, They stood over a meter tall, its huge but slender body created for destruction. it's spine armour plated and it at the end of its tail a massive barbed blade.

Reira finally smiled to herself after spotting her,

"Wow, you are a big girl...but where is your offspring." Reira whispered to herself after realising the size of her intended target. Reira kept her head low, watching the Xanti wander its way across the dunes, followed by its offspring minutes later, walking the same track as its parent.

Reira had tracked the mother and offspring into a small recess in the desert, possibly its den, Reira kept herself as far away as she could downwind from them, if the mother had caught the smell of her, it would be all over. Moments later the mother reappeared out of the den, but wasn't followed by the offspring. This would be Reira's only chance.

Hours had passed, Reira had been tracking the beast through the dunes, and towards the canyons, Reira knew exactly what was going on, was she following the beast into the canyons or was the beast driving her into somewhere where it knew it could strike.

The tiresome tracking of the beast had taken its toll on Reira, she caught her breath, within seconds the beast was gone.

The beast had driven Reira into the perfect place for an ambush. The narrow ledges canyon gave the perfect place for it to strike before jumping away onto a higher ledge. The ledges closer to the top of the narrow canyon had enough of an angle to block out the sun. Allowing the beast to focus on luring Reira into the ambush.

A stone path made a small appearance. Reira looked down at the path

"Not far to the communications outpost. a few hours' hike" she whispered to herself. Knowing that at some point the path would led to a clear opening. In case she needed to make a break for it even though that might still be a few hours walk away.

Reira had been down this canyon many times before, the Xanti (beast) were always predictable,

"As predictable as usual..." she mumbled glimpsing the shadow of the Xanti. Before it disappeared into the shadows again.

This Xanti was huge, she definitely had the upper hand. Strength, power, agility, knowledge of the terrain, this would not be easy.

Reira couldn't wait to get this finished. The sole purpose of this ten-day excursion into the desert was to kill Xanti. The Xanti numbers were higher this year than in previous years. They had attacked a pilgrimage group, killing all but one from the group. They stole food supplies left at retreat cabins scattered across the planet. The beasts deserved what they had coming to them. Reira was the only one who could cull them, her family had the rights descended through law., Only her family or its agents could do what was needed.

There was another reason for Reira to be on this hunt. Monoruanthrophthoxin, known as Ruanox to almost all citizens of the Empire. To Reira it was 'Kalita', the refined venom glad of the Xanti. A potent neurotoxin, deadly to almost all life in the galaxy except Reira and her people.

To them it was a powerful and addictive narcotic with psychoactive effects. A single venom glad was worth one hundred thousand credits. A glad from a Xanti as big as this would be worth close to half a million credits.

In small diluted doses they used it in religious ceremonies across the empire. Supposed to allow communion with the spirits.

Reira's opponent stepped forward. Her steely gaze never wavering as he growled.

"So this is how it goes down..," Reira taunted, her voice raspy because of the dryness in the air

"It's you and me." As she wiped the sweat from her brow. The beast growling again, this time flashing its teeth as it opened its massive jaw.

That was the last straw. Reira had heard enough. Growling with fury, she clenched her fists.

Reira raised it into the air, but the Xanti was faster. She sidestepped the move, towards her by the beast. It lashed out and almost struck Reira's wrist and jumped behind her. She felt its tail crash into the back of her knee. She fell to the floor and rolled away before it could act again.

Reira hadn't managed to stand up fully on her feet before it slammed into her back with full force. In agonising pain, Reira rammed the blade she was carrying backwards., feeling it connect to a bone, with a crack.

The Xanti cried out in pain and fell to the floor. It instantly rolled over and lunged to grab hold of Reira's leg. A swipe with its clawed paw would have ended this confrontation before it had really begun.

Reira kicked its paw away. Grabbing large stone from the floor, She stood over its body. Reira raised the stone and slammed it in the beast's face. The beast cried out in pain, its wail echoing throughout the canyon, scaring away an onlookers. As it wailed, it lashed out with its tail, striking Reira right in the left side of her abdomen.

The only audience to this brawl. Were the small creatures roaming around the canyon minding their own business. Stay stayed in the darkness when they heard the ruckus between them. They'd stop collecting food, look, and stare but not for long, knowing it wasn't worth risking their own lives before scampering away back into the darkness.

To them, Reira and the beast were odd beings, each trying to survive, creatures who would never find balance, who would never live in harmony… And they were right! They had hunted Xanti like this for countless generations, and it would not change.

The Xanti was growing fatigued, Reira knew it, but she was exhausted herself.

Night time crept up on them, though that didn't discourage the Xanti, they saw better in the dark. Reira punched at its blood-covered face.

It's head bounced to the left, its tail catching her unaware. Her knee slammed into the cold, unsympathetic stone ground. She thrust the blade deep into the beast's chest, them both screaming out in pain.

Reira picked up the blade and was about to deal the final blow. Before she had the chance, the beast pushed her off with a single swipe of its paw, and it arose to its weary feet. They glared at one another, circling at a steady pace, neither of them breaking eye contact.

Secretly they were both trying to rebuild their stamina. This intense fight had them both breathing hard. The sand soaked in blood. Reira's white blood mixed with the dark blue blood of the Xanti, making the sand beneath their feet black.

"Come on" she growled, calling out the Xanti.

"Are you going to make me wait?", taunting the beast. Hoping for it to make a mistake and she would seize the opportunity to end this.

Her voice echoed throughout the narrow canyon. A gust of wind blew the sand into their faces, sending both of them into a hopeful situation.

For an instant Reira couldn't see. before she blinked with her third eyelid, a wound on her head trickled blood down, dripping down her nose. She wiped the blood away, flicking her wrist sending the blood towards the sands. Within seconds the Xanti was back in her line of sight.

Reira momentarily looked around the canyon. The wind died down and there she was, standing in front of her, snarling and bearing her teeth. In the distance the shrill gawking of the Hawks broke the silence,

Reira attempted to make another move, her body exhausted from the ordeal. with the little energy I had, but it was useless. The Xanti lashed out with its tail catching Reira in the left side of her torso again. The nasty wound she received making her light-headed. It wouldn't be long before she would pass out from the pain and the venom from the wounds it had inflicted her with.

She scrambled to her feet. Grabbing hold of a rock to steady herself, the beast came close, this was it a chance to strike, she pulled out a blade and prepared to strike.

She grinned as the blade flew down and clashed with the beast at great force. She wanted something great from this hunt, she would be it. She knew this Xanti deserved this great final battle. There was no way for her to recover from this blow, she tried to recover, as Reira rolled to the side as the beast lashed out.

The beast groaned and Reira knew at that moment that the battle was over. She swung up with the blade and slammed the blade into the beast up to the hilt of the blade. The beast went down, hitting the ground. With such force she unsettled the dusty floor that caused the entire area to disappear into a haze of dust.

The beast knew the world was going dark. It lashed out with its tail, catching Reira unaware, striking her in the left side of the chest for a third time, knocking her to the ground.

Reira struggled to her feet, winded but okay. She glanced over at the beast, its eyes flickering open, this battle wasn't over. Reira steadied herself, waiting for the beast to attack again, being aware of its barbed tail. A strike to the head from its tail would mean certain death.

But it didn't move, its eyes glazed over, it let out one sickening wail before collapsing onto the floor. Reira reached over, knife in hand in anticipation of it striking out, she placed her fingers on the wound on its neck, the blood from the wound flowed over her fingers; it was turning cold.

The Xanti must have died moments ago. The adrenaline must have kept her going before she died of blood loss. She could have left her there, but after what had transpired between them. Even she deserved a proper burial. Reira pulled the body by the shoulder, with each pull she cried out in pain and every time her corpse heaved more of the dark blue fluid ebbed out; Reira's hands now covered with it.

As Reira dragged her body through the narrow winding canon. She was alternately cast in light and shadow, her skin paler than it had been in life. The creature was both elegant and terrifying; this one was decades old. That was the only way to explain her tremendous size, there was no other way for a Xanti to grow as big as this, she must have been fifty years old Reira thought to herself.

Reira dropped her to the floor, looking down at her own

hands, she wept. First quietly, before sobbing openly. She clasped her hands and tried to wring the blood from her hands.

She sank to her knees, sinking slightly into the sand before stopping. The sand darkening with blood. Reira stopped crying, wiping her eyes with her forearm. Before reaching to grab a small blade from its holster on her hip.

She reached over to the breast and followed its vertebrae up to its shoulder with the blade, tracing a line a few inches away with the blade before carefully plunging the blade into the beast.

She cut away at its flesh; the blood pouring out, covering her hands before dripping onto the sand.. Her hands delved into the open wound, rummaging around before stopping.

She carefully pulled out a dark blue orb, which glistened in the light. The orb was connected to the inside of the beast by a plethora of veins, which Reira carefully cauterised via a small device she pulled out of her bag, before placing the orb into the bag.

She made her way to her feet and continued to drag the beast through the canyon. Stopping often to rest. The sun rose higher in the sky, rising temperatures to over 140 degrees, causing Reira to stop, exhausted.

She stopped at a small pool of water, a luxury in the desert of Ateki. The shade of the narrow canyon keeping the water from evaporating completely. Reira plunged her hands into the water before scooping up enough water to throw onto her face.

"I can finally get rid of all this blood..." she whispered to herself, pausing for a second. Looking around before dipping her face completely into the water and stopping. Opening her eyes in the water Reira hesitated for a few seconds. She could see the blood dispersing into the water before she raised her face out of the pool.

When at last Reira arrived at the mouth of the canyon, her legs gave way beneath her. She held her hands to the sky and chanted her voice not louder than a murmur. She watched the streams of blood on her arms flow towards her shoulders. That's when the tears came again, her entire body collapsing as if it meant to join her prey in the afterlife.

"Xi-Shala, I praise thee for a successful hunt. Please take this offering and return her to the land in which she was born. Take her bones and fortify the underground streams, return what she was and give life a new..." Reira claimed before collapsing into a heap on the sand, her bag spilling its contents onto the sand, a few vials of a dark blue substance followed by a delicate and beautiful mask strewn themselves across the sand.

Many Hours later

Reira awoke, her body having recovered from the strenuous activity of dragging the Xanti through the canyon, the winds were picking up, wiping the sand into little dust devils.

She scrambled to her feet, picking up her items and putting them back into her bag, leaving the mask out, the mask was beautiful, a delicate white mask its features were expressionless, a simple slit where its mouth was. Its eyes were covered in a fine silvery membrane. She picked up the mask and studied it, before looking into the distance, a sandstorm was coming her way. She could feel it.

She grabbed a simpler mask out from her bag and placed it on to her face, the moment she did that the mask bonded to her face, conforming to her facial features. The latest in nano technology. She placed the other mask on top of this mask and it bonded to the inner mask.

Moments later Reira could feel the mask, drawing air into itself and directing it into her mouth. This would be required to walk through the sandstorm, the mask itself filtering out the sand and other particulates from the air supply.

She slung her bag over her shoulder and walked towards the oncoming storm. A wall of sand and dust stood between her and home, as she stepped forwards the wind picked up, blowing a huge wall of sand towards her...

CHAPTER 3

That Night...

Night had come and gone, and the dawn was now a memory, and Reira was still nowhere to be seen.

The rains had returned, currents of rain ran down the curbs of the streets, that crisscrossed the city. Washing away the dust and sand that had been deposited there over be last few weeks of sand storms.

The rain was torrential. The occasional person quickly scurried from one building to another. Trying to take refuge from the rain on their way home. No different to the tiny creatures which lived in the canyons, just on a harder scale.

Countless others stood in the doorways and looked out into the rain, enjoying the moisture which filled the air., ending the usual dryness which permeated the air. Others emerged from their homes or businesses, and sighed, "finally some rain" an old man exclaimed,

"My garden needs a good soaking..." He murmured to himself regarding the drought which had plagued his garden.

On the balconies of one of the apartment complexes which looked out towards the city wall various individuals stood looking out towards the city defence wall. The rain was so powerful near the wall it occasionally overflowed the gutters on the wall. It streamed over them like a waterfall.

Zamir sighed. Rubbed his hand against his furrowed brow and looked out over the city from the watchtower that rose high into the sky, on a clear day he could have seen for miles. Now he could only make out the city wall, any chance of being able to see her return was long gone because of the storm.

Below him the temple gate wall separated the temple from the rest of the city, a little over a quarter of a mile away. He could make out the city wall raising out of the ground. This wall had protected the city for over three thousand years. Even though there were no longer any enemies to protect the city from. Today the wall stood as a reminder of a different age. Only protecting the city from the full force of a sandstorm now and then.

The temple wall and city wall had created a culture of its own. 'Child of the wall' you were called if you had lived within the shadow of the walls.

The gatehouses along the wall had become rooftop gardens for some privileged within the city. No longer were mounted weapons placed across the ramparts. Makeshift canopies crossed over the ramparts, creating a sheltered living space.

Part of the city was desolate. Especially the old ministry buildings, the city needed rejuvenation. It had become a ghost town since the incident. Only visitors on a pilgrimage to the temple caused an influx of city income.

The city had advantages. Being one of the thirty most visited pilgrimage sites within the empire. More important than the temple of Jeha - goddess of the sun, on Gälden II. Yet less important than the temple of Myale- God of Fertility based on Prim. But this wasn't enough, a huge amount of credits would be required to restore the city to its former grandeur.

The storm had brought dark clouds over the temple, plunging parts of the city into darkness, while others bathed in sunlight.

Across from the temple wall, within the residential district of the town. The faint light from a bar shone across the darkness cast by the temple wall. The building was ancient; the paintwork had blistered and cracked decades before. No attempt had been made to repaint, the desert environment was harsh and unforgiving.

The faint sound of music reverberated against the temple wall. Sending the faint sound down the dimly lit street. The street light flickered on for a second before powering down again. Plunging the street back into the darkness. A figure stood at the door, looking out towards the temple wall. Which arose forty meters into the sky, trying to avoid the rain.

A loud thud startled him. While he tended to the flowers cascading down the wall of the gatehouse that had become his home. He squeezed the handle of the scissors he was holding one more time. Finishing the last of the pruning before the thud came again.

"Hey, what's going on" he shouted as he looked over the wall towards the gate.

He was shocked by what he saw. He frantically searched for the gate controls. Finally, finding them behind his prize roses. He flicked the switch, and the gate shuddered, then he flicked it again and finally the gate moved.

He rushed over, knocking over a container of water which

spilled over the floor he stopped for a second, signed at the mess before rushing down the winding staircase leading him towards the opening gate.

"Who are you...?" He quizzed as the figure walked through the gate, pulling a sled behind him,

"Just a concerned citizen, I'm not the one you should be worried about...!" He remarked as he dragged the sled towards the main road leading up to the temple wall.

The figure was shrouded in a white cloak and hood that protected him from the torrential rain. He carefully dragged the sled behind him, lying unconscious on this sled was Reira. Her head covered by a transparent membrane, keeping her dry, her clothes soaked in blood. She was unconscious.

* * *

23rd Hour of the 25th Day of the 7th Month
IY (Imperial Year) 101

The night had returned, but now it was filled with the sounds of triumph. The entire city was out tonight, they could hear music in the streets. People were laughing and joking as they walked the city. The gate to the temple was open and people streamed towards its doors. Some carrying lit candles, giving a prayer to the goddesses for Reira's safe return.

Reira was standing at the doorway to the temple, she smiled as a young girl came up to her,

"Lady Reira, I'm so happy that your back, grandfather told me you might not return, but I told him you would... you wouldn't leave us..." her voice, angelic and innocent.

Reira smiled as she looked down at her,

"Of course little one, I wouldn't miss your smiling face, it was you believing in me that kept me safe while out in the desert." She added as she ruffled the young girls' hair, before sending her off towards her grandfather, who casually smiled and blessed himself as Reira noticed him.

* * *

A loud roar disturbed the conversation in the temple,

It was the juvenile Xanti, Reira could recognise it, its markings were like that of its mother, it must have stalked Reira back to the temple. It had kept itself out of sight. It mustn't have been far away when Reira killed its mother, tracking her scent across the desert. And now it was looking for revenge. Smaller than its parent, but still capable of killing everyone in the temple.

Reira's hearts raced as she gestured for everyone to leave the temple, this was between her and the beast. She reached to her side, wincing once as her wounds handn't completely healed., a ceremonial blade was all that she had to defend herself.

"This'll have to do...!" She exclaimed as she drew the blade and looking at its small stature, against a nearly fully grown Xanti.

Members of the congregation backed themselves to the walls, but could not leave, fear had gripped them tight. They dare not move; they didn't want to provoke the beast. The beast prowled the main hall, the light from the fire cast its shadow against the walls.

The beast lashed out, missing Reira, but caught her with its tail, impaling her in the shoulder with a barb.

She pulled the barb from her shoulder and laughed...

"Was that supposed to hurt" she retorted, Throwing the barb to the ground, her hand dripping with blood. Adrenaline pumping through her veins, the barb had hurt, but right now she was more concerned about everyone else.

Again, the beast lunged at her, its claws mere inches from her face. She dove backward, throwing the beast off balance. its enormous torso falling forwards.

She lunged forward, swinging the blade in front of her, catching the beast in the torso, causing it to yelp in pain. Before it landed on the bloody floor, with a thump. Then darting out of the light into the darkness of the Temple. Its paws skidding on the floor, She wiped the blood from her cheek, and carefully picked up the blade.

She wandered over to Zamir, keeping her eyes out for the beast,

"Try to get the others out, I'll deal with this..." she stopped mid flow, at the same time she pointed the blade at him, his heart raced as his eyes followed the blade as it came to rest on the side of his neck.

Seeming to look straight into his eyes, she spoke.

"Don't...Move..." she implored, the look of fear in her eyes made Zamir uncomfortable.

Behind him the Xanti stood, crouched down, ready to strike, its mouth wide, baring its teeth for all to see.

It was a standoff, Reira looked towards the right-hand side, hoping that Zamir was watching her eyes and would move in that direction, this wasn't to be; the beast lept forward with all of its might, catching Zamir on the side of his neck with its paw as he tried to flee.

The wound opened instantly, blood poured out of the wound as Zamir fell to the floor, every time his heart pumped, gushes of blood poured out from the wound.

The beast looked down at him, then looked at Reira, who was frozen with shock, before it roared and with both paws pounded on Zamir's chest, the sound of his ribs snapping under the pressure of the blows could be heard by all in the chamber.

This is when Reira finally broke down screaming, unable to move, she stood there screaming. Tears streamed down her face, her breathing became shallow and rapid, she was hyperventilating. Her eyes becoming milky white, the startled Xanti, struggled as it was raised off from Zamir's crushed body. He lashed out, but to no avail, before being flung against the opposite wall, killing it instantly, its body slumping to the floor.

For an instant it seemed like time stopped, the beast lay dead, Zamir's body lay crumpled on the floor. Blood poured out from various wounds across his entire body, his bones broken. He gasped for air, his breathing stopped, moments later restarting. Footsteps echoed running up the stairs of the temple entrance.

The Reverend mother arrived first. Seeing Reira standing

there screaming, she realized. She looked over at Zamir as some junior acolytes arrived. She ordered them to get Zamir off to a side room, and to call for a medic.

Reira's eyes were still glowing bright as the Reverend Mother placed her hand on Reira's right shoulder.

"Dear, you can stop now..., it is over..." her voice snapping Reira out of the trance.

CHAPTER 4

Reira walked past the side room its door slightly ajar, she stood curious as to what was transpiring inside, and looked through the small gap in the door, Zamir lay on the floor, a trail of blood lead to him, a young man crouched down beside him shook his head before placing his hand over Zamir's face, before slowly closing his eyelids. He was gone.

The sight of this caused Reira to gasp, startling the young medic who called out into the room.

"Close that door" causing someone else inside the room to closed the door, plunging Reira into darkness. Reira was stunned.

She murmured to herself as she staggered towards a nearby staircase, grabbing hold of the banister as she pulled herself up the stairs. Momentarily reaching a mezzanine floor and darting inside the room before slamming the door shut with such force it shook the window across from it.

Inside the room it was dark, only the moonlight from an adjacent window cast the darkness away, here Reira stood, looking down at her blood soaked hands.

Reira carefully slid off her jacket, now soaked in both her own and Xanti blood. revealing her athletic body, her vest soaked in blood. She winced as she moved muscles which had been bruised and damaged from the recent fights with the Xanti.

She carefully removed the vest before looking into the mirror. Dust, blood, and venom completely hid her face's normal complexion. Upon looking at herself she burst into tears.

She slammed her hands on to the washbasin, her eyes clouding over. They glowed with an unnatural effervescence. Again she slammed her hands into the washbasin. This time a shockwave emanated from her impact and cracked the mirror. She stopped moments later her eyes returning to normal before wincing in pain. Blood still ebbed out of the wound on her left shoulder. That was only one of many wounds scattered across her body.

Her body littered with scars from previous hunts, a tapestry of near misses. Some of them had healed, leaving only a pale scar.

In the light glimpses of unusual markings covered her entire back, only interrupted by two rows of scales that made their way down either side of her spine, around them swirls and arcane symbols could be made out. Reira dragged herself across from the basin to the shower. Removing the rest of her clothes as she stumbled towards the shower.

"Shower on... and make it a cold one..." she hissed before clambering into the shower. As the water streamed against her, she sank to the floor of the shower., allowing the water to cascade over her completely.

Reira sat on the floor, the water slowly washing away the blood and dirt across her body. She curled herself into a ball, here she felt safe. The cold water causing her skin to react, goosebumps slowly appeared across her body, but she didn't care. The cold water numbing her body, but this is what she wanted. To not feel anything, the pain of the last few days was too much for her to take.

She looked up at the streaming water, allowing it to cascade over her face, finally washing away the blood, Reira caught herself looking at her own reflection as the water pooled near her before draining away.

She looked at herself and was shocked by what she saw. For an instant she saw something which shocked her,

"Numarii?" She called out, her voice trembling in reaction to the cold water. As she looked at her reflection, she noticed the reflection staring back at her, it was her, but it also wasn't her at the same time. Reira reached out towards the reflection with her left hand as she touched the reflection the reflection disappeared, she shook her head and looked up, and was startled by herself sitting on the floor of the shower next to her,

"Mari..?, is that you?" She whispered, but got no reply, she looked over at the figure next to her, noticing a pool of blood forming beneath it. Reira reached over toward the figure, just as she was about to touch it, it looked up at her. Its eyes black and soulless, its skin was pale and semi-translucent, a dark liquid could be seen running through its veins.

"It comes for you…" it spoke, before lurching forwards, scaring Reira, who instantly awoke, lying on the floor of the shower, the water still cascading over her, but now it was different, the water was getting warmer.

"Why is this water warm" she cried out.

"Body temperature drop detected, I recommended an increase in water temperature" the shower replied moments later.

Reira slowly clambered herself onto her feet and washed the

remains of the blood and dirt away. every so often she looked over her shoulder before returning to washing herself.

Moments later she emerged from the shower,

"Shower off" she exclaimed, moments later the shower gradually slowed before stopping completely, besides the shower a huge circle was suspended from the ceiling.

As she stood under it, the device activated and the water instantly dried from her body and her hair which she combed back with her fingers. She stepped away and towards the broken mirror, looking at herself. She steadied herself as she looked at herself, lost in thought.

The silence was abruptly broken by a knocking on the door, followed quickly by a second louder knock, before the door slid open.

A junior acolyte entered the room, he kept his head down, looking towards the floor. His heart was racing, he had expected her to still be in the shower, so he could leave the clothes and go. But that would not happen now.

He was young, no older than twenty. He was dressed in a simple cream tunic and trousers; he carried a pile of clothes which he nervously placed on a chair next to where Reira was standing. Before turning back towards the door, Reira stopped his hasty exit as she spoke up.

"No need to shy away, your new here aren't you…" Reira spoke as she reached over and picked up an item of clothing.

He paused as she spoke, still facing the door he spoke, looking at the ground.

"Sister Abrasar is correct, I've only been here for a few days…" he replied, his voice trembling.

"It's disrespectful to address me while facing the door." Reira replied.

"It is only done out of respect, Sister. I didn't mean to offend, Accept my appo..." he replied, but could not finish. Reira placed her hand on his shoulder, he froze. She grabbed at his shoulder and turned him around. Reira was standing there in front of him wearing a silken robe.

"Jisal Mal, that's who you are, Zamir mentioned you before..." she stopped, tried to compose herself before speaking again.

"Yes Sister, I arrived while you were finding yourself out in the desert." He spoke, his voice shaking with nerves.

"Well, Brother Mal, it's nice to finally have some young blood here in the temple, it's been many years since we had any new acolytes."

He smiled innocently before looking away nervously.

"Thank you Sister Abrasar, if there is anything else you need, they have assigned me to tend to your needs..."

Reira paused.

"That's fine, go back to your studies, I'll be ..." Reira replied, gesturing for him to leave.

"Reverend Mothers Orders...., I'll be here if you need me." He replied with conviction as he stood to attention.

Reira looked at him and smirked.

"Well, can't be going against her orders now can we..." she smirked, looking at him before making her way out of the room, she paused in the doorway, looking over her shoulder she replied.

"I will retire to my quarters for the night, I've got a lot of soul searching to do..." before leaving him to follow behind moments later.

He quickly grabbed the bloody soaked clothes and dropped them into a basket near the door, he would deal with them later. For now he needed to make sure she was okay.

He followed quickly behind, bowing slightly as other acolytes walked past him.

"Sister Abrasar..." he called out, loud enough that she stopped walking, and spun on her heels, looking straight at him, causing him to stop suddenly.

"Sister, the Reverend Mother..." he piped up, before she cut him off.

"I know she means well, but I can deal with this....alone" she scowled. His posture changed instantly, his shoulders dropped and his head lowered.

"I'm just..." he stuttered. That's when it hit her.

The Reverend mother knew exactly what she was doing, Having someone to listen to her, innocent and none judgemental. Someone she could just talk to. Reira let out a sigh.

"Brother Mal, It might be worth your time and mine, If I help you with your scripture, it might keep my mind off... you know" a small tear trickled out of her right eye, as she tried to stop herself from breaking down completely. He looked up at her, sighed a little before smiling.

"I'll go and grab my copy of the scripture from the library..." he added.

"No need Brother, my copy is in my room. But you could grab us both a cup of root tea, it's going to be a long night..."

she implored.

He smiled,

"Of course Sister." He replied as he bowed to excuse himself before turning away from her.

Reira smiled,

"Goddesses, give me the strength to deal with these challenges in my life, I don't think I'm strong enough to deal with them without you..." she whispered. As she turned around and walked down the moon-lit corridor.

* * *

6th Hour of the 27th Day of the 7th Month
IY (Imperial Year) 101

Morning had finally arrived, the night had been a night she would have rather have forgotten. The sun shone over the mountains. The shadows from the mountains stretching across the desert. Like a normal day, but things were far from normal.

A small shuttle had landed across from the entrance to the city. This shuttle would have been Zamir's sisters shuttle. She lived a few days travel from the Aaelonia system. Reira knew she would have to meet her at some point. Preferring to leave that emotional meeting for another time.

Reira could see this shuttle from her room in the temple. She had looked at the shuttle's arrival and had made her way towards the tower. From here she could see everything.

She looked out at the city, sighed and looked into the distance. The air was cold today, a familiar cold, it reminded her of home. Her ancestral home.

Reira had grown up fifty-two years before on Antaria VI, in a city on the planets most northern lying continent. A settlement that included a spectacular mountain range.

Followed by lush forests and a city on its outskirts where the forest met the plateau. Two moons were visible in the sky most nights. Almar and Alnet, Almar was so close that on a clear day she could still be seen even during the daytime.

The city of Kamet had been her family's ancestral home for over ten thousand years. Even though she had been born while her family had been visiting friends in Tsoris Provence. They had stationed her father at the local garrison for the first ten years of her life. Only visiting her true home during holidays and when the council had met at her home.

In a city of twelve million, seventy-five percent of them were Impiri. The rest a mixture of Balirian, Antarian and a small population of Zathians. The Zathian population never mixing with everyone else. Confining themselves into a small town near the forest.

For as long as she could remember Reira had longed for peace, Tsoris Provence was a typical imperial military Provence, and the infrequent visits to Antaria VI were not long enough for her to settle, before being yanked back to Tsoris, and her education at the on base school, and all of this before that fateful summer, she had just turned eighteen.

* * *

52 Years Before

3rd Hour of the 27st Day of the 8th Month
IY (Imperial Year) 49

Morning had finally arrived, the sun shone over the mountains. The shadows from the trees were stretching across the plains. Mist rolling in from the nearby forest, rising just a few meters from the ground.

A small shuttle had landed near a large house on the outskirts of the city.

The door to the shuttle opened, sending in a cold rush of air and wisps of mist. Waking Reira up from her nap, luckily Numarii had woken up early.

"Rei, Come on sleepy head, always the "Bad'dar Sha-Ne" - princess of dreams' as she smiled at Reira. Gesturing for her to follow.

Reira was confused, a little disoriented, but that subsided.

"You know me, Marii travelling always makes me tired." She replied, shaking her head to wake herself up even more. Rubbing her eyes slowly.

"What was that nightmare about? Shouldn't have listened to grandmother using the divination cards. The Dual Priestesses, The Trickster, Eternal Justice and Death Cards, an unusual combination." She murmured.

When these came up a veil of dread and fear descended upon her mind. The foreboding death of someone close, grandmother couldn't say who it was, that the spirits chose to not reveal to her. 'Good thing it was only a Nightmare.' She thought to herself as she wiped the sweat off her forehead before grabbing her bag.

She then exited the shuttle. Stumbling over one of her father's bags as she exited.

"I need to stop eating Alamen root right before taking a nap, always gives me such vivid dreams." She joked to herself. Somewhat unconvinced by her own comments.

She looked over at the clock as she exited; The time read 07:50. She was finally home, the home she felt comfortable in, not that other place called home on the military base.

As she walked the path towards her ancestral homestead, she stopped to admire her home. A large building, decorated in traditional Impiri style, the house covered a huge area; it sat cut into the ground, with the rest of the surrounding area starting on the first floor, the ground floor cut deep into the bedrock, it was wide and spacious, the upper levels had all encompassing large windows, which looked out towards the back of the property.

The property rose three floors above ground, with at least one level below ground. On the top of the property a huge rooftop garden was the main attraction, from here the grounds of the home could be seen, further out the rest of the plateau. Ornately carved wooden and stone embellishments and hearths were scattered across the home.

Reira walked up to the front door, she hadn't been home in such a long time, not since her parents had the home renovated and expanded, she walked through the main door and stopped in amazement; She found herself in a large lobby. Twice the size it had been previously, it was more spacious than before, but still felt homely.

The floors were made of colored tiles arranged in jagged

patterns, and the walls were partially made of glass, and stone, allowing a sneak peek into its interior, countless pieces of artwork covered the lobby, pictures she could not even remember seeing before, paintings of her ancestors, going as far back as ten thousand years.

The walls were a light grey, but mostly bare. A frosted glass partition separated the lobby from a private office. This was her father's study, the smell of flowers caught her attention. She looked around for them, but noticed none, she shrugged.

Reira looked up, the ceiling for the lobby was the actual roof of the house. Silk banners and embroidery hung from the ceiling.

"Father said things had changed, I think everything's changed, except the front door." She whispered to herself.

Looking down past the staircase, Reira caught sight of the ceremonial heart of her home, its solid wooden doors were closed.

Either side of the huge doors, polished stone pedestals held golden and silver statues portraying members of the family, her ancestors who had died during the darkest hours of her people. Everything in the lobby was rich and lavish; Reira knew this place was home, it felt opulent, but upstairs in her room, she felt safe.

Outside Bal'jar Malites' - roamed the plateau, Reira couldn't wait to ride one again, these magnificent beasts were over two-and-a-half meters tall to their backs. Their long elegant mane's of hair made its way down their spine towards their two tails.

They were perfect animals to ride; she had learnt to ride

them before she was old enough to walk unaided. They were a throwback to her family's heritage. Countless millennia ago her tribe had rode these beasts across the plains of Imperis, long before they had discovered any other form of travel. Long before space travel, this was the only way to travel.

She thought, loosing herself to her own thoughts.

"What if grandmother was right, she had a good knack of getting these things right? The things that she had seen when she was younger, they couldn't be explained. Yet they couldn't be discounted, maybe that wasn't a just a dream, but a warning." She thought loosing her train of thought before shaking her head and laughing at herself for even considering the option.

Reira couldn't shake that nightmare. Reira's thoughts caused a shiver to run down her spine. she ran up the stairs and into her room, her room was always the first on the left, father had made sure that during the immense renovation, her room would be where it usually was.

She entered the room and closed the door behind her,. She lay on her bed, here she felt safe. Her room was basic, it contained just what Reira needed. A bed, books, an incense burner, a large mirror in the room's corner, an on suite bathroom and a wardrobe. Its walls were a nice surprise, a view of the grounds played across her walls, the latest technology from Prim. The image was indistinct from actual reality, she stood there in amazement, the view instantly made her hearts slow down.

"Thank you, father..." she whispered, knowing he had arranged this for her room.

She didn't even spend time with her cousins and relatives who were staying at the house; she needed time to clear her own mind.

Reira had secluded herself in her room, the sound of music could faintly be heard emanating from her room.

After a few hours she went downstairs to where her mother was singing and cooking dinner. Outside, she could see her Bad'dar Malite. It always seemed to know that she was home, this was a wild Malite, roaming miles away from here. But it had still wandered over a hundred miles to find her, somehow it knew, this pleased her.

"Is everything okay, Rei" Her Mother said as she put pancakes on a plate.

"I need to tell you something," Reira said. She wasn't sure how her mother would handle this, but she tried to explain herself anyway, her lip trembled as she spoke to her mother, her hands even shook.

Moments later...

Her mother held back the tears.

"Are you being serious right now, I can't believe Nissa - grandmother. Told you that, especially at your age. I know she likes to communicate with the spirits, the divination cards have never lied to her before, they have never let her down. She should have told me and your father, at least kept us informed."

"Mother, I'm worried." Reira sheepishly replied.

"Then why didn't you tell me this before. But don't worry, nothing going to happen to my daughters. You, Numarii and

Ilaria, the goddesses will have a serious battle on their hands if they try anything. They better not try anything against my family." Her mother responded, her voice stern but caring.

"I know, I know." Reira lowered her head.

"I didn't believe her at first, but after the nightmare I had, I'm just worried."

"The council soon might keep your mind off it, it always keeps my mind off of things I didn't want to think about." Her mother added, trying to sound jovial.

CHAPTER 5

Word had come to the house that the council would arrive a few days earlier than expected. One of Reira's uncles had heard through channels, 'security concerns, that's why they are arriving earlier than planned' her uncle had mentioned, causing a stir within the family.

The exact nature of these channels had always puzzled Reira. Her working in import and export, but these channels, they were always secretive and that sparked her interest, all she knew was that her uncle was an importer and a broker, arranging export shipments from Prim to the outer colonies. He ran his side of the family business. It involved him a lot with the Amarlit Alliance, these were the most profitable contracts.

Reira couldn't really remember him that well, only seeing him once since she was born, but being her only uncle had its rewards, she always received gifts on the anniversary of her birth from him, usually a trinket from a far-off colony or something he had received as a gift for arranging a lucrative deal.

Mostly she had heard about him in conversations, well more like whispers. He was generally not mentioned unless it involved him and father.

Members of the extended family ran around the estate like ants. The council would have a meeting here. Reira stood in the middle of the doorway, cousins and uncles. Well, not really uncles, more like great cousin, removed once or twice, buzzed beside her.

Each of them could easily knock her over, without trying.

They were typical young Impiri men; they were the height of masculinity. Perfect specimens of Impiri genetics, strong and intelligent. However they spent more time trying to attract one of the daughters from another related Impiri household, than anything else, unless it was working for one of the security contractors off world. Where they were seen as being the best of the best, worth the hefty contract costs to employ them.

Reira shook her head,

"Why is he talking with her again..?" She whispered to herself, looking across the grounds. Seeing her cousin Tycho walking towards the grounds with a young Impiri woman, her skin the colour of caramel, her eyes were a beautiful emerald green, and a smile which lit up her face as she talked to Tycho.

"Aunt Jysell would never approve, mingling with a girl from the blue....never," She scowled.

She looked at the girl, and felt jealous, the young woman was beautiful, her hair was long and pale blonde, her skin a luxurious caramel colour and those emerald eyes, for an instant Reira could see why he was infatuated with her.

She looked across from herself in the mirror situated near the door. She sighed as she looked at herself; She was pretty in a conventional sense, but different from almost everyone, her silvery grey hair singled her out among other Impiri, but it was the eyes, those amber hued eyes, a telltale sign of her abilities. They were bright blue as a child, until the awakening, the event had been traumatic and she was unprepared for its consequences.

"Stop staring at yourself, someone's bound to find you attractive, one day. Once you've grown into yourself." A young man shouted at her, interrupting her train of thought, she looked over at him, it was her cousin Rysi.

"I'm glad I don't always look at myself, not like you Rysi…" Reira scowled, cracking a small smile at the end.

"I only do it because I know people enjoy looking at me…" Rysi joked in return, gesturing for someone to look at his physique.

Rysi was young, mid-twenties at most. His chiseled jaw and high cheekbones gave him an appearance of somewhere close to the descriptions of the Demi-gods of old. Lean muscles showed that he was a military officer or a ladies' favorite.

His dark brown hair was cut short on the sides and sculpted back on the top. He stopped and watch others moving things around the house. His full lips occasionally pulled a smirk of arrogance before easily lifting boxes which others did not lift. Rysi's blue eyes were full of playfulness, yet also wisdom, like he knew things that you wouldn't believe, and would be happy to tell you tales of wonder, especially if you were one of the single daughters of a neighbouring house.

Reira's cousin rubbed his hands and smiled back at Reira, before grabbing another crate full of bottles and carried it into the house,

"Show off..." Reira sneered at him, before cracking a smile, wider than before.

Rysi-Tane had always been her favourite cousin, he had always made time for her. Not like his brother Tycho, even though they were cousins, Tycho acted like he wasn't part of the family. That the family embarrassed him, which would always be difficult for him as to an Impiri family meant everything. He always pushed the boundaries of what was acceptable. He never acted the same as every Impiri Reira had met, he always like to cause a situation. Maybe that's why Numarii hung around him, she always tried to rebel a little.

Reira looked over at Rysi and shook her head. He was one of the few Impiri she could actually get along with, others were arrogant or distant. He rushed past her after dropping off the box in the kitchen, as he lent over to grab the other box it shifted across the floor, just out of his grasp. He stopped perplexed for a second before the notion dawned on him.

"Rei…" he cursed under his breath.

"Yes…" she replied, looking at him seriously, before breaking down into a fit of laughter.

"I'm sorry, I couldn't help myself.." She added, this time the box lifted a meter off the ground, straight into Rysi's hands.

"You made me do all this, when you could move it all by yourself." He remarked.

She stopped laughing, smiled at him, pursed her lips and winked.

"But then I wouldn't get such a good show of strength, and I know you like to show off." She added before walking off into the house.

A few hours later...

All members of the family sat at the table set out in the back of the house. The summer breeze sending around the table the smell of bread of different kinds. Reira's Mother was an excellent cook. It was all cooked the proper way

"No matter replicators can make the bread the way you do Mother!" Reira declared, smelling the freshly baked bread sitting in front of her.

"Thank you, dear..." her mother replied.

Reira was sitting at her customary place. To her father's right side, with Numarii to her side, across from them their mother.

Reira and Numarii were quiet at the table unless the extended family were around. Reira reached across the table and grabbed at a Yuis Fruit. It's bright purple flesh glistened in the evening light. Reira brought the fruit to her mouth before slowly taking a bite, stopping to savour the taste, she scrunched up her face as the sour juice hit her taste buds.

Her mother laughed at her openly.

"I don't know why you eat those, you've always made those faces." She laughed.

"I only get them because you seem to enjoy it." Her mother mocked as she continued to laugh at her. Reira opened her eyes slightly,

"I don't know either, but thank you for getting them anyway" she added.

Down the other side of the table, a heated conversation started between Reira's cousins and her Aunt.

Reira always hated their arguments, they were quite opinionated, each one trying to outdo the other. Reira's father would not take much more of this, his chair creaked as it moved back as he stood up.

Reira's father spoke, his voice calm and gentle. A relief from the argumentative tones of her cousins.

"Let's not get drawn into this conversation again." He commanded, the tone in his voice caused everyone to put down what they were holding and listen.

He shook his head in disapproval

"Orys has never led us astray. however, he found out this information, we must not speculate. He has always kept us safe. He's always protected his family" He paused

"Don't forget, he is my younger brother, he helps provide for his family. Isn't that right Rysi and Tycho those years in the private school were not paid by the empire, but by your father?" he scolded them.

But her cousins fretted again,

"Why does he always keep himself away for so long, he always promises that he will be here, but is then always called away or cannot attend because of an important meeting.." Rysi added, his emotions running over.

Reira father always had a calming effect the family. Grandfather had always had the same skills. That's why he was once the Impiri ambassador to the Amarlit Alliance. But those times were long ago, he had died the previous winter.

"Uncle, when are the council due? And why have they chosen us to host this year, wasn't it supposed to be a turquoise family hosting?" Rysi enquired.

Reira's Father reached over and poured himself a drink before answering.

"They are due sometime tomorrow, and why us this year, there has been a health scare in the turquoise family lines, so I asked that this year, we take over the hosting duties, it's too much stress for our friends in the turquoise..."

He paused for a few seconds, drinking from his glass before continuing.

"You do remember, the story of how we and our turquoise cousins used to support each other in ancient times...?" Father enquired, already knowing the answer, but trying to change the subject.

"Of course uncle, but you do tell it so well, let's hear it again..." Rysi announced, playing to his uncles vanity.

It was a time-honoured tradition, stories from the olden days back home on Imperis, even though this story had been told countless times before.

This story was even older than that. The red and turquoise houses had respected each other for the last fifty thousand years. Even though they were two houses, they acted as one, especially in council votes proposed by each other.

Reira's family were from the eastern plateau and the Turquoise were from the southern shores. There had been intermarriage between the two tribes over the years. These would be the only intermixing that was allowed. A red could marry another red, or even an unmarked, or a turquoise as long as the tribal elders allowed it.

This is how supportive they had been to each other over the years. Reira's Mother was a lady of the Turquoise, her father was the brother of the current turquoise Lord. Around her wrist were two different tattoos. A turquoise tattoo intertwined with a red tattoo. She had met Reira's father many years before when they were children at a meeting of the families.

"It happened a long time ago, fifty thousand years ago, give or take a generation.... our ancestors had traveled the long journey to..." he began.

CHAPTER 6

The day had arrived; they opened the gates to the estate, and the doors to the house were open. The door to the main hall was even open, Reira had only seen these doors open once or twice in her entire life. The main hall was for ceremonial use, usually the birth or death within the family. Occasionally it was used when someone was being struck from the book of records, that hadn't happened in generations, not since the civil war happened five thousand years ago.

Everything about this made Reira nervous. She stood sheepishly at the door to the hall, staring into its depth. The hall could hold a few hundred people. Great torches hung on the wall, their light glowing. These were traditional flame lit torches, their light cast out into the room amplified by mirrors casting the light around the room, bringing the room from darkness into the light..

Reira was even more disturbed by this, why the torches, normal lighting would be easier.

"It's tradition..." her mother always told her.

Mother was standing at the door. She was dressed in the most elegant attire. She wore a dark red dress, which went down to her knees. Her legs covered by black stockings, with an ornate pattern on them. Her shoulders were covered with a dark turquoise jacket. Which had the same pattern as the black stockings.

She looked out across the plateau; the city was a few miles away, but here it was peaceful, the families land stretched a mile in all directions.

"They are coming, everyone ready" mother declared, her voice firm but laced with nerves. This would be a strain on her as well, Reira ran towards her mother. Nearly slipping on the polished floor, managing to save herself.

"Shouldn't have worn these heels" she murmured as she stopped herself from slipping. She was dressed in similar clothing, but less opulent.

Her jacket was a muted turquoise, the dress was black, with hints of embroidery. The dress was longer, just over the knee. as tradition dictated for a daughter of the house. her legs covered in light white stockings, the same colour as Reira's already pale skin. On her wrists three gold bracelets, which were slightly too big for her were resting on her hands. A black leather collar with horizontal cutouts decorated with small golden embroidery, rested around her neck.

"Where's your sister...?" Her mother called out, looking around for Numarii, not seeing her anywhere.

"She's got ..." she spoke, stopping before finishing.

She paused as Numarii came running down the stairs, fixing her hair in a ponytail as she descended the stairs.

She was dressed similar to Reira, but ever so different, her dress was shorter, just above the knee, with a split up the side of the leg, that just slightly revealed her long legs, her legs were covered in the same stockings as her sister, her bracelets were equally large.

Her mother looked at her disapprovingly.

"Elit'to, where is it?" She barked.

"I know mother" she scowled, smiling when she looked at

her mother.

“But where is yours?” Numarii replied sarcastically, gesturing at her own neck before laughing.

Her mother quickly grabbed at her neck before sighing, she had forgotten her own. Resigning herself to not having time to grab it from her room after thinking for a second.

The council member were here, they slowly walked through the door. Each of one them flanked by an aide, and a bodyguard or two.

Reira looked up, the bodyguards were daunting. The first council member through the door was of the white. He was a tall gentleman, his skin the colour of caramel, his black hair cropped short, his eyes were dark, his stare piercing, causing Reira to recoil as he scowled while he looked around. Reira could easily see his tattoo on his wrist, his jacket cuffs finished in the middle of his arm.

He was not afraid for anyone to see his tattoo; he wore it with pride. He carried himself expertly; he was dressed in all black, in stark contrast to the bodyguard who wore a light cream suit, sifted expertly to his daunting frame.

The member of the White House looked around the entrance as he walked in, his expression turned to disgust. “Basic” Reira could hear him whisper, she looked at her mother who kept smiling, she had heard everything, but it was easier to ignore it.

“Lord Jido-Arkin, Such a pleasure to see you in our humble home, please…” as she gestured towards to main hall…

He didn't reply; he continued to walk.

Charge of the arrival of the council members was always left to the lady of the house. This was an old tradition from millennia's ago. Following behind the council members were their families, and their partners.

Reira's nerves finally calmed after the council members had arrived. They had taken hours to arrive, not arriving together, for security, but spaced out over the morning. Reira had hated the waiting, there were other things she could have been doing, especially today. Replying to a recent correspondence with the Temple at Ateki was at the forefront of her mind.

The doorway was empty. Then instantly it was not, the family members and partners arrived. This was an opportunity for the families to try to get along. Some families never got along, especially from the white and the blue. Reira had been looking forward to seeing a friendly face. Someone she remembered from a few years earlier. Her family had always gotten along with the turquoise. But it was the council member's daughter that Reira got on with.

Reira stood as members of the council and their aides walked past her, not paying any attention to her. She stood, staring out into the distance, waiting to glimpse a familiar face, in the hustle and bustle her mind travelled, lost in thought. Those nightmares were still there, gnawing at the back of her mind. She shook her head, trying to banish those thoughts away, just as she did her focus returned.

"Look at you…" a voice echoed from behind her…

Reira shook her head again, startled by the voice coming

from behind her, as she turned around she smiled.

"Lost in thought again, It is the weakness that we must rid you of." The voice joked, Reira looked straight at her,

"You can try, but I doubt it will work… Nalae" Reira responded, Nalae was shorter than Reira, even though they were both the same age. She smiled at Reira as she spoke. Her emerald hue eyes glistened in the light.

"It's been a while, seems like that growth spirt happened, she looked down at herself… I'm still waiting for mine." She laughed, her laugh was infectious, Reira burst out laughing, before quickly quietening down as others in area stopped their conversations at looked at them.

Reira nodded at her and placed her right hand on Nalae's left shoulder and grabbed it gently, she closed her eyes for a second, as she cleared her throat.

"Nale, I'm sorry to hear about your father. How does he fare?" Reira enquired.

Nalae looked at Reira, sighed a heavy sigh before trying to muster a smile.

"He's… He's, trying his best not to worry me… which…"

Reira interrupted.

"Worries you even more… Mother does that also, seems like it runs in the family." She joked, trying to lift the mood.

CHAPTER 7

Hours had passed, Reira's father had mingled with the other members of the council, 'appeasing the beasts, against my better judgement' he called it, this made Reira laugh, she had followed around her father. She had been introduced as 'my youngest daughter' most of them surprised by her age, given her shy demeanour. Compared to most Impiri who were not afraid to express their own opinion especially after reaching the age of ascension at 18.

However, she was shy around people she didn't know, but that didn't mean she was weak, she could be as stubborn and as forthright as her sister if she needed to be. She kept everything bottled up, never wanting to cause offence, a stark contrast to her sister.

It would be at least a decade before they would see her as a fully fledged adult, she was in the limbo years, an adult by traditional standards, her coming of age ceremony having been a month earlier. But not an adult by the more modern standards, she would still be schooled for another decade before taking her place within society.

Numarii had disappeared into the other rooms in the house, talking to one of the young Impiri men who had turned up with the council members., as she talked to him she curled her long hair around her finger, gently playing with her hair, every so often she bowed to a member of the council that walked past, with each bow she revealed more of her leg through the side split, with glimpses of her stocking tops being seen.

She smiled innocently when anyone had noticed them; she knew what she was doing. She had always been the one to push the boundaries, much to Reira's embarrassment.

Reira had left her father's side to search for Numarii, finding her talking quite intimately with the son of the turquoise house. In one alcove towards the back of the house.

"Marii, Father is looking for you…" She called out.

Numarii laughed gesturing at her sister.

"I told you they would send her, always sending the obedient daughter to find her wayward sister…," as she spoke, she looked directly as Reira, and with her eyes fixed on her she leaned over and kissed the cheek of the young Impiri man she was talking to, leaving him surprised, he seemed as if he would speak. Before he had the chance Numarii placed her finger against his lips. His face perplexed.

"Don't speak, I'll be back soon" she paused, looked him up. at down, admiring him.

"You can be assured of that..." she whispered, at the same time she placed her right hand on the back of her neck and sighed as she rubbed the edges of the scales on the back of her neck.

"Always spoiling my fun..." she quipped as she walked away slowly, fixing the length of her skirt which had ridden up slightly during her time leaning against the wall of the alcove. She reached down and wiped dust off of her stockings as she walked.

"He's quite the catch don't you think?" she asked, not waiting for an answer before adding "do you think mother would approve?" She asked jokingly, Reira wasn't sure if she was being rhetorical, but she replied anyway.

Reira looked back at him for a second before turning away.

"He's okay, if you like that rough-and-ready type, looks like he is in the Imperial Guard.., and I do not know whether mother would approve?"

"Well, it's not like I'm planning on settling down with him, he's not really the type to get 'bonded' with, I mean he's quite nice to look at..." she laughed as she looked over at him, he was standing flustered in the alcove as they walked away.

"Not too smart though, he would be a bit of fun though." She added.

"Marii, really? Now I'm sure mother wouldn't approve of that!" She replied, embarrassed by her sister's brazen attitude to promiscuous activity.

Reira looked at her sister, her expression confused and disapproving, she took a deep breath and sighed, in the air a lingering hint of something sweet hit her senses, for a second she lost her train of thought, a strange tingling sensation traveled down her spine, before shaking her head to snap herself out of it. She grabbed hold of her sister's arm and marched her towards the front of the house and the main hall.

Certain members of the council didn't talk to each other, the rivalry between members of the twelve were endless. Centuries had passed, wounds had healed. Peace had been held between the twelve. Some grudges held were as deathless as the gods and goddesses themselves.

Reira's father stood up and recited a poem written by his ancestor. This had been written during the last Impiri civil war.

Many had died during that decade of distrust. Close to seven million Impiri had died, most of them from the red.

"Upon these shores we came upon, our ancestors saved our lives. Other sacrificed themselves to the darkness during the fall. All we honour them with is strife. The darkness is here. But it is not same, this darkness we bring within, my life, my love will end tonight, destroyed by thine own kin."

Reira had heard her father reciting this poem over the past few days, he delivered it flawlessly. His voice was commanding and emotive.

Lord Castyl-Alon stood up.

"Thank you Lord Abrasar, we must not forget what has transpired between us. The whole reason this council exists is to keep us as one. No longer fighting between ourselves. I thank you for your excellent rendition of part of the poem of Duradim."

Reira's cousins stood by her father's side, as he entered the room, they were situated at the furthest part of the room. Reira and Numarii were allowed into the room. Normally the daughters of the house were forbidden from council matters. Unless they were the only children of the Lord.

Ilaria would have normally taken this, but she was out serving her people, protecting the colony on Daxie VII. So it fell to Reira and Numarii to take her place. Reira sat behind her father, listening to all that was being discussed.

There was a lot of ceremony. Once everyone was seated, An unmarked Impiri gentleman entered the great hall, he was smartly dressed, he spoke with grandeur and melody in his voice.

"Since time began our noble people have convened the council. Here today, we hereby give council again, it has been 407 days since last council. In attendance are:

Lord Inis Abrasar - House of Red
Lord Castyl-Alon -House of Green
Lord Jido-Arkin - House of White
Lady Eslor Sobyl - House of Purple
Lady Nalae Jaeihai - House of Turquoise
Lady Sama De Loret - House of Orange
Lord Daymont Daivaal - House of Black
Lady Carmya Ajik - House of Grey
Lady Jama Vene - House of Blue
Lord Malik Honall - House of Yellow
Lady Drinna Cyone - House of Brown
Lord Deli Adoth - House of Pink"

He recited, his voice rising and falling in melodic cadence. He looked around the room, which had fallen into silence. He cleared his throat quietly before raising his hands into the air, palms up and chanted, as he spoke most of the council members bowed their heads in respect, Reira closed her eyes and bowed her head graciously.

"To the Darkness we give our doubt, to the light we give praise. To all the Gods and Goddesses, we your humble servants, are meeting today to conduct matters of business. Guide our hearts and our minds in the spirit of fairness, right thought and speech. Impart your supreme wisdoms upon our activities so that our affairs may reach a successful conclusion. We give thanks today for your source of guidance." His voice boomed across the hall.

After the recital, he turned around and walked out of the great hall, closing the doors behind him, the sound of the lock being closed echoed throughout the hall.

Reira's father smiled.

"Brothers and Sisters" he proclaimed.

"What is all this talk I hear regarding manoeuvring against Lord Jaeihai. I will let you know now, the Red will have nothing to do with this. The turquoise are our closest ally. do not take my generosity and demeanour here as an acceptance of any supposed actions,". His voice calm but firm.

The other members were silent, Lady Jaeihai sat in the seat her father would have sat in, behind her, her uncle,

"Now, you can, my Brothers and Sisters, understand that any move against Lord Jaeihai is a move against me, my house and all red across the empire, I wouldn't want to have to call in old debts, that some of you, here in this very room have..." he stood up, banging his hands firmly on the table in front of him.

"There is to be no discussion regarding this, there will be no vote of no confidence in Lord Jaeihai..." members of house Turquoise banged their fists on the table, to support his comments. Inis looked over, at Nalae Sacrabam and gestured to her,

"I offer our honest true wishes for his recovery to his daughter Nalae Sacrabam. At only eighteen sitting in what one day will become her seat at this council. The next time you see your father, tell him he always had, and will always have our loyalty."

"The bonds between us will never fail." He added.

Lord Jido-Arkin of house white did not bother with any pleasantries. He was the heir to the great White House as he kept referring the sound of his voice booming through the great hall.

"Whatever sources you have Lord Abrasar, are mistaken, no one here in this room plots against Lord Jaeihai I for one am glad to see someone sitting in his place..." he paused, before correcting himself,

"As the representative of his noble house." The look of relief flashed across his face for a split second.

"Father, he sounds like the old recordings of Telmadus Arkin, except without the calls for mass genocide..." as she mimicked Lord Arkin's gestures and posture. Her father glanced at her, and gestured for her to be silent with his index finger, while trying to hide a smile and failing miserably.

"Did you have something to add to this proceeding?" Lord Jido-Arkin sarcastically implored as he heard Reira's comment.

"... I thought not.." He added before Reira interrupted.

"I did, if someone would allow me to speak it...?" She uttered sarcastically before standing up and walking towards the part of the circular table that Lord Arkin was sitting at, she was seething, he had ignored her completely.

"I was commenting to my father that even though you act like you care about the welfare of Lord Jaeihai. You don't, and you're acting just like Telmadus Arkin, or as my family would call him; Mala Tomez - White Devil,"

The members of the council discussed. Lord Arkin stood up and walked towards her, his anger was easy to see, his face couldn't hide his contempt for her.

"You, the 3rd daughter, dare to speak out of turn, even contradict me..." he spoke, his voice becoming angrier by the second. He was standing three feet away from Reira, As he spoke, he raised his hand in anger, as he did this Reira's father stood up, but as he did, Lord Jido-Arkin's hand froze motionless in mid-swing, Reira's eyes were glowing as she shielded herself with her forearm.

"Nobody raises there hand in anger...only a ....." she spoke, her voice echoing across the hall.

"Enough!" Lady Eslor Sobyl of the Purple House commanded, as she banged a gavel on the table. Reira's eyes faded quickly from white.

"Lord Arkin, Sit down and don't frighten a child for being the only one here brave enough to stand up against you...". Lady Sobyl added, placing the gavel back on the table.

Lord Arkin turned to her, regaining his composure before straightening his collar before replying.

"I will sit, once this child is properly informed, if I may graciously finish..."

"You, child do not understand the intricacies of our people. You still haven't finish your schooling. You are decades away from understanding the basics of our people. What makes you think you know more about our people than I?" The arrogance in his voice irritating Reira.

"Don't even bother answering. I think we need a small recess, it would be useful if you would go and get us something to quench our thirst,". He added sarcastically.

Reira turned towards her father, he carefully glanced at her, and smiled a nervous smile

"It's okay, you can go..." he whispered.

Reira's breaths came as fast as she was walking. She exited the great hall, the sound of her footsteps echoing across the hall.

"Why did he make an example of me..." she thought to herself. She walked towards the back of the house, towards the dining hall. They were filled with the children and partners of the other council members. There were echoes of laughter and discussion. Reira could make out her mother's laugh, this reassured her. A voice of reason amongst the madness.

She walked into the kitchen, the voices of others were louder now, being just a few meters away from the dining hall. Reira reached into a cupboard and pulled out a large tray and several glasses. Her hands shaking nervously as she placed the glasses on the tray. She was about to reach into another cupboard when she was interrupted by a sound.

"Rei, what are you doing here? I thought you was with your father?" Her mother commented when she entered the kitchen, surprised to see a Reira there.

"Just getting a few drinks for the council members, thought I would help out. I've got to set the right example..." she nervously replied, hoping her mother would not notice.

"That's good my dear, just don't take too many, you'll drop them..." her mother replied before walking out into the gardens behind the house, leaving her to do what she needed to do.

Reira was still nervous. Her hands trembled as she poured the drinks, to make sure she didn't drop it. She reached into the cupboard again and poured in a small amount of a clear liquid into one glass before returning it to the cupboard.

"That'll teach him..." she murmured to herself.

What would she say if someone stopped her as she returned with the drinks. Would she say that she had taken her time due to questioning by her mother, or that she wasn't able to carry drinks for all the members.. Or that she had soured the drink as a punishment for Lord Arkin for speaking disrespectfully about her family..

She arrived back in the main hall. Her father was silent as other members were in a heated discussion. The moment she entered the room, the room fell silent, an eerie silence. Each member of the council looked at her, except her father and Nalae Jaeihai of house turquoise. They glanced at each other before finally glancing at Reira.

"You May speak..." Jido-Arkin declared as he saw Reira put the drinks down on the table at the side of the room. She turned around and addressed the room, she bowed gracefully before she spoke.

"I'm guessing that my honourable father has informed you of my ambition not to serve the empire and our people by joining my sister in the military, as has been a tradition for generations..."

"I am the third daughter, my elder sister is already serving our people, and hopefully my sister Numarii gets accepted into the Cloisters, I thought..."

Lord Arkin cut her off..

"It is against tradition..." he scolded.

"Act..." Reira was cut off by her father, he gestured for her to be silent before continuing.

"Actually, it is an even older tradition. Long ago before we had even discovered that we were not alone in this universe. The youngest daughter of a house would be given up to the temple. To give back to the community in which she came. Her responsibility to observe any other tradition was ignored." Inis proudly declared.

"Child, your father has shielded you from my question, but before this council can abide by your honoured fathers decision, please explain to me...why we..." he trailed off, clearing his throat before continuing

"Why I should agree with you..." Lord Arkin quizzed, staring at Reira. He grabbed the drink that Reira had placed beside him, and took a quick sip of the drink, before nearly spitting it out, much to the amazement of the other council members, before composing himself again.

"I'm sorry my brothers and sisters, just a little tickle in my throat, must be the climate here." He excused himself after his outburst.

Reira walked into the middle of the floor. She glanced over at her father, who nodded gently. before looking straight at

Lord Jido-Arkin with a smirk on her face.

"Do you understand Death Lord Jido-Arkin...? "she questioned,

Lord Arkin stared at her, the council members began whispering,

"Quite a defiant young Impiri we have here". She could hear a member of the blue whisper, loud enough that she could hear.

After pausing she spoke again

"Of course you don't Lord Jido-Arkin, it could be said that the white have lost their way." The fury in Lord Arkin's face could easily be seen, being challenged this openly by a child, had irritated him. His eyes narrowed, his lips drew in and his eyebrows sank.

"Punish me for my observations, but by doing so you admit that I was right". Reira added sarcastically. The atmosphere in the room was palatable,

"To some there is no single answer to the question I asked you. There is no particular understanding, in concept. Except the childish notion of rebirth, but don't forget I am still a child. In accordance with the old traditions, But I know what I believe"

"But I do not understand deaths nature, to You our bodies crumble and are returned to the soil, our souls do not even exist, and that is it..." she replied, the tone in her voice changing, she was getting frustrated by his questioning.

"But some of us still understand and appreciate our heritage. Yes our bodies crumble and return to the soil, but our souls. Forgive me for sounding like a child, they are reborn. If we have lived our lives well. If we haven't, they journey into darkness." She paused to clear her throat. "There in the darkness they consume nothing, all food and drink are an illusion, Everything is an illusion created by shadows. There dreams disappear in-front of their grasp."

"But that's just my belief. I do wish to serve our people, but not just our own people. I wish to serve all, that's why I've discussed with my father my acceptance into the temple at Ateki as a junior acolyte." She moved over to the centre of the area where they were sitting and placed her hands on a podium that was there, withdrawing her hands slightly , shocked by its Ivey cold surface. She looked at the council, reading their expressions as she spoke.

"To study the great works from our history. Such an honour is not bestowed by the Temple of the Enlightened Flame lightly." She proclaimed proudly.

"Father?" Reira asked, her voice just above a whisper. "It is I who challenged Lord Jido-Arkin the dishonour is mine alone. I cannot stand by while he disrespects our culture with every turn"

All around her the other members of the council gasped,

"Brash child, but she does speak up for herself..." the member of the black house challenged, Numarii stood up, before being gestured to sit down by Reira.

"I couldn't stand for the disrespect that Lord Jido-Arkin had labelled me with, made his drink bitter with Almar Root, I did this selfishly, to give him a taste of his own bitterness, and I did this by my own conviction and I should face the consequences of my own actions..."

"Reira....?" Her father pleaded.

"Yes Parshai - father, this dishonour is mine alone, he won't ever have to deal with me again, he thinks I'd be better off in the temple anyway..." she replied looking straight at her father.

"Child..." Lord Jido-Arkin laughed, as he paced backwards and forwards. He stopped, Reira's shoulders sank, her posture becoming small. Awaiting his onslaught.

"No one would dare challenge me in such a way..., not even my own children would argue with me..." he cursed, scrunching up his brow as he spoke.

"However, I can't condone your actions, Never the less." He paused, coughing gently to clear his throat

"I can see they were done for a reason...." he replied, these responses stunned the council. Murmurs from members of the council could be heard, Reira herself was stunned into silence.

"I had spoken ill of you and for that, with the rest of the council as a witness, I apologise..."

Reira's father banged slightly on the table, the glass on the table began to rattle, Lord Arkin looked over at him sternly before cracking a small smile.

"I challenged your reasoning for rejecting tradition, for a reason, you do things which don't only effect only yourself, or your family, but the greater community at large..." he added, as she walked closer to Reira, she stood there in shock.

"And yes, I do think the temple would be the best place for you..." he joked, mocking her slightly.

Reira stared at him, her expression confused. He was about

two meters from her, expecting a physical reaction she drew her arms in towards herself for protection.

"It will focus your mind, maybe even bring something to our community, but I say this now, I will keep a keen eye out..."

Reira nodded her head slowly, not really sure of what she was hearing, her mind rushed a response.

"You give me permission...?" Reira stuttered, it was hard to accept.

"The vote was tied, you needed to convince one of us to side with your father, he knows I've stood against him many a time over the years, but for once, maybe he is right, maybe your thinking in the grand scheme might benefit us in the future..."

"So yes, I amend my decision, I side with you...don't make me regret my momentary lapse in judgement..." he scowled.

Reira looked up at him, and for the first time he wasn't menacing, he was still physically impressive but his demeanour was jovial. Members of the council banged on the table in support.

"So finally this matter is closed" the member of the purple house decreed standing up, he gestured over at Reira.

"Lady Abrasar, you may now go..."

Reira looked over at her father who nodded his head and smiled. Reira couldn't contain her excitement, she was about to rush out of the hall but before she got to the door she turned around, and bowed, gesturing backwards with her arms, her palms facing forwards.

Reira was leaving the great hall, Numarii followed shortly after, a big smile on her face, she walked over to Reira who was standing outside the door, the same unmarked Impiri who recited at the beginning of the session began to lock the door.

They were undertaking a small recess. The nights discussions were to be private, only the twelve would be allowed to enter. Not even their aides would be granted access. Somethings were always going to be secret, known only to the twelve, only the affects of these conversations would have implications to over three billion Impiri.

Reira stood there in silence, a huge grin on her face, her eyes sparkled, she was ecstatic, Numarii reached over and hugged her.

"Never though you had it in you sis, I mean that's the kind of thing that I would have done, just never thought I'd see the day that you would be so...brash." She mocked.

What Reira had known about her father was changed that day. He was not only her father, a business leader, a soldier and a honest Impiri. He was a member of the council of twelve. He had tried to keep that from them until they were old enough to understand, and now was the time to tell the truth, to show her what it meant to have this responsibility.

Pride, the first and only thing Reira thought of her father, she was so proud, that she left the great hall with a bounce in her step.

Reira didn't even notice or respond to her sisters words or hug, Reira was so happy she was in shock. She ran up the stairs and into her room, shutting the door behind her,

Numarii stood at the bottom of the stairs looking up, she

smiled before catching the young Impiri man she had spoken to earlier out of the corner of her eyes, before making a quick walk to him, grabbing hold of his hand and dragging him and leading him off towards a quite room in the house.

"Hello Diary, Numarii had told me to use you one of these days, and today it is.

I can't believe what's happened, I mean, I've never been this insolent before, He challenged me, and this is something that got the fire inside me flared up.

Bless the goddesses for today. Father told the council about my acceptance. I should be going to Ateki to study under The Reverend Mother of the Temple of the Flame. He stood up for me, the council were not pleased. I didn't follow custom and tradition. Everything has now been set in motion, but I'm still worried. Nissa had told me those stories, those premonitions. I can't shake them...maybe it's nothing, crazy thoughts in my own head.

Eritrea - Joyful Wishes

write again soon...."

smiled before catching the young Indian man she had spoken to earlier [illegible] of her eyes, he [illegible] a [illegible] walk [illegible] hold of his hand and dragging him and [illegible] leading him out towards a quiet room in the house.

CHAPTER 8

4th Hour of the 3rd Day of the 9th Month
IY (Imperial Year) 49

The mountains were shrouded in darkness; it was a clear night, no clouds covered the sky, the sky was lit up by the stars and the moons, a perfect night to gaze at them.

Reira and Numarii had hiked to the best vantage point to see the relic and the sunrise. The woods had trees to block out the sun, so that viewpoint was out of the question. From this view with the city behind them and with the sun rising in front of them. With the relic in the valley below them, it would be a perfect sunrise.

Numarii had gone on ahead, allowing Reira to rest for a second. This had been an eight-hour hike, in the dead of night, with little sleep on Reira's part, her mind had been active all night.

'Just to see a sunrise and some old relic', she thought. A stone path led to a clear opening below them was a clearing within the trees the ancient relic stood. Thirty feet tall, resembling an obelisk. It was covered in inscriptions across its perfectly black surface. it could be barely made out in the darkness of the early morning

No one was around to stop them. This was one of the few times that they would get on, they both enjoyed sunrise. There were no buildings to get in the way, no people to cause any distractions. Just being able to focus on the sunrise and the full reveal of the relic. With no authorities to stop them from getting as close to the relic as possible.

The sisters knew the area well. Their father had taken them hiking into the forest every year since they were old enough to walk. Much to their mothers disagreement.

Numarii definitely had the upper hand. She was the Stronger one; she had great agility, she could remember every turn on the route to the top. Reira always forgot this knowledge, Numarii was always the first to the top.

Reira had given up trying to beat her, it was nice to be able to do something together. Especially here, at home, before the school semester started again.

Reira couldn't wait to see the sunrise though. The sight would steal away any conversation. There were other places to see this sunrise, but this was their place. The breeze was blowing steadily, causing Numarii's hair to whip around and covered her face.

"Thanks Malanet, why couldn't you have been the god of sunshine not wind" she cursed jokingly, as she again brushed her hair away from her face as the wind continued to swirl around her.

"If he was he'd shine so brightly into your face that you'd find another reason to argue with him". Reira remarked back sarcastically. Reira being prepared for the wind she had tied her hair back into a ponytail.

"Marii?" Reira called out, as her sister continued to walk ahead picking up pace..

"Rei, come on, it's not going to be long until the sunrise. We have about twenty minutes, and it's at least a fifteen minute hike to go!" She replied, eager to get to the viewing spot, before the sun arose.

This realisation caused Reira to jog towards her sister. Within a second a misplaced step caused her to catch her foot on a large stone and fell towards the floor. Crashing to the floor face first and catching her head on a boulder. This nearly knocking her out and causing a large cut on the side of her head which had started bleeding . Reira drifted in and out of consciousness, moments later Numarii was there.

"Rei..." she called out before repeating..

"Rei are you okay?" She called out, staring at her sister, holding her sister's hand close to her chest, her own hearts beating rapidly.

"I'll be...fine" she responded as she tried to get herself up, before sinking back down to the ground.

"Maybe I need a bit of help.." She sheepishly replied.

Numarii laughed. Realised that she wasn't joking and then sighed before grabbing under Reira's arm. Helping her sister up to a sitting position.

The darkness was shattered, rapidly diminishing was the nighttime sky, the sunlight chasing the night sky away. The sunlight was glistening giving the grass below their feet a glow like fire. A feeling of peace and serenity over took Reira. She smiled and took a deep breath, She could hear the cries of the birds in the distance and the sound of the leaves of the trees which swayed in the morning breeze.

The sky resembled a quilt of colours; the colours bleeding into each other, To Numarii it was as good as dreaming. This is when she felt at peace with herself, nothing else mattered at this time, not the views of her parents, not her friends at school, nor her ex boyfriend who she was trying to forget about. Right now in the here and now all that mattered was she was here in this moment with the only person she could trust, watching the sun rise.

Reira and a Numarii sat cross-legged on the hilltop, Numarii's eyes wandered across the horizon, She pushed back her windswept hair and admired the view. She looked at the rising sun. She had seen countless sunrises, yet they always startled her with their immense beauty. She looked over at Reira and smiled

"It's as beautiful as always, I've missed this..." Numarii quietly spoke, she grabbed Reira's hand and squeezed it tightly,

"If everything goes to plan, this will be the last one we see together for a while…" Numarii added, she looked at Reira and gave her a gentle smile, before gesturing that they should go.

They both stood up and wandered down the hill towards the obelisk, the grass was lush and thick, their feet sinking into the grass.

"Marii, I've missed spending time with you...", Reira's commented as she rambled down the hill, she stopped for a second and took in the sights. It was beautiful here. She spotted Numarii walking off towards the obelisk, but she stopped, looked back and saw a Reira, she smiled before picking up pace to make their way to the obelisk.

The obelisk stood in the middle of a clearing in the nearby forest; it had recently been re-erected after being discovered toppled over, buried under thousands of years of rubble from subsequent buildings made on top of the ruins of the ancient temple which stood in its place.

"Can't believe that this had been here all this time..." Numarii exclaimed as she looked at the obelisk which rose 20 meters into the sky. She froze looking up at the temple, trying to make out the inscriptions etched into its surface.

"We had played around here for years without even knowing it had been here. It's strange that when the temple here was being renovated a fire broke out, gutting the temple. Seems like an eerie coincidence." Reira replied as she stood behind her. The bottom sections of the obelisk were protected by sensors, placed by the imperial archeological society. Reira looked at the obelisk, then down at the sensors, before looking over at Numarii.

"Marii. Some of these look Impiri in origin, but how, the reports said that this was dated back to before the fall of Impiris..." she paused, leaning forward, straining to read the inscriptions.

"I can't make it out, not this far away, maybe we can inspect more." She added as she carefully stepped over the sensors and smiled.

"Rei, really?" she mocked, laughing at her with a smile on her face.

"Maybe I've been a bad influence" she paused for thought.

"Next you will tell me that you have a secret boyfriend." she joked as she climbed herself over the sensors.

Reira's smirk changed instantly, she blushed.

"Not likely" she joked laughing off the remark.

Reira slowly placed her hand on the obelisk, expecting the bare stone to be cold to the touch, but it wasn't, it was pleasantly warm. She pulled her hand back in shock.

"Marii, this feels weird..." she added as she touched the obelisk again.

Numarii placed her hand on the stone surface and pulled her hand back almost instantly,

"Good goddess that's cold, how can you still be touching it Rei...?" She cursed, staring at Reira with a confused look on her face.

Before Reira could even respond a noise and wave of vibration emanated from the obelisk. The sound growing before Whoosh! A loud noise sounded from the obelisk, more powerful than before.

"I don't like the sound of that?," Reira announced. Even though the sound of her voice was drowned out by the sound emanating from the obelisk. She had jumped and had nearly lost balance, managing to stabilise herself, not wanting to land face-down on the floor for the second time in an hour.

The entire night before she was alert. The day before her grandmother had told her that something or someone would cause her life to change. She had divinated the future through the cards of Adras (God of Fortune), the messages were not clear; they were not threatening, but an indicator to things above her own control.

Most didn't trust the cards of Adras, but Reira did, her grandmother had been reading these cards for over two hundred years, some of her prophecies had come true, she normally told no one about what she had read int he cards, but this time she couldn't hide the concern she had regarding the reading from the cards. It involved her granddaughter. She didn't normally take what her grandmother said seriously, but the concerned look on her grandmothers face made Reira begin to second guess herself.

Everything she said had already come true, to some extent. Her grandmother asked her earlier how was her head after the fall, she hadn't fallen over until now. Her thoughts were running riot, how could she have known about something that hadn't happened yet. Was there some truth to the divination of the cards of Adras?.

She was lost in thought, ignoring Numarii until she turned around, looking straight at her sister but didn't the sound of her sister speaking, but could see her mouth moving, something was wrong. At the periphery of her vision she caught a glimpse of a strange black mist flowing from out of the obelisk. Seeming to dissolve from the surface of the obelisk into the air, with every gust of wind more of this mist disappeared from the surface.

Numarii turned around, puzzled by Reira's nervous expression. Glimpsing the black mist, which moved as if it was alive, flowing out into the surrounding air before stopping and changing course, directly towards them. Reira reached out towards her sister in desperation to save herself.

"Marii..." Reira cried out, but nothing could be heard. Time seemed to have stopped for an instant. The black mist moving as normal speed but with them now moving in slow motion. Reira panicked and breathed in deeply. At the same time which was happening, the mist travelled between the sisters.

Seconds later the mist seemed to separate. One stream of it making its way to Reira and the other towards her sister. Reira's eyes widened with fear, the same as her sisters, before the mist rushed towards them and disappeared into them, knocking them backwards.

Then there was nothing, just silence. As quickly as it happened, time returned to normal. Reira and Numarii both fell to the floor, unconscious. Their eyes fixed open, within them a black swirling liquid was present. Moments later Reira blinked, and the liquid dissipated.

Reira eyes blinked first. looked over at her sister, who was still unconscious, she tried to move, but it was as if all the energy in her body was gone. She dragged herself the two meters between them before she grabbed hold of Numarii's jacket. This sudden jolt caused Numarii to quickly sit up, she looked down at her sister, her brow furrowed and her lips pursed with confusion.

"What in the goddess's name was that, and why are you ...crawling on the floor...?" She spoke.

Reira looked up at her, and for an instant her eyes were black, not their normal amber hue. She blinked, and it disappeared, returning her eyes to normal.

Fear ran riot throughout her mind, her darkest thoughts were seconds from the surface. Reira could feel her hands clenching, her teeth ground together. "You know she isn't strong enough, she is strong willed, but against me, she knows nothing...but she will try..." a voice echoed inside Reira's mind.

A look of fear spread across her face, who was this voice, it sounded like her subconscious, but different, more sinister.

"Marii, are you okay?" Reira pleaded as she looked up at her sister.

"I'm fine, a little disorientated, but I do have the strangest urge to leave this place." She replied, as she struggled to her feet and made her way from the obelisk, picking up speed.

"Okay, but can we..." Reira tried to reply, her voice trailing off when she noticed that Numarii wasn't listening and was quickly picking up pace. Reira picked up her bag and chased after her sister, trying to catch up, still trying to process what had happened.

Reira spoke to her, but her words fell on deaf ears, Numarii didn't reply, she just kept walking, occasionally grunting a response to Reira's questioning.

Yet, Something was wrong with Numarii, very wrong, normally she would be the first one wanting to see what the cause of this was, always inquisitive. But now she didn't seem to care, it was like fear had taken over and was driving her away from it.

Reira didn't want to leave this place yet. how could you explain it, the black mist, the feeling of dread and malice, the voices in her mind, maybe her subconscious was playing tricks on her, what if the black mist was dangerous?

For all she knew either this mist was a figment of her mind. Yet how could it be if they both saw it, this mist could be deadly, or it was harmless?. She and her sister could be perfectly fine and she would have overreacted.

Maybe the blow to her head earlier had caused concussion, maybe the Kalic from earlier was playing with her mind, a common consequence of its usage by those as young as they were.

Not a minute later after being in deep thought, Reira knew something wasn't right. The longer she waited, the barrier between her and her sister became more noticeable. Something was wrong, and she couldn't put her finger on it.

Numarii was secretive normally, but she seemed distant. Reira suggested that they take the quick route home. As there would me less of an opportunity to seek help if they went the same way they came.

Reira, still recovering from the mist, rubbed her eyes and shook her head as she walked after her sister. She walked slower than usual, lost in thought, the journey home was unnerving. Numarii was lost in thought and it concerned Reira.

When they arrived home hours later, Numarii went straight to her room, ignoring all others, even her mother, she brushed it off saying "they must tired". Numarii slammed her door.

Reira did the same. She wanted to talk to her mother, but she needed to get this sorted in her own head first, she went to her room, closing the door behind her, she sat on the floor, staring into the middle distance, trying to figure this all out. She couldn't rest; she got up, paced around her bedroom.

Contemplating if she should walk out and have a word with her sister or not. She stopped mid walk, turning towards the door, should she go and talk to her sister, she stopped, frozen in thought before resigning herself, this wasn't the right time, give Numarii some more time, give herself more time, time to understand what had actually happened, to process the information. She turned back towards the centre of her room before sitting down on to surface.

"System, activate room emersion system, Meditation Veranda at the Temple of Tsan circa 2805 on the Impiri calender." She uttered, the room was silent, before the walls and everything around her changed, she was no longer sitting on the floor in her room, she was sitting on a cold stone floor, feeling the chill of the cold stone on her legs, she sat looking out onto a plateau, the sun setting behind her, she could feel its heat against her back, a gentle breeze brushing against her skin.

This had always been her favourite recreation, the Temple of Tsan on Impiris, one of the most holy sites on Impiris.

She sat looking out into the distance, trying to make sense of what had happened, to clear her mind of the fear she harboured. Her breathing was still elevated, she looked down at her hands, noticing that her hands were clenched, her knuckles white, she breathed in deeply, closing her eyes, after a while her hands unclenched and found their way to resting in her lap.

Finally, she took the leap of faith and got up to knock on her sister's bedroom door.

"System, end emersion" she announced, the room quickly returning back to being her room. She got up from the floor, making her way towards the door, Before she took a step out her room, she took a deep breath and sighed. She looked at the clock on the wall of her room before leaving, 16:30 it read.

She had gotten herself worked up for the last four hours, not the thirty minutes she thought it had been. "Great," she said out loud.

"I better not be loosing my mind, something is wrong with Marii, if I'm wrong I will look like I'm going crazy"

Reira made her way downstairs, going to see her mother before visiting her sister. As she walked into the kitchen Reira stopped, her breathing became shallow, there was a feeling of dread, the entire place had a bad feeling, like an omen of something bad going to happen.

Reira's face was flush, her usual white skin was pink. "Something defiantly got you spooked" her mother commented, As she checked her temperature with the back of her hand.

"Are you feeling okay dear?, you're running cool..."

"Did Marii look at that bump on your head?, go and rest and we will talk about it in the morning..." her mother commented, rest was always her answer to everything, it usually cleared her mind and resolved a lot of issues, so she always suggested it to her daughters.

"She did mother, she said I'd feel a little off, and to be honest I do feel a bit strange, I just can't shake it" she replied, before stretching her back, her brow furrowed.

She turned around and made her way back up the stairs, she would go to her room and think about this, 'Mother could be right' Reira thought to herself. But first she would see her sister, she had to clear the air.

Reira made her way to her sisters' room, the door firmly shut, she rapped her knuckles against the door, twice. The knock echoing across the mezzanine floor.

"Let me in, Numarii. I'll even make it quick', just let me talk to you, come on we are sisters." She pleaded

"No!" Numarii replied, her voice aggravated, Reira knocked on the door again.

"I just need to talk to you, I cannot talk to mother about this, it's about Castin you know that..." she pleaded quietly, not wanting anyone else to hear the topic of their conversation.

"The unmarked you met while at school ...?" Numarii replied, still not opening the door. She sat behind the door on the floor, curled up in a fetal position.

"I didn't think he was your type." she joked, Reira could hear her getting up from the floor and walking slowly towards the door.

Reira laughed, a typical insult from her sister.

"What do you mean not my type?, I don't even know if I have a type ?" Reira responded, rising to the occasion, even though she knew her sister was winding her up.

The door to the room unlocked, and the door swung open, Numarii was standing at the door, she was already dressed for bed; she was wearing silk pyjamas. Her hair tied back into a ponytail, keeping the hair away from her face, her eyes were red, she had been crying again.

"He's not very religious, you know you need someone as into the religion as you..." she mocked, as she rubbed a tear away from her left eye.

"Can I come in and talk about it, I don't want Mother and father finding out?" Reira responded.

As she spoke she barged past Numarii, into her room...

"Well, it seems like you can make yourself at home." Numarii sarcastically replied, gesturing for her to come in.

"So, what about this guy?" Numarii asked, her attention was on Reira, and she didn't like it.

She immediately reacted,

"Firstly, your room is a wreck, you could of at least cleaned it up, there's paper and ink everywhere." Trying to change the topic of the conversation.

"Had I known I would have unexpected visitors knocking my door at this time I would have." Numarii replied as she picked up the overturned chair, righting it before grabbing hold of a pile of paper from her bed and moving it to her desk.

"And where's the Kalita?, I can't find anything in here..." she retorted, Reira always trying to attempt to lighten the situation.

"So, what are your feelings towards this guy....?" Numarii deflected.

"Hey, no changing the subject, I know you've got some of Fathers Kalita.." pointing at a small incense burner in the corner of the room. The air in the room slightly smokey, the incense burner attempting to hide the smell of the atomised Kalita.

"How do you know what that's for?, who's been telling you..?", has Erlu been talking about me behind my back?" She replied defensively.

Reira shook her head as she sat down on the bed, "Your not the only one keeping secrets from mother..." Reira replied as she pulled out a small atomiser from her pocket, within the atomiser a light blue liquid could be seen.

Numarii's face changed instantly, she laughed to herself.

"Seems like I've not been paying attention in school these days, when the good girl is a Tweaker and even the rebellious daughter doesn't even know about it!"

"Does father know?" Numarii asked,

Reira shamefully nodded her head, embarrassed by the revelation.

Numarii chuckled to herself before replying

"I bet, what's his name?...Castin, he got you into this?"

"Actually, it wasn't, it was Nythish, she's helped me out a few times"

"Nythish, my friend Nythish, I didn't even know you went in the same circles as us." Numarii protectively replied, they shared none of the same friendship groups, so this took Numarii by surprise.

"We took Molecular Chemistry together last year, she helped me source what I needed, but I've been doing this for nearly six years, with father's permission..." she replied, her voice trailing off...

"Wait, what, father knows about this?..."

"Enough of the questioning about our habits, do you want the answer as to why I hang around with Castin?" Reira asked, her voice frustrated.

"Okay then, Miss Abrasar, why do you hang around with that Dakta - unmarked?" Numarii sarcastically replied.

"Don't call him that..." Reira's voice trembling.

"Most of our kind our unmarked, don't discredit him

without knowing him.", Reira replied defensively, her brow furrowing, her eyes brightened, her anger rising.

"Oh, defending him are we? Sounds like my little sister is in love, finally." Numarii joked, for once her smile was genuine, she was enjoying teasing Reira.

"Love, I'm not even sure myself if it's love, but he treats me like no one else, he actually listens to me when I have a problem, you know the way we used to talk?" Reira replied, nervously twisting her hair around her finger.

"What do you and him even talk about, your the daughter of a Lord and a marked Impiri, and he is ...a 'Dak.." she paused, correcting herself before continuing "he is unmarked"

"We talk about my desire to..." Reira replied before being cut off by her sister.

"Your desire, ooh, getting a bit frisky are we, I'm sure mother wouldn't approve." Numarii joked, smiling her eyes wide open.

"To join the temple, nothing perverse..." Reira quickly added, trying to deflect the conversation.

"Is he supportive of what you want to do?, have you talked to him since the council and father agreed to it.?" Numarii changed her tone, sounding concerned about the recent change in circumstances.

"I talked to him last night, he was...supportive?, kinda." She answered, her voice nervous and unsure of itself.

"But enough about me!" Reira remarked.

"We've not really spoken since, the obelisk..." she asked getting cut off before completing her line of questioning.

"Rei, for once I don't want to talk about it, I can't wrap my brain around it. Maybe I don't want to wrap my brain around it, leave it as one of those unexplained situations, it ..." Numarii answered, her smile disappearing by the second, her eyes looking down, her entire demeanour changing as she talked about the situation.

"Shook you up?" Reira chipped in,

"Yeah, shook me up, yeah, in a way, it ...Made me think things that I don't really want to think..," Numarii added.

"Did you hear the voices when it happened."

"What voices...." Reira replied after a delay, trying to hide her own understanding of the voice she had heard in her own head.

"Maybe it was just the voice in my own head, but it must have taken a knock, it suggested some dark things to me, some painful and disturbing things..."

"Like what, all I heard was the sound, something like a scrambled voice, but I couldn't understand it..." Reira announced, unsure of what her sister would think.

"Well, I heard it and I understood it." Numarii becoming agitated, her posture becoming protective, she folded her arms, close to her body.

"I'd rather not talk about it, talking about your situation helped me forget about it for a while..." she added.

"So, did Castin get a reaction out of you?" She teased, changing the topic again.

"What?" Reira responded, unsure if she had her the question correctly.

"Did he get a reaction out of you, come on you know what I mean, did the scales on your back tingle?, I'm sure they did, you know you can't hide it from me..." she joked, reaching over and taking Reira's hand in hers before spinning her around, before attempting to look down the back of her top.

"I'm not sure what you're talking about..." Reira replied shyly as she tried to stop Numarii from looking.

"Really Rei, since we've been talking about him,..." Numarii exclaimed, seeing down her top, the scales ran from the base of her skull all the way down her back. They were hexagonal and ran in two parallel lines down the side of her spine, they were slightly recessed into her skin, the ridges surrounding the scales were greyish.

"So I was right, they have been tingling, your scales are becoming light blue even now, you might not know if it's love, but your body wants him." She laughed,

"He should be able to smell your pheromones from a mile away.." she replied before breathing in deeply, her eyes closing slightly.

"I can smell them from here, quite the aroma," she spoke as she exhaled slowly.

"Luckily no one else at the school other than our own kind could smell them. You know the effect they have on our kind." She stopped and breathed in deeply again, savouring the tantalising aroma.

"Right now it's very intoxicating and stimulating, I can't think straight. I can imagine how they must drive him wild, I bet he would do anything you asked him to," she spoke, her voice calm and relaxed.

The smell of the pheromones affected Numarii, even her own scales tingled, the sensation travelling all the way down her spine in stages from the top all the way down her spine. She sighed as she found it difficult to concentrate.

“He must have had one hell of an effect on you," she spoke, her voice slow and breathy.

“You could easily get drunk on them if you was on Kalita, the mixture would give quite a euphoria...” she added as she reached her hand to the back of her neck and felt the scales that ran down her own back, even the simplest touch sent strong shocks down her body.

Numarii was lost in thought before being shook back into reality by the sound of Reira speaking.

“Marii?, what’s wrong...?”

“I… I have something to tell you, and I’m not sure how to say it.” She replied as the sensations in her body died down.

“You’re scaring me now, what’s going on?” Reira replied.

“I really hope the Cloisters accept me, I mean..” she stopped, then sat down on her bed. She looked up at Reira who was still standing.

“Because of what we are.?” She murmured.

“We’re special..” Reira replied, trying to sound upbeat, as she sat next to her.

“Mother always had a way with words, but you know what we’ve been called...” Numarii smiled as she spoke, a fake smile that Reira could see straight through.

“Freak, flawed, psycho, mutant, degenerate, reject, abomination..I know them all” Reira answered, with every word her body retreated into itself, her shoulders dropping.

“Every time that happens to me, I just ignore them” Reira added, trying to ignore the hurt from each of the names they used to be called.

"Maybe you can but the pressure on me is so much worse, it feels like it's tearing me apart." She stopped, as she couldn't die her emotions anymore, the tears streamed down her cheeks.

"But it's been worse since the obelisk, it's like..." Numarii replied, wiping the tears from her eyes with her forearm. She paused for a second, looking out of the window, the sun was going down, a rolling mist was approaching the house.

Reira reached over and wiped a tear away from her other eye.

"It's like they have flipped a switch, and I'm afraid of what I can do, I mean..." Numarii spoke, her bottom lip trembling.

"I just need to get out sometimes, I'm afraid of myself..." she mumbled.

"The thoughts that run through my mind, they are so dark, that's why I've been crying. I know I said I couldn't tell you, but..." she stopped, clenching her hands together, she looked at Reira, her eyes filling with tears again.

"There is no one else I can talk to that would understand.." Numarii whispered.

"I've tried everything I can think of to distract myself.", locking myself away in here, writing out my thoughts into a diary, meditation even." She stopped, blushing slightly.

"Recently self stimulation of my scales, everything, all other experiences fade quickly and I'm left with these same thoughts. Pleasurable emotions are the only way I feel normal" she replied quietly, seeming to be ashamed of herself.

"It's been like this for... years, but recently it's been getting worse, why did you think I kept disappearing when we are back on the base, I've felt to alone, trapped within myself," she replied her voice returning to its normal volume.

"I thought you were coping with the abilities?" Reira replied looking at her sisters face, trying to get a sense of her emotions.

"Mostly, but sometimes it's too much, I need that release, a need to feel 'normal' , whatever that is." She joked, trying to push back tears.

"But now it's worse, since the obelisk it's becoming harder to control. I've tried everything. The Kalita didn't even help, it made it worse." She added, beginning to cry again.

"It's like I cannot feel anything." She slowly began rubbing her right forearm.

"I'm just numb.." she added as she wiped a tear from the end of her nose.

Reira just stood there, listening. Not interjecting, just listening, she was worried, her sister was normally strong, but this was a side that she hadn't seen in Numarii in years.

"Only your pheromones have made me feel anything since the obelisk. Just the simple sensation of pleasure made me feel great, otherwise all I want to do is cry, and.." she looked over at her right arm, and pulled her sleeve back, revealing three semi healed cuts which travelled across her forearm.

"Marii, what did you do?, why?" Reira cried out.

"Because it's like there is something inside me and I cannot get rid of it, I try to force it out, but it's still there..." she stopped, her voice becoming quieter.

" It tells me things, some of them perverse, but most of them dark, terrible things. It tries to get me to release it from me, I try to forget about it and it's still there sitting in the back of my mind. It's like it wants to leave me, but won't leave, everything I've tried doesn't work." She broke down again, angry at herself for getting angry she quickly wiped her tears away with her forearm.

"The feeling of pleasure seamed to allow me to feel normal again, I couldn't sense its presence.",

"Is that why you've been secluding yourself?" Reira questioned.

"Because you feel like you cannot control yourself?" Reira added,

Numarii put her head in her hands, before rubbing the tears away,

"I'm afraid of hurting someone.." she sighed.

"Most of all I'm afraid of hurting myself..." she added after composing herself.

"Not these scratches, I mean really hurt myself, the thought crossed my mind once.", Reira gasped as she realised what Numarii was suggesting.

"Also, it makes me want to lash out, when you first banged on the door, it wanted me to drag you in here, kicking and screaming" she snapped, before realising and withdrawing back into herself.

"Why?" Reira asked.

"It wanted me to tell you these perverse things, to drive you away from me. Even now it's there listening to everything, it's difficult to repress." She answered.

"I can't be alone, it's getting my insecurities and making them worse...Your the only one I trust." Numarii pleaded.

"I don't know if I'm going crazy? She added, her breathing

becoming laboured.

"But you believe me? Don't you ?" She hastily added.

"Of course.." Reira replied as she grabbed her sister's hand nervously and gripped it tightly.

"I know some things you feel, it's taken a long time to get to this point, you remember why I got into religion in the first place." Reira confided.

"To help me come to terms with these gifts that we have. That's how and why I got into using Kalita, the Kalita has even helped calm me down when I got agitated. I mean i was using every day, sometimes twice a day. Just trying to keep myself in check, otherwise I've been a nervous wreck." She joked, as she pulled her sister close to her for a hug.

"There are times when I wish I didn't have these abilities, you know, be normal once, I can't even remember what it felt like to not have these abilities. But I always knew that I had you there, you were always so strong, so determined, I never knew that you were struggling." Numarii whispered.

"You won't tell mother and father!" Numarii added, her voice full of concern, her parents couldn't find out about this, it would ruin the family's reputation and standing in the community, the embarrassment of that would be even worse.

"I promise...always" Reira added, tears streaming from her own eyes.

"You remember when we always made these promises, I've never broken one, and I don't aim to now." Reira added she reached over and pulled Numarii close to her, hugging her tight.

"I will always be here, no matter what, that's what sisters are for." She whispered in her ear.

"If it gets bad, just tell me" she added as she broke away from the hug, looking at her sister in the eyes.

"If I ever disappear, it's so that I can let myself go, and not be afraid of hurting someone, the woods or the city are always so useful when we are home." Numarii added, trying to reassure her sister.

"I might sneak away at times, just to get some perspective, some sense of normality, just to get away from it all, mother and fathers protective nature, sometimes it just feel stifling and i just need to be me, find some sense of pleasure in being somewhere else, with someone else." She added before sighing.

* * *

6 Hours Later

Later that night Reira was fast asleep, a cool summer's breeze wandered through the window of her room.

She could not make sense of her surroundings. The dream kept fluctuating instantaneously; she was standing alone in the middle of the great hall, the fire pit had been uncovered but hadn't been lit, a single black coffin lay resting on the coals, the air within the hall was hot and restless.

Reira walked over to the coffin, the lit to the coffin was open, she nervously leaned over the coffin and looked in. She jumped back; she saw herself, eyes open, staring back at her.

"Why didn't you save me" it spoke, she looked at herself again after recovering from the shock and it was still herself, but now her eyes were closed and her body was charged and burnt, it barely resembled Reira.

The dream transformed, gone was the grand hall, replaced by a dark corridor, people busy brushing past her, "Where?" Reira thought to herself, It took a while for Reira to understand where they were. It was their old school, they had left that school six years previously.

They were both popular and bright girls, Everyone loved them, She was just an ordinary girl like everyone else. That all changed one winter's morning when they were 12.

For Reira it happened when Numarii was rushing across the hallway at school when she accidentally fell and was about to collide into someone. Moments before she fell on top of him, Reira fell into a deep trance, her eyes glowed brightly, Numarii stopped in midair, after she recovered they exchanged glances, Reira's was upset, she didn't know what was going to happen.

Reira stood watching these events unfold, bringing back painful memories, she stood watching when people in her own class found out about the situation from that morning and had caused her to run away from the situation; she stood crying as others at the school labelled her as an abomination, causing her to leave the school. Running out of the school buildings, out of the surroundings grounds, off into a remote part of the school which had been closed off because of fire years before.

She didn't care about the rain which was falling heavily, as she ran through the rain she cried, pulling off her jacket, throwing it to the ground next to an old tree, before sitting beneath the tree, trying to escape from the rain, which started pouring torrentially from the dark clouds above,

She looked like a mess, her hair was disheveled, something which instantly annoyed her, normally her hair was perfect. Her clothes were soaking wet, her blouse was rain soaked in places, she looked down at her hands, they were shaking, even when she clenched her hands they still shook. She opened her small shoulder bag, it's dark blue leather was saturated with rainwater, as she pulled open the flap on the bag rainwater ran off the bag onto the floor. She delved her hands into the bag pulling out a few different things, finally she stopped searching, pulling out a small compact mirror, opening the mirror she looked at herself, dropping the mirror in shock, she reached over and grabbed the mirror again, looking at it again intently, her dark blue eyes were no longer blue, staring back at her were dark amber coloured eyes, the colour almost glistening with iridescence.

Numarii later found her sitting unde the tree, the rain having stopped, she had been scowering the school for her for over an hour, she was surprised in how fast she had made her way to the far reaches of the school grounds.

"Rei...what's wrong..." Numarii exclaimed, seeing Reira sobbing under the tree, Reira turned away as she heard Her sister call her name,

"Go away, Mari leave me alone, go...I don't want to hurt you...please..." Reira called out.

Numarii wasn't going to take any of this, she walked over to her sister and knelt down, staring at her sister. Numarii's hands were clenched, her left knuckle was slightly inflamed

Numarii was angry that others had dared call her sister names such as that. She had punched one of the boys in the face, breaking his nose because of what he said. No one would ridicule her sister.

"Tell me what's wrong, I'm not going until you do...!" Numarii pleaded, grabbing at Reira's hands and pulled them away from her face, before looking at Reira, she stumbled back in shock as she saw her sisters eyes.

"Rei, they're..."

"Golden, it's true then. I'm one of them...the gifted.." she cried out, not knowing her life was going to change that day.

Reira awoke sweating and breathing deeply, she tried not to cry; the dream had brought back some painful memories, the only constant at that time of upheaval in her life was Numarii

"Now it's my turn to be there for you..." Reira murmured to herself.

CHAPTER 9

3 Days Later

1st Hour of the 6th Day of the 9th Month
IY (Imperial Year) 49

The city was quieter than usual; the rains had dispersed the crowds from earlier in the night; the sidewalks reflected the neon lights that decorated the buildings in this district of town. A hooded figure made its way down the sidewalk, its jacket was semi transparent, stopping at the figures knees, the jacket was open revealing the figure underneath, her long pale legs stood out against the black skirt she was wearing, glimpses of her white blouse peaked out from the done up sections of her jacket.

The jacket was quite fitted, hugging her figure in all the right places. She stopped at the door to a building and looked up

It was Numarii.

"This looks like the place" she murmured to herself. She looked over, a security guard.

"Well, what do we have here?" He grumpily spoke, looking down at her, the rain bouncing off the transparent hood of her jacket, her silvery white hair could be seen, underneath the reflections of the neon lights from above his head.

She looked up at him; he was much tall than she was, his shoulders broad and imposing.

"I'm sure you're not supposed to be here little girl." He added as he realised she was far to young to be in this part of the city at this late hour.

She looked up at him, smiling before adding

"I wouldn't keep calling me a little girl , you do not understand what I'm capable of."

At this moment her eyes glowed, the guard coughed, he quickly reached for his throat, pulling at his collar his neck was closing without his control. He looked down at Numarii, her eyes were changing from glowing a brilliant white into a dark grey before turning black. She looked at him and smiled a devilish smile,

"You see what I mean, now let me in before I really get annoyed and end up killing you for just the fun of it." She added, before the pressure on the guard's neck released.

Numarii blinked and her eyes they had already returned to her normal colour, the guard fell to his knees as the pressure was released, she quickly moved over and tried to help him up.

"I'm..I'm sorry, sometimes I can't control..." she stuttered as she tried to lift him up. Her stuttering was interrupted by his gesturing for her to enter the establishment. She tried to help again before the guard pushed her away and towards the door.

She stepped nervously into the building; the building was beautiful, an elegant bar with seated booths scattered across the vast room, the room was bustling with people, individuals from all across the empire. The bar was busy the air full of the scent of various drinks and the family smell of Kalita.

On a small mezzanine floor in the bar a young woman was singing, accompanied by a small band. Numarii looked up at her, mesmerised by both her voice and her beauty. As she stepped into the room, she pulled down the hood from her jacket, taking in all the surrounding sights.

She looked at him from across the room; he was muscular, over six foot tall and handsome, his hair, which was dark and lustrous framed his chiselled facial features. His appearance, he reminded her of the hero's from the tales her parents told her as a child, she couldn't look away, she was fixated on him.

His eyes were green and clear like emeralds. Numarii felt a tingle down her spine, she wanted him. But did she have the nerve to approach him?

Forces beyond her control made her wander further into the room, the sights and sounds were enthralling, the smell of Kalita smoke filled the air, causing Numarii to lose focus for a second, which caused her to stumble, crashing into the young gentleman whom she had been admiring, knocking them both over.

She apologised instantly, Bowing her head and gesturing behind herself with her arms.

"I..I'm sorry, I don't know what came over me,".

He looked at her, lost in admiration, he admired her figure for an instant, before replying

"It's my fault, but are you okay?" He replied.

"No, I'm alright, are you hurt?" Numarii replied reassuringly.

"I'm fine, I'm the one who should ask you if you're hurt, I can be quite uncoordinated at times." He spoke, a concern look flashed across his face.

He smiled at her as she helped him onto his feet before she asked him curiously;

"Please let me make this up to you..." she pleaded, giving a sultry smile. He stared at her amber eyes, which sparkled in the light of the bar. she was beautiful, but much younger than him.

He replied, "Savis" she smiled at him lost in admiration "What ?" She replied, not hearing his reply.

"Savis, that's my name, and who may you be?" She smiled sweetly and said,

"My names Numarii," before she suddenly walked off turning her head back to take a firm look at him as she walked closer to the bar. He stood there confused, was she teasing him? He could faintly smell a floral aroma, it seemed to seep deep into his nasal cavity, awakening his senses. He couldn't resist. She had got him right where she wanted him.

She perched herself on a bar stool, crossing her legs in front of her, her skirt riding up, revealing her long legs. She took off her jacket and placed it on the bar.

She glanced over at him and smiled, gesturing for him to come over with her fingers.

He didn't hesitate to follow her lead.

"So, I know what you will say, what brings an innocent young girl like me into a place like this.?"

She said as she gestured around the room.

The cacophony of the room sometimes made it difficult to hear,

"Well, I'll answer you, I'm young and yes", she held the side of her blouse and pulled it back, emphasising her curvaceous body and ample breasts.

"I'm a girl, but the innocent part, that's where you've got it wrong." She joked, laughing slightly before smiling seductively at him again.

The singer's voice rose high, following the piped notes from the musicians flute, a soft silence fell across the bar, her voice enthralled them, from the depths of her soul she sang, the song rose and fell into melancholy. It seemed as if all the audience could feel her sorrows and joys. For a moment Numarii let out a tear, the music having got to her, Savis reached over and wiped it away from her cheek with his finger.

"Not always the tough one then..." he joked with a smile.

"Not always, but then again, maybe it's all part of my plan to get what I want from you..." she joked seductively. Taking a sip from the glass of drink that Savis had placed on the bar.

"Quite a sweet drink, for a guy...I'm guessing your got a sweet tooth then..." she joked.

"Always got a thing for anything sweet..., not just drinks..." he replied, as he licked the tear from his finger.

"I'm sure you're sweet enough for me...maybe too sweet, you'd take my breath away" he added, looking straight at her, she blushed.

'Damn he's good, I'm sure he knows what he's doing' Numarii thought to herself.

Her scales were tingling even more now, she reached over and grabbed his hand, pulling it close, and licked the rest of that tear from his finger, looking at him straight in the eye she whispered.

"I just need to feel something, and I'm sure you're thinking the same..." she enquired.

"Are you sure you know what you want?, your only young and naïve" his response hitting her emotionally. She felt she could open up to him, maybe only slightly but enough to give him the benefit of the doubt.

"I've been in a lot of pain recently, only being somewhere like this brings me any kind of normality." she explained.

"And I might look naïve, but I know what I'm doing," she added.

"So, do you like what you see?" She commented brashly, gesturing for him to look at her toned body. He glanced at her, she smiled back as he looked at her, she was beautiful. She laughed as she followed his eyes glancing over her. Her hearts beat faster, she enjoyed this.

At the same time she was looking at him, he was in her mind, perfect. Muscular but trim. His hands was large but the skin soft that discounted him from being a manual labourer. She looked at his shirt. Noticing that it was fitted tightly to his body.

She placed her hand on his chest.

"Getting you excited are we." She spoke, her voice becoming innocent and light.

"Maybe I am I, maybe it's those ..." he stopped.

"Maybe it's my senses, but right now, the only thing I can think about is you." He added as he breathed in deeply, her pheromones were doing their job.

"I'm glad I'm having that effect on you, because right now my scales are driving me insane and I need ..."

She stood up from the stool and leaned in towards him.

"Hopefully you know somewhere close by, I need a little private time...to get to know you better..."

"Well, I live around here..., somewhere" he joked,

She smiled, winking at him.

"I hope you know what you're doing?, you know how fiery us Mak's are." She added as she grabbed her jacket.

He led her down the dark corridor that was in-front of her. She stumbled for a second, her eyes unable to react to the change in the light before becoming accustomed to it. he grabbed her hand, her hearts racing. Where was he taking her. Fear and excitement coursed through her veins, her scales tingled, sending waves of pleasure down her spine. He pushed open a door which she could barely make out in the darkness. A set of stairs lead up to another door at the top.

"Close your eyes, I'll keep you safe" he spoke as he grabbed her hand, pulling her close behind him.

She closed her eyes almost instantly, her foot giving way as she made her way up the stairs, holding onto his hand.

Numarii felt his heartbeats through his hand, the warmth of of hand contrasting with the cold breeze which brushed against her face.

"Are you okay?" He asked as they stopped at the top of the stairs.

"I'm fine, a little...anxious." She responded.

He reached into his pocket then began to speak while removing something from his pocket, a keycard.

"Dont worry, you're somewhere safe, somewhere where you can be yourself. My little piece of paradise in a city like this," he responded as he slid the keycard against a small panel beside the door.

He opened the door and flung the door open, the smell of flowers catching Numarii unaware, she struggled to keep her eyes closed.

"You can open your eyes", he said as he placed his hands on her shoulders, he smiled as he looked at her, she looked innocent, in stark contrast to the way she had been acting downstairs at the bar.

She opened her eyes, taking a few seconds for everything to come into focus. She fluttered her eyelashes before it all made sense. She stood there in amazement, hidden between the different buildings was a terrace garden, large enough for a wide range of flowers to grow. It was private and secluded enough that no one would notice the space being used,

Looking up into the darkness she could make out the stars which sparkled above her. For a second she felt as small as possible before reality set in again, she was here, on a small terrace garden

On the far side of the terrace was a door, the light in above the door flickered on.

"That my dear is home, I wasn't lying when I said I lived around here somewhere." He added jovially while gesturing to the surrounding area.

"It's a small place, but..." he spoke, but was interrupted by Numarii planting a tender kiss on his lips, as she did she pulled him closer by the collar of his shirt.

"For our needs right now, it's perfect..." she trailed off as she reached behind him and slowly caressed the ridge above his scales, causing him to close his eyes with enjoyment.

"And I told you I know what I'm doing...there's more to this..." she paused for a second before continuing.

"Naive little girl, a lot more" she added sarcastically. Her hand slowly travelling around to his neck, caressing it before slowly grabbing it, he flinched as she grabbed hold of it.

"It might even frighten you..." she added with a smile.

He handed her a glass, Amarian wine she could smell it. reminding her of times she caught her mother drinking it. she took only a small sip, Wine would only suppress her senses, and right now they were on fire, every sense triggered by something, the music being played; the adrenaline running through her veins.

She stood in the doorway looking out into the garden, the scents from the flowers causing her mind to race, everyone of these flowers specifically grown to heighten an emotion, the fragrances were mesmerising. Kadandris Blossom smelt sweet and lingered in her nose, Prixasis was more seductive, a fragrance so thick she could physically taste it, mixed with her own pheromones it was intoxicating. Her mind and emotions were doing somersaults, flowing backwards and forwards with every inhale of breath.

"It blows your mind, if you let it..." the sound of his voice bringing her back to reality, she opened her eyes and looked at him, she looked at him in awe, mesmerised by him in entirety. He caught her attention and he smiled back, he gestured to all that was around him before speaking again.

"I brought you here...because I wanted to show that I'm not just a .." she stopped him mid flow by placing her finger on his lips.

Before she pulled him closer to her, his lips meeting hers, she draws him close, pulling him by the back of his neck before pulling away. Leaving him confused.

"You know I'm only here for..." she whispered, her head lowering, and her eyes looking up at him seductively. She knew exactly what she was doing,

"I know..." he replied, a sense of regret lingered in his voice, before the adrenaline in his body and the smell of her pheromones overwhelm him.

"I won't be here in the morning..." she added, as she spoke this, she could tell that this slightly crushed his spirits. He paused for a second before reassuringly smiling.

She looked at him, her hearts pounding, dangerous and naughty thoughts travelled through her mind, she wanted him and he knew it, he gave her a delicate smile and that was more than enough. Numarii looked up and stared out into the expanse above them, hundreds of stars shone down on them, sounds from the sprawl of the metropolitan city around them echoed around the walls.

He pulled her close by her waist, cradling her hips, she could feel the heat radiating from his body. His hands were slightly cold, causing a shiver to run down her back.

Even though she was mostly inexperienced in these situations, she could read the situation perfectly, her first thought was to run, this was getting real and quickly, she had played around with others her age, but this was different, everything felt different.

At times she wanted to race back home to safety. She never normally did things this wild, but the voices in her head encouraged her to act out, and for one she didn't feel like resisting their suggestions. The voices whispered in her subconscious, she tried her hardest to send them to the back of her mind, but failing to hide them completely.

These thoughts of fleeing are quickly replaced, by thoughts of finally being able to feel something. Not being afraid anymore, pushing the darkness and her pain behind her, if only for a fleeting moment. This experience giving her a rush that she had only briefly experienced with her ex-boyfriend, there was a certainty about these new feeling, a total lack of fear. She wanted him more.

He kissed her again, his tongue reaching just the tip of hers, he pulled her closer. Her emotions are running high, "maybe this is what pure passion feels like" she thought as her instincts kicked in, she could feel herself getting even more aroused, the scales on her back tingling. Her thoughts became erratic. But a familiar darkness still lurking in the depths of her psyche, she forced the darkness deeper, trying to forget its existence.

His thumbs slowly caressed her cheekbones, his fingers catching her hair before slowly brushing it back, his other hand stroking the ridges of her scales at the back of her neck. The pleasure was building, suddenly the kiss stopped he pulled away, and she felt herself moving forward trying to recover the kiss, as they broke the kiss, she sighed.

She had never experienced something as pure as this; she was accustomed to being the seductress, and most males her age were easily led, and she always dominated them, if they wanted to be close to her in that way, she led, they followed. With the others, it was animalistic, over before it really began.

But now, she felt she was out of her depths; she was submissive. He stood in front of her, his hand on the back of her neck as she looked up at him. His fingers slowly caressing the ridge on the top scale. This is when she realised that he knew what he was doing. He wasn't some naïve Impiri male her own age, but a male with experience, the ten-year gap in their age made all the difference.

He wasn't afraid of her; he knew how to handle her. But did he? Numarii could feel a darkness growing inside her, a raw and unbridled darkness. She was afraid to allow this darkness out, but it screamed out within her mind.

"He doesn't know what we can do for him. We could bring him to the edge of life and he would still allow us to go further..., you know you want him, you want all of him. You want him to think he can control you, but you know better" the voice screamed in her head, the voice kept repeating, as she tried to force the voice to stop.

These thoughts were silenced when he spoke.

"I think we better do this inside..." he suggested.

Almost like he could hear her thoughts, he turned gently and gave her a breath-taking smile. Spying her sultry smile he grabbed her hand and spun her around pulling her closer to him, he rested his hand on the back of her neck, his fingers caressing it gently, the scales on the back of her neck changing colour slowly from the colour of her skin to a light blue.

A wave of pleasure cascaded across her body, his hand gently pressing the ridge around her scales, making her shoulders sink followed by a sigh. His fingers circled the scales and skimmed their surface three, four, five times Before stopping, her breathing became shallow.

He spun her around, dazzling her with a smile of triumph. Raising his hand, he beckoned to her with one finger, mouthing 'come on!'. Her heart racing, she had done nothing like this before. She had played temptress with some boys at school, they were innocent and unskilled. He was different.

He picked up up and fell against the door in a passionate embrace before they both made their way to the floor; she jumped slightly because of the sensation of the cold stone floor brushing against the already sensitive scales on her back through the thin material of her blouse, her blouse rising up against the floor, the cooling sensation driving her wild. She could feel the heat from his body as he slowly kissed her neck, gradually working his way down to her collarbone.

Numarii sighed, she could feel herself loosing control, the darkness inside her growing.

Saris slowly got up and reached down as he carefully scooped Numarii off the floor. At this moment she grabbed ahold of him, wrapping her legs around him. He staggered backwards. Against the wall of the entrance. She held on tight and kissed him again.

"Now it's my turn..." she whispered as she broke the kiss.

"What am I doing?" She thought to herself, her mind full of different thoughts. She could feel his hands moving up under her blouse, she instinctively let out a moan as his hands caressed her body, they slowly sank to the floor, her on top of him. She sat on top of him and looked down seductively. She smiled,

"I told you I'd take the lead..." she whispered as she pulled on the buttons of his shirt, before sliding her hands underneath his shirt, feeling his warmth, she pushed her hands up further with both hands on his chest, she felt powerful. At the same time he slowly unbuttoned his shirt, exposing his bare chest.

She placed her hands on the centre of his chest, she could feel the twin beats of his hearts, the rush of endorphins overwhelmed her. Her hearts stop beating for what feels like an eternity before restarting.

"I don't know what I'm doing" she thought to herself. Before the darkness inside tempts her again. She looks down at him, she focused on his face, it's beautiful shape, his chiselled features.

His tousled dark hair, his amazingly bright green eyes, that she had never fully noticed before. As she is looking at him, his eyes are following hers. His hands holding her hips, his thumbs stroking her pale soft skin. She gradually leans forwards and moves her hands further up so they are resting on the ground beside his head.

She is mere centimetres from his face, she smiles, her breathing quick and shallow. At this moment she stops and stares at him.

"Numarii?" He questions, breaking her concentration. Her name sounds so different this time, he sounds concerned, different from the firm and defiant tone he mentioned her name earlier.

"Are you sure about this?" He asks. She jumps back a bit, halfway between sitting up and lying on him and smiled a seductive smile before quickly removing her blouse, her young body being exposed to the elements, the cool breeze sending sensations across her skin. She can feel his hands moving down and caressing her thighs. Moving higher, going under her skirt.

"No..." she snapped at him,

"Let me help you with that..." she pleaded, her voice calm, trying to hide her emotions from him, but failing badly.

She reached around to her back and undid the fastening on her skirt, which she then whipped around removing the skirt in one swift movement.

There she was, magnificent. Beautiful and powerful. Her hands caressed her own body from the tops of her shoulders down, past her firm and pert breasts down her taut stomach and slowly down onto his body. He body was on fire, the heat from his body warmed her thighs.

"I told you I was hiding something..." she spoke, shaking her head slowly, her silvery white hair bouncing on her shoulders.

"And I was now wondering what you think after the grand reveal.?" She asked inquisitively, looking down at him, pursing her lips gently.

He didn't respond he just smiled,

"I think you can tell..." he smirked.

She felt his fingers tracing the lace edges of her underwear; she sighed as they worked their way down, pressing gently against her most intimate areas, the sensations of pleasure travelling across her body, mixed with the sensations she could feel from the cool breeze in conjunction with the heat radiating from his body, she was in paradise.

These sensations went into overdrive when his fingers slowly caressed the bottom scales which ran down her spine. Her scales were the most sensitive now, her body began heating up, she could feel the burning deep inside her core, this was normal, but different this time.

The darkness inside her felt angry that it had been kept locked away. Numarii kept it locked away but now it was seeping to the surface.

She moaned as her pleasure escalated, her hips began rocking against his hand, she looked down at him; she placed her hand on his neck, at this moment he stopped what he was doing.

Her hand quickly moved and slapped him across the face.

"I didn't tell you to stop, did I." She snapped, her voice different from before, the darkness had finally emerged to the surface.

She shook her head playfully before smiling and looking at him.

He smiled at her and then gradually returned to what he was doing; the sensations began building again. Her breathing rate increased.

He carefully held her by the hip, steadying her, and with the other hand he gently caressed her inner thigh. The pleasure inside her was mounting, she couldn't resist him any longer, and the darkness knew that, she reached down and guided him into her. She closed her eyes for a second to savour the rush of emotions,

"Now it's my turn..." she murmured,

"What did you say?" he replied. But she didn't respond, he looked at her eyes, but they were closed,

"Numarii" he called out, as he spoke she opened her eyes, gone were her amber eyes, replaced by darkness, her eyes like pools of black liquid, he froze.

"Now I'm going to get my pleasure out of you, either way...." she spoke, her voice deeper and forceful.

His head was full of confusion, what had just happened, all of reality seemed to be disjointed. she reached down and held onto his shoulders, carefully rocking herself on him.

The pleasure overwhelming them both, he couldn't stop himself, be grabbed hold of her breasts, carefully stroking her nipples with his thumbs, she leaned back, and laughed.

"Now this is what you really wanted isn't it..." she laughed to herself, her voice slightly distorted, echoing.

"And I'm not talking to you..." she added before he could respond.

"This young body was uncertain about her own needs, but me. I know what this body wants, what it desires, the sordid dark and despicable feelings, that's what I'm craving..." she laughed as she continued to ride him.

He stopped moving, buried deep inside her.

"What's going..." he spoke, before being stifled by Numarii's hand over his mouth.

"Ssshhh" she whispered looking deep into his eyes,

"If you're not silent, I must silence you..." she added.

A look of fear spread across his face, but Numarii didn't move, she continued to ride him, the pleasure building within her.

"Well…" Numarii whispered into his ear, having stopped for a moment. A wicked smile crossing her face. "You said that I took your breath away, and I couldn't leave that as a simple exaggeration." Her eyes glowed, he tried to struggle to push her away but could not. She was controlling his movement, he tried to push against this unseen force, but she was too strong for him.

He moved again, against his better judgement, like he had lost all control of his body, his instincts having taken control, lost in the moment.

He thrusted faster, sending a wave of pleasure deeper into her. Her whole body was focused in that moment, the intensity of the sensations becoming unbearable, her shoulders tensing, her body tingling all over.

Her scales becoming a deep blue, pulsing with black, until she cried out. The pleasure exploded into a wave of heat flooding through her, out to her hips, her legs, up to her hearts, her breasts, her throat, her entire body radiating in this heat, sweat beading across her entire body.

She collapsed into his arms. He breathed a huge breath as she uncovered his mouth, partially suffocated, his hearts beating rapidly, Numarii's senses were still electrified, she smiled to herself, her eyes still closed.

Eventually she opened her eyes, her eyes returned to amber, her breath slowly returning to normal.

She looked at him and smiled a nervous smile.

"I hope you enjoyed that as much as I did..." She quizzed, he looked at her, still taken back by what she had done, but smiled slowly before laughing.

"Wasn't exactly what I expected but..."

"Yes, I enjoyed it a lot...but there is more from where that came" he whispered as he pulled her close and kissed her passionately.

"Then maybe I'm staying the night." She replied, with a smirk on her face after she broke the kiss.

He looked at her, deep in thought before smiling.

"You can stay as long as you want..." he replied, knowing all too well that she would be gone in a few hours and that we better enjoy the time he has with her.

"Saris, I know you mean what you say, but you know that I'll be gone, so for the moment, no regrets, lets just enjoy each other's company..." she replied as she lifted herself up, looking down on him.

"Hopefully you can keep up with me..." she joked, as she placed her hands on his bare chest, looking down on him before smiling.

He looked up at her; she looked radiant. Her hair was a little disheveled, she knew it and she didn't care; she lifted one hand and ran it through her hair, tousling her hair. She sighed.

"I'm sure I can keep up with you..." he trailed off as she came in close to him, her face centimetres from his, she smiled, and laughed a wicked laugh.

"I do hope so..." she laughed before planting a delicate kiss on his lips.

He looked at her as she got down and lay her head on his chest; she lay there listening to the sound of his hearts beating, the rhythm of the hearts was mesmerising, her head rising and falling as he breathed in and out.

"Numarii?" He whispered.

"Yes, my dear." She whispered back.

"Why did you pick me...? For tonight's..." her response interrupted him.

"It just felt right, then again you are definitely the most impressive Impiri I've seen..." she trailed off as she relaxed on his chest.

Three Days Later

It was obvious she had a hard time with facing reality. The moment Numarii got the news about the Cloisters, she nearly fell over, dizzy. The shock had knocked her; she had already planned what she thought would happen, she'd go and study somewhere across the empire, enjoy the sights and fall into a career of sorts, enjoying herself along the way.

She never expected to be accepted, this was only the beginning but being chosen for this was an honour, there was only fifty places, with over five hundred thousand applicants. Reira herself had received her rejection letter a few months prior, the letter declared that it wasn't fair with a family having two applicants; she passed all tests but knew that her sister wanted it more. Reira was actually glad the pressure was off her, it allowed her to do what she actually wanted to achieve with her life. Unlike her sister she wanted to disappear into a life of devotion, not the debauchery her sister would enjoy.

Numarii stood at the door to the living quarters, almost falling over, catching herself on the side of a chair, steadying herself she laughed, passed the dizziness off as shock, but Reira knew better. She knew how to read her sister, and Numarii knew it, as she nervously looked at Reira.

She focused on Reira, deflecting the questions she was asked.

"Her head looked like it hurt; good thing she didn't hit it too hard, I won't always be there to look after her..." she exclaimed, joking, she laughed, but the laugh seemed empty.

Their parents were ecstatic, Inis had given Numarii a lengthy hug, her mother sitting there crying,

"They better look after my daughter well..." she kept repeating.

Usually Numarii had a tough exterior. But it was always something that Reira could get through. They were sisters, so naturally they knew how to understand each other. Being twins was the bond that no one else could break. They only had each other, their older sister Ilaria had taught them that when they were young.

Numarii stood looking at Reira, she smiled nervously, Reira slowly walked over to her sister, grabbed her and hugged her,

"I'm always here if you need me..." she whispered, quiet enough that even her parents couldn't hear her.

"I'll be fine, you know me..." She replied, as she nervously ran her fingers through her hair.

That tough exterior had not been broken in front of anyone other than Reira. She only talked to her, not even mother and father, she never wanted to worry them. She had recently had a rebellious streak, more rebellious than she normally was.

Sneaking out of the house at night while back home and disappearing off base, only to return in the early hours of the next morning, covered in unexplained cuts and bruises. Her visits out had even shocked herself, surprised at what she could subject her mind and body to.

Even in front of her parents her demeanour was tough and she let no one take her down, yet, this day was different. Fear controlled her like nothing else; it kept her quiet and hopeless.

Reira grabbed Numarii's hand and dragged her out of the door out into the kitchen.

Once they arrived in the kitchen Reira turned around and looked at her sister straight in the face.

"Tell me what's wrong!" Reira pleaded, shaking her fist at her sister.

"Nothing..., just a lot of things going on in this head of mine..." Numarii joked, tapping her head with her index finger.

"You should try it sometime..., can't just have your head in the clouds all the time..." she replied sarcastically, trying to protect herself and deflect the conversation.

"Is it that voice, the nightmares again..?" Reira asked, trying to get some sense of what was going through her sisters mind.

"There are things I have done, things that would shock you, they shocked me. I acted out when I didn't think I would. I lost control again. It frightens me... make that terrifies me." Her shoulders dropping, the bravado failed, she knew she couldn't lie to her anymore.

"I know you can do this, they will help. Maybe it will help you focus. Keep your mind off of these thoughts."

"Okay, I'll give it a shot..." Numarii replied, her bottom lip trembling.

CHAPTER 10

2 Weeks Later.

The house was plunged into darkness. Clouds made it even darker, no moonlight, just darkness.

Numarii had awoken early that morning, the house was quiet and dark, it would be at least an hour before the sun arose. She quickly disappeared into the bathroom and ran herself a bath.

Moments later she was sunk deep into the bath. This was one of her favourite pastimes, first of all the cleanliness. That was always a favourite of hers. Second, It was the only time she felt she could control her emerging abilities. She lay back into the bath, submerging her head until her mouth, nose and eyes were above the water.

She slowly calmed her breathing, and blinked a long blink, her eyes becoming a cloudy white. As she did this the water in the bath shifted, droplets of water began to rise above the bath. Making their way into the surrounding air. Moments later they stopped and crashed back into the bath, Numarii's eyes returning to normal.

After relaxing in the bath for a while, the water having turned cold, causing Numarii to get a chill, she got out slowly.

She slowly clambered out of the bath, grabbing a towel off a shelf and dried herself. The quick bath had cleansed her body, she felt better than she had prior. Even though it was quick, it was enough for her.

She darted out of the bathroom, wrapped in her towel, nearly loosing her footing as she ran down the corridor into her bedroom, shutting the door behind her.

Moments later

Numarii sat dressed in a dark floral dress, sitting on the floor next to her bed, she looked down at her right hand, a dark bladed knife sat in her hand, she slowly grabbed hold of the handle, brandishing the knife she sighed a deep sigh.

The knife shaking as she held it; she took a deep breath, the shaking subsided as she carefully drew down her left forearm with the blade, she winced in pain, biting down on her bottom lip, splitting her lip.

Blood trickled down her mouth. That was nothing compared to the blood pouring to from the wound on her forearm as quickly as the wound was created. It ran down the sides of her arm, with every passing second she drew the blade down her forearm. She paused midway, taking in sight, sound and smell of home, one last time.

Her room smelt like Dassin Orchids, as always, mother had always put a plant in her room. She smiled a slight smile looking at her window and seeing the sunrise. It wouldn't be long before everyone would be awake, so she had better get this finished she thought.

She took a deep breath and continued, wincing in pain as she drew the blade further down her left forearm. The blade making easy work of her skin, the blade had been stolen from her father's collection. The blood now streaming out of her arm, pooling on the floor, her right hand shaking. She paused again for a second to help steady herself; she clenched her left fist. Drawing more blood to her arm before continuing again. Her hearts pounding, with each beat of her hearts, even more blood pumped it way out of her arm. Her breathing started to become laboured.

She lay down on the floor next to her bed, her blood already pooling beneath her. She sighed a large sigh, taking in a deep breath and slowly closed her eyes, this was it, finally the pain would be gone and the voices would stop.

Across the mezzanine;

Reira didn't know that day would be the day that changed her life, it would cost her emotionally, and physically. She had just woken up and had gotten dressed. The sunlight was shining into her room, eliminating all darkness from her room. She walked casually towards her bedroom door. A small folded piece of paper lying on the floor near the door caught her attention. She bent down and picked it up,

She looked at the note, all it read was:

"I'm sorry,"

It wasn't long before Reira started running. What would have been a cryptic message to anyone else, was as clear as day to Reira. She ran down the corridor, and stood at her sisters' door, it was slightly open. Something that would never happen. They both respected their own privacy, they hadn't shared a room since they were younger. Each of them had different tastes and likes, but one thing they had in common, the door was always closed. The lack of this caused Reira to breathe deeply. She pushed open the door, her heart beating fast. Immediately on the floor just inside the room was a letter. Reira reached down and picked up the letter; it read in Numarii's handwriting:

Reira,

The other half of me, yep that's you. I'm sorry that it has to be you that finds me, well, what's left of me. My light has finally gone somewhere where it doesn't hurt anymore.

Reira cried, slowly at first, with each line she sank to her knees, not making a sound. She continued to read:

If I don't return to this universe, then maybe I'm in a better place. Tell mom I love her. Tell dad I'm sorry and Reira. I want to say even though I'm the older sister. I know being petty again, older by 3 minutes is still older, I've always looked up to you.

Reira paused, her expression changing, unable to hide her emotions, the tears running faster down her cheeks

I hated you being able to deal with this gift that we were born with; You have everything I wished I had and more. Mom and dad loved you unconditionally; I felt like I had to compete. Maybe it's because I always acted like I was fine with everything, but it was never true, I'm scared.

This shocked Reira the most, her sister was afraid of nothing. Even when they were younger, she was never afraid.

But I came to a conclusion that I just can't cope with this, I always feel

like I have to keep these abilities under control. The pain is sometimes too much. That's why I always disappeared into the forest, I couldn't hurt anyone there, just the trees and me. They don't control you; you control them. But I can't do that, maybe the Cloisters would have helped with that, but I can't risk the chance they can't help.

I'm sorry, please don't blame me for this.

See you on the other side. May the goddesses find it in their powers to allow you a life good enough for the both of us.

Numarii

This is when Reira finally broke down, screaming, she couldn't move. She sat screaming, tears streaming down her face, she hyperventilated. Her eyes becoming milky white, for an instance it seemed like time stopped. Before moments later restarting and footsteps could be heard running up the stairs. The clink of mother's shoes followed by the sound of father's boots. Then the footsteps of Master Baelin far behind.

Her mother arrived first, seeing Reira sitting there screaming, she realized, her face becoming full of emotion, she sank to the floor next to her daughter and grabbed her and shook her.

"Why didn't you stop her..." she screamed. Not blaming her but just trying to vent her frustration, unable to control her emotions. she pulled Reira close to her and they both sat on the floor in the doorway, sobbing. Her Father arrived seconds later,

He looked over towards the bed. From his viewpoint, the legs of his daughter lay sticking out on the floor next to the bed. a pool of blood spread across the floor. He seemed to leap over his daughter and wife on the floor and rushed over.

Getting to the bed before breaking down, he semi-kneeled next to the bottom of the bed and wept. He stumbled over to the body of his daughter and pulled her onto his lap. He sat there holding her, his clothes soaked in her blood. He stroked the hair away from her face,

"I'm here, please don't go, please," he whispered, the colour draining from his complexion.

Master Baelin entered the room, looking down at Reira and her mother, and drew his hand to his mouth. He knew what had happened, a tear slowly fell from his eye, he looked over. Keeping his distance, others in the house arrived at the door. He turned around and gestured for them to keep their distance, and for someone to call for a doctor, before deciding to find one himself.

Reira's screaming had stopped. Her throat hoarse from the screams, she looked over at her father; he glanced over at her and spoke.

"Please." His eyes were watering.

"Reira, help me get your sister onto the bed, I need you to do this for me." His lips trembling.

Reira nodded, leaving her mother crying in a heap on the floor. She couldn't bring herself to look, not like this. Unwilling to see her daughter in this state, she resigned herself to crying to the goddesses.

"Goodbye, Marii," Reira said as she knelt down in front of her father. She reached out her hand and slowly caressed her sister's face. Pulling her hand back in the first instance. She was still warm. Tears still running down her cheeks. She put her arms underneath her father's arms and they slowly lifted her onto the bed. All of her clothes were soaked in blood.

"Thank you" her father spoke, his voice breaking, before falling to the floor. This was a shock to Reira, her father was always the strong one, and even he was broken now.

Reira looked down at her hands, now soaked in her sister's blood, she tried to wring it off of her hands, but to no avail. She looked at her sister, her expression peaceful as if she was sleeping.

Reira spoke to herself as she walked off.

"She was the only person who understood me, too, yet somehow we didn't get along all the time, not in the past few years. I never knew the reason...until recently."

Reira looked back at the room. Her mother was sitting in the corner of the room now. A neighbour had heard the screams and had come over, and they were sitting with mother comforting her. Father was knelt next to the bed. His skin was pale and his eyes red. He reached out his right hand towards his daughters face and stroked her face with the back of his index finger.

The Doctor was an elderly Impiri man, His hair as white as the winter's snow and his eyes a dark blue. Doctor Khirlai had been a friend of the family since Reira's father was a child. He looked over at Reira's father and spoke, his voice cam and soothing,

"Inis, I'm..."

Reira's father looked up, noticing Dr Khirlai, but not hearing what had been spoken.

"Thank you for being here, how did you get here so quickly..." he stuttered. The Doctor looked over at Master Baelin,

"Kotam, he flagged me down on my way past your property ." The Doctor replied.

"He was lucky that I stopped, but when I saw the expression on his face, I knew I had to stop." He added.

"Kotam, my friend, as always you look out for me and my family, even in times like this..." Inis spoke, his voice trying to regain itself as he still kept stroking Numarii's face.

Kotam Davanii Baelin, an Impiri man of a similar age to Inis stood at the door. He had been Reira's father's aide, his hair scattered with white hair, creeping through is golden blonde hair. He was an 'unmarked man', no allegiance to any household. He had sworn himself to a life oath when Inis' father had saved his life when he was a child. In accordance with an old Impiri tradition.

"You know there is nothing I can do...I can just seal the...wounds." Dr Khirlai spoke, his voice calm and gentle.

"I know, just fix her please." He pleaded, Dr Khirlai looked over and nodding his head slowly, before getting to work. Knowing that fixing the wounds would at least calm Inis down, seeing his daughter with her arm split open was a sight that he would rather not see.

A Few Days Later.

The door to the room was shut, wailing echoed throughout the house. Reira sat on the top stair, as close to the edge of the staircase as possible, her face buried into her hands. She raised her head from her hands, and tried to wipe the tears away, but they were going nowhere.

She glanced down at her hands, her hands soaked in tears, her hands shook as she cried out. But no sound leapt from her mouth. The tears were running down her cheeks, dripping onto her blouse. The tears soaking into the embroidered fabric. turning it from light turquoise into a deep and dark turquoise as it became saturated with the tears.

"Mari, You know I can't do this without you. I knew things were bad, but I never..." she sobbed as she pulled out a small locket from her pocket, as she opened the locket a small hologram of herself and Numarii appeared emanating from the locket, they were younger. A time before their abilities had manifested their eyes were still a dark shade of blue. It was a time when they still told each other everything. In the background of the hologram, a waterfall could be seen.

"You remember this, don't you?, Mother got so angry, we had soaked our new jackets, but father couldn't stop laughing. I wanted to go back to Jasini Falls with you, one day I'll go back and take a part of you with me... I promise." she murmured to herself, trying to calm herself down. She closed the locket with one hand and the hologram disappeared. She looked at her reflection on the locket, her eyes were puffy and red, her makeup was ruined, mascara lines running down her face.

"Must fix this..., what would mother think...?" She laughed to herself knowing what her face looked like. She stood up and wandered into her room, closing the door behind her.

Moments Later

As was tradition, the elders of the family were wailing, in the lower levels of the house. An old custom, letting the goddesses know that an Impiri was about to join them in the afterlife. Hopefully, to be reborn to restart the circle. Reira had been shut out of the room, her role was different. Once again she was sitting on the top of the stairs, looking down.

Reira would first step in front of her family and recite from the book of fate. She would make this journey to her family with no one by her side, adorned in the traditional garments of her tribe.

She stood up and carefully made her way down the stairs. Entering the main hall, the light from the sun shining through small windows. Which allowed great sections of the hall to be cast into darkness.

In the ritualistic garment of her forebears, she bowed as she entered the room. Which was filled by the cacophony of the family, their words unable to be made out. But by the tone of the conversation, something important was being discussed.

The discussion in the hall died down as Reira entered further into the room. She tried to ignore the stares that she received. Especially the stares from her mother, her eyes bloodshot and tired. Her eyes adjusting to the darkness in the room.

Reira could make out her father, Master Baelin; her father's aide and sworn guardian of the family. Her Aunt Lesla, her Uncle Garan, a few of her cousins and finally her grandmother Lady Jenssi Ensil Zalto-Abrasar. who was close to four hundred and twenty years of age.

Even her older sister Ilaria. who was a Sargent in the Imperial Guard had been given dispensation to return home. She stood at Numarii's urn, a single tear made its way down her cheek, she slowly nodded at Reira as she came closer.

Reira looked at Ilaria, place her right hand on her sisters left shoulder. Her eyes closed for a second as she composed herself before breaking the gesture and turned around.

Reira smiled a shy smile in front of her family and the guests in attendance,

"You know," Reira whispered while looking down. "even though we occasionally fought, Mother and father would attest to that, I loved you." Her voice quivering.

"You were the only one who knew what I was going through. You knew because you were going through the same and that reassured me that I would always have you to..."

Father held up his hand for her to stop.

"Say no more. I won't tell anyone. We had always made these promises. We always asked each other not to tell..." she pleaded,

"Promise, always... you would say,"

"Numarii, that's what sisters are for." Reira announced, her voice trembling, fighting back her emotions.

Father smiled, stood up from his chair and walked over, and gave Reira a huge hug and spoke quietly to her

"She won't forget what you did for her."

Reira finally regained her composure,

"That was something that I wanted to say, so everyone would know, 'Marii' was my sister ..." she looked over at Ilaria, then added.

"Our sister and she always will be..." her voice trailing off...as her voice began to break.

"A Reading from the book of fate." She added, after a moment of composing herself.

"Sayif had journeyed to the ends of existence. Through the challenges set to him by the elder gods, these challenges had broken his spirit. His faith was all that kept him from the darkness and the fire. But he wasn't afraid, it comes to all. The goddesses appeared to him" she proclaimed, reciting the tale from memory. She tried to not look around, trying to avoid the look from her mother, such a look would have broken her resolve and cast her into a downward spiral.

"And her voice was unto him: Sayif, Sayif Son of Nasesk. Behold, I am Ishara and I have heard thee. There is no shame in returning to the darkness, being consumed by the fire. Your embers will be blown into by my sister who will grant you a rebirth. I will carry your essence forward into the next. I have come down to deliver thee a choice, life in the here and now or Rebirth. To take thee away from thy father's house, and from all thy kinsfolk and into death." She spoke, the room was silent, only the crackle from the flames from the small fire behind her broke the silence.

Reira paused trying to give the recital more meaning.

"Sayif looked at her, at first staring in disbelief, and realised, it was no trick. The goddess Ishara was sitting on the rock beside the road, weeping. Her words the truth, she had become concerned with his troubles and the challenges set by the elder gods. His lack of spirit wasn't ever a problem because he had faith and that was unwavering."

She finally broke down, the tears streaming down her cheeks,

"I'll miss you..." she added as her father helped pick her up, guiding her to her seat. She sat beside her mother, whose eyes were puffy from all the crying she had done, not caring about the mascara lines running down her face. She tried to be strong for her mother, but she couldn't this time.

This part of the funeral would be the hardest. They had uncovered the Fire pit beneath the great hall. The flames casting out huge amounts of light and heat. Around the room members of the family stood, their faces lit by the flame. by the side of the fire pit a solitary man stood, his hair was grey and his face weathered and old.

Three drummers stood at points across the hall. they occasionally beat their drums, the sound echoing out of the hall into the surround area.

He stood shaking rhythmically; they attached beads to a sceptre. With every occasional beat of the drums he shook it, the beads clashing together.

He stood looking at an enormous fire pit; the flames illuminated his eyes. The skin on his face was wrinkled and dry. His wrinkled skin broken by a white satin line that was smeared down both of his cheeks from his eyes to his jawline.

His dark red robes, seemed as close to black in the darkness. Only the occasional flare of the fire revealed their true colour.

The rest of the hall was unlit. Only the rising flames cast

light onto its walls. Occasionally revealing intricately engraved scripture and ancient tapestries

Eight large statues stood in semi-darkness around the corners of the room. The drummers cast completely into the darkness as they faced away from the pit. The beat of the drums seemed to dance between bass filled and a lighter more melodic cadence. The smokey haze of burnt Incense drifted across the space between the family and the solitary man. its scent delicate and addictive.

One solemn figure dressed in a long white dress stood at the door to the hall. Her face half painted white, the other half painted black. The flames flaring up enough that her completely white eyes could be seen. She seemed to speak. The crackle of the fire and the changing beat of the drums drowning out any chance of hearing what she was saying.

The beat stopped as she raised his hands into the air; the drummers relaxed their arms and put down their batons. The figure sighed before speaking, her voice cutting through the silence.

"I sense a connection in this room" her melodic voice echoed.

"A bond which cannot and will not be broken." She declared.

She turned away from the fire pit, into the darkness, before speaking again,

"Goddess, your guardian of the deceased wishes for your communion. Give me guidance in this time of need." She stood in silence, Reira's Mother looked at her, her expression perplexed, this wasn't normal.

"I sought the guidance of our goddess, to help with Numarii's journey into the flames..., but she..." she stopped, her eyes filled with a brilliant white glow, as the candles in the room flickered out all at once. Different members of the family gasped as the candles went out, this was followed by cool chill descending on to the hall, followed by an eerie silence, Reira looked around the hall, her breath froze in misty clouds as the Guardian spoke.

"Nidiri Reira Abrasar..." she screamed, breaking the eerie silence.

Her voice booming with unnatural reverberation, her voice breaking slightly as he spoke. Her eyes opened wider, everyone was taken back by this turn of events. Everyone seemed frozen in place, except Reira. She moved herself closer to the Guardian.

The fire died down as the guardians' eyes closed. Reira was three feet away from the guardian when she spoke again in her own voice.

"May the goddesses accept our sister into their embrace, may she find happiness in the next life, may she..." She stopped as the fire roared into life. The flames swirling towards the ceiling as the flames rose higher. Arcane symbols appeared within the ceiling of the hall out of nowhere.

"Rei...Rei is that you, I'm sorry for doing this to you, the choice wasn't mine, I couldn't take the pain any..." the guardian spoke, her voice was Numarii's, it echoed from her mouth, but it was distinct, it was Numarii's voice, but how?

"It's me, Marii..." Reira pleaded, her voice trembling, the shock of hearing her sister's voice again, her mother ran towards her,

"Marii, my beautiful daughter, go into the flames my child, don't linger in the darkness..." she cried, sinking to her knees.

"Don't leave me.....I can't do this without you..." Reira screamed, her eyes glowing white. Just as the flames died down and the arcane symbols dissolved into nothingness.

Reira turned towards her father, he carefully glanced at her, and smiled a nervous smile

"It's okay, Rei, I think Marii heard you...I don't know how this has happened, but I'm sure in my bones that she heard you..."

"I hope so, I truly hope so..." she pleaded, her emotions running high, she was having trouble dealing with this, her mind going crazy with what had just transpired.

"You can go..." her father whispered as he looked at her, seeing her emotions swelling inside her.

Reira's breaths came as fast as she was walking, She quickly exited the great hall. The sound of her footsteps echoing across the hall.

"Why did you leave me..." she thought to herself, she walked towards the back of the house, towards the kitchen. Her mind was still filled with regret. From the great hall Reira could hear the echoes of crying and wailing. Reira could easily make out her mother's cries.

Upon hearing this she stopped, Reira was still nervous. Her hands trembled slightly as she resumed walking into the kitchen. She needed to be alone, to breathe, everything was a whirl of confusion.

Something was wrong. The ceremonial burning of her sister's ashes, something was out of the ordinary. The Guardian had even decreed it so, there was nothing about this in the many books she had read. What did it all mean?

CHAPTER 11

21st Hour of the 27th Day of the 7th Month
IY (Imperial Year) 101

21st Hour of the 27th Day of the 7th Month
IY (Imperial Year) 101

Nighttime had returned to the city, long gone were the memories of just a few days earlier. As if someone stole the life of the city, people walked throughout the city, not making much noise, just living the day-to-day life.

As was tradition. Reira would begin this journey into darkness adorned in the ritualistic garment of her ancestors. She sat on a solitary chair in the middle of the great hall. Her head covered by a black sack, her hands tied together behind her, and then tied again to the chair. Her shirt gaping open to reveal her pale chest, her legs were tied to each of the chair legs. Around her neck was a woven gold choker, a known as an 'Elit'to (Mark of Respect) a symbol of her heritage, abandoned by almost all most but the most orthodox. Her family never gave up this tradition, it was a sign of who they were.

The great hall was lit by a series of precisely arranged candles. The smell of incense filled the air, the incense filtering the light emanating from the fire.

She was asleep, her breathing gentle. The light from the roaring fire behind her casting the other side of her body into darkness.

Standing around the fire pit were five robed and hooded

figures. Their presence casting long shadows across the temple hall. Three of them were dressed in dark purple robes. The other two in white robes, their faces facing towards the fire.

A solitary crash of a gavel against a sound block, causing Reira to stir,

Her breathing became deeper, and a muffled scream could be heard.

Out of the darkness of the temple, a single figure dressed in a plain white robe walked towards the chair. Her hair grey and platted peaked out from out of her hood. She reached for the sack covering Reira's head and pulled the sack off in one swift motion. Casting the sack to the floor.

Reira struggled against the binding on the chair. She lifted her head. Letting her gaze drift up the distinguished white-robed figure standing before her.

"Reverend Mother..." Reira questioned. The Reverend Mother was old, at least one hundred and twenty years old, in the last years of her active life within the order, before retiring to the monastery on Gatis Prime. The end of a long journey of devotion. Her robes were all white, but they were anything but plain. A signal of her role and the privileges she had.

Delicate embroidery covered every inch of the material of her robe. The embroidery occasionally glistened in the firelight. She stood in front of Reira and removed the silk from covering her mouth.

She continued to look at the individual standing in front of her, and the struggling subsided.

"Child..." the old woman spoke, her voice as frail as her

body.

Reira looked up at her, "Reverend Mother..." she replied.

"It is the tradition of our Order to follow the request of a dying Priest. Our Brother Zamir made a request moments before he died, and I have considered that request..." the reverend mother announced; her voice carried across the great hall, causing a murmur throughout the other members of the order who were present.

"Normally a request such as this would never be accepted, not without the tribulations. However. Because of your service to this order. After consulting with your brothers and sisters here at the order" she paused, gesturing to the heavens, and after communing with the spirits in divination, and based on their insight into the task the goddesses has given you in your life. I have granted this final request."

Reira's expression was perplexed, what had Zamir requested?

"I Ilyaria, First Mother of the order, Daughter of the House of Baear. Bestow the right and privileges of High Priestess on you, under the rules of our order."

"Lady Nidiri Reira of the House Abrasar. Third Daughter of the House, Priestess of the Order of Ehji-Ha. One of the Chosen, do you accept the responsibilities and privileges of this role?" The Rev. Mother decreed as the gavel was slammed again into the wooden block.

"Yes," she paused.

"Only if I go through the tribulations," Reira added nervously.

"We thought you might say that..." one voice behind Reira announced, causing Reira to turn around.

"Then give yourself to the goddesses and let them take you through the Tribulations". The Reverend Mother Proclaimed. As she sliced through the ropes that tied Reira to the chair.

Reira stood up, shifting her athletic frame around the chair and turned her back to the Rev. Mother. She turned her attention to the five figures standing in front of her. The flames seemed to dance differently, almost alive. Reira looked at them and cleared her throat.

"I, of free mind and will. Submit my mind and body to the tribulations" she proclaimed. her mind clear, adrenaline pumping through her system, her hearts were racing, her scales tingled and for the first time in days she was at peace emotionally, beads of sweat formed on her brow, her eyes opened wide.

The first of the three figures in purple spoke; their face still shrouded in their robe.

"Where have you been?, Confess your secret..."

The second figure then spoke,

"Where are you? And what do you want?" Followed by the final figure.

"Where are you going?"

Reira stood the heat from the fire radiating through her. The chamber fell silent, and she could feel all of them watching her, waiting for her response,

"My goddesses, demigod Children of Life and Death, Nuwai, Suwai, Ilwai. (Past, Present, and Future)

"Nuwai, I have been on a journey, I have occasionally taken

the wrong path" she stopped, bowed graciously then began again.

"Suwai, I am here, I am at the moment, I never want this moment to end," she stopped, took a deep breath to compose herself then continued.

"Ilwai, I go where ever this journey takes me. My light comes from the darkness and travels to the fire. Only to be reborn from the darkness, without one the other cannot exist. I give myself truly to the fire, let it consume me if my journey ends then it will only begin again"

Reira was about to turn towards the Rev. Mother, when she felt a sharp pain in her neck. Grabbing at her neck she pulled a dart out of her neck.

"What is the meaning of this?" She gasped, she could feel something travelling through her veins, her body reacting, a tingling sensation travelled down through her neck out towards her extremities.

She staggered towards the Rev. Mother, her legs giving out before she could reach her.

"My child, it's not that simple. To survive the tribulations..." Reira gasping for air interrupted her, Reira slammed her hands onto the stone floor. A shock-wave burst from the impact blowing out the incense and extinguishing the fire. Plunging the hall into darkness, only the moonlight from above lit the room.

"You must die" the Rev Mother exclaimed as a Reira fell unconscious and collapsed onto the floor.

* * *

The goddesses, were impossible to summon. But the darkness, that would be easier, especially for the three. The darkness being summoned to judge the soul of a priestess. Especially the wayward daughter of an Impiri Lord, for the darkness this was an offer too tempting to resist.

The stone floor had the markings of a conjuring circle drawn onto their surface, made from the ash from a cremation and the blood of a Xanti.

"I Seek the council of darkness, I make this offering to you, I hereby require you to judge..." the Reverend Mother exclaimed, the three chanted quietly. Enough that they made a sound, but not enough that you could actually make out what they were saying.

Reira woke up in the middle of the conjuring circle. Her eyes flickered open, her breathing shallow, she looked up. The Reverend mother standing over her.

"To test the faith of one of her children, the Goddess has given us many ways to subject her ordained child to push her to her limits, to subject her to the darkness to see if she emerges from its grasp and is reborn. To see if she truly believes in the faith she preaches!" The Revered Mother Preached, a flash of fear streaked across Reira's face before disappearing.

"I shouldn't tell you, but I know your secret. I've known it for a long time, only now will you understand the course the goddess has given you. Your path is not of your own creation even though you may think it it. The darkness will test you, hopefully you will survive." The Rev. Mother spoke, her voice echoing throughout the chamber.

"I remember when you were horrified at the sight of Zamir's broken body, his death, which you had a hand in, was tragic. However, he saw something in you which merited his final wishes before he joined the flame to be reborn." The Rev. Mother spoke, before changing her gaze from Reira to looking out into the rest of the chamber. Her hands raised, a swirl of dark blue dust and vapour worked its way around the Rev. Mother's arm as she spoke, the vapour moved as if it was alive.

"et in nomine adhibuerunt deas. Educam et qui erat, et qui est, et qui unum sint, ego magna voco tenebris. Offerre sacrificium, si forte ego indignus ea iudicare. - in the name of the goddesses. The one who was, the one who is and the one who will be. I summon the great darkness, I offer a sacrifice if you may judge her unworthy"

"The great unclean, I demand your council." The Reverend Mother commanded.

"I am here" it's voice disembodied and melodic. The flames danced like they were alive.

Reira stepped into the Flames of Tribulation and was instantly engulfed by it. The flames burned the bottom of her robes; she flinched with pain as the flames scorched her skin. Clenching her fists she took a deep breath before she chanted

"May the flames consume me and let me be reborn" she kept repeating. The flames began to move. Gradually making their way across her clothes before engulfing her entire body. The flames burned her flesh, Reira screamed out in pain as the flames burnt her alive.

"I am ready judge me worthy..." she screamed as she sank to the floor,

As quickly as the flames engulfed Reira, they disappeared. Sinking into her body, a massive Shockwave emanated from her body. extinguishing the flames on each of the candles around the chamber, knocking one of the three to the floor.

Reira's burnt and blistered body sank to the floor, by the time she landed on the floor she was already dead. It had drained all signs of life from her already burnt body. Reira's eyes were open, her hands clenched tight towards her chest. It has burnt her clothing off, only a fragment of fabric remained, which was seared into her flesh. The smell causing one of the three to cover their mouth.

Her body shook, first small shakes before an uncontrollable seizure. Her arms flailing around her body, her eyes still open. Her burnt and blistered body rose above the floor. Twitching and jerking in an unsightly manner.

"Nidiri Reira Abrasar...are you there..." Reverend Mother claimed, as she flung the contents of a glass of water at Reira's body. The water hitting her body and evaporating almost instantly, causing a cloud of mist to surround her, before dissipating.

Reira's burnt and blistered skin bled. The blood running from every possible place, her eyes, her nose, her ears, her mouth. The scars on her back bled, her skin charred and bloody. The seizures slowly becoming less severe with each passing second and as quickly as the seizures started they came to a standstill.

"She is no longer here, I am Darkness and...." a voice emanated from Reira's mouth, but it wasn't her voice, the voice was disjointed but female and it echoed across the hall.

"I am here, but I am not alone. She is here, and she is strong. The things she has done, the darkness it is overwhelming .." Reira's voice exclaimed, her voice laboured.

Reira's mouth slowly opened, she tried to speak again. This time she slowly exhaled a breath, the air in the chamber became cold. Reira's breath hung in the air before disappearing. She coughed blood before a continual stream of blood trickled out of her mouth, this lasted for a few moments before stopping. She smiled at the Reverend Mother a mischievous smile.

"This one is mine, she is strong, I can see into her, she has suffered much in her existence, there is something here, I have known of her for a long time, ever since..." the voice then stopped.

"It is strong, but it is.." she paused

"Afraid." Reira added, regaining control.

"It is afraid of something, something hidden, I can't see what it is, but it is afraid...it is afraid of...me..."

Within her consciousness Reira could feel everything. Immense sadness, uncontrollable rage, pride, but also fear. Its wasn't her own fear that fear was close to the surface. This fear was hidden, her own fear was that she was now dead. She could feel her life ending and all her memories fading, for a second she could see herself. She could see the fear in the eyes of the Reverend Mother, and in the eyes of each of the three.

For an instant Reira could read all of their thoughts. Their minds were a jumble of thoughts and feelings. The Reverend

Mothers thoughts were hidden, her mind trained, but she emanated fear. She could not hide this most basic and primal of emotions.

The three all had various emotions and thoughts. One was concerned about the amount of blood Reira had lost since the tribulations began. The second was thinking about making sure the tribulations went well.

This had been their first tribulations and the summoning of the darkness had taken a lot out of her. The third, was the most puzzling. His thoughts were fear, but he wasn't scared, he seemed to enjoy the fear, in some perverse way, the fear excited him.

Her mind opened up to the voices. Not just the voices of those around her, but the voices of those in the city. Just as her mind was opening up, the darkness returned.

"Join me in the darkness, in dying, you shall not die. Even the goddesses know that my offer shall tempt you. Give yourself up and I shall open your eyes, and you shall be like darkness. There is no good and evil, but the darkness and the flame, without me there is no flame." She decreed, her voice boomed.

This realisation shocking her, trying to move Reira struggled. But her body was paralysed. She fell to the floor, her body resembling a dried, burnt husk., Laying on the floor completely motionless. Feeling the darkness slowly course through her body.

Her nerves being overwhelmed with sensation. As if each of her nerves were being triggered at the highest levels all at once.

She screamed out, inside her own mind. The pain was unbearable, her thoughts changed from being afraid to just wanting the pain to end. Hoping that she would pass out from the pain, but it continued.

Until she screamed out in pain the flames rushing out of her throat. With each passing moment the pain becoming slightly less severe. As the flames left her body, her body healed. The burns disappeared, and the blisters dissolved into nothing.

One of the three picked up a robe from next to him and covered Reira.

Reira looked up at him, her eyes filling with tears, "Thank you" she stuttered, her body still covered in blood, but the burns and blisters were gone.

The reverend Mother crouched down next to Reira and spoke to her.

"The darkness manifested in you was stronger than I've ever seen before. What worries me is that you said the darkness was afraid, the darkness is fear, how can it be afraid." She whispered.

"I don't know, but somehow I survived..." she cried out, her body shaking, as the breeze caught her skin.

There were many answers she could have given. But she was unable, she couldn't comprehend what had happened herself. So she could not explain it to others.

The Reverend Mother looked at her as she pulled the robe tightly around her.

"Child, the darkness has left you alive..., take from this what you will, but you have been judged..."

In the hours that followed, Reira was visited by the three. They treated her as if she was sacred. They had never witnessed a Tribulation as violent and visceral as hers. No one in the chamber had seen one as violent as that before. Some had been in the temple for over a hundred years, and this was worse than all previous tribulation on record. Kesi D'Korra offered her a place to rest, somewhere desolate but peaceful, somewhere far from the main hall, somewhere at the far reaches of the temple.

The fire in the room was freshly stoked. it was a rare occurrence for Reira to feel cold, especially when it was over 90 degrees outside that night. The glow from the fire warming Reira's face, its glow mesmerising. At times she was lost in thought looking at the flames, watching them dance.

Occasionally when she closed her eyes, she could remember the burning. The pain she endured, and the unusual peace as her hearts stopped beating. This was a heavy toll on Reira's mind, sometimes she lashed out. Screaming at the walls in different languages, sometimes in standard dialect, other times in the old tongue, even times in other unknown languages. sometimes she was caught banging her hands against the surface of the fall or the floor. This was the only way she felt she could let the anger inside herself out.

Shoan had nervously enquired about the severity of the burning and had she felt anything. of course she couldn't describe it in full detail. The three would never go through the tribulations, not until they were no longer acolytes. Which would take years, Reira had only progressed through the ranks so quickly was because of the forty years she has spent studying scripture in her free time at the cloisters.

She knew every word of scripture, every hymn. She knew more at times than the Reverend Mother. The three would have to work through the ranks from Acolyte to Master of Ceremonies. Junior to Master, then finally priest to High Priest.

Reira didn't want to scare him, he had only been in the temple for the last year; he was young and naïve. He had brought her pills to take away any pain, but they weren't working.

Her head was still pounding. Reira shook another pill from the bottle beside her bed and put it away. She couldn't keep swallowing pills. Something would have to give, one way or the other. Either the pain was going to go away, or she'd find another way to get rid of the pain.

Shoan Rene who'd brought her the tablets earlier was staring at her at her open door. He looked at her with a concerned expression. Was it so obvious something was wrong with her? Reira thought she was hiding it well.

'Let me in, Reira. I'll even make it quick' maybe as quick as your sisters' a voice echoed in Reira's head. This voice startled her. She shook her head and cursed under her breath. She remembered the voice it was the same voice that had occupied her during the tribulations.

"No!" Reira forced the voice away again.

"I did it once before, and I'll do it again..." It was growing insistent, slowly creeping up in the back of mind until it surfaced again.

'You can't win, you know. I will take you with me. Give up this charade. If you don't come I'm going to kill one of them, take their soul instead...And you will watch, as I'll make you do it.." it laughed.

"You're not going to win," Reira moaned.

'Is that what you really believe? You know they think you fought me off, that I left you, I stayed because you wanted me to. Because you wanted me to see beyond this consciousness into that bit of darkness inside you. You know that darkness that your sister couldn't take. That's the real reason why she killed herself you know, what was inside her was worse than I could ever be." It mocked, the mention of her sister scared her. She tried to hide those memories.

"Why do you say that, what do you know about my sister...?" Reira screamed.

The pain was overwhelming. It was hard to concentrate on anything. Shoan was moving toward her now, he was calling to her.

'I know that she couldn't take the darkness that was inside of her, she sought the only way out.' The voice laughed.

"Your Eminence are you okay?" He called, before walking into the room, a concern look appeared on his face.

"Your Eminence , are you okay?" His voice seemed distance and faint. Then she realised she couldn't hear anything else any better. He closed the door behind himself, this should have made a noise, but it made hardly a sound.

Darkness was closing in at the edge of her vision. A spreading tide of black that would mean the end of her own existence as well as Shoan's.

'Here I come, Reira', you will watch him die tonight. The voice giggled inside her head.

"I don't think..." she answered, before being cut off, her whole demeanour changing. She smiled a demure smile, her eyes inviting him closer.

"Shoan, my dear Shoan, always wanting to help me, isn't that sweet. You know I heard your thoughts during the tribulations..."

".. you.. you did.." he stuttered as he got closer,

"Such dark thoughts for someone so innocent, I never knew you thought about things, about me in such a way..."

'Stop it' Reira thought to herself, unable to stop the darkness acting out using her as a conduit.

Reira gestured for Shoan to sit on the chair next to her, while she sat on the side of the bed,

Shoan carefully sat himself on the chair, he leaned forward and listened to Reira intently.

"Shoan, I knew you were always polite to me, but I never knew you had a motive behind it..." she teased.

"I didn't, I mean..., I didn't know you knew..." he nervously responded.

Reira leant forward, placed her hand on his shoulder, then slowly stroked it, causing him to lean in closer.

"Maybe I never appreciated what you did for me,..." She

replied, her hand slowly making its way to under his chin, she began slowly combing her fingers on his chin, causing him to recoil gently.

"It was always for you...I thought you never noticed me..." he replied,

All the meanwhile Reira was screaming within herself. Still unable to stop the darkness acting out. Being locked inside herself while she toyed with the emotions of Shoan. She knew what was going to happen.

Instantly her hand grabbed at his throat. The shock of this sending him off the chair backwards. Reira following, her hand grasping at his throat.

"And I know you like pain like this," as she said this he slowly nodded.

"You are such a deviant, your perverse nature sickens me, compared to you I am a goddess." Her voice booming.

The look on her face showed a playful disgust at his perversion.

His expression changed instantly. this wasn't Reira, but he couldn't cry out, she had hold of his throat and with her other hand she smothered his mouth.

"It won't be long, she won't come with me, but I'll take you instead, I'll enjoy tormenting you for an eternity" she added.

Before Reira could even scream out, a bolt of light hit her, emanating from the top of a twisted wooden staff. Holding it was the Rev. Mother, she struck Reira in the chest with the staff, a moment later. Shoan lay on the floor, gasping and clutching at his throat, he struggled to move out of the way.

"Don't go too far, my darling, I'm coming back for you..."

Reira yelled at him.

Reira's face turned towards her, she hissed at her, bearing her teeth,

"Think you can save her old woman. Many have tried before, they have failed, and they were much more powerful than you." It laughed.

The Reverend Mother kept the staff pointing at Reira,

"That may be so, but I'm sure our sister wants you gone also, so begone..." she roared.

"In the Name and by the power of Our goddess. May you be snatched away and driven from this place and from the souls made by the grace of the gods. Be redeemed by the Precious Fire of the Divine Flame." The Rev. Mother commanded,

Reira looked her and laughed. The laugh changing from Reira's voice to the voice from the tribulations,

"Nice try, you will have to try harder than that...in the name and by the power" she mocked.

"I, keeper of the Faith, Servant of Idara, and Ishara (Goddesses of Life and Death) commands you. They whom, in your great insolence, you still claim to be equal." The Rev. Mother recited, before reciting it again.

Reira's expression changed, the laughing stopped and a look of concern crossed her face.

"Help me, ...please..." it was Reira's voice, not the voice of the darkness.

"Most cunning serpent. The darkness incarnate, wanderer of the dark places between life and rebirth. You shall no more dare to deceive our sister. Persecute the Temple in which she dutifully serves. Torment the goddesses children and sift them like wheat in a field." The Rev mother commanded, her voice echoing though the room.

"I command you to leave her and leave her you will.." she exclaimed one final time as she had grown tired of its resistance to scripture. This failed, a final bolt of light left the staff and hit Reira straight in the chest, sending her crashing towards the wall, screaming loudly before falling down onto the bed unconscious.

The atmosphere in the room was charged. The lightening strikes from the staff had cooked the air. Mixed with the roaring fire, it was uncomfortably hot in the room, causing the Reverend Mother to sweat.

The Reverend mother sighed. dropping the staff to the floor, before falling to her knees, the exorcism had taken a lot from her. The protection spells she was thinking while trying to perform the exorcism were strong enough. Strong enough she didn't succumb to the darknesses thoughts.

Shoan was dragged out of the room by Airal, he was coughing, his face still red from the rush of blood to his face. He kept his head won in embarrassment. Meanwhile Kesi helped the Rev. Mother up onto her feet and they left the room, Reira still unconscious on the bed.

After the shock from the staff, and the attempted exorcism her body was unwilling. Reira's body ached, she could barely get out of bed, she slowly sat up. Pulling the tablets from underneath her pillow.

Reira shook another pill from the bottle before put it away.

She couldn't keep swallowing pills. She wanted to block out the pain, thoughts of ending it all coursed through her mind. The easy option she thought, but they would have won. She would not let that happen.

Reira had spent the night awake. Her nightmares had awoken her screaming or waking up in a trance. Reciting scripture in multiple languages before passing out again. Airal, Kesi and Shoan came and went keeping an eye on her, but they came and went as they wished. there was always someone watching her.

She couldn't leave, not until the nightmares and visions subsided. The Rev. Mother had ordered a protection sigil be placed a round the door and window of the room. The door was always open, but Reira knew she couldn't leave.

She scared the three; she threatened them, but she had no power to do anything. The tribulation had screwed with her mind, left her mind tormented and her body drained. It had been a miracle she had even survived.

At some point the darkness would leave, by the morning light it would be over, as long as she survived the night.

Early the next morning.

Shoan was staring at her via her open door. He looked at her with a look of fear. His throat was blackened by a bruise where a Reira had attempted to crush his windpipe. Reira saw him and tried to show a thoughtful smile and look of wanting to apologise. But she shied away.

She felt terrible about what she had done; she tried to smile again. Trying to hide the pain and guilt from her face. He sighed before walking away from the door. Reira thought she was hiding it well before the Rev. Mother appeared at the door.

"He won't be able to face you for a while. He is ashamed that he was tricked by the darkness. if this was his tribulation, in his current state he would have been given up to the darkness." She commented bluntly.

"Hopefully one day he can forgive me, for what I did" she paused.

"And what I said, I said some terrible things to him, using some things personal to him against him, I couldn't stop it, I knew what it was doing, but I wasn't strong enough." She broke down crying.

"You must have been strong enough, you're still here..." the Reverend Mother replied.

'I remember everything. The things I said, the things I did. I mean, I could have killed him, I could feel his life slipping away. I resisted, even when you knocked me out, I could hear her talking to me, she was convincing, but I knew that I couldn't let go.." Reira responded through the tears.

"We have all heard her voice, to me she used the temptation of seeing my mother again..! Rev. Mother replied.

"I forced the voice away, it came back, I forced the voice away again. It was growing insistent."

"Did you believe that I would survive?" Reira asked.

"Over the years, I've grown to believe that your stubborn enough to survive anything, even though you might cry about it later." Rev. Mother replied with a knowing smile.

"But just in case, I was willing to sacrifice you to stop the darkness from taking hold" she added after a short pause.

"I had made sure that all the scripture had been read, the correct offerings made, I knew the darkness would come." She arrogantly replied.

"Zamir's death might have brought forward your ascension within our ranks, but you proved by yourself that you were willing to sacrifice yourself for the temple."

Reira nodded her head as she drank from a small glass.

"For you to have gone through that, especially with all that's happened to you recently. I think you'll become a better person because of it." For the first time, the Rev. Mother sounded caring, she had grown to see Reira develop into a full-fledged member of the order.

"I had never thought about anyone in the ways that she made me think, the needs of the flesh had always been a mystery to me, they were a mystery when I was in the Cloisters and they are a mystery now." Reira added after trying to calm down.

"She always delves into the darkest parts of our personality, bringing them out. What she did was all of her, but how she did it, that was using parts of your own personality that had been repressed."

"So you mean, the things that I said, the way I acted, that was from me?" Reira questioned.

"In a way, a subconscious way..." the Reverend Mother replied.

"It's hard to believe that I was capable of such actions, I

mean flirting in that way with Shoan, it's.."

"I'm not saying it's a desire of yours, but there must be something in how you acted with him that the darkness picked up on and brought to reality."

"But the true question is, how do you feel?"

"I'm fine, of course, what could be wrong with me...?" She responded, the Reverend Mother looked at her,

"Those visions and the voices, the ones which kept you awake at night..." she questioned.

"What about them?" Reira replied, her expression full of worry.

"Those are the same visions that everyone who has been through the Tribulations has. They once wrote these visions down , started by one of my predecessors. these scriptures are forbidden to be read. Not even I have read them, it's against our highest laws."

"Why do you tell me of this?" Reira enquired, she had never heard of this, not even rumours, she had seen every book within this temple. Except the ones in the Rev. Mothers Personal Library. These books and the Rev. Mother's office was off limits. Punishable by expulsion from the order and being silenced from disclosing temple secrets.

"Because a vision told me to, a vision I have had since you first came here..."

"And I mean the first time you came here, with your father. I was but a Master of Ceremonies, but the visions came to me during a series of meditations." The Reverend Mother declared.

This made Reira even more confused that had occurred

nearly sixty years before. Her memories from that point were a mess, she didn't want to remember those times. Numarii's funeral had occurred about a month before she visited the temple. When she had to decline her offer of taking up residence at the temple to take Numarii's place at the cloister.

In the days that followed, Reira tried to recover her strength. It was a slow and painful process, spending a lot of time meditating, even consulting the divination card of Ardos. Which was against the advice of the Reverend Mother, communing with he spirits so shortly after a Tribulation of such magnitude could be dangerous.

Reira passed the main hall, but never stepped in, it was her right now. She was one of the High Priestess of the order, a hundred of these existed across the empire. It was a great honour to be at this level. She had wanted this role for years, but in the back of her mind she knew she was a decade away from it.

Zamirs death had sped up her standing at the temple, Yes she had survived the tribulations, but at what cost to herself, she had witnessed the ancient darkness take over her body and exposed her to its perverse ideals, but even more frightening was the darkness that still dwelled inside her was something that the ancient darkness was afraid of.

She stood at the doorway and looked in. Zamir's coffin was lying in state at the entrance, here she froze. Kesi eyed Reira at the door, but did not speak to her, he just bowed slightly, before resuming his activities. Reira didn't even notice, the coffin transfixed her, but she was too afraid to venture closer. Her hearts raced again, this would be difficult to deal with.

She walked out to the front of the temple; the day was drawing to a close. Tomorrow would be the day she had to do something she never wanted to do.

Zamir's Funeral

"May I have a word with you..." Reira's asked while standing at the half-open door of the Reverend Mother,

"You may come in..." the Rev. Mother replied, her voice cutting through the silence.

Reira stepped through the gap in the door, the Reverend Mother was sitting at her desk, looking at a book.

"What is it my child, is it those visions that you've been having..." she enquired.

Reira looked at her and nodded,

"I must confess, that I have had those visions again. but these were not circumstantial, I did it knowingly. I could easily have lied about this but you would know, anyway. I had never been good at lying, Zamir knew this, and the goddesses would know it also, and that I couldn't live with."

"That my child isn't a problem..."

The Rev. Mothers calmness lit a fire in Reira,

"Is that all your going to say. Everyone seemed to want to avoid me, even Kesi. did I say something during those night terrors after the tribulations?"

"It's not what you said, it's what happened after you said it. You said thing that you should not have even known." The Reverend Mother replied. Her voice stern, not liking the tone of Reira's voice.

"You talked about our weaknesses. Weaknesses that I didn't think we all have come to terms with. Things that only the darkness and the goddesses know about. The darkness left a mark on you, don't you remember..." the Reverend Mother exclaimed,

Reira stood there in shock.

She looked at the Reverend Mother, scanning her face for any hint of what kind of answer she was looking for, but finding nothing.

Reira's mind was full of thoughts, she stood there lost in thought.

CHAPTER 12

That night came quickly. Everyone in the temple had already gone to sleep. Not Reira, though. She lay on the bed, in the room she had spent the last two days. It was about two o'clock in the morning when she realised she had Zamir's funeral in a few hours.

How could she think about the funeral when she had other matters to attend to. She couldn't just forget about what had happened over the past few days, in Reira's mind it felt like the fate of the world was to be rested on her shoulders and She didn't know how she could juggle this dilemma with Zamir's funeral.

Reira finally forced her mind to cooperate. Her body was exhausted but her brain was not. She slowly but surely fell asleep. This room had made her feel comfortable, the fireplace still roared, its glow making Reira remember the fireplace at home, and that was the only place she considered keeping her safe from harm's way.

Reira pulled a warm wool blanket from the bottom of the bed and covered her legs, a thin silk top, which elegantly flowed across her torso covered the top half of her body.

"How could I ask for more? The perfect silence of the temple at night and the crackle of a fire. As long as this brain of mine lets me sleep?" She whispered to herself, smiling a wry smile.

She gradually shut her eyes, all she could hear was the sound of the wood in the fire crackling, the faint sound of the wind as it blew down the chimney, causing the fire to crackle more. Through the open window in the door she could make out the sound of the city, even at this time people were still out, but it was faint and calm and she did not mind. This gradually sent Reira to sleep.

Moments Later

She awoke, and the room was a brilliant white; she looked around slowly, everything was so bright it caused her to squint, she was standing in the middle of the room; she looked down and saw her bare feet on the cold stone floor.

A black spot appeared on the floor, catching Reira's attention, the spot growing bigger and bigger, big enough that she had to move out of the way, afraid that the spot would have allowed her to fall through the floor.

The spot opened out into The room, getting quicker and quicker until Reira had nowhere to go and she slowly stepped into the darkness, the room going black instantly. All She could do was hold on to her half as she felt like she was falling. Reira's hearts pounded in her chest, She nervously called out into the darkness.

"Where, Where am I?" She asked, her voice dissipating into the room, there was no echo, the sound of her voice just dissipated. The room then appeared out of the darkness as this happened Reira grasped at her shoulder when she saw something out of the corner of her eye.

A Xanti tail barb was sticking out of her shoulder, it didn't hurt as she didn't even notice it impale her shoulder, but blood was pouring out of the wound. Soon the light turned off again and when it changed back to a bright white, the barb was gone again.

It was so bright that Reira was blinded by what was up ahead. Then it started to become dark again, this time stars appeared on the ceiling, they looked as distant as the stars in the sky that night. The stars twinkled in the sky; the room was amazing, Reira stood in the middle of the room, looking into the ceiling, out of the corner of her eye the stars in the sky were being absorbed by an approaching darkness.

Several of the golden stars disappeared from all around her even though the darkness hadn't spread that far. She looked around, as she turned a pack of Xanti came into her field of view, Reira jumped back, these Xanti were ferocious, their teeth were dripping with blood,

"Will I survive?" She thought to herself.

"Xanti have never scared me this much before, I've had enough run-ins with them before.." she whispered. She thought "Is there anyone that can save me." Nothing made sense anymore; She closed her eyes and prepared for the worse., she could hear the Xanti growling and hissing as they made their way closer.

Just when she thought her life was over the bright light turned on once again. All around her light then darkness again and….. seconds into the darkness, the light turned back on, but this time everything was black and white. Plain. Nothing had colour. The Xanti were gone, and the stars were gone, but the colour…. no more.* everything in the room was muted in colour, Reira could hear the embers of the wood crackle in the fire, she could smell the burning wood but everything was muted in colour.

That's when It all dawned on Reira, a moment of crystal clarity. In the darkness, where she only had thoughts of fear, The darkness was something that she had faced before; She had been absolutely absorbed by it; it had tried to take her life many times before, but she had escaped it.

The stars that went out, she thought, they must have been those in her life which She had lost, the darkness had taken them, Grandfather, Numarii, Father, Ilaria, Zamir...

A few hours later Reira awoke suddenly, she sat up, the fire in the room had died down, its glow still illuminating the room, she reached over to the side table and grabbed a small device and her fingers began tapping on its screen.

It read ;

"Live Your Own Life...",

She spent the next few moments staring at the screen; she smirked as things started to make sense in her mind. Looking over at the clock on the table, it read 06:13. As she looked at the clock, she could hear the sounds of people starting to move around the temple. She would have to get up and get ready for today. She clambered out of bed and stood up and stretched.

"Well, today's the day..." she murmured before walking over to the window, she stared out into the city, people were already wandering around the city, she had less than an hour to get ready before the funeral. Her stomach rumbled, she needed to eat something. She hadn't eaten in nearly two days, her body was now craving food.

"...okay, okay, I'll eat a little something" she replied to herself as her stomach rumbled again.

* * *

8th Hour of the 29th Day of the 7th Month
IY (Imperial Year) 101

It was early morning, people from all across the city were walking towards the temple. It was the day of Zamir's funeral, and everyone was out to pay their respects in their own way.

Right before the service, various dignities from across Ateki gathered at the gatehouse. Zamir's sister Mazur was sitting on the floor next to the entrance to the temple. her head in her hands, sobbing.

The hearse arrived at the entrance of the temple. Zamir's coffin was draped by an intricately decorated cloth, inscribed with arcane inscriptions. The cloth looked ancient; it emblazoned a family crest in its centre.

A young girl approached the coffin as the gates to the temple were slowly opened. She laid a single orchid on the coffin. Zamir had always enjoyed Orchids, she turned around and shyly ran back to her grandfather who was waiting by the gatehouse door. He looked down at her and ran his hand through her hair and whispered, "Good Girl...."

The wooden gates to the temple slowly retracted, occasionally creaking, before finally stopping. The guests and dignitaries stopped what they were doing. Carefully bowed their heads as the hearse passed them. The old man and his granddaughter were the first to follow the hearse as it made its way to the temple entrance.

The rest of the guests followed them. Each of them carrying a beaded chain, some made of gold or silver, some of them made of precious stones. Others were made of various types of wood or ceramic.

Everyone came, the first minister of Ateki, his wife and their daughters. They lived on the other side of the planet. The local doctor, people from all walks of life. Even a military general that had argued with Zamir years before came to pay respect.

At the door to the temple, Reira stood, initially looking out at the procession making its way towards her. She then looked over, Mazur was still crying, unaware that Reira was only meters away. Reira stepped forward, wanting to console her, but hesitated, before stepping back. It wasn't the right time, and her mind wasn't in the right place.

Reira was in full ceremonial dress. her white dress covered in red embroidery, partially hidden by a white robe. Her hair free to blow in the wind, very different from her usually tied back hairstyle. Her eyes still red from all the crying, she had done over the last 48 hours.

She shook her head and sighed, trying to snap herself out of the emotions she was currently feeling. She now had a job to do, a job she never wanted to do, not under this circumstance. Presiding over the funeral of her predecessor. She had presided over the funeral of many people over the years. Yet this was different, never had she presided over the funeral of a friend and mentor.

"May the goddesses help me through this tough time..." she whispered as she looked at the approaching hearse. which was slowly making its way up to the temple, she had maybe a minute before they arrived?.

Reira nervously clenched her hands. clenching enough that when she released them she left nail imprints in her palm.

The sun was shining, a perfect day, even the wind had died down, seemly in respect for the situation.

The grand hall was lit by a series of precisely arranged candles. The smell of incense filled the air, the incense filtering the light emanating from the fire. Ceremonial banners decorated the higher levels of the temple.

In the grand hall, there were rows of chairs. Each row made a circle towards the centre of the temple. The fire pit crackled, the flames were low and flickering slowly. Closer to the fire there were three chairs; each of the chairs was covered by a dark purple cloth. No one was to sit in those chairs. They were reserved for the goddesses, out of respect.

Next to the fire stood a single pedestal, it was intricately decorated, a small book sat on the top of the pedestal. The book lay next to a single ornate blade. The blade looked new, not a single mark could be seen on its surface.

Suspended above the fire pit, was the coffin. its suspension chains went up to into the ceiling and then down into the mezzanine. Where four temple aides held the ropes. Between each of the aides, two drummers stood waiting. Their drums covered in purple silk, the drums were silent.

Huge black candles lined the walkway to the seating, remaining unlit. Reira walked slowly into the grand hall. The hall was now filling with guests.

Once the guests were seated, the drums slowly started beating, quietly and rhythmically. Before stopping, Reira looked around, all eyes on her,

"Ishara and Idara, Please come and take your honoured servant, Zamir, back into the light..." she preached.

"Traditionally I would recite a passage from the book of Fate" she announced, her voice ringing out into the crowd.

"But that wouldn't do justice to the light we are committing to the fire. I have chosen to express this in an ancient Impiri way. A way reserved amongst my people for the death of a great leader,"

"Although Zamir wasn't an Impiri, he was a Vasari, he definitely was a great leader to us all. Hopefully, you can all agree with how I honour him..." she preached, before banging the sceptre which was next to the podium three times onto the floor. Which sent an echo reverberating across the great hall. No one moved, not a sound was made.

The audience sat watching, silently. Two Impiri dancers entered the hall, took their places within a space left for them near the fire pit. Waiting for the drumming to begin once it started they took a step backwards. Bowed to Reira, then turned to Mazur and bowed again, before blessing themselves in front of the three empty chairs.

They then turned to each other and walked in a circle around each other slowly. Their gazes remaining locked on each other, one of the dancer's places his hand on the woman's back. With her hand on his shoulder. Together they danced to the beat of the drums, their bodies moved rhythmically to the beat of the drums. They seemed to be in perfect sync with the music, then they parted.

The sound of a flute broke through the beat of the drums, their smiles changed to a sombre expression. And the dance changed, from being close to each other to facing away from each other, moving further apart as the music grew. Still moving to the music but carefully drifting away from each other. Then quickly returning within inches of each other to be finally cast out.

Each of them was dressed in the most intricate clothing. The clothing emblazoned with embroidery. The pattern seemed to mirror each other, his clothing embroidered on the top half of his body. While her clothing was embroidered from the middle of her torso down.

He looked at her, his eyes not moving, he turned away from her, in tune with the drumming. There was a harshness to his movements, like a story of life and death was being told, at this point betrayal. She looked at him, her face full of emotion, as she pulled him closer to her.

Their eyes met, and his expression changed, pulling each other closer. She pulled a red rope from her dress. slowly tying it to his wrist, and he tied the other side to her wrist, they were connected. His fate and hers tied to each other, her breath short and ragged. He looked at her, and the drums stopped. The melody of the flute changed from emotional and full of energy to pure sadness.

He guided her in a slow dance, their bodies close to each other. She slowly danced lower to the floor, he kept his eyes fixed on her, yet he still knew exactly where to take her. With every moment the emotion of the scene could be felt. Everything had been rehearsed and planned down to the gestures made by their hands. They forced nothing; they were in unison, then the flute stopped.

"The Cycle Begins again" she spoke, her voice raspy and breathless. He turned to the audience that was stunned into silence, some in the audience quietly crying. Reira looked at the dancers, a solitary tear running down her cheek. Once that first tear broke free, the rest followed in an unbroken stream. But she didn't care; the emotion of the situation was uncontrollable.

The male dancer grabbed his partner's hand, and she fell graciously to the floor. Her eyes closed, To hushed gasps from the audience.

"She has been given back to the goddesses" he implored. Before gesturing to the red rope signifying the bond between them.

"And this bond will never be broken, hers in the realm of death and mine in the light of the living. We are two that have been bonded together by the goddesses as one. Life and Death the eternal partners.

It was then when her body went limp; she let go of his hand

and lay motionless on the floor.

The drumming began again. This time returning to the background noise of earlier in the ceremony.

Reira carefully made her way from the podium, towards the staircase to the side of the hall, the audience following her movements.

The audience sat watching, silently, as Reira nervously made her way up a spiral staircase leading to the mezzanine floor. Her robe flowing as she moved. Mazur followed slowly behind. Reira made her way to a precipice overlooking the crowd below. A rush of fear came over her as she looked down. The casket being suspended at the end of the precipice. She approached the end cautiously. Her heart racing, she hesitated, momentarily before leaning towards the casket. With Mazur standing a few meters behind.

"You know I don't know how to say this...especially to you..." Reira whispered her face as close as possible to the casket. She brushed away a few strands of hair away from her face. Tucking them behind her ear, She placed her hand on the casket, and ran her fingers across its surface. Her fingernails painted bright red, a stark contrast to the black casket. Her hand slowly caressing its glossy exterior.

"I know you won't let me say this! You would scold me as you normally would...", she paused, seeming to force back tears.

"It was my fault...and this is something that I'm going to have to live with..."

Mazur slowly put her hand on Reira's shoulder, startling her.

"My dear, Zamir would be the first to tell you that this wasn't your fault. If the roles were reversed, I know he would be feeling the same way that your feeling" her voice close to breaking. She spoke in the same melodic way as Zamir and for a second that familiar cadence brought Reira a flicker of joy. Before reality set back in, replacing that glimmer of a smile that was working its way across Reira's face.

Reira stood up, turned to Mazur, and slowly nodded her head. Mazur reached across the small gap between them and pulled Reira in close. Shocking Reira for a second, the warmth of Mazur's hug, comforting.

"He may not judge you, in all of his wisdom. But the goddesses will judge you for what happened. So will I." She whispered, her voice changing from warm and caring to scathing and resentful.

"But since we both have a special part of our lives linked to my brother, I allow you to grieve for him. Maybe even grieve for yourself for the life you had planned, but know this" she hissed.

for an instant Reira feared for her life, she was close enough to the precipice that Mazur could easily have pushed her to her death.

"I may come to terms with his death...but I will never forgive you for allowing my brother to be taken from me..." She stepped back. Her eyes overflowing with tears and stormed away towards the staircase.

Reira struggled to fight back the tears, her hands shaking. She again leaned towards the coffin, in silence, the crowd below becoming restless.

A quiet disturbance of whispers made its way through the crowd.

"I have to admit, your sister is right to judge me. I mean, my reckless attitude and failure in judgement are why you are here, instead of me. Maybe it should be me," she paused.

"I mean who am I, a daughter of a Lord trying to become a priestess. I mean I failed my father after spending 40 years in the Cloisters, and I failed in my duty to you.." she stopped, her expression changed as she recalled a fragment of a happy memory.

"Who would I tell my jokes to? You were the only one who ever laughed at them... Who would I pour my heart out to, Tell me who! No one, that's who" she declared, her eyes filling with tears, her lip trembling.

Reira gestured to the rope bearers who began to slowly lower the coffin. Simultaneously, the fire pit roared to life. The flames reaching higher and higher. Before coming to rest in the pit, Reira's face was full of emotion. Her eyes filling with tears, which she was fighting back. Her lip still trembling, Her hands clenched. The casket began to burn, slowly at first, the wood cracking its surface blistering before being consumed by the fire.

"You know", she whispered, looking down at his slowly burning casket.

"Even though we had differing opinions, and sometimes didn't see eye to eye at times in the past, I respected you. Everything you did for me, you listened to me." She paused.

"You cared about how the setbacks in my life affected me, and you never judged me. Even though I may have initially thrown your generosity and kindness back at you. You accepted me as me, you didn't see an Impiri, everyone else did, but you didn't.." she raised her head and forced a smile.

"I might have never told you, but I hope to the goddesses you knew..." she drew a deep breath "that.." she stopped, cautiously looked to make sure no one was within earshot,

"I love ... you."

She grasped at a necklace that lay around her neck and clenched it tight.

"And I always will..." she whispered as she slowly turned away.

* * *

A Few Days Later

8th Hour of the 30th Day of the 7th Month
IY (Imperial Year) 101

High Priests Office

With the realisation sinking in of Zamir's death, it finally drove Reira to the edge. She slowly clenched her fists, digging her nails into her palm. Not once caring about the damage being done. As she sat on a small bench in the office's corner, the office was vast, decorated in a very minimalist way, its far wall was covered by a large selection of robes and religious paraphernalia.

Any normality in Reira life seemed to slip away. With Zamir dead, she lost everything and gained everything in a moment.

She sighed

"Suwai, why is this fate destined for me. Haven't I suffered enough" she hissed through clenched teeth.

Carila sat there next to her, watching, not interrupting, just letting it happen, it was for the best. Reira looked at Carila, she flickered her eyes, trying to force back tears.

"I've lost everything" she screamed, causing Carila to sit upright in response.

Again Carila didn't speak, he knew Reira well enough to just let this occur, to get it out of her system.

Reira reached for a small necklace that was around her neck. Twisting it between her fingers and holding it close to her lips which were slowly trembling,

"Parshai, what should I do, if you were here you would know actually what to do. Curse the goddesses for taking you away from us, from me," she cursed.

This startled Carila, Reira had been angry before but never had she blasphemed, especially after her time at the temple.

Reira cried, silent tears, occasionally mumbling to herself. She shook, she closed her eyes, forcing away the tears. At this point Carila got up. Reira looked across at Carila, and spoke, her voice fragile and childlike,

"Please don't go...does it ever stop hurting?" She pleaded, wiping the tears from her eyes,

Carila looked at her, reached over and attempted to wipe a tear from her chin, her hand phasing out of existence.

Carila paused, looked at Reira straight in the eyes,

"No, not really, you just make room for it...I just wish I was there to wipe those tears away" she whispered.

Reira looked at her, her eyes still streaming with tears.

“I know, but for an instant I forgot that you were so far away, too realistic those holographic projectors...” she paused, lost in a thought.

“It’s, it’s just that, first my twin, then father, my older sister and now Zamir is gone, and...” she stopped.

“And with everything happening, I don’t think I could take...” she continued before being stopped by an intercom message...

“Lady Abrasar, you have a coded priority zero message from...” the voice announced over the intercom before stopping abruptly.

Reira reached over and pressed a small tear-shaped device laying on the table across from her,

“Who is the message from...” she enquired, tears still slowly rolling down her cheeks,

“The message is from Aterix...” to voice carefully replied.

“From the Office of the...,” he added before being cut off.

“Reroute the message to my office please...” Reira enquired, her voice trembling.

Carila looked at Reira,

“Aterix. Why would someone from the Cloisters be messaging you after all this time?..”

“Sorry for the interruption to your day Lady Abrasar. I send this communication with utmost urgency. At 04:01 Imperial Time this morning. An imperial convoy carrying Ildise Baeil was attacked by Ankari Rebels on its way to Rebels on Prim. They destroyed the entire convoy. There were no survivors...”

"I must convey to you our regret in the circumstances in which I must inform you of this information and what I'm sure you are now aware of..." the voice trailed off, before resuming.

"Today, on the 8th Hour of the 30th Day of the 7th Month, 101st Imperial Year, in the Name of our Emperor Isalnesh. I Eerain Gahal Minister of the Ministry of Truth. Proclaim that you Nidiri Reira Abrasar, third daughter of your house." He paused

"Are elevated to Codex in waiting. With all the rights and privileges, the role entitles...An imperial carrier will arrive in 3 days to escort you to Prim...". He paused for a moment before adding.

"The reason for the urgency in the shuttle's arrival is to be expected. Given the codex's situation." Then the communication ended,

Reira sat looking into the middle distance, unblinking. Her breathing deepening, Carila looked at her, unnoticed.

"If you ever need me, you know where I am..." she whispered, Reira sat transfixed on the now blank display. Carila stood up slowly, this movement caused Reira to blink, her eyes now looking down. A tear formed from her left eye and slowly ran down her cheek.

"Please..." she spoke, her voice breaking.

Carila looked at her,

"Listen, you know where I am. It's getting late here I've gotta be up in a few hours. Message me later. You've got to give yourself time to let this sink in..." she said looking at Reira straight in the eyes.

Reira looked at her, smiled a nervous smile.

"You are always right..., aren't you.." she replied, taking a deep breath.

"I'll talk to you later...okay...?" Reira added as she stood up.

"Talk to you later..." Carila replied before disappearing into nothing.

Reira sank back down onto her chair, looking at where Carila was standing only seconds ago.

The Next Day

"You said you would always be there if I needed you..., and I know the rules, since your role in the diplomatic corp..." Reira replied, her voice firm.

"You can't be asking what I think you're asking ...." Carila interrupted.

"I've had all night to think of this, and you are the only sensible choice...." Reira replied instantly.

"I'll need a friendly face in all this, who better for me to choose..."

"Reira, we have known each other for ...50 years, and you know I would do anything for you, but how can I be the right ...you know that I'm only a junior assistant to the Altarian Ambassador, ...I mean, this role is... it's above my station." she stuttered.

"And that's why I think you're the perfect choice..." Reira pleaded.

Carila was sitting in front of her, her eyes open wide in amazement.

"After we talked last night I got another message, it was

asking me to approve my aide, someone that I'll be working with on a daily basis. None of them were suitable." Reira added.

"I mean they were suitable based on record. But really you expect me to work daily with someone I've ever even met..." that's what i told the Minister this morning. So he allowed a special dispensation, he's already approved your transfer. I just wanted someone who I know I can trust." She pleaded.

Carila replied

"Is that why I've got a meeting with the Ambassador this evening? Telling me I've been reassigned." She snapped, before looking at Reira.

She sat there looking at Reira's face. She knew she couldn't turn this down, of course this was a better career. Instead of being an assistant to an ambassador. She would be the aide to the second most powerful person in the empire.

She looked at Reira and smiled.

"Okay..." she relented, "I'll do it..." she added.

"Than..." Reira was about the reply before she was cut off by Carila.

"I know, I know...these perks better be worth it..." she joked, causing Reira to burst out laughing.

"Definitely worth it.." Reira added mid laugh.

CHAPTER 13

5th Hour of the 33rd Day of the 7th Month
IY (Imperial Year) 101

The Morning sun shone through a small gap in the heavy curtains of a small room. Casting a beam of light which cascaded as it shone into a small glass ball situated on a table just next to the window. The light split into its different compositions. Red and blue and green fragment's of light lit up a young woman's face as she slept in her bed across the room.

Her skin was the pale and her complexion nearly perfect, resembling a porcelain doll. Not a blemish marked her skin, her auburn hair tied into a braid running down her back, shone in the morning light.

After a moment, the sunlight caused a stirring. The young woman turned away from the light that caused her to squint. As she turned away facing the darkness of the room again. The room was silent, an eerie silence filled the room, an unnatural aura. Something would happen, but nothing occurred. Only the sound of the young woman's shallow breathing disturbed the silence.

This silence was shattered in an instance by a loud knock on the door which reverberated around the room. Causing the young woman to open her eyes, which were a bright green, and slowly turned towards the door. As she was nearly facing the door another knock broke the remaining fragments of the silence.

The young woman slowly reached up to her eyes and slowly

rubbed them.

"Such a weird dream…" she thought to herself. Reminding herself of the dream which woke her up during the early hours of the morning. Fragments of the dream still stuck in her mind as she slowly tried to get out of bed.

She sat herself up on the bed and looked over at a small bedside table. Which was still shrouded in darkness only the light emanating from a digital clock could be seen. It flashed 05:00, the young woman looked over at the clock briefly. Before clambering out of her bed draped in a purple nightdress, still in a state of sleep. She stumbled over a book lying strewn on the floor next to her bed.

"Carila, why did you put that there, you knew this would happen..." she cursed at herself as she rushed over towards an open door. Entering another room and closing the door behind her.

Minutes later Carila rushed out of the room, she was now dressed. She was wearing a smart formal uniform; she wore a large silver Ornate charm on a chain around her neck. Her fingernails were painted a dark blue and her lips a dark, near a black shade of red. Her hair still slightly wet she grabbed a medium-sized satchel

She approached the door and opened it, stepping out into the corridor.

"Forgive my lateness" she announced as she turned. Jumping back for a second when faced by the shadow of an imperial guard standing next to her.

He looked down at her, not speaking and gestured down the corridor.

She gulped slowly before taking a step down the corridor; the corridor stretched as far as the eye could see. Every fifty meters an imperial guard stood watch.

As she walked past the first guard, he stood to attention and saluted. Instantly shocking her, causing her to stop. The guard behind her stopping instantly.

"Sorry, Ma'am" the still saluting guard spoke,

She looked at him, nervously at first, then smiled..

"It's not your fault..." she paused, looking for his rank insignia, before speaking again.

"Sergeant"

"It's not every day that a lowly girl from the backwaters of the empire is saluted by an Imperial Sergeant." She innocently joked.

"And If I can speak freely ma'am, it's not every day an Imperial Sargent meets the Appointed Attaché to the Codex." He replied sheepishly. Before regaining his composure.

"Not yet, Sargent, her Eminence is still on route and I still have to be sworn in..." she smiled,

"But thank you for the gesture..." she added.

"Protocol Dictates you deserve the rights and pleasantries considering your status, so I only followed Protocol..." he replied, nervously.

"At ease Sargent, your attention and knowledge of Protocol will be much needed by myself and her Eminence when she arrives, I will count on your support..."

His demeanour changed instantly; a proud smile came across his face.

"Yes, Ma'am" he replied whilst standing to attention.

She smiled and continued to walk down the corridor, her guard following a few meters behind.

He smiled, sidestepping other members of the guard. Amused with his own thoughts, he wandered the corridors. The citadel was full of dignitaries from across the Empire. Everyone was on high alert, not just the guards. They had recalled the members of the second legion from fortifying the outpost on Kalarnan VI on the outskirts of the empire. Their task was of utmost importance, the second legion was the Codex's Legion. The founder of the legion had pledged the legion to support the codex, in any endeavour they were asked to serve.

* * *

6th Hour of the 33rd Day of the 7th Month
IY (Imperial Year) 101

Eladris Nebula Jump Point

The silhouette of a pair of Tramiri escort fighters buzzed along the sleek lines of the Nevarian Class Imperial Cruiser. They were gliding as close to the shields as possible, mere meters from the shields, keeping as close as possible to fool any sensor scans from passing ships. The cruiser had just jumped into normal space, its arrival displaced a reddish white plasma in its wake. Compared to the escort fighters the Cruiser was enormous.

This slowly dissipated into nothingness. Starlight from the nearby nebula reflected off its near black reflective hull plating. The ship was new, top of the line, only the best and newest ship of the line would be designated as transport for the codex. Light blue markings accented the sleek contours of the ship. Reira stood looking out of the window, lost in thought. She had spent countless hour staring into space, admiring its grandeur. She had walked all the levels of the ship. No where was new, the last two weeks of Sub-light and Jump Point travel had allowed her to prepare for her arrival on Prim.

'Only twelve more jumps until Prim' she thought. That would be another two weeks. They could jump instantly to Prim, but doing it this way was preferred; for security, the ship couldn't be tracked through multiple jump points. This also allowed the ship to complete its shake down tour before being assigned to guard the furthest reach of the empire.

Reira didn't mind this, she had time to enjoy a few things. The regular day-to-day happenings on a cruiser of this size were interesting to her, completely different to the life she had lived before.

She stood staring out of the window of her quarters onboard the ship; they were not basic quarters, quarters like this were reserved for admirals and commodores but they were more than opulent enough for Reira's needs, she continued to stare out of the window, sipping tea from a small cup as she looked out.

She was shaken by shock-wave before noticing three huge cruisers appear out of her window.

"Who are..." she spoke before noticing a wave of small ships disperse from out of the three cruisers, like tiny insects escaping the nest. A huge energy blast rocked the ship causing Reira to drop her glass of tea onto the floor.

The support cruiser behind the ascendant Justice engines exploded in a flash after being struck by a huge blast by one of the enemy cruisers.

Reira turned around and ran across the corridor. The observation lounge she was standing in was across front the main bridge, she rushed through the doors which opened as she approached them.

The first casualty reports came in, the second cruiser had taken the brunt of the initial attack. It knocked out their engines. Drifting freely in space, they were doomed.

The jump engine was flicking between operational and offline. The squadrons of attack fighters were surprised by the initial attack. The fighters were in a Free for all. The telemetry readings and communication which came from the second cruiser were severed. Causing the fighters to aimlessly attack any enemy fighter, without purpose. They were easily picked off by the enemy sentry guns, blasting them as soon as they came into range. Their shields unable to withstand the power of the enemy guns, their numbers were dwindling.

Missiles were tracking the Ascendant, it was impossible to evade them all. the shields were holding, Every time the shields changed frequency, the enemy misses would explode on impact with the shields, moments later the next volley of missiles and energy blast would rip through the shields like they were not there.

Perhaps they would hold long enough for any help. The communications officer sent a distress call just before long-range communications were blocked. They must have known imperial procedures, they disrupted all frequencies used.

Captain Ralis, was quick to learn this as every manoeuvre was countered with a countermeasure. Captain Ralis, was a middle-aged Nekordian, his feline features were expertly groomed. His dark brown fur seemed to absorb the light shining on him. he commanded a great presence across the bridge of the ship, when he spoke, others listened. right now he was in the thick of it.

"Fire all sentry guns" he exclaimed.

The Ascendant opened fire with each of its sentry guns. There was not enough time to power up the rail gun before the generator was disabled by an EMP blast, crippling some of the ships' systems, sending backup systems into overload.

The first of the enemy cruisers could not withstand the sustained punishments inflicted by the Ascendant. In a flash the enemy cruiser exploded. This blast crippling one of the other enemy cruisers, leaving one cruiser and fifty attack fighters.

Captain Ralis

"Focus all fire on the lead cruiser...full power..." he ordered before he was thrown from his command chair.

The ascendant Justice rocked as a missile was destroyed in close proximity to the ship. The shock-wave damaging a few of the ship's systems before the backups kicked in.

A concussion missile exploded on impact with the port side

shields. Captain Ralis rocked in his command chair, some terminals on the bridge flickered. He waited for the report from Damage Control.

"Port shields are down to 46, make that 45 percent" the engineer reported. "Secondary systems are down on decks four through 8. Jump engines are..." he stopped, double checking the system. "Offline."

"Navsys is also offline" he added.

The helms officer's hands buzzed quickly across the console in front of him. The ship banked hard to port. Softening the explosion of a secondary missile which exploded on contact with a missile fired from the Ascendant Justice.

The weapons officer was thrown out of his post resulting from an explosion on his console. He lay on the floor, dead, a chunk of shrapnel impaling him through the chest.

Reira stood near the navigation terminals, their screens blinkering off and on. Her eyes adjusting to the rapid changes of light. The bridge was chaos,

"Captain Ralis?," she called out.

"This isn't the right time Your Eminence" he yelled over the sound of another impact.

"Drop a missile without arming it..." she screamed back, over the sound of the alarms sounding.

Outside the ship, the escort fighters were being picked off, the three Ankari Capital Ships were blasting them out of existence. The shields of the Ascendant just managing to keep the ship from being destroyed.

"Once the missile drifts behind their shields, detonate the warhead..." Reira recommended, fighting her way to the tactical position behind the captain's chair.

The captain looked over at her

"My father said never argue with an Impiri involving strategy." He paused,

"and I will not start now..." he laughed,

She looked over at a terminal beside his command chair, and his expression changed.

"But the launcher you would need to use is the probe launcher on deck 7, primary power is out, and secondary systems are pretty much none existent..." he replied, he paused for a few seconds, lost in thought.

"Lieutenant Prax, go down to deck seven, and make it work..." he ordered, gesturing towards a member of the bridge crew on his left side.

"Yes, sir" he responded, "but if the power is out how are we going to load the missile..."

"By hand, if you have to..." the Captain responded.

"Captain, I'll go down and help him" Reira coughed,

"I can't spare a security escort right now..." he replied to her question.

"Don't worry Captain, I know my way around this ship..." she replied, as she followed the lieutenant out of the bridge.

"Transport lifts are out of commission ma'am, we shall have to take the access tubes..." the young lieutenant responded, as he failed to get the transport lift doors to open.

"Never had a problem getting my hand's dirty" she answered, smiling.

Outside the bridge, it was chaotic, even though this ship had a small crew's compliment, a crew of about seventy. It looked as if it had a crew of hundreds, multiple crew members were busy repairing terminals. Some crew running between different sections of the ship.

The lights on deck seven were flickering off and on. Occasionally flickering off for a few seconds. Plunging the deck into complete darkness, deck seven was empty. It looked completely different to the ship from a few hours earlier. Gone was the peace and tranquility. Replaced by shorting out terminals and a power grid on the verge of collapse.

The occasional body lay on the floor of the deck, a young man lay dead. A power conduit nearby had exploded; he never stood a chance. His body lay blackened by the fire, within the few seconds before the fire suppression system kicked in, extinguishing the fire.

Reira reached down and placed her hand on his neck, checking for a pulse, he was dead; she placed her fingers on his eyes and closed his eyelids, reciting a prayer as she did. She was about to stand up when another shock wave hit the ship, causing a power relay to explode, throwing Reira across the hallway into a bulkhead. Her head cracking against a section of the bulkhead, her arm taking the brunt of the explosion.

Blood poured down, covering her eyes for an instant, the ash in the air stinging the eyes, more blood dripping down, covering her face. All around her was nothing but chaos, a blur of colour, and of disorder.

Reira coughed, her throat collecting the dust-choked air.

Again, another explosion sent a blast of sound, throwing Reira to the ground. She looked around, dazed and confused, the blast was deafening, all sounds were distorted. her own heartbeats drumming inside her head, enough to drive a person insane.

Another explosion ripped through the corridor as a power relay exploded. The sound of the explosion, was enough to obscure the cries of Reira. As she was thrown across the corridor into a bulkhead her body thundering into the metal of the bulkhead. Further down the corridor, more screams of injured crew echoed through the ship. Reira's eyes flickered open, barely able to see, she gasped for air. her entire left arm burnt from the explosion. Pain from other wounds was nothing in comparison with the throbbing pain from the arm. Which lay unresponsive on her left side.

She looked at herself on the screen of a fallen display terminal, lost in thought, contemplating the meaning of existence and why she was even here. Reira sighed and tried to crack a small smile

"This is how it end's..." she coughed, her lungs filling with fluid. she coughed again spitting blood across the floor before falling unconscious.

* * *

Half an hour later...

They rushed Reira to the medical bay. Medics tried desperately to revive her, but life seemed to have left this damaged husk. The doctor reached over and slowly closed her eyelids, which slowly reopened. Captain Ralis entered the room at the time her eyes reopened, his expression was that of hope. Quickly changing to distress as he witnessed the medics.

Her robe had been removed and was discarded on the floor beside the bed. As he reached to pick up the robe another blast hit the ship.

"Captain Ralis to the bridge, respond..." he screamed.

"Demaris here sir" a voice replied.

"Is the missile tube on deck seven ready..., " he paused waiting for the response.

"System is coming online sir..."

"Launch missile when ready. Detonate the warhead when it's inside the lead cruiser's shields"

"That should give them a nice surprise..." he cursed.

He reached again for the robes; he lifted up the blood-soaked robes and walked towards the lead doctor. Gesturing with the robes in his hands.

"Show some goddamn respect, you do know who she is...was," he hissed. Shoving the robes into the doctor's hands, before storming off out of the medical bay. Before stopping behind the closed door

"In the goddess's name, Please guide our sister to..." he trailed off as members of the crew ran past him.

Back in the medical bay one of the doctors shook his head, the doctor opposite sighed. The other doctor had only joined the crew earlier that day, transferring from Prim on a routine transfer, well, that's what he had been told.

The doctor looked over at another doctor, who was sitting in the corner of the room. an Impiri Doctor, a rarity in itself, as there were few Impiri Doctors. He sat on the floor, head in his hands, his hands stained by blood. Glimpses of a turquoise tattoo circled his wrist, he lifted his head up to look across the room.

Reira lay on a solitary bed in the middle of the medical bay. Her face covered In blood and ash, flash burns scattered across the left side of her face, charring her skin. Her left arm was badly scorched, hands were hanging slightly off the bed. Her shirt gaping open to reveal her pale chest, her robes soaked in blood lay on a chair next to the bed. Around her neck was a woven gold choker. Her eyes were fixed, staring into nothingness, her usual amber eyes a milky white. She was gone, her body still, no longer did her chest rise and fall with each breath, just silence.

The medical bay was lit by a series of precisely arranged screen and instrument panels. Casting a light blue hue across the black floor of the bay. The ship rocked again, another shock wave from another concussive missile. Causing the lights to flicker on again before turning off. The smell of ash and burnt skin filled the air, the ash filtering the light emanating from the screens.

Outside the medical bay, it was chaotic; it looked completely different to the ship from a few hours earlier. Gone were the clean lines and diffuse lighting, replaced by shorting out terminals and a power grid close to complete systems failure. The medical bay was isolated from the adjacent compartment.

The doctor in the room's corner stood up, the other doctors walked right past him and left the medical bay.

Just as an announcement for.

“Any medical personnel to make their way to the bridge," echoed through the communications channels.

He reached the side of the bed and slowly looked down at Reira’s now lifeless body. He looked at her eyes and his expression changed from disappointment to a glimmer of hope. He slammed his hands down on the side of the bed.

“In her name, this better be right” he proclaimed, although there was no one to hear his message. He rushed quickly over to the far wall and pressed a button, and a drawer popped open. He reached into the drawer and pulled out a medical device which resembled an epi-pen.

A six-inch needle protruded from a cylindrical tube a further six inches in length. he rushed back to the bed, stumbling over a fallen portable terminal. He regained his footing, and stood next to the bed again, he looked down. Rested the tip of the needle on Reira’s chest, moving it down towards her second heart, and hesitated.

“I hope this works. .” he whispered to himself.

“Here we...” he exclaimed, being interrupted by a massive shock wave knocking him off his feet.

He stumbled to his feet and looked at the window looking out towards the back to the ship and was shocked. As a second shock wave hit the vessel, just as a vessel appeared into view from nowhere. His expression changed, he recognised this type of ship, this huge vessel appeared. Right between the Ascendant and the three Ankari warships. All weapons on the ship fired a spread of torpedoes, and a swarm of fighters launched within seconds of the ship jumping into battle.

“An Impiri Flag carrier, here now... thank the goddesses...” he roared, before turning back towards the bed, as he turned he caught a sight that caused him to sink to his knees. From the floor, he looked up at a figure sitting upright on the bed. Reira was alive, Her eyes fixed on the window.

"They have come" she spoke, her voice seemed disconnected and out of phase as she spoke the words.

She sat upright, legs hanging off the side of the bed, her eyes still milky white.

He looked up at her, "how..., how..." he stuttered

"I pronounced you dead....". He added.

"I had to get them to come, the only way to save us was to get them to come...." she replied, before repeating it again.

"I had to get them to come, my death was only temporary, in the goddess's name I returned from the void." She replied this time.

The enemy cruiser was capable of defeating a single cruiser, but an Impiri Flag Carrier, this was a warship. Twice the size of the enemy cruiser, and with a full complement of over eighty fighters, it wouldn't survive long against this onslaught.

"10 second until missed within Shield range..." the officer replied.

Captain Ralis looked out of the view screen, as he pressed a few buttons on his control panel, "who ever you are...get your fighters out of the kill-zone..." he screamed, as he saw the missile drift closer to the enemy shields.

A voice echoed throughout the bridge.

"Ascendant, we confirm..., all fighters are disengaging from the kill-zone...." the voice echoed

"Light them up..." it added.

Captain Ralis looked puzzled, how did they know what they had planned.

But now wasn't the time to ask the question. He'd save that for later.

"Do it..." he exclaimed.

The commander's hands flew across the console in front of him and seconds later the missile exploded.

The enemy cruiser suffered huge damage before the shock wave imploded back in on itself before going critical. Ripping the enemy ship in half, the final shock wave hitting the Ascendant Justice which had just moved into a safe range.

The resulting shock wave destroying most of the remaining enemy fighters, the remaining fighters scattering before jumping away. The last of the enemy cruisers was being punished by the Impiri warship, which was inflicting serious damage, the enemy cruiser exploded just as it was trying to jump into subspace.

* * *

An hour later

"How did you know?" Captain Ralis spoke, his voice conveyed his confusion, the commander of the carrier stood in front of him, he was a tall middle-aged Impiri, his jaw was sculpted and clean shaven, his features confining the lines of his eyes, which glittered with a self-pride of a man who thinks himself the best in the world. A typical trait for an Impiri, known by many to be the most strategic minds in the empire. His face was offset by thin lips, which looked liked he hadn't smiled in years. His skin was a beautiful caramel hue, his black hair cut short and styled to perfection, as it moved his hair stayed in place. He was much taller than most Impiri. Captain Ralis moved around his captain's office, drawing back his shoulders, enlarging his chest, trying to intimidate the commander.

"You will never believe me if I told you!" The commander replied, brushing his hand through his hair, smirking slightly.

"Commander Aryal Try me!" Ralis demanded, slamming his hands on the table as he got behind his desk. The lights in the office occasionally flickered as repairs to the main power grid were underway, the ships would take days to get back to being jump ready.

"About an hour ago, I received a random scrambled message on a secure channel." He paused, leaning closer to the Captain.

"The usual procedures were followed." He added calmly.

"At first my communications officer thought it was a degraded communication message from an old Impiri relay station in the Auris System, we were only a nine light minute jump from the system. So it was a valid presumption" Aryal replied sternly.

"So as protocol dictated we jumped to see the cause of the message." He described.

"That's when we received the second message." Aryal added

"What second message." Ralis enquired,

"Well, not a normal message by any conventional means." Aryal cryptically replied. Looking around the room.

"Sir, the things I'm about to tell you are..." he paused,

"How can I say it...classified under the terms of the Impiri

Military Act of?.."

The Captain looked at him, pressing a button on the side of his desk. The door to his office shutting and the lock being activated. Captain Ralis gestured for the commander to continue.

"I received reports from a few of my crew of a shared dream. The weirdest part, none of them were asleep at the time." He exclaimed pounding his fist on the desk in jovial excitement.

"All they saw in the dreams were sequences of numbers. The numbers were 31.9.251.918.7.28.012 Followed by an image of a family crest. That's when it made sense." Aryal preceded to explain.

"How can that make sense..." Ralis exclaimed, studying Aryal's face to try to glimpse any more information, the numbers making no sense to him. These numbers not following any known sequence.

"To almost everyone in the empire that would make no sense" he commented mockingly.

"I'm not surprise Sir that you haven't heard about it, this knowledge is generally not shared to any Maladesh - 'None Impiri'. But in these circumstances, and with her Eminence on board. I think you need to know the full story." He continued, nodding his head slightly.

"See Sir, to an Impiri, this message made all the sense it needed to make." Aryal replied, laughing to himself, looking at the confused look on the Captains face.

"How, I'm not following your train of thought..., what are you hiding from me..." Ralis ordered, banging his hand on his desk.

The commander shook by this action stood up straight.

"Sir, nothing is being hidden. But it's been Impiri tradition for countless millennia that a sequence of coordinates followed by a crest was a call for help." He emphasised.

"What co-ordinates...?" Captain Ralis insisted.

"Those co-ordinates, 31.9.251.918.7.28.012 "he replied exuberantly.

Captain Ralis looked at him with a confused look on his face.

"Not in Imperial nomenclature, something a little older. I mean 'we' used this style of spatial co-ordinates forty-five thousand years ago, we were told stories as children using 01.3.901.001.1.02.125 as the co-ordinates for Impiris, no Impiri would forget that" he joked, remembering the stories he was told as a child.

"No right-minded Impiri would ignore such a message..." he replied, he now had to explain everything. He pulled at his collar nervously.

"Not when the crest was..." he added reluctantly.

"Hers..." Ralis murmured, it all seamed to make sense.

"Yes", he looked down at his own wrist, a basic red tattoo circled his wrist.

"You see Sir, my people take loyalty as a serious matter, betrayal to your house is the worst kind of dishonour. So you see, I might be an imperial officer, but first amongst all loyalties, I'm loyal to my people, especially her family."

"I couldn't let something happen, not on my watch." He proudly exclaimed, looking down at his wrist again.

"So I consulted with my senior staff, plotted the jump point and jumped in, and here we are..."

That still doesn't. Explain where the message came from, our comm system was down, there is no way we could have sent a message to you..." Ralis enquired.

"The thing was, these images that we received, were not received by any systems in the ship, our doctor confirmed that something implanted them, someone imposed those memory engrams on our consciousness." This revaluation confused Ralis. He furrowed his brow and drew his hands into a fist, cracking his knuckles.

"Only a member of the "Daln' Saldar' - Gifted Ones" could do such a thing. Once you informed me of who was onboard, that's when it made sense to me."

"You see Sir, to the rest of the empire, those with these powers are sometimes seen as freaks of nature. But to us Impiri they are the rarest of the rare. Maybe one in a hundred million are born."

"Tales of the Abrasar Sisters ring though out my culture, twin girls with such abilities, are unheard of. A genetic impossibility. The odds are so remote..."

Ralis was curious, he leaned towards the commander and spoke. The commander had piqued his interest; the Nekoidians were very statistical creatures; they loved games of chance.

"What are the odds.?" He whispered,

The commander knew he had got the Captain's interest.

"Roughly, 1 in a trillion." Aryal added.

"You mean?"the Captain replied after working it out in his mind.

"Yes Sir, statistically it's possible but no sisters have ever been born with these abilities, and I mean never, not in all the forty-five thousand years of recorded Impiri history has this ever happened.

"And that's not the most intriguing part, doing such a thing over such a distance...That's statistically impossible..."

The commander looked at the Captain and watched the Captain's mind working it out.

"Normally these ways to ask for help used to be done over a distance of a few miles, but not this time, she did that over 2 light years. No wonder she nearly died." Aryal added.

"She didn't nearly die, I saw her dead body in our medical bay, then not much later you arrived." The Captain replied.

"As I said Sir, she's a rare gift to this universe....it shouldn't have been possible, but it happened" he paused, leaning closer to the Captain.

"I need to speak to her, Captain, to pay my regards..." he whispered.

CHAPTER 14

6th Hour of the 41st Day of the 7th Month
IY (Imperial Year) 101

Every day she looked at herself in the mirror, lost in thought, contemplating the meaning of existence and why she was even here. She was a failure in her own eyes why couldn't anyone else see this she thought. Reira sighed and tried to crack a small smile.

She looked over at her arm, it still ached from the explosion, the bones had healed but the emotional scars were still there. Only her own quick thinking had helped them survive, she and Numarii had tried sending mental images to each other whilst they were at school. But that was years ago and usually over a few miles. The images bouncing through the consciousness of others until it reached it intended target.

She didn't know how she did it this time; it was instinctual; she lost all control of herself, lost in some near death experience, that what's the doctor had called it. The Impiri doctor had called it a miracle.

"There is nothing good about me. I mean I have no talents that come to mind unless you class the ability to be good at bringing about death. Usually of those close to me" she hissed at herself,

"I mean people don't see the real me, they see what I let them see. Only Carila has seen me, I mean the real me, she notices that I exist." She stopped, and the smile dropped from her face,

"Zamir knew the real me, and that lead to his death...by my hand. If only someone could see the real me continually,".

The next day Reira again sat looking in the mirror, listening to an incoming communication from the Cloisters, a member of the selection committee discussing something about etiquette for the Arrival Gala, and all that Reira could do was stare at the mirror. She slowly reached over and paused the communication. She turned towards the door simultaneously the door alarm chimed,

"I'll be out in a minute, just getting ready" she called out. As she was getting her robe on she knocked over a vase, it fell and shattered, sending pieces of glass across the table.

"Your Eminence is everything okay. I heard a glass shatter.." a voice from the other side of the door announced.

"Don't worry" Reira exclaimed, her hand shaking. She looked at the remains of the glass, shattered into thousands of pieces on the table, her eyes glowed, as they glowed the prices of glass moved, they moved into a heap on the table.

"Ma'am, the Captain has radioed for you again..." the voice echoed through the door again, his voice sounding concerned.

Reira was lost in thought, the glass finally resting together.

"Ma'am..." the voice called out again. Interrupting Reira, hasn't he heard her response, she was getting ready.

Moments later

The door opened, Reira quickly walked out of her quarters,

“What’s got into her...” a guard mentioned to another as she stormed past him, lost in thought she nearly knocked him over.

Reira turned around, to let them know that she heard them.

“Sorry..” one of them quickly retorted, unable to talk further, his throat visibly constricted. Reira’s eyes had become a glowing milky white, the faint tattoos on her neck glowing slightly.

“Get out of my sight, I had told you that I was getting ready, and sometimes that takes its time.” Reira hissed, her voice distant. The man slowly regained his ability to breathe,

“Please” he coughed, “please forgive my comment, Your Eminence...” he coughed again before staggering away. Reira’s eye faded back to their normal amber hue, she walked off, her emotions were running high, and his attitude wasn’t helping with her nerves. This is when her life would change. Just being on Prim would be different. She knew exactly what would happen, the ceremonial actions she had to perform, that was the easy part, the attention by the media would be the toughest to deal with.

Reira sat looking out of the window of the observation deck, staring at the ever-changing scenery of Prim, from the Snow-capped mountains of Ajinar. Crossing over the sea of silence, the rolling hills of Amaranth and finally approaching Caspria. Locally known as the citadel.

She wondered what was happening below as she squinted as the light from the sun’s reflected off the surface of the river winding through the capital.

Another bright flash of light reflected off the river, startling

Reira. The ship glided slowly across the outskirts of the city; the city was vast. Covering approximately twenty-six thousand square miles. They divided the capital into twenty-three wards, and then Citadel prime, the imperial heart of the city.

The eight gates to the citadel still stood guard as entrance ways even though their role in securing the heart of the city hadn't been used in many millennia. The architecture of the capital amazed Reira, her eyes wide with youthful ambition, forcing back the nervous thoughts from her mind.

"Before the ceremony, I must see some of this..." she said to herself.

"There is a lot to see your eminence," a voice behind her spoke.

"Wouldn't want you to get lost in a city of over a billion citizens, luckily none of them know who you are...l he laughed before adding They know your name, but have no idea about what you look like. You could if the fates allow, slip out of the citadel and take in the sights..." he spoke again, Reira turned around slowly, a young ensign had been standing at the door behind her, waiting nervously.

"Arriving at the landing coordinates in the next 5 minutes," a voice announced over the communications system.

The spaceports main concourse was more like a market, it teamed with people. From all corners of the empire, and some from as far as the Alarlit Alliance, over three years travel from the Empire. The crew of a few Imperial carriers were wandering around the port, probably returning from shore leave, before leaving on deep space exploration missions.

Some people passed the time trading with vendors for all kinds of merchandise from across known space. Carila slowly walked through the crowd, aimlessly lost in thought. 'It won't be long before she is here' she thought, hoping that she would have time to sort out the remaining challenges before she arrived. Forgetting the time, she walked forwards before a message arrived on her communicator.

"Astral Ascendancy has arrived at main concourse bay 3." As she read this message she sighed, she wouldn't be able to get all the things sorted before Reira arrived.

Meanwhile, across the main concourse.

"Belief in the will of the goddesses empowers my every moment," Reira said aloud, as she walked through the docking port of the ship she had taken from orbit to the surface, a small ship, with a crew of no more than thirty, in comparison to the Ascendant Justice.

She was followed by two imperial guards who kept a close eye on all surroundings. Reira stopped, and the guards stopped immediately behind her.

"Your eminence, is everything okay?" one of the guards inquired, his eyes scanning the area for any potential threats.

"Just admiring the sight! My first time on Prim, would you believe..." she joked, before walking. She entered the entrance hall of the spaceport, the hall was busy. The hustle and bustle of many races, all making their way through the spaceport. The guards sensing danger, cautiously moved forwards. Allowing Reira to drop back, not once did they break concentration.

Reira looked around, listening to every sound and breathed in deeply, wanting to savour the smells.

"Your Eminence" a voice echoed.

The guards turning towards the voice, drawing their weapons and training them on a young man. He was covered by an intricately embroidered green robe; his head covered.

"Stop where you are" one of the guards ordered.

"Stand down" Reira ordered,

"He's been sent by the order to assist me.." she ordered.

"Ma'am, are you sure?" The young officer enquired.

Reira turned towards him, nodding her head, her hair blowing in the cross breeze.

"If you want to confirm his identity, I'm sure he wouldn't mind. But as you can see he's wearing the ceremonial cloak of my order, but if..."

"Ma'am, we're only doing our duty," the lead guard replied urgently as he removed his finger from the trigger, resting it on the safety.

Reira smiled at him before gesturing towards Rako.

"Rako, could you please show yourself to these careful young men, they are a little worried for my safety." She spoke with a smile on her face.

"If that's what they need me to do, then of course I will oblige" he spoke slowly as he revealed himself, pulling back the cloak which cast shadows across his face. He pulled out a small card from his pocket and presented it to one officer, the other keeping his weapon trained on him.

The first officer pulled out a small device and swiped the card across its surface, instantly a holographic representation of the young man appeared, his details appeared floating next to his image, after a few seconds waiting the image was amended by 'Verified identity." appearing below the image.

Rako sighed a heartfelt sigh as the guards lowered their weapons,

A voice interrupted this quiet lull.

"Rei?" The voice called out, Reira turned her head quickly, trying to locate the voice.

"You've never been good at this..." the voice mocked, the guards looked around before being pushed aside by Carila who walked between them.

"I see the security detail I assigned turned up..." Carila spoke, gesturing at the security guards who immediately lowered their weapons.

"At ease, I'll take it from here..." Carila ordered.

"Yes Ma'am. The guards replied before moving further out, allowing Carila to take responsibility.

Reira looked at Carila and smiled,

"Seems like you're enjoying this new role..." she joked.

"It's taking a lot of getting used to, but then again, I get to boss around the security details. And they are so nice to look at, she bit her lip and smiled.

"Typical Cari..., you know you're not supposed to enjoy the hired help, especially my security detail." He laughed in return.

Reira gestured for Rako to come closer, he carefully walked closer, they were now a few meters from each other.

"Rako, I'd like to introduce you to Carila Parluet..."

"Cari, this is Rako, the order has sent him to give you

whatever help you need until the rite of Tasir. I know you will be under a lot of stress, with a lot of things to organise. So I asked the Reverend Mother, and she sent him." Reira explained.

Carila smiled and laughed to herself,

"Thanks to the goddesses, I'll be glad to get help, I've got so much that I'm having to deal with, it would be good to get some assistance..." she gestured at Rako.

"Of course, I will deal with whatever you need me to do, my time here is short, so I better make the most of this experience." He replied sheepishly, he bowed slowly.

"Your Eminence, your are required to make entrance to the citadel in less than thirty minutes, we must be going..." the guard spoke up. As he looked carefully around the area, people were noticing the official military presence and this worried them.

Reira looked at him and smiled,

"Cari, I'll see you tomorrow morning for breakfast?, I think I can still make those pancakes you loved that my mother used to make..." Reira mentioned as she turned around, noticing her guards were gesturing for her to follow them.

Carila looked at her and smiled.

"I'll be there...you better be going..." she replied as she smiled.

"Lead on..." Reira replied to the guards and she gestured for them to lead her to where she needed to go.

As Reira made her way down the corridor, her two member security detail followed in pursuit. The sound of her walking echoed throughout the wide corridor, bouncing off the walls.

Individuals stopped as she walked past 'is that...?" Someone whispered.

Reira's pace increased, with security trying to match her pace. The primary corridor from the west gate was littered with offices and accommodation for some of the highest-ranked individuals in the capital.

At the end of the corridor a security detail waited, from here access to the central citadel could be gained. Protocol dictated that Reira must present herself to the master of the guards. A symbolic rite in which the first Codex was presented to the Emperor. But faced three sets of doors, each door slammed in her face. The first door would be easy, the second and third door would be trickier.

'Luckily this is a private matter, no reporters, but everyone is watching' she thought, her pace slowing.

She reached the first door; she knocked on the door, using a large metal ball that was suspended from a chain next to the door. The metal plate which she struck had been worn, countless times by the same ball. It's surface smooth and dented in the middle.

The door opened slowly, behind the door two members of the Imperial Guard stood watch, in the middle was the master of the guards.

The man was a middle-aged Hakarian, which put him between sixty and seventy years of age. His chiseled jaw and high cheekbones gave him stern appearance. We was heavyset, but had weightlifters physique His dark brown hair cut short on the sides, and sculpted back on the top. He stopped and watched the other guards opening the door. His full lips occasionally pulled a smirk of arrogance. He bowed slowly as he noticed Reira at the door. He was dressed in a black and red suit. Embroidered with exquisite detailing.

He carried a five foot golden staff, which he pointed at Reira before walking slowly towards the door. The guards beside him stood to attention as he reached the door. He proceeded to hand the staff to a member of the guards hidden behind one of the door just before he forcefully slammed the doors closed at the same moment. Shocking Reira with the sound they made.

“I Nidiri Reira Abrasar, present myself to the master of the guard. I demand that this door be opened.” Reira declared. Lifting the ball from the door and slamming in against the door again. The door shook as she slammed the ball against its surface.

Moments later the door opened again. Three guards stood behind the door, in the distance the master of the guard stood with his back towards her, as she walked in he walked away down the small hallway leading to a second set of doors. He stood a meter in the second room and turned around. Banging the staff on the cold marble floor.

Reira stepped into the hallway further. Lining the hallway were various members of the parliament. They stood in silence as Reira made her way into the room.

“She’s quite young...” Reira heard someone whisper, as she passed them.

“Quite a looker though, a bit of a difference to the previous codex's...” a colleague whispered in return.

Reira tried to ignore the comments that were being made, she walked towards the second set of doors.

She looked at the master of the guard straight in the face. They were no closer than six meters apart when the second set of doors was slammed in her face.

This time two guards appeared out of the periphery of her view and stood in front of her.

"Why do you seek entry to the citadel?, only those with Imperial business may proceed." One guard spoke.

Reira looked at him.

"I stand here, seeking entry to the citadel, I have been chosen from many to aide and guide the Emperor, to be his voice when he is unable to speak. To be his eyes when he cannot see and hear all that is addressed to him, no matter where he is..." she declared.

After she spoke she could hear a murmur from members of the crowd lining the hallway.

"And in his name, I demand entry..." she boomed, her voice forthright and emotive.

The two guards stood to attention and sidestepped, allowing Reira to push the door open. The doors creaking as they opened.

This hallway was more opulent that the last, the hallway was a hundred meters long, on each side it was lined with people, in some places in was lined three people deep.

Reira slowly stepped forward, closing her hands into fists she nervously continued to walk. In the distance she could see the master of the guard, he stood at the third and final door, a ceremonial sword in his hand held out pointing at Reira.

"You speak the words, you know the actions, but do you really understand what they mean..." he declared, his voice booming down the hallway.

The members of the parliament stood in absolute silence, watching every movement Reira made. Her hearts racing Reira approached the master of the guard, she walked closer and closer, stopping in front of the sword which was only a few inches away from her throat. Her neck drew in close, muscles tightening. Her breathing slowed.

"I do know the words and yes, I do know the actions, and with the help of the goddesses I will truly understand what they mean." She spoke, her bottom lip trembling.

I would also appreciate "Your guidance in such matters, with all due respect. I am inexperienced in such matters, if you don't believe my honest words, it is your right to walk towards, run that blade through my throat and end this. If you do accept my words, please open the third door and allow me to serve." Her voice trembling. The Master of the Guard stood in silence before drawing down his sword and placing it within its scabbard attached to his waist.

"Your words ring true..." he replied, gesturing out with his right hand.

Reira held out her hand and grasped his hand before, shaking it.

"Let me take this honour" he added as he let go of her hand before turning around and pushing the door open. This door lead into a huge chamber, stained glass panels lined its walls, the sunlight illuminating the panels which cast multi coloured light streaming into the chamber. The master of the guard stepped forwards followed by Reira, who stepped into the light of the chamber as the doors closed behind her.

She stood in the stream of light and sighed a sigh of relief.

"You did well, Lady Abrasar..." the master of the guard spoke.

His demeanour transforming. His sullen and stern expression changed into a jovial one. He smiled as he looked at her.

"That was the most terrify things I've ever had to do..." she exclaimed.

"They say it's all ritual, but it's the parliament, it's the watching by each of them, it's like they are watching to see if I fail."

"My Lady, they are watching to see your conviction in performing your role, don't forget that you will go through this ritual every year after the New Year Festival...." he replied, placing his hand on her shoulder.

"Don't remind me..." Reira joked in reply, before smiling at him.

That Evening

She knocked on the door twice, then again for good measure "who is it" a voice echoed in a hushed tone.

"It's me..." Carila replied

"Who?..." Reira replied, her voice slow, the sound of her yawning could be heard from the other side of the door.

"Carila" she paused, wondering why Reira couldn't recognise her voice, then she realized, she would be sleep, so she was probably still half asleep.

She could hear her yawn again, "... it can't be, you're not here yet..." she responded, with a bit of confusion in her voice.

"This cannot wait until morning, Reira, it's...," the next thing she knew the door was open and Reira stood there, draped in a white silk gown. Half asleep.

When she realised that her security guard was standing next to the door she quickly pulled the gown closed, to protect her modesty. Even in those few seconds, anyone would have been able to see her toned physique.

She gestured quickly for Carila to enter before sidestepping allowing Carila to enter the room before the door closed shut again.

"I'm sorry for waking you," Carila said in a soft voice.

"No worries." She smiled, and for a second Carila stood there looking at her, mesmerised.

"What can't wait until morning?" She enquired, her voice tired she yawned slightly.

Carila stood, trying to glance away from Reira, Reira looked down and quickly tied a ribbon around her waist pulling the gown closed. Blushing for a second.

"I, um, overheard from one of the security detail that a spate of random encoded messages were received. From what they have made out" She turned away from Reira's intense stare, using a shaky hand she brushed her hair behind her ear.

"They are worried about an attempt on your life." Carila confided,

"What Life, I don't have one?" Reira joked in return.

Carila arched her eyebrow as she watched Reira go to her

closet. Inside, she grabbed a small hand held disruptor and walked back out. Carila's mouth dropped open.

"I'm not taking any chances then," she continued, as she checked the pistol.

"I thought they might, since the attack on the convoy."

"What?" Carila managed to speak, taken back by the latest revelation.

"Well, I could say my journey to Prim was eventful," She smirked, as she placed the pistol on the table. Her room was dimly lit, multiple cases were scattered around the room. This was a temporary location until after the ceremony, so Reira hadn't unpacked completely.

"Just that we were attacked by raiders, watched some good people die", she paused

"and I died, for just a bit..." she laughed, making a face which resembled her dying.

"Reira don't make such a face, and what do you mean, why wasn't I informed by security..." Carila spoke, her voice concerned, her eyes welling up with tears, her eye lashes holding back her tears.

"Ongoing investigation, probably. Salis, the Captain of the second legion has taken this under advisement, his legion is responsible for all of my security arrangements, well, that's what I've been told anyway..." she paused and yawned again.

"Reira, as your friend, you must keep me in the loop about this, I'm worried about you" she gushed, pausing for a second before adding

"As your aide, I must be privy to all security concerns, I'll have a word with this Captain myself..."

"Seems like you've already gotten yourself ready for this role, and you said you wouldn't be able to do it" she chuckled, and instantly Carila's guard fell.

"Rei, You know what I mean..." she spoke, her voice calmer than before, the anxiety in her voice fading as quickly as it arose.

"Haven't heard you call me that in a long time", Reira replied, a smile appearing on her face.

"Let me get dressed, and I'll tell you all about it, I was having trouble sleeping, anyway. It's too cold here..."

Carila nodded.

"Well, it's not Ateki, you've been spoilt by the heat over there." Carila added jokingly. Reira smiled at her before getting up and walking into her closet.

"Yeah, I had thoughts about my life being at risk, since I was home, I mean the convoy was destroyed and as usual I acted like It's not a big deal. Heck, I can't leave this apartment without being followed every second of the day." She sighed, lamenting her ability to walk freely around the citadel.

"If I leave the apartment, someone replaces the guard and watches the door of the apartment, even when I'm not here....just as a precaution."

Carila sat in awe of what she was hearing.

"Now, Carila," she announced as she walked out of the closet, stood and stretched her neck side to side.

"Is there anything else I need to know? Any more sinister plots to end my life?"

'Anything else you need to know?' Carila thought to herself

"Uh, no," She ended up replying.

Shocked by Reira's laid back attitude to the threat on her own life.

Moments later she appeared, wrapped in a thicker robe than earlier, as she walked out she ran her fingers through her hair.

Usually, Reira had a tough exterior, only crying when alone, her sister had taught her that when they were young.

That tough exterior had not been broken in front of anyone other than Carila in decades. Even in front of her parents her demeanour was tough and she let no one take her down, however, this day was different. Fear controlled her like nothing else; it kept her quiet and hopeless.

"I can't believe this is happening!" she said as she and Carila sat on the couch. Unlike Carila, Reira was very jovial, even regarding her own life.… at least that was what she said.

She had tied her pearlescent white hair, into a rudimentary ponytail, with the occasional strand of hair framing her face. She wore a deep red fitted catsuit, which emphasised every inch of her model-type body. She smiled at Carila as she spoke, occasionally distracting Carila.

Reira had always been a lucky girl, surviving the awakening of her abilities when she was twelve. The accident at Kamet, multiple run-ins with Xanti over the past decade, and even the attempt on her own life by raiders days before.

She hadn't had many friends because of her upbringing. Moving between military installations and the occasional trip home. She could count her true friends without going into double digits. Carila was the only one who was willing to walk side by side next to her, unafraid of what others thought. Carila had been there since the first day at the Cloisters when although they were competitors, they never saw it that way, and that was over fifty years ago.

Carila knew Reira's personality. Being her friend for over fifty years had taught her a lot. The attempt on her life had forced her to reevaluate everything, even though she joked about it, it had shaken her, and Carila knew it.

"Honestly, all my people believe it to be a death sentence. How would an empire of over 800 billion, treat an individual whose species represented 0.1 percent of the population..." she mumbled.

"I would be speaking a view of the few to the many, I mean my kind are scattered across all corners of the galaxy." She added.

Some would see this as a change of the times, the Impiri were so rarely seen, most spread themselves to the far reaches of the empire. Some people had never seen an Impiri before in their entire life. Stories about the fall of Imperis was told to children all across the empire as a story of ultimate sacrifice.

Carila explained that might happen after the ceremony of Tasir was over, she would become the media's and the Empires symbol of unity. That people would do anything sometimes in order to get to Reira, and that would be the most challenging,

Reira, however, knew exactly what would happen. the journey of the Codex was a difficult one, especially the first two years, travelling the empire. Something that one of her predecessors had started on ten thousand years before.

A stop on every world within the Empire, in order of date of admission to the empire. The journey to the forbidden zone would be the most harrowing, three months travel from the forbidden zone was the Impirian system. A stop at the Calipras Station would be a symbolic stop, being unable to cross into the forbidden zone and thus unable to reach Imperis. This stop would occur within a few weeks of the twenty-three thousandth anniversary of the fall.

Reira coped with the whole ordeal, knowing full well what she was about to step into. At least, that's what she told herself. Besides, Reira needed Carila just in case someone did something stupid, she was always level-headed even in a crisis.

"Listen, Cari," Reira said when getting up from the chair.

"I'm going to get a small pick me up, would you like one?. It helps me relax when times get as stressful as this."

Carila sighed.

"Okay," she replied, in a sarcastic way

"Of course, I better make sure a medical team is on standby since it would likely kill me within minutes..." she added, smiling.

"I still can't believe your kind can take that, most other species get violently, sick, trust me to have the worst reaction." Carila replied, she stopped smiling, a look of worry flashed across her face.

"I'm worried about the second legion, they are supposed to be your eyes and ears. But now you told me about the raid on the convoy, I'm even more worried."

Carila questioned, Reira stood still, looking at the concern look on Carila face, she knew something was up, Carila was genuinely concerned.

"The only people that knew of your journey to Prim was the Imperial Chamberlain, his office and the Captain of the second legion. I had accidentally received reports into the attack on the first convoy. The same people were involved. In planning that journey..."

"I just can't shift this feeling I have, I have no evidence, but it just doesn't feel right..." Carila pleaded.

"I think a change in your security arrangement would be prudent..., maybe another unit within the second legion." She added after pausing for thought.

"You have the option of using Red Section, I've a few connections since my time in the diplomatic corp." she proudly added.

"I can request a change in detail, as a matter of precaution, but Red Section would be a stretch." Reira replied, realising it was easier to allow Carila to go with her instinct, she had always been prudent and careful.

Later that day.

Outside the Official Office of the Codex in Waiting

Carila approached the door, Carila and was taken back, seeing Captain Salis walking towards her.

"She called you for this meeting as well?" Carila remarked.

As she got closer to the door, she saw the guards who were

in attendance.

"RS, are here... I only put through the request this morning..." she exclaimed.

Besides the door two members of Red Section were present, these were the best of the best. The elite team from the Second Legion, their uniforms were black, minimal detailing. Their tunic jackets were made of a material which absorbed light. Only a single red badge referred to their position, this badge located on their left lapel, and on the right label the emblem of the Codex.

These guards were for her protection, after the discussion with Reira earlier, Carila had requested a security detail from the Second Legion. A detail not previously involved in her protection, hoping for but never honestly expecting Red Section.

As she got closer to the door the two guards stood to attention,

"Ma'am, as per your request they have assigned us to guard her Eminence, Major Kattor Elar will forward to your office our rota for your attention and for further discussion with her Eminence." The guard spoke before saluting.

He was a young Lathiosa, is must have only been in his mid-twenties, Carila was reassured that such an individual was on the security detail, the Lathiosa were a recent addition to the empire, only a few decades before, but they were already known for being loyal, and excellent strategists. Most Lathiosa had moved into Impiri districts and were met with little hostility as honour and loyalty were a similarity they both shared as a core belief in their cultures.

“We’ve been called to her office together, that’s what’s more worrying," Salis replied with a wry smile,

“Her Eminence must have a reason for this, calling her Aide and the head of Citadel security, and now we can see that Red Section have been assigned as her security, I’m more worried about my role in this.” He added.

“I wish I could have seen the look on the faces of those Imperial guards were previously on her detail then these turned up. There was no way they would have let this slide. I’m sure to have to deal with repercussions of this for the next month," he joked,

“The unions will have me up in arms...” he added, laughing slightly.

“Sir, your Guards took the news, the way they would have been expected to take the news, they were a little...disgruntled, but orders are orders...” the other guard spoke, his voice husky, he was a lot older that the other guard.

Carila laughed, before realising it wasn't the time to laugh.

“I’m sure you’re going to be fine, after they have had a word with you.”

“Let’s see what her Eminence wants, then” she said turning to face the door, the guards watching every moment.

She raised her right hand and knocked on the door.

“You may both enter...” Reira’s voice echoed from behind the door, one guard turned and opened the door, gesturing for Carila and Salis to enter the room.

Carila entered first, the room was spacious but simple, a desk stood in the middle of the room, the walls decorated with artwork, a wall of books covered the left-hand wall.

As they entered the room Reira stood up from behind her desk, placing a computer pad on its surface. She was elegantly dressed in an intricate wrap around blouse covered her top half, a body fitting pair of black trousers covered her legs, followed by dark brown boots, which went halfway up her calf.

"Captain Salis" Reira spoke, bowing graciously, before turning to Carila, and gestured for her to take a seat, winking at her.

Carila proceeded to take a seat on one of the two chairs in front of the table.

"First off all, I'm guessing your wondering why I asked you to come to this meeting..." Reira spoke, sitting on the edge of the desk, just after fixing her blouse, with Salis standing a few meters in front of her.

He stood there studying her expression, trying to gauge what this meeting was about.

Reira sat looking at him, trying to gauge his possible reaction to what she was about to tell him.

"This investigation, it's over. At least your involvement in it is..."

Salis Looked at Carila first, shook his head and then looked at Reira, it was hard for him to hide his malice; it was etched across his face.

"I've given you, the decency of informing you this way, instead of it being done and you be unaware" she commented, her voice calm and clear, She looked at him sternly.

"I've respected the boundaries of what you can accomplish, all internal investigations are still under the remit of your office and the second legion will still compile daily reports to be sent to your office. Reira commanded,

"But any investigation. That's impossible for you to deal with, that's why the decision was made." She added.

"I wanted to debate with you in a civilised manner, get your input on who you would want as a liaison between the investigation and yourself, but, I can see from your expression, that maybe that wasn't a good idea" she commanded.

"This isn't any normal investigation..." Carila added, Salis pivoted quickly to scowl at her.

"You knew of this..." he cursed. His fists clenching, beads of sweat appearing across his brow.

"Not exactly how, but I had an idea, I wouldn't be a good attaché if I didn't keep abreast of all situations, I only suggested that she kept you informed, that would be the decent thing..." Carila added before being cut off.

"The decent thing is to let me do my job" Salis snapped at her with fury in his eyes.

"This is a vote of no confidence, I do not see how a newly appointed Codex with little experience in the citadel's running could overreact to a situation like..." Salis declared.

"I might be new here in the citadel, but don't forget, I've spent the last forty years understanding every nuance within the citadel, every department, every meeting, especially the remits of each department, and you're stretching your remit as far as

I'm willing to allow..." Reira replied sternly, forcing him to back down.

"And you, you were acting all innocent in all of this, maybe exploiting this situation to advance your own aims...standing at the door, waiting for me, claiming that you knew nothing but, it was all hypocrisy" he scowled at Carila as he turned towards her.

She turned and scowled at him

"I said nothing, because you didn't ask the right questions. I knew what would happen, how it was going to happen, that I did not understand." Carila replied.

Reira paused, nodded, and then spoke,

"I expressed more concern that my security detail, where also responsible for an investigation into an attempt on my life, something which is out of their remit, was I right to be concerned?."

"Potentially?, but who else could run it?" Carila enquired.

"I'm getting to that, I looked into who would be the best, but without making it obvious, as if someone was out to kill me" she paused, the words sinking into her consciousness.

I mean using a high-ranking member of the security services would tip them off to your investigation, we need someone who would be off the radar." She added.

"Now, the only person my father had ever talked about as someone he could trust, someone known to most as 'the ghost of the citadel'". Carila looked at Reira in surprise.

"Him,..are you being serious, I know we read about his cases while we were in the Cloisters, but he went off the grid years ago, how would you even find him, and convincing him to help would be almost impossible..." Carila replied with a confused look on her face.

"In normal circumstances that would be correct, but he owes my late father and I know of a way to contact him, it's a long shot" Reira declared, looking at them both.

A Few Days Later

Captain Salis' Office - Outer District - Ministerial Quarter.

The office was small, the ideal office for someone as busy as Captain Salis, he stood in his office; the walls covered with computer screens, from here he could monitor all security incidents in the citadel.

Carila stood beside Reira as she looked at an elderly gentleman, Praetor Damar's jaw was sculpted but was hidden by a six inch beard. His features confining the lines of his eyes, which glittered with a self-pride of a man who thought of himself as the best in the world, and according to some, he was the best legal mind in the empire.

His face was offset by thin lips, and a stern expression. His skin was a rich dark hue, of set by his white hair cut short and styled to perfection, as he moved his hair stayed in place.

"It's unbelievable, how can a security service not pull records on everyone in a case this important. It like your waiting for an attempt, so you can pinpoint the assailant, correct?" Praetor Damar enquired.

"It's the only way to keep this investigation under wraps" Captain Salis responded, gritting his teeth, he didn't like the inquisition by this outsider, under minding his judgement.

"Ah, yes, see I was right, and that is why her Eminence called my office, she was worried about being used as a pawn in the capture of whoever is trying to assassinate her. Right!" Slamming his hand on the table, startling everyone.

"To think she might have to spend the rest of her life in such a state, if you don't find out who it is, and that's something that I'm not comfortable with.," Praetor Damar said as he was walking around Captain Salis's office.

"If only there was a way to find out when they were going to act...." Damar grinned, rested his hands on the table and nodded.

"Oh, I know, and I think you do too, It's all too clear, the first public speech, that would be the ideal time, it's a small and intimate setting, if I was going to do it, that's when I would do it. All we need is a confession from their contact in the citadel, you do know who that is, don't you?."

"Not to my knowledge…" Reira replied, looking at Captain Salis.

"We have some clues, some things that I haven't briefed her Eminence on…but nothing confirmed.." Captain Salis sheepishly answered, Reira looked at him, her expression turn from shock to anger.

"what do you mean, that's not what you told me yesterday…"

"I wasn't going to brief you until we had more evidence, but since the investigation is being taken out of my hands, I might as well share it…"

A spate of random scrambled messages had been passed through various communications systems in the citadel, at first our communications team thought they were just completely random, but they seamed the occur more and more frequently, with no change in security credentials. That's when it came to me, these were requests for a meeting. A simple message which could be repeated. But still use the same security credentials.

"I have a clue of who our culprit is, but without any confirmed evidence I can't move against them."

The media briefing must go ahead, only then can we confirm our theories.

"To everyone not in this room, you must openly discuss not attending the media briefing in a few days. That should help motivate the culprit to move their plans forward. ..." Damar suggested as he wandered around the room.

"Promise me..." Damar added.

Reira paused before replying

"Yes,"

Carila nodded her head, before looking at Captain Salis, who struggled his shoulders before nodding.

CHAPTER 15

3 Days Later
8th Hour of the 2 Day of the 8th Month
IY (Imperial Year) 101

Reira stood in the middle of the courtyard, lost in thought, as members of the local government office walked past her, not paying any attention to her. She stood underneath a massive tree; the flowers blooming on the tree sent waves of aroma across the courtyard its scent tantalised her senses.

She stood staring out into the distance, waiting to glimpse a familiar face, in the hustle and bustle her mind travelled, lost in thought. Her mind was full of chaos, those nightmares from long ago had returned, they were more prominent in the moments between thoughts; they were still there, gnawing at the back of her mind. She shook her head gently, trying to banish those thoughts away, maybe for just a minute, just as she did her focus returned.

"Look at you…" a voice echoed from behind her, snapping her out of her daydream.

Reira shook her head again, startled by the voice coming from behind her, as she turned around she smiled.

"Day dreaming again, my darling." The voice joked, Reira looked straight at her,

"Just lost in though, a lot of things going on, how are you Mother" Reira responded, her mother was elegantly dressed, even for citadel standards she was a sight to behold, her auburn hair was tied up, into a bun at the back of her head, a single white leather collar elegantly caressed her neck, it was covered in a beautiful brocade made up of gold, with highlights of sapphire. She looked up at Reira, her mother was shorter than her now.

Reira had grown a lot since the last time they had spoken. She smiled at Reira as she spoke. Her emerald hue eyes glistened in the light.

"It's been a while, seems like that growth spirt happened, she looked down at herself… I'm still waiting for mine." She laughed, her laugh was infectious, Reira burst out laughing, before quickly quietening down as others in area stopped their conversations.

Reira nodded at her and placed her right hand on her mother's left shoulder, she closed her eyes for a second. As she cleared her throat. "Mother", Reira enquired, a lump appearing in her throat, causing her to stop.

Her mother smiled a closed lip smile and pushed away tears with the flick of her eyelashes.

"I'm fine, dear, I've been kept busy since…" she stopped, trying to push the tears back again.

"I'm sorry that I couldn't be there, to help with the arrangements.."

"Don't be silly" she scowled, trying to hide her sadness, deflecting the conversation

"I didn't want it to interfere with your studies…" her mother replied, trying to put on a brave face in front of her daughter.

"But they would have allowed it, Reverend Mother would have sanctioned it…" Reira replied, trying to force back tears.

"I know she would have…" her mother replied nodding her

head approvingly.

"It was a nice small ceremony, Master Baelin presided over the formal part of the ceremony, almost every member of the council turned up, except Lord Arkin." She stopped,

"Him and your father had fallen out a few years ago, when your father didn't sell his controlling shares in the family business to him."

"I didn't know father still had the controlling shares… especially with his role in the military and the nature of our business.…" Reira replied with a puzzled expression.

"Well, your father said 'I'm only the guardian of these shares, with only one heir these are now my daughters, when she's ready she will take them…' of course Lord Arkin wasn't happy."

"But that's not the reason for our chat…" she laughed, changing the subject.

"They want to speak with you…" she added, the tone in her voice dropping, her smile disappearing quickly.

"What do you mean?, they want to speak with me…!" Reira replied, her expression was full of confusion.

"It's not my place to question the council, you know that dear?"

"My schedule is already so packed..." Reira replied, thinking for a second about the many things she had to attend that were in her already busy schedule.

"They are not requesting an audience...." her mother added sternly, reaching forward and brushing a few loose strands of hair away from her daughters face.

"What do you mean, not requesting?" Reira quizzed, the tone in her voice becoming concerned. She looked down at her mother, even now with all that had happened she was still worried about things like the council.

"It is an official summons, you cannot refuse it," her mother added.

"To do so would undermine the entire family. They would seize our lands, our assets destroyed. We would be cast out of the council." Her mother added, a look of concern flashed across her face, her eyes welled up with tears.

Reira looked at her and smiled, nodding her head slowly in acceptance of her fate.

"I tried to delay them, allow everything to run its course, then they could summon you, but they voted me down," her mother declared.

"I know, you always try to protect me, even now..." Reira declared as she pulled her mother close and hugged her. Her mother hugged her tight.

"You the only one I have left, I'd go to the ends of the universe for you...you do know that..." her mother whispered.

Reira gulped, trying not to cry.

"I'm not going anywhere...." Reira replied as they broke the hug.

* * *

19th Hour of the 2 Day of the 8th Month

IY (Imperial Year) 101

Evening had finally arrived, Reira had been nervously walking around the grounds of the capital building, trying to shake the nerves she was feeling. This would be her first social unveiling, she had to make an impression. As she walked around the capital building a member of Red Section was only ten meters away, watching every move.

Reira walked along the corridor towards the Great Hall, the sound of her shows echoing throughout the corridor. The corridor between her quarters and the Great hall were restricted, only she would be allowed the entrance, it was easier that way. Even though it was only a short walk to the great hall, Reira took her time, spending time looking at the statues and artwork which lined the corridor.

The great hall was a massive structure, with magnificent views out of its tall windows, views of the rest of the citadel always impressed, it was on the itinerary of most of the tours of the citadel, the legendary views of the citadel from the Great Hall. Reira didn't even have time to admire its beauty, there would be time after the ceremony, but not much, the tour of the empire would keep her busy.

The great hall was a masterpiece in Hakanarian construction, and in the best tradition, it merged countless cultures into one message.

"The Empire Binds us together and strengthens us..."

An orchestra played within an alcove, their music cascading throughout the hall, even the acoustics of the hall had been meticulously designed to show the opulence of the empire.

The great hall was decorated with vast paintings and murals, from all corners of the empire. A large image of the fall of

Imperis was cast into the darkness behind the main entrance to the hall.

The fall of Imperis had occurred fifteen thousand years before, orphaning the Impiri species from their home world, scattering them to every corner of the empire. As little as million had initially survived the fall, from a population of 12 billion.

A middle-aged Impiri delegate looked up at the painting, lost in thought. He could feel a longing for home, a home he had heard about in countless stories. Stories the only thing that survived its destruction, passed down from the survivors, only twelve of the Impiri houses survived, they absorbed some smaller houses that survived. Each of these houses kept the Impiri culture alive.

The destruction of their home world triggered a civil war, for their own survival each of the twelve houses worked together in the Jinal Council, an organisation from forty thousand years in Impiri history. When each of the houses were struggling at resolving ancient grudges, the council mediated between the representative houses, now the council concerned itself in all matters of tradition, protecting rituals and the purity of the bloodlines.

"Blessed are the twelve" he whispered. He looked down at his wrist; a dark red tattoo surrounded his wrist. A sign of his allegiance to an Impiri house. He turned around and walked away from the painting towards his wife who lingered behind him.

The doors to the grand hall swung open and Reira stepped

in, she made hardly a sound as she entered the room, her feet seemed the glide across the marble floor, her movement precise and graceful. With each movement, her hooded robe emblazoned with intricate embroidery flowed revealing a dark layered outfit underneath, with glimpses of her athletic figure being occasionally seen.

The room watched with amazement, the orchestra quietened, conversations stopped and heads turned. The occasional whisper broke the hushed atmosphere before the orchestra regained their composure and the conversations returned.

She slowly made her way through the crowds, surrounded by friends, admirers, and well-wishers, every few seconds she commented to a guest or dignitary, the sounds of the wind echoed throughout the great hall.

Occasionally drowning out the sounds of the band playing, she bowed graciously to the occasional military colonel.

Stopping once and giving a sultry smile to a young admiral who caught her eye, startling the young officer into blushing, she smiled to herself. 'naughty me...' she thought, as the sounds of a thousand conversations seemed to merge into one encompassing sound occasionally, then falling back into individualised voices,

She stopped, a familiar voice caught her dead in her tracks,

"Your Eminence..."

Reira turned, that voice was a soothing reminder of simpler times.

Stood in front of her was a middle-aged Impiri man, his hair on the cusp of becoming grey, he smiled, and Reira's facade fell, her expression radiated kindness and familiarity, her bright amber eyes seemed to glow for a second and she allowed herself to smile, a real smile, not one for the dignitaries and Prelates. A genuine smile.

"Master Baelin... what.," she spoke, her voice filled with surprise.

"What am I doing here?" He cut her off, his voice full of emotion and joviality.

".... Many years ago I promised your father, that I would always be here if you needed me..." he retorted.

"And I think, now being the time when you need me most,", he added, smiling.

Reira's eyes watered, the facade completely destroyed, she fought back the tears and nodded.

"I definitely do..." she replied sheepishly,

"I thought you were back home on Aaelonia...", she paused again, her emotions running high

"Especially since your duties to my father ended..." she added.

His smiled stopped, a look of concern now replaced it,

"Listen child, serving your father..." he paused, "and thus serving his family, for over 70 years was, and is the most important part of my adult life, Looking after his family when he was on the far-flung corners of the empire, I grew to see things from a different point of view..." he paused again, now his eyes filling with tears and emotion.

"Your father wanted me to be there at the times when he wasn't, and over the years I've grown to see you not as the daughter of the man I have sworn to protect and serve but..."

he stopped and wiped a tear from his eye.

"...but as the daughter, I never had..." he spoke.

Reira's smile returned a truthfully honest smile.

She stepped across the space between them and embraced him; she leaned in and whispered into his ear,

"I hope I've lived up to your expectations..."

She stood back and smiled.

He nodded, smiled a wide smile and gently nodded again.

"But what kept you away for so long..." Reira spoke, her voice full of concern.

His eyes lowered,

"Since the attack and your fathers passing, and my guilt at surviving it, all I wanted to do was keep you and your family safe, so I waited. Observing the Rite of Mourning, spending that year away, allowing you time to grieve..." he added

"My intention was to respect the promise I made to your father, to... using your father's words 'keep an eye on Reira, she's destined for great things.' So I'll always keep an eye on you" he concluded.

Reira smiled.

"We must arrange a time to catch up..." Reira asked.

Baelin smiled a wide-eyed smile.

Nodding in acceptance,

"I'll be here on Prim until after your speech... then I'll accompany your mother home." He replied.

Reira looked at him,

"I'll be free tomorrow afternoon, well I won't but I'll make it know that I have an important engagement that I cannot turn down." Reira jokingly replied.

Later that evening

After minutes of talking to an ageing praetor, regarding royal etiquette not being what it used to be.

Reira paused, a wave of nervous emotions battered her senses, she knew who these were from, she politely excused herself and glanced over, looking at the crowd and finally noticing her aide.

She spun around on her heels; her robe fanning out for a second before gracefully walking towards her aide. He was a young man compared to Reira, of no more than 25 years, he had been sent on behalf of the order to help Carila with anything she needed to get sorted, releasing the pressure she was under in arranging all of Reira's schedule between her arrival to the ceremony of Tasir.

He was smartly dressed in a toned down tunic, his light blonde hair slicked back, he was clean shaven; he carried himself well, at times Reira could tell he was nervous, even though he tried to hide it.

Rako Alik had sensed this was not the right time to bring up this matter but, it had to be done, he gathered his thoughts as she got closer.

It was of utmost importance that he conveyed the message in a manner fitting of its intended recipient, but also with the grandeur of who the message was from. His heart raced, pupils dilated, breathing became shallow, her clenched his fists to stop his hands from shaking.

Within seconds, she was standing in front of him.

He hesitated for a split second, and she was about to speak when he regained his composure.

"Your eminence..." he spoke, while gracefully bowing.

"Go ahead, I can tell there is something you need to tell me..." she commanded, with slight concern in her voice.

She could tell Rako was having trouble with his new role and the gravitas of the information he was now in receipt of.

Rako sighed quietly before he spoke,

"She has requested your presence, her attaché has informed me that she wants an 'off official records' conversation with you and that I'm to escort you to her residence in the citadel immediately"

The tone of Rako's voice caught Reira off guard, causing her to step back a half step. But, the manner in which he spoke caused her to anger.

Her expression was as if she was disgusted with what she had been told, did he just say what she heard him say...'she' she thought. Even though her aide was young, innocent to a fault, probably unaware of all due protocol; she said quietly to herself.

He should have known not to use such a common language when speaking about her. She thought to herself, all of this in the second after he spoke.

Her anger arose, it was hard to hide the thinly veiled anger in each of the words she spoke,

"You mean, Lady Yueari-Dhar of the House of Idralur, Minister of Truth, Guardian of Secrets, The Sacred 47th Codex, Elder of the Praetorian Guards, High-Arbiter of

Justice, Praetor of the Royal House" she replied, her voice sounding threatening.

Rako was taken back for an instant, Reira had never spoken to him in this manner, even when they were back on Ateki, when he was a Junior Acolyte before he transferred from the temple to the mountain retreat to allow him to complete his studies.

He knew that things were different now, the pressure on her more prevalent than ever. Rako closed his eyes for a split second in acknowledgement of his error before speaking again.

"My apologies your eminence, it's just the nature of this message has caught me unexpected..., "he paused for a second, then continued

"Lady Dhar of the House of Idralur, has requested an audience with you, and you alone..."

The final words in this sank into Reira's subconscious, All meetings with the Codex were normally highly managed affairs, and planned many months in advance and never alone, She thought.

"Seems like things are not always as they appear to be" Reira spoke quietly, catching Rako unaware.

"Your Eminence?" Rako quizzed not fully catching Reira's words.

"It's nothing, just thinking out loud..." she paused. Rako waiting on every word.

"We can't leave Lady Dhar waiting, and its bad etiquette if her successor doesn't grant her every courtesy...lead on.," she added.

Rako gestured for Reira to follow him, as he slowly walked back through the crowds, She followed slowly behind, glancing around the hall as she walked, watching the glances of others, and getting glimpses of whispered conversations

"It seems important if she is leaving now..." she heard from a conversation between a Valarai General and his aide., the tone of the General's voice gave Reira prangs of fear which ran through her already nervous mind

The voices of the people surrounding her faded, slowly into nothingness, only the sound of her own heartbeat could be heard.

The music slowly faded as she walked through the hallway leading out of the great hall, the sounds of her footsteps echoed across the marble floor and ricocheted off the wooden-panelled walls. Rako walked behind, carefully, his footsteps making barely a sound.

Rako walked over to a huge ornately decorated door and knocked loudly on the door, the sound resonated throughout the wood, and again, he knocked, followed by silence, nothingness.

Reira stood a few meters behind him, she brushed her hair away from her face, then opened her eyes wide when the sound of a voice echoed throughout the corridor,

"You may enter..." the voice spoke, the voice firm but frail,

Reira glanced at Rako and smiled a shy smile and then walked to the door and pushed it open.

* * *

The doors opened into darkness, Reira took a deep breath and walked into the room, the darkness was only broken by the light from the twin moons shining in through a vast veranda.

It took a few seconds for her eyes to adjust to the darkness, finally, she could make out the layout of the room, the room was vast, the light from the moons was shining enough light that Reira could see a figure standing in front of the veranda looking out to the rest of the citadel. She took a step forward, stopped and spoke carefully.

"Ma'am, you requested my presence." Her voice trembling with nerves.

The figure moved to her, revealing itself in the light of the moon, an old woman, her skin wrinkled, she was far into the later years of her life, she cautiously walked out, without speaking.

"So, it is you my child who comes to replace this frail old woman, who I have become..." a voice spoke, but her mouth didn't move, Reira smiled, and thought.

"Not so frail ma'am, you know my place in the scheme of things, and your place in the scheme."

The old woman smiled then spoke, her voice caring and more informal than the voice Reira heard in her mind,

"You are from Tsoris Provence I believe," she asked,

Reira stood perplexed, for a few seconds she thought, before speaking,

"Yes Ma'am, I was born there, but I grew up on Antaria VI ... a more traditional place for an Impiri like myself to live. It's as close to the climate and conditions as living on Imperis as possible according to some." She replied.

Lady Dhar looked at her, smiled a wry smile, trying to remember.

"ah, yes, that is true, I haven't been there for many years my child, are the summer storms still as traumatic as I recall..." the old woman spoke, Reira laughed a muted laugh and nodded her head in reply.

"As expected, they come and go with such regular frequency., but with more intensity over the past few years, last seasons storms were the worst in my mothers lifetime..." Reira added.

"Come sit my child..." she gestured to Reira, two high-back chairs sitting facing each other were sitting in moonlight. Reira bowed slowly before walking towards the seat. Lady Dhar slowly following her. The chairs were beautifully embroidered, Lady Dhar sat on the chair first and sighed.

"Everything takes a lot out of me these days," she cursed, her breathing laboured.

Reira looked over at her, seeing someone in the last years of her life, Lady Dhar had been the Codex for over a hundred and fifty years, being sworn in under the rule of Emperor Isalnesh.

Those times were seen by some as the golden years of the empire, expansion had occurred, peace with old enemies had finally been agreed and everything was great with in the empire.

Lady Dhar coughed again, her voice was dry and raspy, she grabbed at her throat; the pain was immense. Next to the chairs on a small table was a small bottle, Reira recognised this bottle, it was Kalita. Reira was surprised by this, to most this would kill them, but not in small doses. Lady Dhar shook a pill from the bottle beside her and placed it into her mouth.

"Is that Kalita?" Reira enquired, worried about Lady Dhar's health.

"I know I couldn't keep swallowing pills. Small doses of Kalita numbs the pain...Something is going to have to give, one way or the other. That's why you were rushed here... "

"It's that… I'm.." Lady Dhar added, pausing for a second to steady herself.

"I'm dying" she blurted out.

"I'm going to tell you something that they don't want me to tell you, the Kalita gives me more control now, sometimes it makes these voices easier to handle."

"What do you mean? They don't want to tell me?" Reira asked.

"Reira, open your mind..." Reira heard in her mind.

'Let me in, Reira. I'll make it quick', maybe then you'll understand that I had no choice in this..." the voice spoke again this time louder than before.

"No!" Reira forced the voice away again. The voice pleaded with her "I don't have a lot of time to tell you these things..."

"Can't you tell me in person?" Reina asked.

Lady Dhar's face was wrought in pain and sadness, she shook her head.

"This is the only way" she pleaded again.

Reira listened to the voice, its pleasant voice drawing her in. Something about this voice felt familiar, it was welcoming but haunting; it felt familiar even though she had never before today met Lady Dhar.

"Okay..." Reira answered.

"The circumstances in which you became my successor we're not by chance..." the voice explained.

"Wait, what?" Reira responded in shock.

"I can't explain how, but something in me has known about you for a long time. I cannot tell you more than that, it would jeopardise your life. I can tell you that I've had visions the last 50 years, they were fragmented, but they involved you." Lady Dhar exclaimed.

"Soon you will understand more, but I won't be here to help you, all I can say is that I'm sorry..." the voice added, the voice full of sadness.

CHAPTER 16

"Hopefully, I was up to her standards" Reira muttered, clenching her hands, as she left the room, closing the door behind her, the clank of the door closing caused a rising in Rako, he had fallen asleep sitting on a chair next to the door.

"I hope news of this meeting hasn't been leaked out of the citadel. I don't think I could deal with the news networks getting the wrong end of the story." She mumbled, shaking her head.

"I suppose a meeting between the Codex and her successor wouldn't be too much of a headline," Rako replied, with a small amount of joviality in his voice.

Reira rubbed her temples and shook her head as she slowly walked down the corridor.

"At least she didn't have you thrown out, that could have been the most embarrassing thing to happen." He added while grabbing his things, before following Reira down the corridor.

* * *

8th Hour of the 3rd Day of the 8th Month
IY (Imperial Year) 101

The next day Reira sat in a chamber, with Carila sitting just behind her, the walls were covered in books, as far as the eyes could see, as the professor goes on and on about protocol.

"I'm sure we went over this, back in the Cloisters' she thought.

"All I'm doing is staring at the wall, really. Why is he not treating me like someone who already knows this, I didn't forget everything during the last ten years? Does no one notice?" She rested her chin in her palms and smiled.

"Rei, are you all right? You're doing that thing again," Carila said. Reira turned her head and nodded.

"Funny how you like to point out a flaw" she whispered mocking her. The professor still mumbling on about the 'accident of Iladrisa' which happened three thousand seven hundred years ago when the freshly appointed Codex made a grand error by not bowing before turning around, which was a massive sign of disrespect to his excellence, luckily that protocol changed a few generations later, even though some still do it out of respect.

"So, does that make sense?, Your Eminence?" he exclaimed, causing Reira to sit up straight.

"Yes, it's a different way than how I learnt in in the Cloisters, however the premise is the same," Reira said with a tense smile as his question startled her, as she had been focusing on something else.

The bell as the temple next door rang out, three rings, in rapid succession, the running echoed throughout the room, the professor sighed.

"Every day at the same time..." he mumbled to himself, cursing the interruption to his day.

The ringing finally died out, and the professor spoke again.

"Now, Pardon my language but if I may be so blunt.". He paused.

"This initial meeting with the Emperor is basic, stick to the rules and you will be fine." He explained,

"However, it is a tradition that the Codex must face scrutiny from the council, and they will see any sign of weakness as a way to discredit you, maybe they discredit you now, but in the future" he replied, his voice lined with concern.

"I must advise you not to give those bastards any leverage..." he seemed to be flustered by the whole ordeal. He bowed, slowly.

"I'm sorry Your Eminence, the council and I don't see eye to eye, so to speak." He added, as he loosened his collar. The conversation having heightened his emotions.

"The council members are all members of the social elite, they can be cruel, especially Lord Rix, the Zathians find any way to use your weakness to their advantage." He declared, the near though of it seemed to make him uncomfortable.

"My Mother mentioned that Lord Rix has a grudge against my house, an old grudge. It's been a family story for many generations."

"This would probably intimidate me normally, however, I'm not in the Cloisters now and I'm all the wiser" she paused, she grinned slightly.

"I'm prepared for him, I've felt with people like him before, I dealt with Lord Jido-Arkin, it's been a while but I dealt with it" she added.

Carila and the professor looked at her, Carila cracking a smile, know that Reira had a plan and it would be a good one.

"You argued with Senator Arkin and won?" The professor enquired.

Reira was taken back for a second before she realized.

"I forgot he had been elected to the senate..." she replied jovially.

She sat with a look of concern on her face for a minute, before leaning forwards, a small smile formed on her face.

"So here's the plan," Reira spoke quietly.

"I will let Lord Rix try his best, mother had reminded me of an obligation that his family has to mine, an old obligation, near twenty thousand years old obligation, it was to be saved for when it would be most useful, and being the first Impiri ever to be Codex, and the highest ranking Impiri ever, I'm thinking this would be the best time to use it." She smirked.

"However Your Eminence, he might not even know of this?" The professor exclaimed, his voice excited by the possibility of shaming Lord Rix.

* * *

A Day Later

8th Hour of the 4th Day of the 8th Month
IY (Imperial Year) 101
Imperial Council Chambers

The Chamber was huge, wood lined the walls, ornately carved wooden columns broke up the dark red leather covered seats. The chamber was well lit, Reira stood in the middle of the council chamber, with members of the council sitting on each side of her, only the members of the primary council were int he chamber, if it had been a full parliamentary questioning there would have been over eight-hundred members present.

Reira placed her hands on the podium in front of her, her hands shaking.

"During my time at the Cloisters, it was clear to see that the study of the history of the Empire, the past affects the ability to govern in this age." Reira proclaimed, the members of the council staring at her in silence.

This silence confounding Reira, she nervously clenched her fists.

"To gain an understanding of our past, we must first understand who we are as an individual that being an individual entity, or as an individual species." He recited from memory, this speech having bounced around in her mind of the previous few hours. Driving Carila insane with her constant recital.

"Only can then we harness the innate benefits of each species and achieve a common good" Reira preached. She stopped speaking, nervously, realising that all voices in the room had gone silent, and only her voice echoed throughout the chamber.

"Seems like our 'little girl' over here feels as if she has a better understanding of our empire than the rest of us..." Rix scoffed, his eyes narrowing, as he lazily gestured in Reira's direction.

"Maybe she believes that this council is a circus, full of parlour tricks and that we are out of touch with the empire, he added.

Everyone was still silent,

"I propose in stripping this child of the position, she isn't ready, she cannot be ready, spending the last decade stuck in some far off dust bowl of a planet, she has no loyalty.

"I must object Lord Rix, if I know my Impiri history, as well as I, do, you must remember that.." Reira snapped back, taking him by surprise.

"Adarus Abrasar, My ancestor came to the aid of the Zathian House Ranes, which if I'm not mistaken, is the parent house of your lineage. Diluted by its merger with house Danis, not a generation before the fall of Imperia"

"So yes, this 'little girl' does know her history, especially when it comes to claiming loyalty" she snapped back, before he interjected. I invoke 'Na So Ladj'..." She declared.

"A loyalty pledge..." a few members of the council whispered, startling Lord Rix.

"Sorry if my Zathian is a bit weak, but I'm sure you know of what I speak" Reira added.

Lord Rix's expression changed, his frown disappeared, his eyes lowered, he placed his hands on the banister in front of him, sighed then nodded his head.

"If evidence can be shown within six days...then I may consider it..." he spoke,

"Didn't anyone tell you to not argue, a strategy with an Impiri, a photographic mind made them the best strategic minds in the empire, especially if they are a pureblood family. Her family, Lord Rix, stretches all the way back to the first Emperor, some believe that there is some Impiri blood in the imperial bloodline, going back over thirty-five thousand years ago." Another member of the council added.

"I for one wouln't challenge her in any way. She's got my

support." The council member added, banging his fists on the banister in front of him.

This sent a ripple down the banister, multiple members of the council banged their hands in support of Reira. She had convinced them.

She stepped down from in front of the podium and made her way towards the door leading to the throne room.

In the next chamber surrounded by the Praetorian Guard, and flanked by his personal attaché, and clerics from each of the sects within the faith. His Imperial Highness Calidral Dominius Ekaram Valnesh Amarii, known to all as Emperor Valnesh. Sat on the imperial throne. The light from the sun shining through the easterly window, casting multicoloured light through the stained glass window, he was a Hakanarian male in the latter years of his life, gone were all traces of the bright blonde hair of his youth, replaced by a full head of white hair, which hung perfectly to his face. Beady brown eyes, set handsomely within their sockets, watched the proceedings with the council via a hovering information display., he stroked his moustache and goatee while in deep thought. He gave a small smile and awaited her arrival; he looked up and stared into the distance; he leaned forward and paused, listening to her footsteps as she walked across the marble floor in the corridor between the parliamentary chamber and the throne room, a small grin appearing on his face.

The Emperor, was a true hero among his people, more so

after the unexpected defeat of the Dar'asul, who had launched devastating attacks on planets on the fringes of the empire, in his youth. He sat elegantly among others, despite his narrow frame.

His attaché stood behind him, stern faced looking into the distance, ready to interject with pertinent information if and when it might be required.

Reira stepped forward, her hearts beating so loud in her own chest she thought others in the room would be able to hear them.

Scanning through her memory, she tried to remember all the etiquette she had learnt at the Cloisters, hoping that she wouldn't step over the line, any failure here would end her life, the tactic used by the council wouldn't work here, respect would keep her alive, she wasn't just doing this for herself, this was for everyone who tried to get to this point, she thought.

She nervously walked towards the Emperor, she bowed gracefully as she approached, her hands open and facing forwards in traditional Impiri style.

Reira remained bowed in front of the Emperor, awaiting her formal introduction.

"Your Highness, I hereby introduce, Her Eminence, Lady Nidiri Reira Abrasar, Third Daughter of House Abrasar...." a voice called out. Reira slowly arose from her bow, keeping her eyes lowered.

The Emperor smiled,

"Lady Abrasar?" The Emperor spoke as the room fell silent.

"Finally, I get to see the individual who I will be working so closely with..." he spoke gently.

He cleared his through before speaking again.

"I was told stories, about the fall of Imperis by my father, and of those who fought to save your people." He paused, trying to remember the exact details of a story he had heard decades before.

"He told me of the legion who had fought the darkness at the end of the fall, before being overrun by it, all members of the legion fell that day." He recited.

"Twenty thousand died in the fallout from the fall, but that was nothing in comparison to the loss of your own home world, and the deaths in the billions."

"After witnessing the way you spoke with conviction to Lord Rix not more than a few moments ago..." he paused.

"I do apologise your highness, I hope I didn't offend..." Reira quickly replied.

The Emperor smiled before chuckling,

A reaction that no one in the room expected, even his children leaned forwards and looked over at him.

"My dear girl, I would hope..." he stopped.

"I would expect the codex to be as forthright and occasionally as passionate about the truth as you were, I do hope that our conversations will be as eventful. I do like to be challenged, if you think you are up to the task..." he questioned with a smile on his face,

Reira raised her gaze slightly,

"I graciously hope so your highness.." he spoke, her voice trembling.

The emperor stood up from his chair, grabbing hold of a cane situated on the side of the chair, and carefully stepped forward, his attaché trying to move to help him, before the emperor quickly shooed him away with a wave of his hand.

The emperor stood in front of Reira,

Her hearts beating as rapidly as if she was going to face an enemy in battle.

She felt a soft warm sensation on her chin as the emperor slowly tilted her head to face him.

"Your highness..." she spoke.

"I can't have a codex who won't look at me..." he whispered,

Reira nodded gently, raising her gaze and looking at the emperor face to face.

He looked at her, studying her expression before he cleared his through before speaking,

"You speak about the hope for your people, and I for one, agree, the Impiri have spent too long as looser in the schemes of this empire, and I don't agree with it, I know it has been discussed for generations the possibility of your people finding a world to call your home. Now this is going to change" He declared,

This took Reira by surprise, she gasped, did he really mean what he was saying,

"I believe your people have suffered enough and a home world of their own would allow you to grow. I have already discussed this with my ministers, and they are in unison with my ideas. In consultation with the council of your people, it is now a policy of our government to help your people chose a world, either from a world already inhabited by your people, or one you would find suitable to be declared as your own."

The members of the various sects clapped as the emperor made this decree, much to the surprise of both of his children, who had not even heard of this from their father before he announced it.

"This is my gift to you...This is just the first step, and it might be a step that I never see completed myself, but it is a start..." he added.

Reira looked at him, trying not to cry.

"Thank you, your highness, I speak for myself as well as all of my people when I thank you from the bottom of my hearts for your gracious gift," she jubilantly replied as she bowed, her heartsbracing. What would this mean for her people, would this be a new beginning for them, where would be home. Where would they want, where did she want.

CHAPTER 17

The Next Night

The moonlight through a crack in the curtains covering the windows of the chamber, casting light into the eerie room, the atmosphere of the room was stale, nothing had been in that room for quiet a long time. Layers of dust covered the tables scattered across the room, those tables were piled with sketches and manuscripts, a wine glass stood alone on a small table next to a high-backed chair, the light from the moon reflecting off the glass and the remains of a dark red liquid stained the bottom of the glass.

The sound of a lock being opened broke the quietness of the room, before the door creaked open, Reira looked into the room,

"Now this is the ideal location for my official offices," she paused

"It needs a..." she added before she was interrupted.

She looked over at Carila as ran her hand across a surface, pulling a disagreeable faces as she saw the dust on its surface.

"It needs to be destroyed, you know it hasn't been used by anyone in..." Carila paused as she looked at a small handheld device

"About eight hundred years...this section of the citadel was rediscovered a year ago, it had been closed off by order of the 43rd Codex."

"And the only one able to rescind that order would be... me, luckily the 47th had already rescinded that, that's why she gifted me the apartment." Reira joked, enjoying that Carila hated the place.

"It's also close to the temple of the flame, so I get to have the best of both worlds..." he replied as she looked at a small layout of the citadel which beamed from a holographic generator she was holding in her right hand, before she flicked a switch which turned off the generator, putting it away in her pocket as she looked over at the manuscripts on the table in front of her.

Fascinated by the documents which were left out in the open, picking one up and blowing the dust off the manuscript, causing a huge plume of dust to swirl around her, blocking her vision before slowly clearing.

"This complex was used by the 43rd as a private residence, before it was moved to its current location."

"The 43rd wrote these himself" she commented as she looked over the documents.

"Alice, Why aren't these lights on?" Carila announced, but nothing happened.

"Cari, this place is probably not connected to the main grid, I mean, parts of here were designed about two thousand years ago, which means that the Artificial Living Information and Communications Entity isn't set up."

Carila looked around,

"You're probably right, I mean if the A.l.i.c.e system was installed, it wouldn't have let the atmosphere get this stale.." she coughed, the dust in the air causing her to cough.

"It won't take much time for a team to get this whole section back up to our specification, Ninety days at a stretch..." Cari spoke through the cough as she typed commands into a handheld device.

"I'll let you get this sorted...but I thought you were against it" Reira spoke, just before sneezing, sending up a plume of dust into the air.

"I'm not going to be able to change your mind, so I might as well go along with it..." Carila responded, as she made her way back towards the door, brushing the dust off of her clothes as she approached the door.

Across the city, on the outskirts of Caspria.

Far out of the city, away from the hustle and bustle of the citadel, in the industrial sector of the city a solitary figure walked down a dark path.

The path long and winding, disappearing down one dark alleyway, before reemerging on another street entirely. This time of night, not a single person remained in the sector. The night sky above gave light, the street lights occasionally flickered on before quickly flickering off again, in complete contrast to the pristine citadel, this area was almost abandoned.

Other than the moonlight the street was dark, the atmosphere was still; the wind didn't stir. Nothing at all. A figure ambled slowly, walking between the light of the moon and the shadows cast by the buildings next to them.

A quiet echo of music, pulsated behind a huge dark metal door, the building was old, slightly rundown. It had seen better days, the whole area was in need of rejuvenation, but that was not likely to happen in this district. The area was home to most of the factories which provided for the rest of the capital.

The figure slowly walked up to the door, his long rich red jacket flapped as he walked towards the door, he reached over to a large black door knocker on the door, raised it then let it go, causing it to slam into the metal door, the sound resonating throughout the street, before dissipating and returning the street to silence.

Nothing happened, the figure went to grab the door knocker again, but before he could grasp it, the door opened slowly.

He slowly stepped in, the room was quiet, nothing made a sound, even though moments before music was being played. The figure walked towards the bar, looking around he grabbed a bottle which was sitting on the end of the bar and opened it, its contents a light blue liquid. "Romariam Ale, I might as well" he mumbled, before pouring the contents into a glass, he sat there in silence, unaffected by the eerie silence.

This kind of eerie silence would normally send a chill down his spine, but he had grown accustomed to it. The occasional overhead light, brought light to sections of the room, the room was lavishly decorated, with intricately designed coving and statues, other than those lights the room was plunged into darkness.

The light of the moon cast light onto a figure standing in the corner of the room, not moving, just watching.

The figure then moved quickly, disappearing into the darkness in the room, a great burst of flame erupted from the hearth situated in the left-hand side of the room, it's light escaping into the very depths of the room, bringing the room in an instant from the depths of darkness into its warming glow. The person located at the bar towards the back of the room exclaimed,

"Still a fan of the dramatic I see..." as the heat from the fireplace finally warmed him.

The figure slowly walked out from the darkness, the light from the fireplace casting shadows across the figures face, the figure was masculine, his face was sculptured in all the right places, his cheekbones well defined and jaw was well defined, no light emanated from the figures body itself, but his eyes disappeared, they were completely black.

the figure, standing tall slowly walked out in front of the fire, only now the figures full stature could be seen, he was an average-sized man in height, young in his years, his mid-twenties. His attire matched the room's design perfectly, he was dressed exquisitely in a black suit. He cast a strange aura as he walked; the atmosphere changed like all the life in the area was somehow drained.

The figure walked closer to the figure at the bar, as he got closer the lights came on, flickering for a moment before fully illuminating the room.

Standing a meter in front of the shadowy gentleman was Rako, he stood there looking at the figure, before smiling.

"So, I'm here as you requested, I don't have long, what do you want from me this time..." he nervously questioned as he drank from the glass.

"You said that Reira made a deal with Carila, that she wouldn't do the press event, before the ceremony. Isn't that right?" He questioned, staring at Rako, his stare piercing.

Rako nodded his head nervously.

"Tha...that's what I heard..." Rako replied as he ran his left hand through his hair.

"I've heard that she said this to her friend not to say anything about it to anyone, even the media until just before the event." He smirked,

"All the media is aware is that there will be an announcement regarding the codex but YOU, Rako never made such a promise to her. With that said," a grin surfaced on his face. This grin made Rako gulp, afraid of what was going to be said next.

"I believe it's best for you to tell the media she's planning on cancelling the announcement, that will force the Chamberlain to force her to attend." He laughed,

Rako's expression changed, this would be harder than he thought.

"The position of the Codex cannot be thrown into disrepute, so she will have to attend. As the aide of this young woman, I'm sure you know someone who you can leak information to…" the gentleman sarcastically added as he placed his hand on Rako's shoulder, causing Rako to recoil, but he wasn't going anywhere.

Rako fidgeted in his chair. He brushed his hair back, revealing the sweat on his brow and then released a big breath.

"Look," he finally said,

"I'm not going leak it to the media, that won't work for

Reira. She doesn't care what they think of her." She's stronger than you think..." he postulated.

"Just give me time to have a word with her. I can convince her to attend the event. Just don't put pressure on her. Otherwise I won't do it..." a sense of urgency rang out through his voice.

He stood up straight, his demeanour changing, he scowled as Rako, raising his hand towards him he shook his fist repeatedly.

"Don't use that excuse with me, you have a job to do. We've given you everything you asked for, donations were made and individuals were paid off." He verbally scolded him.

"If you're looking for sympathy, you're not going to get it here." He added.

"We made things go away for you...the Kamarian's you owed credits to have been silenced, a bigger target has been offered to them." He laughed maniacally,

"That target could easily be changed back to you..." he threatened, placing his hand back on Rako's shoulder, Rako tried to step back, but the figure held him in place.

"The items you have asked for have already been delivered to the right people...just do the job your being paid to do" he added.

Rako nervously moved back, the threat was real.

"She has to make that speech, in the right place at the right time...too much is at stake for you to fuck it up. This comes from the highest levels within the empire." The gentleman added.

Rako looked at him, and sighed, nodding his head reluctantly.

"She knows something is wrong, she has no idea of what is wrong, but she's a smart girl, she'll figure it out." Rako added, after thinking about the situation.

"We can't have her figuring it out. Not before the ritual. If she survives this, then maybe we have a chance, but we can't risk her not going through with it." He snapped back at Rako.

"But, really having to kill her, I mean..." Rako replied, after swallowing a mouthful of ale deeply. His eyes wide, a look of realisation flashed across his face

"Why not just threaten her, she has weakness especially, Carila. Can't you just apply pressure to her." He added, after a moment of reflection.

The figure spoke again, this time, his voice was slower than normal.

"A little pressure in the right way, if she survives, and I'm sure she will." He paused, scaring Rako

"It will force her hand, she's stubborn." He stopped, grabbing at the bar,, seeming to temporarily loose his balance before continuing.

"She will go along with our original plans. But right now, she's unsure., we need her on our side for this to work" the figure demanded.

The figure held the bar and looked sternly at Rako,

"We didn't remove the codex in waiting Ildise Baeil for fun, it was a very delicate plan that worked in our favour." He smirked, the tone in his voice lowered even more.

"He was never going to do as we wanted him to. She on the other hand, She's always been the one we have wanted. For longer than she's realised, she has been the one, a few hiccups along the way." He laughed, Rako stood there puzzled.

"A decade wasted in some backwards temple, but that helped her get ready." He added as the thought came to him.

"The time at the temple helped her get ready?" Rako quizzed, grabbing at his glass again, taking a small sip to quench his thirst.

"Well, we know what she will do for something she believes in, I'm sure you know about her tribulations.?" He cryptically replied.

"You know about them...? How?" Rako stammered.

"All I can say is that she lived up to our expectations, all of them. Surprised us in more than one way. But she has a darkness inside her we would like to ..." the gentleman insisted.

"Help her understand..., especially now that her abilities are stronger than they have ever been." His eyes beginning to get darker, stopping what he was saying after realising he had said too much.

"Her loyalty to the empire and to her people will benefit us more than your simple mind can comprehend,".

"She's a puppet and doesn't even know it..." Rako exclaimed as it all began to make sense to him.

"I..., I mean we have been pulling the strings in her life for years. She doesn't even know that the biggest tragedy in her life, was us. It happened because we wanted it to happen." As he spoke his eyes filling with a black substance, his voice deepening.

"She will only realise when it's too late, and there will be nothing she can do, there is nothing the old lady can do about it to stop us." He spoke, his voice deeper than it was before.

Rako was taken back by his tone of voice before his emotions took back control.

"Don't act like you care about her, I didn't forget what you told me that first day we offered to help you out of your...'situation'…" he replied sarcastically.

"Really, I was desperate then…" Rako snapped, trying to defend his actions.

"And now you owe us... if my people can help you with your situation, we can easily undo what we've done."

Rako sighed, giving up any resistance to what he had to accomplish.

"Fine, I'll do it, just make sure that there is no trace back to me.." he sighed.

"Just make sure she's there." The gentleman demanded, his voice getting even deeper and more menacing than before.

"There won't be anything to trace it back to you, as long as you do your job..." he laughed maniacally.

Rako took this as a sign for him to leave,

He nodded his head and turned away from the gentleman, he nervously walked towards the door.

Not turning around, he was spooked by this turn of events.

The gentleman stood at the bar, looking at Rako as he made his way to the door.

"We'll be keeping an eye on you" he spoke, knowing that Rako was still in earshot. Rako didn't turn around, he made his way out of the bar.

Moments later

The gentleman was sitting at the bar, looking at the glass that Rako had been drinking out of, lost in thought.

Suddenly he fell off the chair, landing flat on his back on the floor, as he landed a huge stream of black mist poured out of his eyes and mouth into the air. Swirling around before making its way to the ceiling before dissipating.

The gentleman's eyes returned to their normal colour, his expression bemused,

"Where... where am I...?" He spoke, his voice trembling.

Across the citadel Lady Dhar was sleep, her breathing laboured and shallow, the room was illuminated by moonlight, moments later a dark mist poured through a small opening in a window, travelling towards Lady Dhar, before disappearing into her mouth, causing her to stir in her sleep, before waking herself abruptly looking out towards the window, she shook her head before lying down again,

"It's all going to plan" she murmured, her voice was deep and distorted.

CHAPTER 18

It was late at night; the moons shone their light into Reira's quarters. She was pacing towards the door of her room before turning around and pacing back towards the centre of the room.

"This isn't working out, even Cari can't help..." she murmured to herself. She sighed as she paced.

"I need clarity..." she quipped as a look of enlightenment flashed across her face, she ran over towards a box on the shelf in the room's corner.

She lifted the box from the shelf and carried it carefully across the room towards a lounging chair; she sat carefully on the chair while placing the box on the floor. The box was ornately decorated, its surface was inlaid with various colours of wood, it was expertly crafted.

She crouched down and looked at the surface of the box, a memory flooded back. She could remember the day she received this box, it was the day of her 18th. She had received this box from her father. She smiled as she admired the box; it had lasted fifty years of use and didn't look a day older than the day she received it.

She opened the box carefully, inside the box six, long thin vials filled with a glistening blue substance, lay in one corner, a separator separating them from the contents of the rest of the box.

A smaller transparent box lay to the side of the vials, inside the transparent box a dark blue powder resided. Reira reached in and pulled out the transparent box, she brought it up to eye level and shook its contents, which shifted side to side, there was barley a few grams within the box.

"Not much left..., thank the goddesses for the family reserves. Mother will send more if I ask her to..." she whispered to herself as she looked at a small screen which resided on the top of the container.

'Abrasar Reserve Imperial Year 09,". It read.

She tapped gently on its surface, bringing up a list of information, her family's crest filled the screen before the information appeared. some information so small it couldn't be read easily. She ran her finger down the display, and the information scrolled down, she traced her finger across the information until she found the information she was searching for. She smiled as she saw the information

6,350,293kg Remaining in Family Reserve.

She laughed as she saw this information, nearly 7000 tons of Kalita were in her family Reserve, more than the amount of Kalita that was sold in a single year across the entire empire. She could remember vividly the day her father told her about the family business.

She was 13 years old; she had trouble controlling her abilities, the family doctor had recommended a Kalita derivative to help control her emotions, her father had completely disregarded this, Numarii didn't have any difficulty in controlling them, that's what he had thought.

Her father had taken her and Numarii to Parlis, a small refinery in the Haxis System. Her family had been the sole purveyor and importer of Kalita, they sourced and refined the pure Kalita and sold it across the empire. Every Impiri in the empire knew of her family.

Abrasar Reserve was the purest and most expensive Kalita in the empire. It was even granted Imperial Ascent by the Emperor; they had held Imperial Ascent for over twelve thousand years, becoming one of the most influential companies outside of Imperially controlled companies.

Other companies had artificial version, they cost less, but the effects were inconsistent. Her uncle Orly was in charge of the export of the Kalita across the empire. That's why even now she had only ever seen her uncle a handful of times, he constantly travelled across the empire. If it was Kalita you wanted, he was the gatekeeper.

He could get anything, from the lowest quality to the highest, to various blends. The purest was expensive, upwards of five thousand credits per gram, the family reserve was the highest grade, the purest of the pure.

Her father had taken over the business after his father had passed away. It had been a family business for as long as could be remembered. As she remembered this memory, she chuckled to herself.

"Abrasar Reserve: When only the Best will do" she murmured to herself, reciting the advertising slogan for the company.

She looked at the contents of the box. It was a fully stocked Kalita kit. Two vials of a clear liquid glistened in the box. In contrast with the dark red of the felt which lined the box.

She remembered the first time she had taken some of her father's private reserve, without asking of course. Her father's reserve was of the highest quality, its effects were almost instant and stayed in your system for hours.

She had nearly killed herself, by taking too much. Her father was furious. She remembered the argument she had with her father. He was in tears but he understood, her abilities were too much for her to take, so he had decided to allow her to vaporise it.

Its effects would be weaker, but that would allow her to adjust her levels until she could take the families reserve. Her mother wasn't to know of this, this was their little secret. All he wanted was for her pain to be manageable and for her to feel in control of herself.

She shook her head and reached into the box, grabbing one of the blue liquid filled capsules with one hand and a small silver cylinder with the other,

She placed the two items beside her as she removed her jacket. Placing it neatly on the floor. She reached again into the box and pulled out a folded black band; she pulled at it with both hands and it stretched slightly before contracting again; she slid the band onto her left arm and pulled it up to her upper arm.

With both her hands she grabbed the liquid-filled cylinder and inserted it into the other cylinder, as it was inserted it hissed as the seal on the other was broken, at the same time a thin needle appeared out of the cylinder.

Reira drew her hand into a fist a few times on her left arm, drawing up her veins before carefully inserting the needle into her vein, before pressing a small button on the cylinder. The contents of the vial emptied into Reira's arm. She closed her eyes as the Kalita worked its way through her veins.

A few moments later she withdrew the needle from her arm, and pressed the crook of her arm, stopping it from bleeding.

Her eyes rolled back slowly as her breathing slowed to a near stop, she was out, her arms fell to her sides, dropping the vial onto the floor. As this happened she fell backwards on the chair.

The Kalita was taking effect, her dreams would be traumatic, old memories long forgotten would resurface, but she had to remember.

Her mind was a disorganised mess, flashbacks to better times, echoes of voices lost to time, a face appeared in her memory, a young Impiri man, Reira stood surrounded by all of this, quick flashes of a time long ago became as bright as day. Before jolting her into the disconnected jumble which was her consciousness.

The young man appeared again, reaching his hand out, "Nidiri, it's time to go" he called, before fading away.

"Parshai, don't make me go Parshai," a voice called out.

"There is a someone here, calling out my name, but I don't remember this happening, there is a young girl there, it's me, she's afraid. Desperate to find her way home, she's distraught, she's afraid of failing, there is another person, Father is that you..."

Reira walked towards her father before disappearing in a

blinding light.

A young girl stood in the middle of a gathering of various adults, she looked around; she moved between the adults who didn't even notice she was there, too busy in conversations with each other to take notice of her, she stood in the room's corner, looked down at her dress, the dress was an intricately woven white fabric which stopped inches from the floor.

He breathed a deep breath before reaching out towards her, but she nervously moved away, she wrapped her arms around her torso and sank to the floor. He stood in shock, devastated that she no longer felt safe and that he couldn't do anything about it.

He cast a few glances at her; she sat on the floor, her eyes looking at him, but seeing straight through him, fixed on the middle distance, paralysed by fear, she changed from being the eighteen-year-old daughter and regressed emotionally to being a little girl. She whimpered again until he couldn't take it anymore; he walked over, crouched down and grabbed her in his arms, he looked at her with tear-filled eyes.

"Nidiri, I know this wasn't your choice..." he whispered, forcing back tears.

"But, a chance like this..., it's something you can't turn your back on..., Do it for Marii " he pleaded, even though he could see the pain in his daughter's eyes.

"Parshai, I..I know, something just feels wrong,...what if they...if they don't like our...if they don't like me" she pleaded.

She raised her knuckle to her mouth and bit down hard, resisting the urge to cry out in pain, she was finding it hard to come to terms with everything. Her life had changed so much in the past six weeks, life was unfair, she hated the fact that she had to do this. Give up on her own dreams. She hated her twin sister for leaving her, above all else she hated herself for not being strong enough to say this to her father.

The dream jumped, time had jumped backwards a few hours. Reira and the others were deafened by a loud applause of the audience, before finally dying down.

Reira sheepishly looked for her father in the crowd, she tried to ignore the stares that she received from members of the audience, at last, she found the glaze of her father. He had arrived in time, being stationed at the far reaches of the empire, Master Baelin stood in the room's corner, watching like a Hamarian Hawk, as always. He has always kept an eye on her and her family.

Reira stepped forwards, and took her place within the group, her breathing slowing, waiting for the soft flow of music to begin, once the music started the group stood forward and bowed, their gaze remaining locked on the crowd, a sense of foreboding filled the air. After bowing one by one the members of the group filed out of the room, with Reira hesitating to move, she paused, her breathing deepened, only the feel of a hand on her shoulder brought her back to reality, she turned around and looked up,

Master Baelin stood behind her, winked at her and whispered

"Time to go, don't worry about anything..." his voice calming and reassuring, she smiled a shy smile before walking off towards the open door. He stood back, looked across at her father and nodded, her father sighing knowing that things were hopefully going to be alright.

She looked down at her hands while she walked; they were shaking again once behind the door her hands shook her concentration was immediately disrupted when the door was slammed behind her.

Being away from the prying eyes allowed her to relax and allow a small smile to form on her lips. She stood looking at her reflection on the back of the door; she looked formal; she wore a white spotless suit, around her waist was a single intricate red woven belt, black tassels hung from a knot at the end of the belt.

She glanced at her reflection, not happy with what she wore, everything was neutral, no resemblance to anything from her culture, she glanced over at everyone else, who were busy talking within small groups, there were fifty individuals from over thirty-five different races.

Her glances caught the eye of another Impiri, his eyes as blue as a spring rain, they mesmerised her; she had never seen an Impiri with eyes that colour before; he looked over at her, noticing her wrist and frowned with disgust. She was taken back by this and looked down at his wrist, around his wrist a white tattoo was present, she looked down at her own wrist, a bright red tattoo worked it was around her wrist.

She knew that her parents' generation there was distrust between the houses and the members of each tribe, but she had never experienced such a look on another Impiri's face when they saw her bond.

The dream shifted again, Reira was sitting on the floor, in total darkness, curled up

"Rei... Rei... Rei" a voice called out,

Reira looked up, her eyes were black.

"Rei..." the voice called out again, waking Reira from the dream.

It was Carila; she had gained access to the room and was leaning over Reira who was lying on the chair.

"Rei, are you alright, I've been messaging you for the past fifty minutes..., security had to let me in...I thought something had happened,".

Reira looked at Carila with a confused expression, still coming around from her lucid dreams, her vision blurred, her focus soft.

She blinked her eyes a few times and everything came back into focus.

"What happened...?" Carila enquired.

Reira sat up and grabbed hold of Carila's hand, her hand shaking.

"Cari, I'm fine, I just needed a bit of clarity..."

She sighed, everything making sense now.

"I think I'm going to go ahead with the media event, I've been afraid like this before, it's no different from when we started at the Cloisters.. you remember that...?" She quietly explained.

"Rei, of course I remember that, I've never seen someone so

afraid in my life, and I still haven't, that's why I was worried about you." As she spoke she looked down at Reira.

"Especially when you didn't respond to Alice, she told me you were in your quarters, and your hearts rates were low, I thought you might have taken control again. If you know what I mean.." she gently caressed Reira's hand with her thumb.

Reira looked at Carila, at the same time as gently helping her to sit down beside her.

She held Carila's hand and looked at her face, reading her emotions clearly.

"Cari, I'm sorry. You know me too well." She spoke, her voice laced with seriousness.

"I'm never going back to that place, you're the only reason why I didn't end it years ago. You were my light during that time of darkness. I know I scared you and I'm truly sorry." She grabbed Carila and pulled her close, hugging her, they slowly broke the hug. Carila stopped and looked at Reira, Carila could feel the heat emanating from Reira's body, the sensation of feeling her breath on her skin. She looked at her, lost in thought.

She smiled, Reira had been her closest friend, there was no one else she trusted as much as Reira. They had each been there for each other, during the darkness times in their respective lives.

Reira had been there during the difficult times when Carila's parents had died during a freak accident a decade before. Carila on the other hand had been there through all the sadness that Reira experienced, the inability to cope during the first few months in the cloisters, the times when Reira had spiralled into darkness, stopping her from ending it all. This bond was strong, nothing would break it.

A Few Days Later
18th Hour of the 5th Day of the 8th Month
IY (Imperial Year) 101

Reira shifted her balance from her left side to the right, she was always uncomfortable in her clothing before dealing with the unknown, and this was a major unknown. A meeting with the Jinal Council, was an honour, but also traumatic.

"Cari?, can she tell me how this looks?" She called out while fixing the last strands of her hair. Her hair having been braided traditionally, ornate red and turquoise beads were placed on differing strands of her silvery white hair.

Moments later Carila approached the doorway to the closet, Reira was dressed in a sleeveless dark turquoise blouse, with a v-neck which exposed a hint of cleavage, The highly embroidered blouse tapered tightly around her slim waist, She wore a long dark red dress that ran the length of her legs and stopped, just before her feet.

Carila stopped, lost in admiration, before shaking herself out of it,

"Rei, I think you look...." she trailed off.

"Fine..." she added, just before Reira could respond.

"Hey, do you think I need the jacket as well?" As she held out a delicately embroidered turquoise jacket.

Carila couldn't believe it, she was asking her for fashion advice, Reira had always been confident in what she was wearing, never caring about other people's opinions.

"I've never seen you, looking so...." she paused again.

"I know, it's a little revealing, for the council, that's why I think the jacket would be more suitable." Reira replied.

"I was going to say, looking so much like your mother, but..." she laughed in response.

Reira turned around and looked at herself in-front of the full-length mirror. She smiled,

"You're right, maybe that's the best look for this situation, Mother was always traditional, and this calls for traditional. Except mother wouldn't have gone for this blouse, 'a little too revealing' she would have thought, especially for a Lady of the house" she chuckled.

She smiled at Carila,

"Lady Abrasar, it is 18:05, The scheduled meeting with the council is at 19:05," A.l.i.c.e spoke, interrupting Carila as she was laughing at Reira.

"It's time" Reira spoke, her voice wavering, her hands clenched.

Reira looked at Carila nervously, her eyes welling up. Carila walked over to her and hugged her, pulling her close. Carila stopped mid hug and whispered in her ear.

"I know you've got this, You know I'm here for you..."

Reira turned to her, stroking Carila's face slowly with the back of her hand, causing Carila to close her eyes briefly.

"I've always known..." Reira whispered, looking at Carila in the eyes, lingering for a moment before smiling nervously.

"You'll be here when I come back?" She queried.

"Maybe tonight I'll cook something for you...when you've finished come to my quarters. My treat." Carila spoke, her heart racing. Reira had never looked at her in that way before. Her emotions were running wild.

An hour later.

As was tradition, Reira would first step in front of the twelve, the heads of the Impiri houses, these twelve the most known in Impiri society,. She would make this journey with no one by her side, adorned in the traditional garments of her tribe.

She entered the dark hall, the light from the sun shining through small windows that allowed great sections of the hall to be cast into darkness.

Dressed in the ritualistic garment of her forebears, she bowed as she entered the room; the room was filled by the cacophony of the Eleven, their words unable to be made out, but by the tone of the conversation, something important was being discussed.

The discussion in the hall died down, as Reira entered further into the room, she tried to ignore the stares she received, her eyes adjusting to the darkness in the room.

Reira could make out eleven individuals sitting at a semi-circular table in front of her, each of them wearing distinctively different hooded robes, in front of them a Solitary chair lay in the sun's light which shone through the small windows and cascaded across the room because of strategically located mirrors.

The smell of incense filled the air, the hall was ancient, on the floor layer a carefully constructed mosaic, Reira glanced at its pattern as she walked towards the chair, arriving at the middle of the room she bowed, finally stepping into the light,

"I hereby announce the arrival of Lady Abrasar; Daughter of the late Lord Inis Abrasar." A voice announced, echoing across the hall.

Reira approached the chair, nervously, her head covered by a black headdress, adorned with various colourful beads. Her hair braided into many strands. In her left hand she clasped a beaded necklace which was tied around her wrist, the darkness of the room was illuminated by what she was wearing.

Her blouse was an opulent and intricately brocaded bright turquoise, her dress a radiant rusty red, embroidered with gold and around her neck was a woven gold choker, her face was immaculate, not a single blemish, on her forehead a single red stone lay suspended by an intricate golden chain.

A solitary crash of a gavel against a sound block, disturbed the silent causing Reira to jump slightly,

"Thank you for giving me this privilege, speaking here at the heart of our people." She stopped, taking a deep breath to help control herself.

"Before I answer the questions you have for me, I admit I'm not worthy of such a privilege but I'm here to.." she stopped, her breathing becoming deeper, before returning to a calm rhythm, she spoke again.

"I am here to speak in front of this council, about a great

injustice to our people."

Out of the darkness of the hall, a single figure dressed in a plain white robe walked to the chair. He was a young man, his eyes green, and his skin a sandy white.

"Speak your mind, Lady Abrasar, But be warned. I will scrutinise your comments..." he declared.

She strolled towards the solitary chair pausing at its back.

Her mind was a jumble of thoughts and emotions, she tried to focus her thought before she spoke.

Reira placed her hands on the back of the chair, cleared her throat and spoke. Her bottom lip trembling.

"'The people in this room, are seen as a pillar of strength in the community, the people believe in.."

She was immediately interrupted by one of the eleven.

"'The people believe in what they want to believe in if it suits their selfish needs, but what would you know 'Makhara''' it spoke,

Reira was taken back by the language used, she closed her eyes for a second before trying to speak again, her hands slowly clenching, she was furious.

"So, You are the last remaining daughter of Lord Abrasar, correct?" Another voice interrupted

"I am she" she replied,

A member of the council, still hooded stood up and made his way towards Reira, his voice was familiar. Lord Amadak, she thought, it had to be him. It couldn't be anyone else, his voice was too familiar.

"Ah, okay, to think you are the only remaining daughter of Lord Abrasar, spending the last decade of your life on some godforsaken desert planet, since the disgrace of your failure," he said, walking around the chair Reira was holding onto.

"It's strange, your father kept his distance from you, was he ashamed of you?" He grinned, resting his hand on her shoulder, causing Reira to stir, shocked by his accusations.

Reira looked uncomfortable.

"How dare, how dare you say that," she said in a quiet voice.

"I was I who was ashamed of myself and didn't want it to affect my family."

Lord Amadak arched his eyebrow.

"Although this may be true, wouldn't it be better if he had another heir?"

Reira nodded.

"And wouldn't you agree that if your elder sister was still alive, he'd want his eldest daughter to safeguard his family?"

Reira jumped out from behind the chair, her face tense, her lips pursed….

"Don't bring my sisters into this, you have no right," she said with an intense fierceness in her voice.

He knew that he had hit a nerve so he continued down the path.

"Fine, but you do know that your father left your mother in charge of our families role within our society, isn't it better to just admit that the house Abrasar will fall, However, unlike your twin sister, you probably wouldn't slit your wrists, you probably would just like to disappear into the dust bowl planet from which you came. It surprised us you even survived the first week when you were back in the Cloisters."

"Enough!" She shouted. "You bastard,"

Lord Amadak held out his hand towards her to hold her tongue.

"Listen" he said in a calm, soothing voice,

"I'm just trying to understand why, someone who we hold in such high regard, your mother, pleaded with us to allow you to speak, All I want is the best for our people, Nidiri, but I can't help if you are not willing to help me understand why I should listen to you..."

Reira turned back towards the council, resting her hands back on the chair.

"Why? Because I am his daughter, You speak of my father with such esteem, Am I not as his daughter due a modicum of such respect. I have the right, it is in accordance to the customs you hold so dear" she pleaded, regaining her composure before speaking again.

"Let us not forget that we, the shadow of the Impiri, are still far from a united people. You pretend you are loyal, maybe loyal to yourself, but to to each other." She mocked sarcastically.

"A third of the great houses would leave the council if they could. And the others would break out into a civil war. Every Impiri dreams of home, but none of us have ever seen home, the occasional recreation, and simulation of home might seem great, but don't forget, we, as a people are homeless." She preached,

"But. ." a voice spoke before Reira cut them off.

"Earlier one of you claimed that the people are selfish, but you treat each other with contempt..." she paused,

"'Makhara, you use that as an insult. I haven't been called that since I was a child, yes, I am Makhara - Sandy Blood, But I am proud of my heritage, I am of the house Abrasar, a member of the proud eastern Makla-hara-Dasho tribe. (Children of the Blood Sands). She proclaimed proudly, lifting her sleeves revealing the dark red tattoo which worked its way around her wrists.

The hall went silent,

"You and your traditions" she laughed, her hands clenching the back of the chair again.

"This council is a circus..." Amadak interrupted. If we had any true common sense, we should have disbanded it years ago, all it achieves is the isolation of our way of life"

"Then maybe you are not ready, this 'circus' as you put it, is the only way we have been able to preserve our way of life since the fall, maybe we have preserved too much..." Yarda Amadak exclaimed,

"You still think you are saving our people," Reira mocked, laughing slightly.

"You are blind to the truth. Our people still live on the fringes of society, yes our numbers have increased, but so has our prejudice...

"We have integrated into society, but not really integrated, we would never allow the stigma of a none pure blood. Those Impiri not linked to a great house, what do they really want, they want a culture to be proud of, not afraid of, the infighting must stop," she declared.

"We have turned into packs of Hazan Wolves; we have turned on each other instead of helping each other. Grudges that are thousands of years old are still held by our people. I for one have taken offence when addressed by a member of a grey house, and by your own words, speaker of the house of grey" gesturing to a dark grey tattoo around its right wrist, peaking out from underneath the robe.

"The term Makhara, Ubek-Zunid (Wilderness Child), and even 'Tamir-Zunal' (Cold Heart), were used by our ancestors to drive a wedge between us, to label and separate our people by the location of their birth. It seems like their usage still divides us, even after thirty thousand years..." she pleaded,

"We were once the twenty-four great houses, no, make that the twenty-four great tribes of the Impiri" she stopped, staring at each of the council members there hooded robes still covered their faces.

"We have taken the bloodlines too far, let me remind you that generations ago, a young boy, a member of the White, was abandoned by the elders of his house, and was left to die"

"He was weak and unlikely to survive, my ancestor found him, the matriarch of our house, she saw past his bonding, his upbringing, she saw only Impiri. My family adopted him, forsaking all his upbringing, this child grew up, and was the best of us, he was Tylo Ajith Lanan Abrasar, and he saw us as one people."

"He saw the fractures between us as differences in opinion and differences in tradition, but he was not afraid to discuss this with his brothers and sisters in the White, when he returned to them as a young man, he dreamed of a reconciliation between the houses, and was killed for what he believed in." Her voice echoing throughout the chamber.

"We all try to forget those times, especially the 'Idmin Samis Kalet' (nights of the thousand knives), when countless members of my tribe were brutally murdered, by our own kind." She cast a look around the room, catching glances from members of the council, before they lowered their heads in shame, ashamed of the actions their own ancestors took.

This angered her, their silence was the final straw in their disrespect.

"Why won't you show yourself, are you too ashamed?" She pleaded, her hands clenched. Her breathing deepened, and her eyes turned a milky white; the faint tattoos on her neck glowed.

A hushed murmur came from a few of the twelve,

"Lady Abrasar, what is the meaning of..." just as he was about to finish, Reira's hands opened wide, and instantly the hoods of each of the twelve flew backward, revealing their faces for the first time.

"Now I can see how I'm talking to.." Reira sneered,

The murmur grew into a cacophony of different voices.

Lord Jido-Arkin from the White House was the first to address,

"Lady Abrasar..." he screamed.

"Yes, Lord Jido-Arkin..." she snapped in response.

"Please respect the traditions of this council, you have raised your concern with us, and we will hear you out" his voice boomed in the chamber, before fading into nothing.

"How can I respect it, when you don't even respect me or my house, my people, have sat on this council for thousands of years, yet I see eleven of you, white, green, blue, black, purple, turquoise, yellow, orange, grey, pink, and brown, you spit on the decency of my people, and fail in showing respect to my late father." As she spoke she gestured to the wrists of each of the members in front of her.

The hall grew quiet, the eleven looked at each other, each gesturing for someone else to speak,

"Why..." Reira cried,

Someone stepping out of the darkness into the light broke the silence; she was young, around Reira's age, her eyes a brilliant green and her skin the colour of sand, her hair a dark brown.

"I can see your concern, Lady Abrasar..." she paused, turned to each of the other members and bowed graciously. Reira's face changed as she saw who stepped into the light, a familiar sight, it was Nalae Sacrabam, daughter of the House of Jaeihai, she had changed little since she last saw her, fifty years before. Reira nodded her head slowly, in recognition, a small smile crept upon her face.

"The reason for not having a member of your house present is that you are here." She spoke, her voice calm and understanding, she smiled at Reira as she spoke.

"What do you mean, my mother should be here... especially since my father passed?" Reira questioned, not fully understanding the response.

"Your mother, in her wisdom, has graciously stepped aside. For you..." she declared as she placed her hand on Reira's shoulder.

Reira was shocked, at that moment everything became clear. The reason for the call to the council, the message from her mother, the missing member of the council.

"But the right belongs to her..." she implored, looking around the chamber with concern.

"Your mother had spoken to us in our last meeting a few weeks ago, she had told us about your concerns and said we should hear you out..."

"Traditionally, only the representative of each of the houses would be granted a hearing as she asked" Nalae added.

Reira stood in silence as Nalae explained.

"And she knew that to allow this to happen she would have to step aside, but with the news of your 'promotion', we felt it necessary to elevate your standing under our traditions" he paused, looking around at the council before speaking.

"In recognition of the honour you would bring to the council, You have been 'raised' by your house and by this council, no longer are you third daughter of the house, you Nidiri Reira Abrasar, are Lady Nidiri Reira, Emi'rre (Head of House) of the House Abrasar." She added, Reira stood there in silence.

"House Jaeihai has always shared a bond with House Abrasar, all the way back to the beginning. Thousands of years we have worked together, Our kinship has lasted, all trials and tribulations we have faced."

"My late father" she paused, steadied herself, trying to push back her tears...

"He would have enjoyed being the one to 'raise' the daughter of someone who he called his 'brother'. Since they are both no longer with us, I'm honoured to be the one to address your raising." She smiled and bowed graciously.

"I will now address you, as it should be made known amongst our honoured people across the empire and beyond; Lady Nidiri Reira, Emi'rre of the House Abrasar, of the Honoured Makla-hara-Dasho has been 'raised' by a council of her peers, and by the members of the house she now leads.

Reira was speechless, the room was silent, not even a murmur, she looked around the room, the members of the council were silent, until a laugh disturbed the silence, shattering it into a million pieces. Reira looked over at the source of the laughter, Lord Jido-Arkin had stood up, laughing, a laugh from deep down within the core of his being.

"Finally, someone has managed to silence her..." he laughed, the rest of the council were sat in silence.

Reira looked at him, unsure of whether that was an insult before she noticed a sly smile creeping across her own face before she burst out in laughter.

"He isn't wrong there..." she laughed, completely shattering the atmosphere in the room, Nalae reached out her right arm and placed her hand on Reira's left shoulder, gripping the shoulder tightly before releasing.

Reira smiled at her and proceeded to do the same. A traditional Impiri greeting, something that Reira had never forgotten even though the last time she had done it was when she was at the Cloisters, what seemed like a lifetime ago.

Reira smiled at her, before being interrupted by Lord Jido-

Arkin, he stood next to her. Since the last time she had seen him, he had aged; he was now close to a hundred and thirty years old. The last time she had seen him, he was about her current age, his features hadn't changed, but they had softened slightly. He looked at Reira with the same look he had given her all those years ago when she had questioned him before her time in the temple.

"Lady Abrasar...Reira, I know this might be improper of me, because of the nature of things, but...", Reira's expression dropped, even now over forty years since the last time she had seen him, his presence still over shadowed her. She looked at him and slightly bowed her head.

"Your father would be proud of you, how you defended your family...and stood up for yourself, even against me." He stopped when he realised that everyone had stopped their discussions and were listening to him, "Seems like you have a predisposition to arguing with me...just like you late father," he sternly added, embarrassed by the eavesdropping.

"But maybe I need to be challenged...occasionally." he laughed, cracking a smile.

She leaned over and hugged him; he wasn't expecting this, his shoulders tensed as she hugged him, before slowly relaxing.

"You knew that I would do this", she whispered into his ear,

"But you still mentioned my father. You knew his opinion mattered to me, somehow you knew, I thank you for that!" She added.

He looked at her as they pulled away from each other. He smiled a small smile before speaking.

"Even though we argued, and we argued a lot, over seventy

years of arguments. I miss him. I hope you challenge me as much as he did..."

Then she realized, she couldn't lead her family, being the codex would take so much of her time, they knew that, she would always be absent from all discussions.

"Lord Arkin?" Reira responded as he was about to turn around, catching him mid flow. He quickly spun around, a curious look appeared on his face.

"I'm sure you thought about this, but I won't be able to attend the council. Not after the rite of Tasir"

"It had completely slipped my mind.." he answered, "unless you can find someone you will abdicate the role to. Otherwise we would have to convene council without you.." he remarked in return.

A small smile appeared on his face, he knew that this would happen, this would allow his agenda to be unchallenged within the council, his influence would grow if not counterbalanced by her family.

Reira looked at him, lost in thought. A thousand thoughts ran through her mind, she couldn't hand the role back to her mother, such things would cause an uproar. Then the thought dawned on her, the side of her mouth curled upwards, a slight glimpse of a smile.

"Lord Arkin, as Emi'rre I would like to table a motion, with upmost urgency."

Lord Arkin looked at her, trying to read her expression, Reira gave nothing away.

"It is your right, but what kind of motion would help you in your current predicament."

“It’s something more serious than that I’m afraid, I would like to lodge a Shal’Nha-Cha (Accusation of Intent).”

The other members of the council stopped what they were doing, some gasped, others were silent, their expression said it all, this was serious.

Lord Arkin stood in shock, he regained himself after a moments thought, turning towards the seated members of the council.

“Lady Abrasar has tabled a Shal’Nha-Cha, under council rules and tradition, we must hear her out. The doors must be sealed, no one is allowed in or out until we conclude this matter.” Lord Arkin declared, his voice trembling. Other members of the council dispersed, one went to lock the door.

“Are you sure?, there is no record of a red family having declared one of these, not since...” he added as he turned towards Reira.

“Idmin Samis Kalet’ - (The Nights of a Thousand Knives..), I know, five thousand years and not a single one, but that is all about to change.” Reira replied, a concerned look flashed across her face, her eyes filling with tears. Her ancestor had been subject to a Shal’Nha-Cha, instigated by another one of her ancestors. It had been a time of massive upheaval, a time which most Impiri tried to forget, but she couldn’t, No red Impiri could, stories from that time had been passed down, it had touched the lives of most of her kind, but directly affected everyone associated with red. At least four million members of red houses had lost their lives in the decade of civil war, another two million Impiri from other houses died, the civil war had torn a hole in the middle of the Impiri community, which still hadn't recovered.

* * *

The Next Evening

19th Hour of the 6th Day of the 8th Month
IY (Imperial Year) 101

The evening had arrived quickly, Baelin had spent the day out across the capital, visiting friends he hadn't seen in years, before making his way back to the citadel, Reira had messaged him, she had news to share with him.

The urgency in Reira's voice worried him, he knew that something was up, the sound in Reira's voice was easy to decipher, when he had looked after her and her sister while they were growing up and their father was away, he had grown used to it.

He had booked himself into one apartment that was close enough to the citadel it was within a few minutes walk, but was private enough that he would be left in peace. He knocked on the door, and waited, a few moments later the door slid open, a young boy stood in the opening.

"Baelin I presume.." he quizzed. Baelin looked down at the young boy. who mustn't have been more than 10 years old, before he was shooed away by a much older figure, the man was similar in age to Baelin,

"I apologise for my grandson, he had heard me and his

grandmother discussion your arrival, and he was eager to see an Impiri, he'd never seen one of your kind before, I do apologise again." He gestured for Baelin to enter,

Baelin entered the building, the building was compact, everything had its place, it was a well lit building, a huge skylight filtered light down to the ground floor, a winding staircase led up to a mezzanine floor with three doors in the distance, Baelin took in the sights, looking up. Admiring the artwork on the walls.

"First one on the left is yours..." he added as Baelin ascended the stairs.

"Someone came to see you, but you hadn't arrived, so I told them they could wait in your apartment..." he murmured as Baelin was close to the apartment door. Baelin could just make out what he had said when he unlocked the apartment door and opened it, the apartment was shrouded in darkness,

Baelin heard a loud noise as he opened the door, but thought nothing of it. At first, he assumed it was either the apartment next door or the owner downstairs going to the kitchen for something to eat, however that wasn't the case. After a few more unusual sounds Baelin entered the room slowly, feeling his way on the right side to find a light switch when suddenly he felt a strike against the back of his head, he grabbed at his head quickly to protect himself from a further strike, His vision began fading quick and his strength disappeared even quicker, he tried to look up and could see nothing, before he slowly blacked out.

A Few Hours Later

21st Hour of the 6th Day of the 8th Month
IY (Imperial Year) 101

He came to with a thudding headache, his eyes closed, trying to force the pain away. The back of his skull throbbed with pain, like a beating heart. The rhythm of his heart so loud it caused his headache to get worse. He slowly opened his eyes and there was nothing but darkness, he cursed under his breath and tried to move, but was unable. Something was restraining his arms. His legs, too, were immobilised, as he noticed when he tried to get up. Whatever way was up. With no visible surroundings and being suspended within the air, hanging from restraints clamped to his wrists.

The crackling sound of a fire echoed all around him, but it seemed to come from a single source. He couldn't feel its warmth, but he would faintly hear the wood splitting and cracking, it was unmistakable.

How long had he been out cold? He thought to himself, he instinctively licked his lips, his mouth was dry and his stomach was empty. He opened his eyes wider to better perceive his surroundings.

Darkness continued to engulf his senses, A tremor of panic vibrated in his core. He was sightless, motionless, restrained. His senses battered, What had happened, all that he could remember was opening the door to the apartment he was renting while on Prim, stepping inside and then nothing.

That slight tremor in the core of his being increased in

intensity until he physically shook in response.

"It's all a dream, a nightmare even, Only a nightmare. I'll wake up any second now. This is not real, It can't be real. Definitely not real!" He thought to himself again, the thoughts running wild within his mind. Repeating it repeatedly in his mind.

He tried to wrench his arms free and felt the cold steel cuffs dig into his flesh. He cried out in pain and kept battering at the chains with his forearms, stringing the metal slightly.

With each movement the cuffs dug in deeper, rubbing against his skin before it drew blood, but he was too far gone to notice it. All he could think about was escape, even his instinct forced him to fight this unseen enemy, to escape these bonds, to free himself.

He snapped his head back, the impact dizzying him for a moment. He struggled to move his head repeatedly, struggling to move against his restraints. He yelled out, a shout mingled with fury and panic.

"Where...why am I here" he coughed, the dry air invading his mouth, causing him to gag. How hadn't he noticed before? The metallic scent of blood mixed with the familiar taste of incense.

He knew this smell. A daunting memory flashed across his mind, back to a time when he was just a young man, a few months after his rite of ascension at the age of eighteen. The smell was a 'Shal'cha' - Persecution, an incense burnt during the ritual of an Impiri trail. He had never witnessed one let alone being the subject of one but he had been in a room after one, this smell was familiar, it was that smell. His mind went crazy with fright, he had done nothing wrong, had they got him confused with someone else. Did they not know where his loyalty lied.

His strength was ebbing; he sighed as his poundings came at longer intervals; his feet beat a painstakingly slow rhythm. He drew in a ragged breath after another.

A squeak from rusty hinges came from behind him,; someone was coming in–or going out. Were they going to just leave him here, terrified and alone, or were they going to inflict even more pain onto his aged body.

"No! No, no, no, no! Why? What have I done? Let me go, She won't stand for this" he thought to himself, if he didn't turn up for his dinner with Reira she would search for him, she wouldn't let him go, not after all this time.

He tried to cry for help, but his throat was raw from shouting and his lips were dry and cracked; The distinct sound of swishing cloth reached his ears. It was coming closer. Closer, closer, and then past him, the faint footsteps receding into the other direction.

"Come... ba-..." he croaked as loud as he could.

"No... Don't.. leave me here." He coughed again, coughing up blood this time, spitting it out of his mouth.

He listened for an excruciating moment. A moment which dragged on for what felt like an eternity, the door slammed closed. They weren't coming back. They had left him to rot, to die in the darkness alone.

What had he done he thought to himself, They had left him hanging over the chasm between life and death, between the light and the dark.

His tortured throat let out a pathetic cry as he attacked his bonds with the rest of his strength, knowing it was a waste of his time and energy he had to at least try. He would get free, he would. He'd escape. He'd walk in the sun again. He would die free, not chained in this realm of darkness.

He thrust upwards with every muscle he had, gritting his teeth when the chains tightened around him, trying to overcome his captivity. He could feel the links groan in strain and he pushed harder. Hope. It existed. Just a little more... A few inches. one link popped out of its socket. He clenched his teeth harder as he continued to struggle. A few more links popped, and he'd be free.

"It seems like he will do anything," someone said above him, her voice brimming with excitement.

A set of dragging footsteps echoed into his struggles.

'Maybe they would let me go' he thought,

He let his aching body collapse the cosine which held up his arms taking the full weight of his body; the strain causing him to breathe heavily.

The footsteps had stopped. He heard soft breathing. Something nudged his hip painfully, a questioning prod from the shadows; he shirked away from the sadistic touch the best he could.

"You were right, but is he willing to make a sacrifice for the betterment of others, not just to save himself.." This voice was crisp and cool, all warmth drained by the lack of compassion. He wasn't sure if the speaker was even a living being.

"Well, should we let him see us? My Lady?" The voice added.

"Hmm" she voiced in reply.

The voice stood just out of range, in the darkness where the light from the solitary lamp couldn't reach.

The implications of this request hadn't the time to register in his mind before a hard fist wrenched the rough bag from his head, ripping out some of his hair in the process. He cried out as bright illumination worked its way through his eyes and into his brain, cooking the nerves, causing him to forcefully close his eyes.. He heard the two voices conferring behind him.

"He looks like he is worthy, a fine specimen, a near perfect Impiri and you said he was loyal." The voice spoke.

"Was…" he heard, his mind running wild.

"I am… Loyal… I would never betray my life debt…" he retched, it was becoming difficult for him to speak. But he still continued to protest.

The distorted voice answered to the female,

"Who am I to judge? We hide the darkness inside ourselves; we keep them hidden in the secretive corners of our hearts and souls. But this, this judgement. It's our way to make sure it's done right, that his sacrifice is worthy of our bestowment. We will let him burn in the purging of his dishonour before the rebirth in the fire. He must be going mad, maybe we should let him suffer more," The cold voice grew an edge of pleasure in his torment.

"Even I Tarli, only son of a forgotten house can see that his darkness is close to the surface, he could kill us both if we let him out." He paused, laughed maniacally before continuing

"See him squirm and groan! That is his darker side answering to the caress of the darkness, maybe we should subject him to the flame, burn away that darkness. When he is pure only, then will his true sacrifice begin." Tarli laughed, gesturing at Baelin who was a few meters away from him.

"You can see the confusion on his face, he does not understand what lies in store for him. He would be so lucky to find solace in this time, you will ask much of him my lady before the end..." Tarli spoke whimsically.

"Kotam Baelin" Tarli spoke,

"Kotam Davanii Baelin, You are here because someone has accused you…" the shadowy figure added before being cut off,

Baelin spoke "Accused on what grounds…" a hand silenced him by grabbing at his wrist. Restricting his movement even more.

"You have been judged by a council of your peers…" Tarli added.

"I wish to face my accuser. Give me the dignity of that, if I will face judgement…" Baelin pleaded, his voice husky and laboured.

"You may not.." a voice interrupted his reply, a figure walked out of the darkness, into the light,

Baelin looked up, the glare from the light affecting his view for a few seconds before he could see who it was, as the figure came into focus a look of shock flashed across his face, his eyes filling with tears as his mind realised who it was.

"Reira?" Baelin mumbled in shock. Reira was standing in front of him, she was dressed in all black, her white hair tied back. Around her neck a black collar gently caressed her neck, her outfit was minimal, her shoulders bare, a figure hugging black leather bodice covered her torso and chest. Intricate details glistened in gold, lit by the light overhead. Her skirt stopped at her knees, She held a blade in one hand, the blade pointing at his throat, the light overhead glistening on the intricately enscribed blade

"What are you doing here and why?" He questioned.

She looked at him, before slowly leaning towards him reaching out with her left hand and caressing his face, his eyes closing as she carefully touched his cheek. Expecting the blade in her opposite hand to be plunged into his chest at any moment.

"Master Baelin, My Friend, My Confidant, My Council, My Guardian…" she spoke, her voice serious.

"I have accused you, I have presented my evidence to the council, and they have passed judgement." She turned away, unable to bare the sight of him.

"Your Life as a Dakta - *Unseen is over."

His heart raced, how could she accuse him, he had been loyal to her, memories from the past flashed before his eyes. She turned around quickly,

"I told the council that in this circumstance, I should be the one to pass the sentence of this council." Reira added, she paused, her emotions running high.

"What are you going to do," Baelin had found the strength to speak up. He didn't know how long he could speak as his voice was failing.

"They have charged you with something serious, the punishment will be severe" Reira was coming closer, the cold steel blade of the knife rested underneath his chin, the sensation of the cold steel caused his neck to draw in

"Do you deny the charges brought against you!" She replied inquisitively.

"I Nidiri Reira Abrasar, Emerre of House Abrasar, Find you Kotam Davanii Baelin are guilty of the charges brought against you." Baelin struggled, he fought against the chains as she spoke, his struggling stopped as he was struck across the face, he stopped, surprised that Reira has struck him, he licked the side of his lip, tasting blood. Her strike had drew blood, he looked at her with tears in his eyes.

"If you let me finish..." She coldly added.

"You will no longer be Kotam Davanii Baelin, you will be wiped from the book of our people, your records will be destroyed, your properties will be seized, your life as you know it, is over.." she commanded her voice powerful and forthright.

Second hand grabbed at his right wrist and injected a needle into his skin, the sensation was mild at first, his skin tingling before the sensation grew. It grew worse, from a mild tingle to a burning sensation, the pain centred on his wrist; he winced in agony as the injection took effect; he began to sweat, his breathing became rapid, the pain almost unbearable before it subsided. He was exhausted, he looked up in a daze.

"Why am I still alive…" he mumbled, he was out of breath,

his senses were heightened.

“Because I need you…” Reira added, looking at him, her eyes tearing up. Her eyelashes flickered trying to pushback the tears.

He looked over at his wrist, the burning sensation had subsided, his eyes couldn’t focus his vision blurred.

“What happened…”

“Baelin, my dear Baelin, Do you not know, has it not sunk in yet.” Reira added melodically.

“I’ll make it clear. You are no longer Kotam Davanii Baelin, an unmarked, I have charged you with…” she paused before smiling, looking at his confused expression.

“Being a loyal and trustworthy Impiri, have sacrificed to help my family, my father and myself over the years, countless times, and I couldn’t let that loyalty go unrewarded.

“Kotam Davanii Baelin, no longer exists, Kotam Davanii Baelin-Abrasar exists.”

That when he realized, his eyes filling with tears. his mind going crazy with the realisation.

“You mean…” he spoke, his bottom lip trembling.

“Yes…” Reira added, she finally smiled, a look of relief flashed across her face.

“The council agreed with me that your loyalty needed to be rewarded, this hasn’t been done in my family for countless generations, not since the olden days, has an unmarked been granted a bond.”

He had never had a family before; he had his family, but being bonded, It was above his wildest dreams.

Tears streamed down his cheeks, he looked up at Reira, then back down at his wrist, he stared for a few moments before speaking, mesmerised by the faint red tattoo that circled his wrist, the tattoo gradually becoming darker.

"Are you sure?" he muttered,

She smiled widely before graciously nodding.

"I've come to take you away from normality. I can't lead my family without you." Reira said with a gleam in her eyes.

"What are you talking about?" Baelin looked at her as the chains that held him suspended were lowered to the ground. He tried to get up, stumbling at the first attempt, he arose to his feet, uneasy, he stumbled a second time, taking a step back, looking at the get-up Reira wore. He had never seen her dressed like that before, she looked so much like her mother had done at that age, he had to double blink to make sure he was seeing correctly,

"Listen to me," Reira said abruptly,

"I wouldn't have made this decision lightly, I remember father once speaking about it to mother, but it wasn't the right time, but now, with all that's going on, I wanted someone to look after my..." She paused, laughed to herself for a second, before correcting herself.

"Our family's interests, I wouldn't be able to look after the day-to-day decisions required to make the family successful, you had been with father during all of his trips and you know more about our family's business than anyone and I won't be able to speak at the council, my duties to the Empire require someone to be my voice in the council. That would be you, someone I trust." Reira smiled as she explained the trust of the matter.

CHAPTER 19

45 Years Previous
Iridani System
21st Hour of the 17th Day of the 2nd Month
IY (Imperial Year) 66

"Don't use that excuse with me, you weren't looking for that book, you were snooping," Reira cried out.

They were in Reira's room, Carila sat with Reira, while Tryiar, a young Impiri male was looking at the bookshelf in the room's corner. Tryiar was young, early twenties at most. Lean muscles showed that he spent a lot of time in training, a small gash above his right eye, highlighted that he occasionally got into brawls when he went off and wasn't scheduled to stay in the cloisters.

His dark brown hair cut short on the sides, revealing an intricate tattoo which was inked into the sides and back of his head. His hair was sculpted back on the top. He stopped and took the box off the shelf. His full lips occasionally pulled a smirk of arrogance, before walking away from the bookshelf, carrying to box towards Reira.

"Maybe I Was," Tryiar replied as he walked closer to Reira, as he uncovered a small medical box hidden next to the books scattered on the shelf.

"And maybe I had the right idea…" he replied as he opened a small box, revealing three medium-sized vials of a dark blue substance..

"It's Kalita, and you know it's not restricted…" Reira replied, as she stood up, grabbing the box from him, closing its lid and placing it on her bed next to Carila.

"I know it's not restricted, but we have all noticed it, your distant, you don't seem to care anymore…" he replied.

Reira was taken back by his caring before her emotions took back control.

"Don't act like you care, I didn't forget what you told me that first day we met…" she scowled.

"Really Reira, I was a hotheaded isolated idiot then…" Tryiar snapped, trying to forget his attitude then.

"Don't forget racist…" Carila chipped in abruptly, he turned towards her and scared at her with his piercing blue eyes.

"Ok, fine, I was racist. I'm not proud of it…" Tryiar snapped back, he stepped back towards the wall,

"You told me I was a Dirty Mak, and that I wasn't even worthy of being in your presence…" she remarked, trying to push back the emotions of that event.

"That hurt me, I was going through a lot of… things…" Reira cried out, her eyes flickering , trying to push back tears. Her emotions running close to the surface.

"Rei.." Carila called out, trying to stop Reira from talking,

"It's, it's okay Cari..He needs to know, he needs to understand..I can't keep this hidden forever" she cried out.

"Less than a month before the initiation… my sister, Numarii, she took her own life..." Reira mumbled, her voice straining under the emotion.

"She is the one that should be here, but I took her place, we scored the same during the tests, but they chose her…" Reira added as she fell to her knees, tears streaming down her cheeks. She slammed her hands against the floor in anger.

Tryiar's face dropped, his bravado crumbled. Gone were his broad shoulders, his imposing stature ended, he looked at her. Wanting to say something but knowing it wouldn't be received.

"I was looking for someone who would understand, another Impiri who would listen but you rejected me..." Reira tried to regain her composure, struggling to her feet.

"I could have ended my life that day, I felt so alone. It had turned my life upside down," she turned away from both of them, trying to hide her face.

"That's being polite about it, my life was a total mess." Reira added, walking around the table,

"If only there was a way to get away from our differences, that our similarities would help keep me focused. Having spent years with others, it was nice to see an Impiri face looking out at me during the initiation. But it wasn't a face I expected to see, I had never seen a face of such disgust and loathing, I felt I could cut myself in half." Reira looked up, forced a grin, before resting her hands on the table and nodded.

"Oh, you didn't know that I noticed the look of disgust, don't lie you knew that I felt a connection between us, that we could..." she spoke, her voice calming down, opening up her feelings to him was comforting.

"Reira, I'm...sorry, I didn't know... if I had known..." he stuttered.

"I would have..." Tryiar added, interrupting Reira confession.

"Pitied me, I didn't want your pity, I wanted your support," she interrupted, her voice pithy and full of spite.

"I don't know what I would have done, honestly I wouldn't have been such a..." Tryiar confessed, he couldn't hide his feelings, at that time he was been angry against all from a red house, something had driven him to hate her family.

"Heartless bastard..." Carila added as she comforted Reira, wiping a tear away from Reira's face.

Tryiar looked uncomfortable.

"You know, we come from different houses, but I didn't see our similarities. I had been brought up with our kind, distrusting of others. I should have had my own opinions, but I was young, first time out in the real world" he said in a quiet voice.

"I promised my father I would be true to our people" he added proudly, before realising how it sounded, then lowering his tone as he continued to speak.

"I saw that as anyone from the blue, I couldn't trust a red, not after a member of a red house strung my older sister along, a red called..."

"I thought I recognised her face at the initiation…" Reira interrupted.

"Arantha, my older sister, she was heartbroken, and I promised her that I would never fall for the charms and beauty of a red. That's why you and me were distant for all those years, Because she had fallen for him, and it hurt her when he broke it off, all because of her house. And I..I didn't want to potentially fall for you..." he added nervously, he looked at Reira, before lowering his gaze.

Reira looked at him, it was her fault. She had spoken to her aunt, about seeing Tyco with a girl from the blue. The night before her sister died she faintly remembered hearing a heated argument between her aunt and Tyco.

"I know I shouldn't have done or said those things, I didn't want to get to know you, in case I ever fell for you..." he conceded, raising his gaze again this time looking at Reira, seeing how she was taking his response.

"And you think gave you a reason to completely destroy my confidence."

"Yes I admit it, I had spoken to my aunt, told her what I had seen, knowing she wouldn't approve, but Tyco, my cousin never listened to anyone, I didn't think he would have broken it off. He didn't care about anyone's opinions."

Tryiar arched his eyebrow

"Although this may be true, tell me why would you have done such a thing..." he paused before replying. "Wouldn't it be better if we as a people got over our differences, instead of ruining our lives?" Tryiar added as he nervously ran his fingers through his hair.

Reira nodded in response, staring at the floor, ashamed of her actions.

"Maybe without knowing, our own hatred and mistrust caused this?" He remarked, his own emotions getting the best of him.

Reira jumped to attention as she heard this, she wasn't going to take his accusations without a fight, her face tensed, her lips pursed, she clenched her fists before speaking.

"I never meant for it to break them up, just that my aunt should have been aware!" she said with an intense fierceness in her voice, her eyes glowing, this reaction caused Tryiar to step further away. Objects in the room levitated and swirled around the room chaotically.

"Rei... stop it!" Carila cried out, reaching for Reira, but Reira didn't hear her.

Tryiar knew he had hit a nerve, but he couldn't stop, his emotions took control, he knew he should have stopped, but he continued to goad her.

"Fine, but you do this and you know I was right, you have a problem Reira, I mean you can't do this and expect no one to get hurt" he cursed taking a back step, just as a book from the shelf wizzed past his head.

"You'll end up dead at this rate..." he shouted, staring at her.

"Enough of your lies" Reira shouted, drawing her hands into fists again.

Carila stood up and stood between them, trying to break up the argument, she couldn't condone fighting.

"Maybe I'm not the one who should end up dead" she screamed as the mirror was ripped out of the wall and hurtled towards Tryiar, crashing into his side, knocking him to the floor, before a vase crashed into his skull, knocking him unconscious.

Carila held out her hand for her to stop, putting herself between Reira and the now unconscious Tryiar.

"Listen" she said in a calm, soothing voice, forcing back her own emotions.

"All I want is the best for you, Rei, you know I'm here for you, but Tryiar is right." She stopped clearing her throat, tears forming, causing her to flutter her eyelids to stop them from falling.

"Rei, I can't help you if you are not willing to stop." She pleaded, tears slowly trickling out of her eyes.

Reira stopped, she sank to the floor in a heap, bundling herself into a protective position, drawing her knees up, she slowly rocked, closing her eyes slowly.

The items which had been flying around stopped mid air and crashed to the floor; the room was now a mess, but she didn't care.

"What have I done, I can't do this anymore" Reira exclaimed. She realised the stupidity of this all. It was about time she listened to someone who cared about her.

She sat on the floor; her face covered by her disheveled hair, her eyes were sunken and red.

Across from her the mirror lay on the floor, ripped from the wall and smashed to pieces, she mumbled to herself before raising her hands to her face and wiping the hair away. She stared at the fragments of the mirror with curiosity, lost in thought, she looked down into her lap, there it was, the same blade which had been made years earlier. Tryiar lay unconscious on the floor near the door, a broken vase lay beside him, blood seeping out of a wound on his forehead.

She sat there looking down at the blade, dark thoughts running through her mind, the same dark thoughts that had ran through her mind years before. With one hand she stroked the blade, the stone blade was cold to the touch, delicate chisel marks covered its surface, she could remember the countless hours she had spent chipping away at the blade, trying to polish it with a small strip of leather from one of her belts.

Her thoughts, the same thoughts she had while creating the blade were as prevalent now as they were then, but now somewhat different, darker. The urges to lash out were stronger. She placed her hand on the handle, her fingers caressed the knurled wood. Lost in thought she grabbed the handle, resting the blade on her forearm. Her skin tightened once the blade touched her skin.

"Do it...you know you can, you can control this. Maybe you're not strong enough. I know your feelings..." she murmured to herself, her voice reverberating in her throat.

She stared at the blade again, feeling the urge to slice through her wrist. Release the pent up anger and sadness which had been welling up in her.

Memories of her sisters death flashed into her mind,

Remembering that time was difficult for her, she began to cry, remembering seeing her sister with her arm sliced open, and the blood, she couldn't forget the blood. The pool of blood which she had to clear up once her sister was taken to the mortuary.

She looked at the blade again, the voice in her head whispered to her again.

"Come on, you know it and I know it, you are not as strong as your sister, and even she took a way out, if your not going to let me do what I want, I'm going to make sure that I find someone who will do as I want. You must set me free".

This time the voice had said something which shocked Reira, it had explained what it had wanted with her, to control her, to allow it to fulfil some action, which she would have to be witness to.

Carila looked across the room, frozen with fear. Tryiar was stirring, he murmured as he tried to fully regain his consciousness, grabbing at the wound on his head, he winced in pain.

"Rei, what are you doing?" Carila's voice cut through the room, waking Reira from her thoughts. She looked down, seeing the blade in her hands, before dropping it into her lap. Tears began building in her eyes, her eyelashes flickering as she tried to force the tears away.

"I need help..." she cried.

"I'm here for you, I always will be..." Carila added as she crouched down and held Reira as she slowly cried, Carila held her close, placing Reira's head on her chest, before planting a kiss on Reira's head, as she sobbed uncontrollably.

Reira awoke, tears running down her cheeks, blood slowly seeped from the injection point in her forearm, the capsule of Kalita was on the floor next to the contents of the box which had been strewn across the floor as it had fallen off the seat.

CHAPTER 20

10 Days Later
Outside the Citadel
23rd Hour of the 16th Day of the 8th Month
IY (Imperial Year) 101

Reira paused, sighed, and then spoke, "I...I?." She shuttered, her breaths short, she clenched her fists,

"Ila ek, Nomas Dineh Somanek?" - Young Lady, What will be your method of death' He asked, taking Reira by surprise, he was speaking Onal'ne, one of the Impiri languages, Reira looked at him with a confused look, how did he know Onal'ne, how did he know it was the language of her tribe, this was a language only spoken between people of the same tribe, an outsider would have been spoken to in Okal'na-ni, a generalised Impiri language understood by all Impiri. Countless thoughts ran though her mind before being interrupted by him speaking again.

"Miss, what's your poison?..?" He asked again, this time in Seemdi (Standard Empire Dialect) , Reira stood there in shock.

He made a drinking gesture, that made Reira laugh, a genuine honest laugh, releasing her stress, even for just a moment.

She looked at him, thinking of a response before replying.

"Ila ek?, Dama Manek Silas, Falkdhi Di? Camas di Tai Fabria Onal'ne?- (young lady?, I'm sure I'm actually older than you are...but how do you know Onal'ne?) she joked in response.

He looked at her, trying to access her response before smiling then bursting out laughing, completely changing the atmosphere at the bar.

"Definitely Makla Hara Dasho? Am I right?, and to answer your questions, it's good to know about the people who walk into your bar…." He replied, as he cleaned a glass before putting it on the bar, the small glass was intricately designed, but had seen better days, the edges were chipped and the bottom of the glass was stained black.

"But how did you know I was Makla Hara Dasho, Impiri is a given, but specifically knowing my mother tongue, most wouldn't even know where to start, there are hundreds of dialects and over a hundred primary languages." Reira questioned, totally absorbed by the conversation, ignoring everything in the bar, other patrons stopped and looked at her, before continuing on their way.

He looked at her and smiled, as he poured a drink from a purple bottle into the small glass he had just cleaned.

"Your right, Impiri was a given, as a good bar keeper it's good to keep your eye on things. It's the little details that make the difference. Such as..." he gestured towards Reira's wrists.

"I noticed that you were more likely to be from a red house, only the red houses keep their marking hidden, if you was from a White House, it would be easier to notice." He laughed, as he continued to tidy the bar,

"Now, narrowing it down to Makla Hara Dasho, that's more of an observation, I noticed the Elit'to that you are wearing."

Reira quickly placed her hand on her neck, brushing her fingers across its surface, it was exquisite. Its surface was sculpted out of gold, a few small scarlet jewels were imbedded in its surface.

"Most traditional Impiri would wear one of these?, it's quite common" She replied, about forty percent of Impiri wore an Elit'to, especially the females.

"But a gold Elit'to, only a Makla Hara Dasho would wear something as traditional as that..., so I took a gamble..."

Reira sat herself on a stool near the bar, she looked around taking in the atmosphere, the sights the smells, everything, it was exhilarating.

"By the way, I'm Kala-Linis Cthonall, most of the patrons of this bar just call me Linis..." he added as he placed the drink in front of Reira.

Out from a door behind the bar a young Impiri woman appeared, not more than sixteen years old, she wore simple clothes, with her dark auburn hair tied into a braided ponytail. She kept looking down, not once raising her gaze. She grabbed a cloth from under the bar and cleaned its surface; she wasn't paying attention to anything else, just kept cleaning, she cleaned around Reira's drink, before slowly glancing up, feeling Reira's gazing at her in her subconscious.

She became distracted by the purple liquid in the glass. followed by a flash of recognition appeared across her face. She looked up and locked eyes with Reira; she starred for what must have felt for an eternity, as time seamed to stand still before shyly looking down again, her hands nervously shaking.

"I'm sorry, forgive my intrusion..." she spoke, her voice trembled, her voice echoed her innocence.

Reira looked at her and for a second she saw herself, she smiled a gentle smile before slowly glancing down, the young woman's wrist was wrapped up in a bandage, hiding her wrist.

"Why do you hide it?" Reira asked, carefully placing her hand on the young girls wrist.

"....because I'm afraid that people will think differently about me when they know..." she stuttered.

'I had the same feelings when I was about your age..." Reira replied, as she pulled back her sleeve, revealing her dark red tattoo, the sight of this brought a look of fear into the young girl's eyes....

"What's wrong...?" Reira enquired, taken back by the young girls fear.

"That's the mark of a Lady of the House of Abrasar..." she gasped.

"My Lady..." she replied, bowing slightly, as she unraveled the bandage from around her wrist. Reira was fixated as she slowly unraveled it.

As she unraveled it, it revealed a dark red tattoo; it was a basic design, from a lower status house.

"Is that.., the house of Nalle? I thought that house died out, my mother had told me that all members were killed during a raid on the Ralboe Military Base above Kaelte..."

"There was one survivor..." she pulled back her collar revealing a massive burn scar, which looked like it covered most of her upper body.

"Didn't you get…" Reira's voice trailed off.

"Treatment, some, but the cost of such treatment is so expensive, Linis tries to put some credits aside for occasional treatment, but I've grown accustomed to..." she paused, her nerves getting the best of her.

"The pain" the added nervously.

"You know who I am?" Reira asked, her voice cracking with nerves.

"Yes, my Lady" before noticing a ring on Reira's left thumb, her voice changing tone, becoming even more respectful.

"I mean, Your Eminence" she whispered.

"Linis here was stationed at Ralboe, before the raid, during the aftermath he rescued me, he brought me up. I've been living here since I was 3, he tries to keep me informed about my Impiri heritage, he even learnt..."

"Onal'ne, I've already had the pleasure of his Onal'ne skills, quite impressive, and now I can understand why he learnt it..."

"He must care for you a great deal...?" Reira added.

"He even partitioned the council in regards to my linage. He never heard from them, one of his sources said that the council were even here on Prim..."

"Why would you want to talk to the council?, your life here is good, you'll learn a lot about people, working and living somewhere like this, you at least have the freedom.." Reira enquired, placing her hand on Apairtae's,

"I know they are not much to look at, these Hanakarians, but they are good people."

"I know" she looked over at her father, who was still busy cleaning.

"I want to serve our people. I know they won't accept me, why should they, the daughter of a fallen house..." her voice becoming saddened,

"I want to restore my family's position...I don't want to be the last of the house of Nalle"

Linis glanced over, and saw his adopted daughter striking up a conversation with Reira, for the first time she was holding an honest conversation with another Impiri, Linis grinned slightly, while cleaning the glasses that had been used earlier that day. 'It's about time she talked to her own kind' he thought to himself, it was a nice surprise to see them talking to each other.

"Apairtae my Dear?" Linis remarked, gesturing for his daughter to join him from across the bar.

"Ok father, I'll be over in a second..." she replied, grabbing the bandages, as she began to re-wrap her wrist before stopping, looking across at Reira who nodded gently, before unwrapping the bandages again and leaving them on the counter.

"Thank you..." She sheepishly replied.

That moment a old woman approached the bar, knocking over the glass and stumbling into Reira, taking her by surprise.

"That we should forget that fateful hour in its place for her dead sister knows where she's going. and knows beyond all of us that dreams do come back to haunt, that the child of the blood should divide the sand of her ancestors" she mumbled, startling Reira.

Linis rushed over before gestured for her to go away, shooing her into another part of the bar.

"Take no notice of Gir Lya, she's spent too long reading old scriptures, she's always trying to scare away my customers, but honestly, she is harmless..." Linis added, as he wiped up the spilt drink on the bar.

Reira sat there, staring at the bars surface before glancing over at her own wrist, staring at her own markings, lost in thought.

The next morning, the bar is empty, the chairs turned upside down on the tables, Apartae makes her way through the tables, brushing the floor with a long handled broom, while Linis is rubbing a waxy substance into the wooden bars surface before stopping. Noticing a small envelope sitting at the corner of the bar. He slowly picked up the envelope, turning it over, reading the name inscribed on its surface. "Apartae..." it read elegantly, in a dark purple ink.

"Apartae, my dear there is something here for you..." he called out, as he placed the envelope back on the bars surface. Apartae stopped what she was doing and came over to the bar, seeing the envelope as she got closer.

"Who's it from." She enquired, picking up the envelope, turning it over, no other inscriptions marked its surface.

"You'll have to opened it and find out, I haven't got a clue" he responded jokingly.

Apartae ran her finger nails down the end of the envelope, catching the corner of the envelope with her nail, before slowly tearing it open, revealing a folded letter.

She pulled out the letter, nervously unfolding it, she stood there in silence, her eyes widened, her breathing deepening with every moment. Linis looked at her, concerned by her expression,

"Come on dear, read it out,," he exclaimed.

"Okay, father, it's just...I'll try, it's just a bit of a surprise" she paused, composing herself before reading the letter out aloud.

"Dear Apartae,

Our brief conversation last night, made an impact on me, your courage in your persuit of your families honour rang true with the thoughts of honour and heritage that run through my own mind.

I too am the only remaining daughter. You have suffered more than most would be able to deal with. The loss of your family and the loss of your birthright, the emotional scars as deep as the physical scars you now bare, I can't eliviate the emotional scars, only time can fade those, but the physical ones, that's something I can do.

I spoke with my mother last night, she knew your father well. When I told her about meeting you, it stirred something inside me, and I couldn't let it go.

I do hope you accept this small token from me and my family. Your father spoke to me last night about your treatments after our conversation, so I have arranged, if you are willing to accept. That you are to undergo a full restorative treatment to heal your wounds, eliminate your scars. Don't worry about the cost, that has already been paid.

House Abrasar is honoured to help the daughter of house Nallae. We are of the same blood, you and me, separated by circumstance, it's my honour to help support your recovery. You are welcome to contact me at anytime.

Your sister, - Reira"

Apartae stood there, tears running down her cheeks, she looked over at her father, who tried to wipe his own tears from his face, trying to hide his emotions.

"I can't believe she did that father, but why...", she spoke a she walked over to him, placing the letter on the bar.

"Maybe my dear, she sees someone blighted by circumstances, someone who's life she can change." He stopped, looking at the letter himself.

"Did you notice the details at the bottom, she's booked you in at the hospital today. And it's not the clinic, it's at the medical centre in the citadel." He paused in thought, seeming to be working out something in his mind before continuing.

"I mean that treatments got to be costing more than a hundred thousand credits....and she's done that for you." He looked at her.

"You mean there wont even be scars, and the pain will be gone, forever."

My dear, you won't even be able to tell that it had ever happened." He replied, pulling her close, hugging her tightly.

"Then I better make my way to the citadel then, don't want to miss an appointment..." she whispered as she cried in his arms.

"You go, I'll be fine here until you get back..." he calmly added.

* * *

44 Years Previous

Iridani System
23rd Hour of the 4th Day of the 2nd Month
IY (Imperial Year) 67

The dreams this time were clear, her memories of this time still echoed throughout her mind. But reliving them this way, it started her how vividly she had remembered them, Reira sat looking out into the middle distance, she was gone, her hand clasping the crook of her arm, a small drop of Kalita coated the tip of her finger.

No amount of study or prayers to any of the gods or goddesses would allow her to succeed in this endeavour, the Cloisters were supposed to mould you into being the best you could be, but it was more like perpetual bondage, and who would benefit from such a system, the government, the social elite. But at what cost, her sanity she would question.

Her kind would stand behind her, but not trust her allegiance to her people, being the second citizen was a great honour, but what pride would there be in being Impiri? Would she hold on to tradition, would she be a voice for changes within her people, or would she be the cause of more divide.

At this time in her life, These thoughts ran through Reira's mind on an daily basis, sometimes the pressure became too much, sending her on a downward spiral. Only Carila could pull her out of these dark times.

Reira sat on the edge of the bed, Carila sat beside her, she didn't say anything, she just listened to what Reira had to say.

"The Impiri system is complicated, twelve major tribes ruled over three billion, each tribe comprised thousands of families loyal to the tribal elders, such as my father." She paused, memories of her father flooding back. She spoke again, forcing back her tears.

"Each family was placed within a caste within Impiri society. The twelve finally managed to reunite the Impiri after the fall" she mumbled to herself.

"I know I couldn't change the Impiri nature by myself. I mean many had tried, but none had succeeded"

"Hopefully by attaining the role of codex would allow me to draw attention to the inequality of my people. Revealing to them that even though they work together to call a ceasefire on over a thousand years of civil war, prejudices between the houses ran deep and mistrust had taken over.", she shook her head,

"Maybe we are doomed to fall into it again...that we are close to falling back into open warfare, not since the Idmin Samis Doro'shal - Night of Ten Thousand Deaths which forced the ceasefire of the last war, four thousand years ago."

Carila looked at her,

"You can't be expected to be everything to all Impiri?" She added.

Reira turned over and looked at her, wiping the tear that ran down her own cheek.

"It's not that simple, I should be the one to fix this, a chance like this won't come again, I mean, no Impiri has had such power in the empire, long gone are the days of one Impiri leading our people, but I must try and bring balance"

"All because of our inability to solve the issues that had originally separated us, simple tribal differences, traditions, and language had separated us, even though common similarities had merged us into one people, on the surface things were brilliant, but beneath the surface, simple prejudices still ruled. To reach out to them, to bring them inside would be an achievement..."

The dream shifted, hours had past.

Reira sat on the floor of her room, Carila was out at one of the libraries, Reira was contemplating her future.

A concerned look grew across her face,

"He dared to call me that…" she whispered.

She hadn't been called this name before; she remembered her father mention it to her as something she might be called, but never expected it to happen in the Cloisters, even the hallowed grounds of the cloisters were subject to the racial hatred of her people.

The Iridani system was the centre for learning across the empire, the highest level of academia and research were scattered from the surface of Arkaedia. Reira's mind drifted to the day that she had first seen the sights of Arkaedia. She and a few of her fellow acolytes were granted leave for a few days to see the sights. A privilege that only a few of them were granted.

* * *

She had spent many days studying the scriptures, every nuance in its translation, reading some in their original language.

Some of them updated post-cataclysm, some verses were permanently embedded into her memory, of the three books of her order, the first was the book most memorised.

Finding the scripture marked the beginning of a change in Reira, she threw herself into a pure devotion to the cause, anything that would fulfil her soul, with a focus on the one thing which joined all together, faith. It was a focus on something which was above the petty differences between people; it was on the things that made them similar, it could be simply put as ego.

The basic need of one individual to put the needs of the empire above the needs of even her own family, her house, the tribe she was brought up into and even her own dreams and desires.

This marked a change in her approach to her studies, her grades increased. She saw the knowledge from a wider perspective that before, with a focus on conciliation of ideas into a simple defined theory. However this change in perspective, had consequences, ones to change her life forever.

* * *

The dream shifted again, ten days had past, Reira remembered this time, she hadn't thought about this time in years. She couldn't control her dreams at times, trying to focus her memories onto a specific time in her life occasionally threw out memories of times she had long forgotten. She smiled as she stared out into the distance, letting the memory overwhelm her.

"Now take a deep breath, your doing fine…" a voice spoke, the sound of the voice began to distort.

"Just control your breathing…We are nearly done…."

Reira came to with a thudding headache, this pain was quickly forgotten by even more pain, radiating throughout her back. Every nerve in her back was firing, overloading her synapses, causing her headache, She closed her eyes trying to force the pain away.

Every centimetre of her back throbbed with pain, like a beating heart, the pain travelling across her back in waves.

The pain pulsating in time with her hearts. She tried to move, but was unable, the pain inhibited her movement. She opened her eyes slowly, staring at the floor, her face resting in a hole in a circular pillow, she was suspended mid air. A gentle breeze blew in from an opening door, the second the breeze touched her skin the pain increased, every sensation doubled. She had thought the procedure would be painful, she usually had a high threshold for pain, but this was above any pain she had experienced.

"Miss Abrasar, are you awake?" A voice echoed out throughout the brightly lit room.

"Yeah, Laeanna I'm awake, how long was I out for?" Reira replied exhaustedly, her back pulsing with pain, the simple act of replying caused pain.

"To be honest, you were only out for about an hour, enough time for me to clean up." Leanna replied as she carefully stared at Reira's back.

"I couldn't stand the pain anymore" Reira commented in reply, wincing slightly as the pain ebbed and flowed across her body.

She slowly tried to raise herself from the apparatus, and there was nothing but pain, she cursed under her breath and tried to move, but was unable. The pain was too great,. She gave up and relaxed, easing the pain slightly.

"I was surprised you lasted as long as you did, most never have his done in one session, especially with this type of ink, this normally burns down deep into your skin. I've seen Impiri faint before, having this type of work done." Laeanna exclaimed, admiring her own work which was now emblazoned on Reira's back.

"Especially when having sanctified and blessed inks inscribed into your skin, even the most devout have half the work done in consecrated inks, but you went full." Laeanna replied, still taken back by the situation she had been placed in.

"I've only ever seen one gifted individual have this, and he was unconscious afterwards for about a day." She added.

Laeanna's voice echoed before Reira felt a easing in her muscles after a sharp pain radiated throughout her right shoulder.

"The pain is fading, what happened..." Reira enquired,

"Kalita injection, straight into your nerve bundle. Should take the edge off for a few hours, you should hopefully be okay to go in a few hours." Laeanna paused, as she carefully pulled a needle out of Reira's shoulder, she was lost in thought for a few seconds before continuing

"I honestly have no idea." She remarked quizzically and gradually helped remove Reira from the apparatus, being careful not to touch the inscriptions. Reira winced in pain as she stood up for the first time, looking at a screen in-front of her she could see the detail of the work undertaken, she smiled an approving smile as she nodded her head.

A small flying drone sprayed a faint mist onto her back as she looked at herself,

"I would refrain from using your abilities for a while, and gradually use them, the reaction between your abilities and your inscriptions will be severe." Laeanna added as she inspected the work, making sure it was perfect.

"The enzymes in the ink will react violently the first time, the pain my overwhelm your pain receptors. Don't worry it is normal after a few instances it should be fine." Laeanna commented as she passed Reira a light silk robe to wrap herself in, Reira wrapped the robe around her waist, before slowly pulling up a loose fitting skirt.

"In accordance to your requirements, you have every one of the six incantations inscribed on your back. It is surely a piece of art. Your scales will be sensitive for quite a while, I would avoid any intimate contact with them for a few weeks."

Reira was about to speak, before stopping, trying to hide her emotions.

"It's not likely that they will get stimulated, it's not my kind of thing." Reira replied sharply, trying to hide her emotions.

Laeanna looked at her, quizzically before replying

"Just in case, I can prescribe a desensitising nano treatment, it would block all sensations from your scales for about 3-5 days, before wearing off"

Reira reached back, looking at her scales in the mirror, the scales were dark blue. She slowly caressed the ridge which surrounded the scales, but Reira couldn't feel any pleasurable sensations, the pain coursing through her body overrode the sensations, but she could feel a sense of euphoria, as she touched them the sense of euphoria grew, every time she breathed in the smell of her own pheromones filled her senses.

Laeanna left Reira as she looked at the tattoo, Reira didn't even notice her leaving, she was lost in thought. She had finally made this change, she had wanted this for years, father had surroorted her decision, but her mother had always disapproved, based on fear of her not being able to find a partner based on the level of work she had done.

Reira stood alone looking at the screen which was still relaying images of her tattoo, Laeanna had done a brilliant job the inscriptions were perfect, each of the inscriptions intertwined with each other, creating six individual tattoos but also merged into one singular piece of work. As she looked at the tattoo, she could feel sensations emanating from one of the tattoos, she had been thinking about Numarii, she would have loved the tattoo.

The tattoo started to glow, Reira's breathing became deeper, as she tried to control her thoughts. Her eyes closed she as focused, the pain emanating from the tattoo was now close to the sensation of being burnt. The pain intensified to the point in which the tattoo started to bleed. Her entire back was now bleeding, "arrrrrgh" she cried out, before falling to the floor.

Laeanna rushed in, seeing Reira slumped on the floor, the entire tattoo was emanating light, and bleeding. She quickly dashed towards a wall panel, waved her hand over the panel which then slid open to reveal a plethora of different medicines and medical contraptions.

This threw Reira out of her dreams, she stood her head,

"I couldn't forget that could I, the most pain I've ever experienced." She mumbled to herself, as she reached over to the wooden box which sat beside her, a second dose of Kalita still waiting to be used, Reira grabbed hold of the device, before slowly injecting in into her left arm. She winced as the Kalita took affect, slowly travelling through her body, she could feel her sensations heightening, her vision began to dim, she lay to one side, next to the wooden box, as the Kalita sent her to sleep.

Reira awoke, this sight was familiar....a time she would have rather forgotten completely, but she had to witness it again.

It had been over twenty years since she had gotten herself tattooed, this place was familiar.

Iridani System
Imperial Year 90

Reira sat there looking to her left, the crowd was enormous; it was difficult for anyone to spot members of their own family, she stared, scanning each row before finally finding them, they were 8th row back, father stood there in full military formal dress, next to her mother who was dressed in a traditional colourful Impiri dress. Once she caught Reira's gaze she smiled and waved, Reira smiled a quick smile and laughed to herself, mother was always like this informal events, always breaking from the norm.

To Reira's right everyone involved in their development was seated, the principle lecturers, guidance councillors, drill instructors, tutors and medical staff, each of them smiling, putting on their best formal smile, hiding the fact of how harsh and struggling the time at the cloisters was.

"Let's give our successful candidate a warm welcome" the crowd began to clap as the principal walked onto the stage, followed by Lidise Baeil, Reira's face expressed her emotions, ignoring Lidise's speech about tests and the struggles faced, he mentioned the teachers and us and how we all got on perfectly. 'Such a liar' she thought looking at him with distrust, sabotaging her final test, and forcing her to fail. She should have been the one standing there. She looked down at her hands as they were clenched, her fingernails digging into her palms, a small stream of blood made it's way out of her palms onto the floor.

"Oh, and I almost forgot about this" he spoke, just as he was about to turn away from the crowd, he looked directly at Reira, her hearts beating deep within her chest, "To my friend, the only person who pushed me to achieve, Reira." He smirked, knowing this would enrage Reira but she would be unable to do anything about it.

"May the Empire find a great use for your skills, in whatever you choose to do after today"

She almost stood up, her emotions running high.

"How dare he even..." she murmured, Carila quickly placed her hand on Reira's knee, distracting her.

"Rei, you know he's trying to get you agrivated, let him have it. You know you can do anything now?

"I mean, I'm going into the diplomatic corp, I mean me, you know how hard it is for an Amarian to get into the corp. the. Last one was over a thousand years ago...."

Reira looked st her, and smiled, her thoughts drifting away from the rage she was feeling. Cari, I'm proud of you, you know. I still haven't decided where I'm going, I might look at becoming a historian, the library at Abdax has reached out to me, but so has the temple..."

"You mean?"

"Yes, that temple, I could start again, go back to my roots.".

Reira awoke violently, her dream having kicked her out, she looked around in a daze, her vision still blurred before gradually focusing.

These dream had stirred old memories which she had almost forgotten about, but now they were at the front of her mind, why had her mind shown her these things, why was she seeing the most painful memories of her life. Either emotional or physical pain, it was pain nevertheless.

She reached over to the box, pulling out a small device, her fingers glided effortlessly across its screen.

10th Hour of the 28th Day of the 8th Month
IY (Imperial Year) 101

The normal fare around a media event was disrupted by a explosion so severe that countless members of the media were killed. A secondary podium that was going to be used by Carila had exploded moments before Carila was about to make a speech. She had only just arrived after finalising the plans for her speech to the Empire after the ceremony.

"Reira," Carila shouted as she searched for her, amongst the confusion created by the blast. She coughed as the smoke from the blast permeated the air.

There, lying on the courtyard floor behind the first pedestal was her best friend, Reira. She lay motionless on the ground, semi covered by Sargent Vero, she had been shielded from the brunt of the blast by his body, covered in ash, her arm had been cut by a piece of shrapnel and blood was pouring out, pooling on the floor.

"Rei," she screamed, noticing Reira's motionless body, her voice crying out, she could nearly hear herself, her ears still ringing from the blast.

"Ma'am, please step back, we haven't cleared the area, there might be.." a voice said, walking from behind her,

"I don't care, if there is more, and she is dead, then they better take me too, she's my friend, I..." she trailed off, as she saw Reira cough and splutter as she regained consciousness.

'Don't you dare die on me' Carila thought to herself, "you've come way too far" she cursed.

Tears started to fall from her eyes. The thought loosing Reira pushing her to the edge, someone who had been part of her life for so long. What someone had done drove her mad. Her fists clenching, Suddenly, Rako stepped quickly into her field of view placing his left hand on her shoulder, "Carila, is she ...okay."

"I heard about the blast, while I was observing the final preparations for her residence, I came as quickly as I could..." he spoke, his voice laboured, his breathing heavy.

"I just don't know, she's drifted between consciousness and unconsciousness for the last few minutes, but her breathing has become erratic, the medic told me to not move her, and just keep talking to her...an Impiri Doctor is on his way, he should be here any time now.." Carila explained as she tried to brush the dust and dirt away from Reira's face with her hand.

A Few Hours Later.

From her window to the east of the courtyard, she could see a flurry of doctors and medical staff performing triage on the other survivors of the blast. The lives of some of the citizens were close to ending,

"May the goddesses help them find their way..." she exclaimed.

Death had come quickly to a large number of the attendees, the citizens surrounding the bomb were incinerated instantly, followed by third-degree burns on those further away, and shrapnel wounds caused the death of countless more. A few had been trampled by the rush of people trying to make their way out of the courtyard into the surrounding gardens.

Reira looked down at His burnt body, he had been her

security detail, his body had taken the brunt of the blast, far enough away to avoid the incineration, but the blasts shockwave had broken his back, shielding Reira from the blast.

His eyes flickering slowly. His uniform burnt and bloody, he tried to speak, coughing as he tried, the smoke and damage to his lungs made it difficult.

"You..your...eminence" he stuttered, coughing blood.

"In her name..." he coughed again, before exhaling his final breath.

Reira stood there, looking at him, watching the life finally drain from his eyes, she carefully placed her fingers on his face, closing his eyes slowly.

"In the name of the goddess, please accept the light from our dear departed brother, Vero. He gave his life in attempts to save my own. Please guide him to rebirth so he can be rewarded for his devotion..." she murmured before removing her hand and blessing herself.

Reira turned slowly to the right and made her way towards the door, stopping at a display, and began to watch the news feed of coverage of the blast.

After watching the news feed, and commentaries by journalists debating the merits of having a Impiri as a Codex, or the opposing opinion, expressed by a Zathian political commentator, Reira had become nervous again. Especially when a few people who she had met at the bar, had expressed there views on her, some one had leaked information to the media, and this made Reira fearful. Even more so after the explosion.

"Carila, are you sure you're up for this meeting? She asked.

Carila was standing by the door, waiting for Reira to finally leave, they should have been there ten minutes ago and Carila started to sigh,

"Rei, I mean Your Eminence, you know your in good hands, and as your aide, I'm ready to go into this with you. "We are are ready as we are every going to be, well, I'm ready."

Reira was lost in thought, the news report began covering the explosion again, and then listed the names of those who had died, followed by the speech from the head of security his role as head of the second legion now under scrutiny as this had happened under his watch.

"I wonder why this meeting is so important, that it couldn't be communicated via the comm system. And why the secrecy of the meeting, only you and me know of this, and ..."

Reira stopped her.

"Maybe he found something, maybe I can feel some sort of normality...if they've found out who's behind all of this."

Three Days Later

18th Hour of the 31st Day of the 8th Month
IY (Imperial Year) 101

Carila looked uncomfortable.

"You know you can't do that," she said in a quiet voice. "He will be made to pay, but if the media get ahold of this, we've lost."

Praetor Damar, arched his eyebrow, surprised by Reira's response.

"Although this may be true, wouldn't it be better if he lead us to the others that conspired against you...let's say, we let him know that we know what he's done, and offer him a way to redeem himself....maybe exile for life, instead of life in the harshest prison in the empire. In which he wouldn't last more than five months?"

Carila nodded, looking over at Reira, she was stunned into silence, the only reaction was the sound of her knuckles cracking, as she slowly clenched her fists.

Her eyes were glowing, Carila stood there, frozen with fear against the wall, Reira's expression was of pure hatred, Carila knew what she wanted to do, she wanted to find him and end his life, he had to die, the betrayal was too deep to just forget, Carila jumped in front of Reira as she walked towards the door causing Reira to stop on the spot.

"I don't want to have to move you out the way" she pleaded in a huff.

"I don't care about what you don't want to do, you cannot do this by yourself, there are rules..." she interjected.

"Rules, don't talk to me about rules, he betrayed my trust, plotted to have me killed. He conspired with others to bring me here, how far does this deceit go. Has my entire life been as a pawn in someone else's game..." Reira hissed, her eyes glowing even more brightly.

"Reira, I can't let you do this, if you go out there and do this, they have won. And everything you have sacrificed will be for nothing."

"I'll make sure that he's picked up by security and hopefully, he puts up a fight so they have an excuse to kill him."

"I don't care what you want to do, he's a murderer, I know you're trying to protect me, but you know I can't let this go..."

"I don't expect you to let this go, but you have to let me handle this, this web of deceit goes further than we think, we must find a way to find out who else is involved..."

Moments later

Sensing this wasn't the right time to interrupt her ranting, her guards backed away, maintaining a fixed stare into the middle distance.

"How could they, they planned all of this, guiding my choice..." she grabbed hold of the railing in front of her, clenching her fists until her knuckles cracked. She stared into the distance.

"How...how did they get to him, make the person who I trusted, I trusted him with my wellbeing, one who was appoint...appointed by the Rev Mother to support me during the transition."

She released the railing and turned towards her guards.

"Was it one of you, that betrayed me." She screamed

"Maybe it was both of you bastards.., maybe everyone is against me." her hands clenching again, her eyes starting to glow,

At the same time she spoke, both of the guards began slowly

rising from the floor. Each of them rose about a meter into the air, Reira's eyes now completely white.

"If you admit it, I'll make the judgement quick..." She scorned

"But if you lie and I find out that you had something to do with it...! There won't be any part of your soul to send into the next life, I'll end you, and this time it will be permanently"

Looking up at each of her struggling guards, she slowly caressed their faces, pausing for a second, before slapping them. She turned from them, and began to walk away, both guards fell onto the floor and onto their knees, looking at each other in shock.

* * *

23rd Hour of the 31st Day of the 8th Month
IY (Imperial Year) 101

Rako fidgeted while sitting in his chair, he brushed back his hair which had become disheveled, his hands shaking.

The officer finally spoke;

"I'm not going to give you all the details of what you have been charged with, but the first one is treason, I'm only going to give you a choice..." he looked over his shoulder, sighed Before continuing

"My superiors have intercepted the communication that you made with a conspirator of yours, you are to meet with them as expected, but you must then leave, and when I mean leave, I mean if you are seen on any imperial world, you will be shot on sight. my superiors have granted you this option" he sat looking towards the floor,

"You said there was a choice? whats the other option?"

"My superiors thought you might ask about the other option, in accordance with the imperial statute, for a crime such as this, life in prison, in solitary confinement until the day your heart stops beating."

He glanced at the officer standing in the corner, "I'll tell you my choice, but I'll only speak to you" he gestured at the other officer, "he has to go..."

With a nearly instant motion Officer Creena ordered the room to be cleared, the other officer, quickly made his way out of the room, slamming the door behind him.

"So, what's the decision..."

First, Rako spoke " I need to have your word that I'll be allowed to meet with my acquaintances, and that I'll be allowed to leave Imperial space without any surveillance"

"I can't promise that ..." Officer Creena replied with a smile.

* * *

4th Hour of the 31st Day of the 8th Month
IY (Imperial Year) 101

A loud thud startled Rako as he wandered through the remains of the courtyard, sections of the courtyard barricaded protecting evidence from being tampered with, the flowers on a nearby wall were in full bloom,

'Akarian Moon Orchids' he thought as he caressed the beautifully ornate petals of the orchid.

The flowers cascading down the wall of the courtyard reminded him of home, his gentle and tender touch became a clench of anger as squeezed the flower he was holding, crushing its petals before releasing his grasp, allowing the now destroyed petals to cascade down onto the courtyard floor, again the thud came.

"Hey, is that you" he shouted as he began to walk closer to the sound of the disturbance

He was shocked, he frantically searched for the gate controls, before finally finding them, he flicked the switch and the gate shuddered, then he flicked it again and finally the gate started to move.

A figure appeared from behind the gate, shrouded by darkness, the figure held out its hand.

Rako reached forward to take its hand,

The instant their hands touched, the figure moved her hand and closed her fingers around his wrist, pulling him closer towards her. She quickly twisted his hand, he winced in pain. Even more as she pulled it around his back, pressing his wrist against the small of his back. She kept her self close to him, close enough that she embraced him with her other arm, she leaned over his shoulder and whispered in his ear,

"It's time to finish what you started" she whispered, then his expression changed, her face was inches from his, his face betrayed his emotions.

"Shhhh," she whispered gently into his ear,

"Your expected Visitor won't be coming" she purred.

"She knows it was you..." she added, that's when the look of realisation came across his face. He knew who it was, it was Carila.

"I never stood a chance. Did I?" He smirked, trying to crack a smile.

She spun him around, now they were face to face, she looked up at him, her eyes full of emotion.

"The sad part..." she paused and sighed,

"you did" she whispered, leaning in towards him before stepping back.

"You had the chance to walk away, leave, make your excuses and go."

"But you didn't, you committed the ultimate betrayal, not only have you turned your back on your priestess, your guide, your friend..." she paused, her fists clenching tight around the handle of the knife,

"You turned away from your goddess and stepped away from the light she casts on us, you have sworn to her name and lied directly. You attempted to destroy everything she has been working towards, a lifetime of torment, sacrifice, things you know nothing about. You have twisted and perverted the remarks of someone infinitely more spiritual and worthy than yourself to your own twisted goals."

"In the name of Ilaria, I strip you of your light, and forbid the rites of passage, into the darkness you will go, you walk alone into death"

As she spoke, she quickly plunged the crystal blade into his chest, staring straight at him, he flinched as the blade was slowly twisted, Carila kept hold of the handle and kept it in place, he was going to suffer for what he did, she leant towards his right ear and whispered.

"I do this to protect her, her light will shine and the goddess will be joyous, a new Age of Enlightenment will arise once your darkness is gone... in Reira's name I do this! Anything to keep her safe..." she implored.

"By the Gods ! you love her..." he mocked,

"Don't You. ." he added, screaming. His voice retching, full of anger.

Looking down to his torso, the blood now fully soaking into his clothing and dripping onto the floor.

He watched as the blade was gradually pulled upwards, Carila closed her eyes, trying to get the sight of his impending demise out of her mind. She wanted to remember something but not this, but the only thought in her head was the fact that the cold hand of death was reaching out to him, and she was its instrument.

She looked at him, she needed to feel something deeply, the only thing she felt was hatred, she looked into his eyes to get a glimpse of conviction in what she had done, she stared at him, but there was only fear looking back at her.

She had wanted to do something to save Reira, she needed something that meant something, but the only thing that she could see was the blade, and the look in his eyes the look that he wasn't ready to die.

The blade came close to his lungs, seeming to move inch by inch, taking an eternity, moving closer with the precision that only the end can bring. He knew that it was the end, he had to pay for his crimes.

A single glimmering tear shimmered out of his eye. He knew it was over, when he felt the first sharp sting of the pain in his chest he knew that it was going to be over soon.

She pulled the blade out of his chest and turned around, her eyes wide and full of tears.

"I've loved her since the first day we met..." she sobbed, dropping the blade to the ground, which shattered on impact with the ground, sending echoes across the courtyard.

His breathing was now shallow and laboured, his skin slowly became pale and lifeless

He had something that he needed to say, a curse that he needed to utter, and last words to send out into the world. He parted his lips,

"You know it's foolish... she can never return it..." he retched, wanting to cast that final insult before falling to the ground.

She looked down at his body, He wasn't dead yet, but he would be soon. Only a few more moments existed, She smiled, but there was sadness in her eyes. This wasn't what she had wanted for her time, something that she never thought herself capable of. It wasn't something that she had planned. But here she was, in this place, dealing with this judgement, this betrayal by Rako had caused her so much pain.

She knew that this wasn't his fault. He had been coerced by

other sources, and one day they would make themselves known. but this was a message to them, “we know you exist, and this is what happens when you hurt someone”

She had attacked him first after all. Had he defended himself, she might be the one dying on the courtyard floor. Still, she wondered whether she should have let him go. That is what he had expected to happen, but her own anger had betrayed her.

If he could have done something different he would have done it, but there wasn’t a choice.

"She will never know the truth..., and I'm fine with that..." she quietly whispered as she looked at Rako dying on the cold stone floor of the courtyard,

CHAPTER 21

Three Weeks Later

12th Hour of the 21st Day of the 10th Month
IY (Imperial Year) 101

The day had arrived, the citadel was packed, colourful banners hung all across the citadel, bringing colour to the caitadel, the vibrant colours contrasting with the pale stonework and glass that could normally be seen. People from all across the empire had made the journey, this would be an event to remember, some had travelled from the far reaches of the empire, most of the rentable residences within the city limits had been booked, Reira had only seen a few snippets of the broadcast by the media. This was to be the biggest event since the coronation of the Emperor one hundred years before. An event like this wasn't to be seen again for over a century, Reira was seventy-four, and if she lived as long as her grandmother, she had possibly another hundred and sixty years to go.

The midday sun shone brightly through the windows of the citadel, it was a perfect day.
As was tradition, Reira would make this journey alone. The heads of the Impiri houses, the heads of every great family in the empire, ambassadors from over one hundred worlds and the members of the social elite, would be there. Watching making a judgement, and billions across the empire would see the ceremony, a day like today would be remembered for

generations, some would watch for the sheer fact that an Impiri was to be elevated to such a highly respected role.

She stood still, front of a doorway, millennia old, behind her a transparent door remained shut, behind these doors dozens of people hurried around, making sure that everything was perfect, a reporter stood in the middle of the commotion, A hovering camera recorded and broadcast everything that was going on.

She stood in silence, with her heart racing, her breathing deep but controlled and beads of sweat starting to form on the back of her neck, she remembered how close she had come to ending her own life after failing over a decade earlier, Carila had found her sitting on the floor of her room, crying as she had never cried before, gripping the same sharpened blade that she had created to defend herself years before, only mere moments away from slicing through her own wrists.

So many other members in the Cloisters had chosen this way out, the pressure had always been too much for a child to endure, in their eyes there was nothing to live for, once a failure, always a failure, society had drilled into them, no rejected member of the Cloisters had gone on to achieve any great achievements, usually bouncing straight out of the Cloisters into the military, hoping to be assigned to a patrol ship in the far reaches of the empire, away from anything which would remind them of the ultimate failure.

She shook her head, sending these thoughts back into the depths of her memory, she stepped forward, a slight jingle of the beads braided into her hair disrupted the silence, even for only a second. She looked totally different than her usual self, her hair was braided in the traditional Impiri way but styled in a modern way, similar to a style she had seen on the streets of Caspiri

She was dressed in a fusion of traditional garments of her tribe mixed with a military-inspired modern look. The mix of the clothing just worked, giving respect to both sides, but also being true to her own beliefs, She remained still, the light from behind her shining allowed great sections of the door to be finally illuminated. She could hear a commotion at the door in front of her was opened, sending in a gush of wind which caught her unaware.

She steadied herself, before she bowed, almost ninety degrees before gesturing behind herself with both of her arms, her palms facing forwards, before looking straight ahead. She blinked quickly as she entered the room, the hall was filled by the cacophony of the crowd, their words unable to be made out, but as she entered the room the conversations stopped, and all attention was on her.

She could feel the gaze of billions on her, hundreds in the chamber itself, and countless billions watching from across the empire as communication drones captured every angle, hovering just out of sight. Their slight hum being the only way of noticing that they were there.

Ambassadors representing protectorate states and first ministers of each member race of the empire stood lining the easterly walkway towards the council, on the opposite side, members of the social elite, heads of industry, members of the multiple regions Orders and a representative organisation of Impiri scholars, stood now in complete silence. At the end of the walkway it opened out into a huge amphitheatre, it was an architectural wonder, the amphitheatre symbolic of the parliaments of old, was lit by the reflected light of the midday sun.

Sitting on the seats of the amphitheatre, four hundred members of the various branches of the government, ministers from each of the ministries and the heads of each of the branches of the military.

In the centre of the amphitheatre sat the heirs to the empire, Caldaran Melathusar Eldarni Amarii and Carlisis Marsakash Tarleya Amarii, Caldaran looked like a younger version of his father, his hair dark brown in comparison to his fathers now white hair. He was young and beautiful, but with an air of being able to handle his own in any situation while his twin Carlisis looked elegant.

She carried herself with ease and grace, she was recognised by many as the most beautiful individual in the empire. She had an unfortunate reputation of not being diplomatic with her words and would often say what was on her mind, in stark contrast to her twin brother.

Far ahead a great circle of individuals stood ready, the council of Tasir, the first part of the ceremony. This would be the last journey she would make, as herself, within the hour she would be joined by forty-seven other voices and would never be alone again.

In unison, a small group of high ranking Impiri began chanting "Makla-hara-Dasho", this outburst catching Reira unaware, causing her to stop walking. Her emotions stsarting to run wild, for an instant. She looked across at them and smiled, not sure of wether this was a chant in support or in protest of her heritage. The leader of this group, a middle-aged man, with piercing blue eyes, reached over to his left wrist and pulled back his sleeve before raising it into the air, followed others in the group.

She looked up, noticing a familiar tattoo on their wrists, they were from her tribe. The single gesture of support removed any doubt from her mind, she didn't do this for herself, she did this for them, all of them. For all Impiri. She nodded her head in acceptance and bowed slightly, as she did this they lowered their hands in accordance with tradition.

Reira reached the centre of the amphitheater, The first minister stood at a podium, he smiled when he saw Reira, he placed his hands on the podium and spoke, reading from a ancient book.

"We, therefore, the Representatives of the Citadel of Caspria , and the Empire in General Congress, Assembled, appealing to the Gods and Goddesses of the universe for the rectitude of our intentions, do, in the Name, and by Authority of the Emperor solemnly publish and declare, That." He paused, before reading again from the ancient book.

"Lady Reira of the House Abrasar, Emiree of the House, High Priestess of the Order of Ehji-Ha, Chosen among Many, Tasir Order of Distinction, Is now wholly proclaimed as The Sacred 48th Commissioner of the Codex, The Elder of the Praetorian Guards, The Minister of the 2nd Legion, The Minister of Truth, The Guardian of Secrets, The High-Arbiter of Justice and Praetor of the Royal House." He proclaimed,

There was was silent, only the sound of bird song in the distance could be heard. He paused for a moment before speaking again.

"You Are Absolved from all Allegiances to anything but the Empire and his Highness the Emperor. You now have full Power to levy War, conclude Peace, contract Alliances, establish Commerce, and to do all other Acts which the Emperor and Empire may require of you, do you understand these roles that have been awarded to you.?"

Reira bowed her head and took a deep breath, as she raised her head she spoke.

"In front of all of you, I Nidiri Reira Abrasar, accept and understand the weight of the responsibilities that I now undertake."

As she finished the members in attendance broke out in applause, causing Reira to blush, knowing that this was the first part of a two hour ceremony.

CHAPTER 22

That Evening

Reira stood outside a dark chamber, a hooded figure stood beside her, their face covered by a silvery mask, its features were blank, the eyes were hidden.

Reira stepped forward as the door to the chamber creaked open, she stepped into the chamber slowly, the sound of her shoes echoing across the chamber as she made every step. Her hearts were beating rapidly in her chest, she had been summoned by the hooded figure who had arrived at her quarters. She hadn't been prepared for this, what ever this was.

Reira glanced around as she walked forward, the chamber was huge, the room was filled with candles, she gasped in amazement, there must have been thousands of them, the flames flickered, casting shadows onto the dark grey stone walls of the chamber. As she walked forward three figures emerged from the darkness beyond the candles, the first was Lady Dhar. She was dressed in all white, her clothing was plain, a far cry from the elaborate and elegantly crafted robes she had worn previously. She staggered forward clutching a cane which helped her keep still. She was followed by Carila and another hooded figure, Carila was held by the arm by the hooded figure, the second she saw Reira she tried to walk towards her, but was instantly pulled back by the hooded figure, this figures mask was solid gold, the polished gold reflected Reira as she looked at the mask.

"Rei..." Carila spoke, before being pulled back, the hooded

figure stepped forward.

"The rite of Tasir is to now be concluded, any failure to follow guidance will result in her death." It threatened, turning towards Carila as it mentioned death.

Reira looked at it nervously

"I thought the rite had been concluded..."

"Not until you know know the truth will it be over" Lady Dhar spoke, her voice frail, her lips trembling.

"My dear, I have to tell you something, so just listen I don't have much time left." She added before stumbling forward.

Reira stepped forward trying to catch her, before being stopped by the hooded figure speaking again.

"Leave her..." it exclaimed, Reira cast her glance at it, her eyes glowing white,

"I will do nothing of the sort, can't you see she is frail..." she exclaimed, her voice resonating throughout the chamber.

"I am nothing of the sort" a voice echoed, catching Reira and Carila by surprise, the voice was deep, ethereal.

Reira turned towards Lady Dhar, looking for some sort of answer, surprised to see her standing in front of her.

"This host may be frail, close to the end she is, but I have been here for countless millennia..." she spoke, the voice was coming from Lady Dhar,

Reira stepped back, shocked.

She knew that voice, it had been a familiar part of her life for countless years.

"I...I remember you..." Reira declared.

Lady Dhar smiled and laughed, the smile causing Reira to gasp with fear.

"I thought you might..."

"Rei, Who is this...?" Carila interjected, before being pulled back by the hooded figure, who placed a blade on her neck, causing her to tighten her neck instantly.

Lady Dhar turned and laughed,

"I will enlighten you all, while there is still time." She spoke.

"Thirty five thousand years ago, a Crystal was found not far from where we are standing right now, when the crystal was excavated it was dropped and cracked into many different shards, the biggest of the shards contained me. I have existed in this form since long before your people knew how to even speak, I've travelled across the stars, before being trapped in the crystal by those who I created."

"But you may know of my name, I've had countless names over the years, Galdiar, Mesmonet the all knowing, Defai the keeper of secrets. But maybe you would know this name; Dakr' Hu Val" she proclaimed proudly.

Reira looked at her in amazement, she paused in thought before speaking, trying to remember the tales told to her by her grandmother when she was a child.

"Dakr' Hu Val, the one who birthed the old gods..." Reira replied nervously.

"Yes, you still remember, I'm glad to know my name hasn't disappeared from your people's culture, I've been keeping an eye on your life since ...well you remember when you first heard my voice."

That's when it dawned on Reira, that voice, the one that she had tried to hide in the back of her mind, the one which kept tormenting her, pushing her to the edge.

"What you have experienced was fragment of my consciousness embedded in that obelisk, I had been waiting for you, waiting for thousands of years, only you would be able to reunite that part of my consciousness with me." She paused, looking at how Reira had been glancing occasionally at Carila, before smiling,

"Years ago I bonded with whom you know as the first codex, in exchange for allowing my consciousness to survive, I've given them countless advantages, their lives have been longer, in greater health, all memories are more vivid. When they were close to death I left them and bonded to another, but as I left them, I took their memories with me, all that they knew was bonded to the next, only the chosen would be strong enough to survive the transfer, and that is why you are here. You see this body is dying, and you will be my host"

"You are the one that Numarii was afraid of..." Reira screamed, her voice full of anger, realising she was the cause of her sisters death.

Lady Dhar smiled at her, mocking her

"Your sister wasn't strong enough, that's the simple truth. That fragment of me was from the darkness part of my essence, that's what I've been seeking, to be whole again. Only someone with your abilities, one born from your blood line would could contain my essence, to hold in the darkness to allow me to be whole again."

"The essence that your sister held was too much for her to deal with, it tormented her, causing her departure. But the darkness that resides within you, you contain it. It burnt through your sisters soul, but didn't destroy you, it brought you to the edge, but you resisted. That's why you life has been guided to this day..."

Reira stood there, silent, trying to take all of this in,

"It was you..., all this time, everything." Reira cried as it all made sense, the death of her sister, the attack on the previous codex in waiting, it was all so she would be here, in this moment.

"It will all make sense to you when I am with you..Do you accept..." she spoke, her voice was stern and forceful.

Reira looked over at Carila, fearing for her safety, as the hooded figure held still held the blade to neck. She smiled a loving smile, hoping to save Carila from any pain, before taking a deep breath.

"Yes..." she added,

As she spoke Lady Dhar screamed, a blood curdling scream, as she screamed a torrent of black vapour poured from her mouth, and out of her eyes, travelling straight towards Reira, who turned towards her. Th vapours pouring into Reira, straight into her chest, disappearing, causing Reira's body to convulse.

As the final vapours entered her body, a massive shockwave emanated from her body, extinguishing the flames on each of the candles around the chamber, knocking Lady Dhar to the floor, by the time she landed on the floor she was already dead. All signs of life had been drained from her already frail body, Reira's eyes were still closed, her hands clenched, she slowly crouched down, and lay on the floor. Her body beginning to shake, first small shakes gradually getting more severe, just before an uncontrollable seizure occurred, her arms flailing around her body, her eyes still forced closed.

The chamber was cast into darkness as clouds covered the only source of light, moments passed before the clouds moved, allowing a stream of moonlight to enter the chamber, by this point, Reira's pale skins had been covered by a dark web of veins, with each second the veins seemed to pulse with liquid. The seizures slowly becoming less severe with each passing second, and as quickly as the seizures became they came to a standstill.

Reira's mouth slowly opened, she slowly exhaled a breath, the air in the chamber was cold, Reira's breath hung in the air in a misty vapour before dissipating,

Within her consciousness Reira could feel everything, instant sadness in the realisation that Lady Dhar was now dead, she could feel her life ending and all of her memories instantly clashing with her own, for a second she could see herself, see the fear in her own eyes, a fear she had never seen on her own face, reminding her of the fear on Zamir's face just before he died.

This realisation shocking her, trying to move Reira struggled, but her body was paralysed. She lay on the floor completely motionless, feeling the vapour slowly course through her body. Her nerves being overwhelmed with sensation, like each of her nerves were being triggered at the highest levels all at once, she screamed out, inside her own mind, the pain unbearable. Her thoughts changed from being afraid to just wanting the pain to end, hoping that she would pass out from the pain, but it continued, with each passing moment the pain becoming slightly less severe.

Memories, countless memories flashed in front of Reira's mind's eye, witnessing thousands of years of history all at once, fragments of conversations made centuries before she was born as vivid as conversations she had days before. These rapid flashes of memories, were disjointed, completely out of sequence, remembering the faces of hundreds of thousands of individuals, remembering intimate details of the lives of people she had never met, but worst of all, the torrential flood of emotions, mixed with her own. Her own emotions were magnified, the joy that she felt was above euphoria, but the sadness that she experienced was enough to crush her soul.

Carila pushed the hooded figure away, causing it to drop the blade and approached Reira's body, which lay motionless on the floor of the chamber, the moonlight highlighting her complexion which had gone from porcelain white to a semi-translucent white, the dark veins pulsing, Carila's eyes filling with tears,

Regret began to sink in, what had she let herself in for, nothing is now private, she thought, all of her secrets, her fears, and desires, not really private, but subject to the scrutiny of the other consciousnesses now residing within her.

Flashes of long-forgotten conversations with her father quickly brought a tear to her eye, not just memories, but feeling as she was present in those moments, listening to her father's voice, as if he was in the room with her, brought her comfort, but also crushing sorrow. Her own memories more vivid than ever, but now joined by so many countless memories and thoughts, seeing flashbacks of events that had taken place thousands of years before she was even born.

A while later

Reira was being helped walk out of the chamber, Carila car fully helped her walk back to her quarters, she would need to rest.

It was easy to see that Reira was having a difficult time facing the reality of her situation, the moment she stepped forward she nearly fell over, her head was a mess and her body looked as if it had been broken in every conceivable way and then just popped back into place, it was a good thing that Carila had been there, even more of a reason why the Codex had an aide, a sole person besides the Emperor who knew the truth about the codex.

While she struggled to walk through the corridor towards her private quarters, members of the inner circle wanted to keep their distance, the uncomfortable smell of burnt skin didn't help the situation, Carila was breathing lightly, as the smell occasionally came close to making her physically sick, at one point she had to cover her nose in order to breathe properly, which didn't help much as the smell tasted worse than it smelled.

Carila helped Reira to a railing at the side of the corridor and that's when she noticed it, the scars on her back were gone, not faded, completely gone, only the tattoos remained, but now they were more prominent than they had ever been before. For an instant Reira cried out in pain, Carila stood behind her and embraced her, understanding that the pain must have been too much for her to bare.

Before she could make a single step into her quarters, she staggered forward and fell to to her knees unable to stand any longer and started to cry, the pain was too much for her to take.

A Few Days Later

The first experience of her new life began with a rapid flash of light, followed by a distant muted whisper this whisper kept repeating before finally dissipating - then nothing. Similar to her memory, self-aware - but empty. a cocoon. A mind, processing all that was around her.

Her body savouring the rush of air as she drew breath, everything new, opening her mouth, and sensing the dryness and starting a rumbling in her throat - nothing but a murmur.

Struggling to adapt to her new surroundings, everything was new, her life beginning again, this time she was no longer herself. She lay motionless almost comatose, her body tried to move, but nothing. her hands flinched, not controlled movements, but attempts to move, even the simplest movement was difficult. She tried to move her arms but her hands were strapped down beside her.

A glass enclosure surround enclosed her, she felt trapped, feeling her breath bounce off the glass and falling back onto her face. She blinked several times as she opened her eyes, her vision began clearing, from a complete haze to a smoother and clearer image, then recognition, momentary recognition, a slight reflection within the glass, herself.

Her eyes were darker than before, still amber coloured but with their sparkle diminished, her pearlescent white hair flowed down cascading over her shoulders, every part of her body ached, every movement was agony, her skin pale and dull, it's radiance lost, somehow, drained away by some unknown force.

She struggled to move again, this time she moved her head less than an inch before nothing, the feeling of something grasping her skull and not letting go... it was then that she realised that a restraint held her in place, within seconds the glass cover of the capsule opened out and a cool rush of air quickly rushed in trying to fill the void in the capsule.

Her skin tensed as the cold air graced her skin, sending a wave of sensations across her body, every sensation was magnified, so much greater than before.

The sensation of the cold air touching her skin forced her to gasp, the first time she heard her own voice since the ceremony, memories of which were fragmented in her mind.

"I'm sorry, but the restraint was needed, your nightmares were so violent, you begin to lash out at others, so it was the only way. The imperial surgeon general suggested it as they only to to stop you from destroying yourself." a voice echoed, but Reira didn't recognise it, flashes of memories blinked into existence but disappeared before she could grasp them.

"Just don't move..., your weak..." she spoke, her voice calm, eloquent and understanding.

Reira didn't know why to trust her, whoever she was, but something told her to trust her. Within seconds her eyes opened wide, forced open by the pain which was shooting throughout her body, a deep pain, the kind of pain which wouldn't go.

She moved her head, in acknowledgement, even though the pain was unbearable but forgetting how she knew what to do, her mind full of echoes, voices, images and sounds, items of knowledge stored within her brain, but most of them closed away, just too far away to grasp.

Reira was reassured, her mind calming after fragments of her memory came into focus, then faded away again, without any context , the images didn't make any sense, a roaring fire followed by a mountainscape, then a clear blue sky, kept filling her mind, then it changed again, she looked down at her hands, covered in blood, then in an instant the blood was gone.

In any normal situation this would be frightening, but nothing, no apprehension, just peace. Reira's mind scattered the imagery of into a thousand pieces before coalescing into an image of the inside of an apartment, this image grew until it enveloped all of her vision, then this vision became reality, it was the room she was lying in.

Reira lifted her head off the cold base of the chamber and spoke,

"Can you help me out of here.." her voice nervous, Carila ran over, grabbing a towel as she passed a table in one quick movement, before offering it to Reira, who was still naked at this time, after she unlatched the first of the wrist supports, followed by the second wrist support.

Reira smiled and nodded her head as she tried to clamber out of the chamber, she managed to lean forwards and tried to step forwards, but nothing, her legs buckling under the stress, Carila grabbed underneath her right arm and helped carry her towards a sofa nearby.

Her muscles aching, Reira screamed, a strong tingling sensation worked its way up her legs, starting at her toes and working its way to her hips, the pain becoming unbearable, she cried out in pain, unable to hold to pain in any longer, she tensed her muscles as the pain sent strong shocks across her body.

Carila placed her on the sofa and grabbed a dressing gown from the table in-front of her and wrapped it around Reira and she writhed with pain, the bright red dressing gown contrasting against Reira's pale skin. "Th..thank you...., Wh...why does it hurt so much.." she winced.

Carila looked at her, her eyes wide, almost about to cry,

"Rei, it was the only way to allow, that thing to bond with you, the doctors said you resisted it, that's why you were lashing out, don't you remember...?"

Reira looked at her, trying to focus through the pain, she clenched her fists, trying to regain control of herself and spoke,

"They are all here, all of them. I hear all of them..and it is here, oh Cari, it's here, it wasn't lying, I'm finding it hard to keep it back there, but it's there." she hissed through the pain.

"The doctor said that the pain will go, it should only be a few hours, your body is just adapting. I have no idea, honestly, I just thought I was going to loose you..."

Reira looked at her, and smiled a forced smile.

"It's gonna take more than this to kill me off, you know

that..."

"Especially when you still owe me dinner.." She retorted, trying to laugh.

Carila looked at her surprised by her response, before smiling,

"I thought you might have forgotten about that..." she mocked, stroking the side of Reira's face with the back of her right hand.

"There is no way I'm forgetting what you promised, no matter if I have forty seven other codexes in here, and the essence of something unbelievably ancient rolling around in my head." She laughed, trying to hide the pain she was experiencing,

Carila smiled,

"As long I as I know I'm talking to you, not who ever else is in there I'm okay with that..."

CHAPTER 23

Three Days Later

12th Hour of the 23rd Day of the 9th Month
IY (Imperial Year) 101

As she walked out towards the podium, Reira stopped, glanced up at a camera drone which was too close for comfort and double blinked, and gestured with her right hand, a simple elegant gesture, the drone then flew off at great speed before crashing into a nearby tree. Moments later another drone took its place. The media outposts were not going to miss a single angle of this event, and She knew it.

Here it would happen, the first Impiri Codex of the Empire, would give an iconic speech. To her left and right were to members of the second legion, lined up in an honour guard, as she walked past each one of them in turn, they turned away from her towards the crowd, the crowd cheering with delight. Reira smiled as she walked through the honour guard. Nothing would ruin this speech, no attacks on her life, or the lives of anyone here. The strongest telepaths and kinetics in the legion were constantly keeping watch, a kinetic field protected Reira, and this was being reinforced by her own abilities. Everyone one of her senses were heightened, she was calm, on the surface, beneath the surface she struggled to keep the darkness at bay. "It could all go wrong now couldn't it" be kept repeating. Imperial Spell-casters were also present, they could be seen at the four corners of the pavilion, each one of them casting protection spells, they moved elegantly as they cast the spells, beneath them arcane symbols circled them on the stone floor, these spell-casters were from the Emperors personal guard, the Veteri - the best of the best, from all corners of the empire.

...

The camera drones captured the embrace between Reira and Minister Clabar Eenkar, aide to the Emperor, as if he was an old acquaintance, a strong two handed handshake followed. Before she was gestured to make her speech.
She stood at the podium, the flood of emotions becoming overwhelming, she sighed as she looked around 'Marii, this is for you..." she thought to herself.

The sun shone through the clouds, casting rays across the pavilion, it was a perfect morning, she looked around, again, all around her many different faces looked anxiously up at her. She glanced over at the crowd to her left, pausing for an instant, for a moment, Numarii was looking back at her, having not aged since Reira last saw her, she smiled at her and bowed slightly before disappearing into the crowd. Reira's hearts raced, she continued to look in that direction, noticing Apairtae standing in the crowd, in traditional Impiri clothing, her wrist bare, only her Red Tattoo was visible. She smiled as she glanced down at her wrist, before smiling back at Reira.

Reira cleared her throat before speaking, her voice clear and precise.

“We will not fail we will not falter we will not disappear into this dark night that looms over us.” She paused, the crowd stood in stunned silence. The translators taking a few moments to translate what she had said. Reira looked down at the crowd, noticing the confused looks appearing on their faces as the translations came through. Reira’s throat tightened, causing her to cough gently before beginning again.
“Some of you have heard rumours, I have been advised to stay silent about this matter, but with good conscious I cannot remain silent...”, the recording drones lowered, trying to catch every expression that appeared across her face.
Countless billions stood in silence across the empire. Stopping what they were doing for a moment. Reira’s gaze tracked down, looking at the podium in front of her. Her speech was lying in front of her. The words written on the page were meaningless right now. The words began to blur as she got lost in her train of thought, she could betray her own feelings and write what was written, or be true to herself.

‘May the goddesses be the ones to judge my actions’ she thought to herself as she raised her gaze towards the crowd again. Seeing past the drones and looking at the eager looking expression of the members of the crowd.
“Yes, There was an attempt to silence my voice, but I stand here before you. As determined as ever to serve you, the people. I may not be as wise as my predecessor, but that will come with time and your support.” Her hearts racing, the cacophony of

her own heartbeats caused her to pause and take a deep breath. "I wish to thank you all for being here, and that is a personal thank you, from the bottom of my hearts, I feel such pride seeing you all here. But this thanks isn't just for today." the crowd cheered.

Carila, who was standing off to the side in the area reserved for dignitaries, closed her eyes and listened to the words, she knew how nervous Reira had been, she had helped her calm her nerves earlier in the morning, this part of the speech was different, it came from deep inside her, these words were not scripted, and her nerves were gone.

"The history of my people is a fragile thing, our links to our past kept from us by time and", she paused, reconsidering her next word before continuing.

"Long ago people thought my kind would be wiped from this universe, but from that darkness light came." She paused, she flickered her eye lashes, trying to force back tears. "You were that light" she opened her arms, gesturing to the crowd, who were enjoying all of it in silence.

"This shall never be forgotten, but this empire has given us, and me so much more than we ever deserved. You welcomed us as members of the empire in the early days, before the fall, you helped us settle out own differences and we thank you for that", she smiled and gestured out with open arms again to the crowd who erupted into applause, she gestured for silence and the crowd quietened.

"Many say this darkness sleeps inside all of us , well I say it lives in the hearts of those who wish to destroy what the goddesses have created." She paused in thought before continuing.

"Even if the destruction comes from within ourselves, The fighting between our kind must end now, it has been many generations since the civil war between my kind, but we cannot forget the sacrifices that we all made... Centych Vale, Ledo Braji, Hysio Denau, Carmiya Nalle', Aurin Dystraay and Tylo Anita Lanan Abrasar. a few amongst countless others who died to we could have the freedoms we have now, but the grudges between us still remain, Otherwise we will be the last generation and none of us wish for that." She paused, trying to push back tears before continuing.

"I call for the houses red white blue black purple turquoise and pink to find it in your hearts to put down old grudges and grievances which we all had with each other. It's been 35,000 years since we lost our home, has't it been long enough to forget about these ridiculous quarrels. I can remember when I was young being told of the horrors of the darkness when Imperis fell, the billions who sacrificed themselves so some of us could survive." She smiled, lookingas tthe adoring crowd, who were stunned into silence, Reira could notice the drones flying around recording everything.
"You stood with us, you welcomed us. We were refugees, we didn't have a home. We were a mess, 754,912 of us survived, we thought we were alone. But we were wrong, we were never

alone, we had a home, a different home, but a home nevertheless". The crowd were still silent, the drones captured every moment of this, in all angles, a full holographic recording would be used in schools across the empire within the coming days.

"We were scattered across the empire, things were difficult, but you made us feel like we could belong, and things were okay for a while. Then those old grudges came back, we started fighting amongst ourselves, there was disinterest." She stopped, then voice in her head spoke,

"Go on, tell them, show them what your capable of..." it whispered, for once the voice in her head wasn't trying to destroy her, but was guiding her, for once she chose to it.

"The stories of the darkness who were soulless creatures who only knew how to inflict pain on us, were not forgotten, but relegated to stories we told our children, it wasn't always easy being different, our culture was embraced by some and rejected and alienated by others, but we survived." A few members of the crowd cheered, before realising and stopping to allow Reira to continue.

"Why did we survive, because of you, the citizens of this great empire, and I thank you. And that if why I wanted to give back to you, why my life will be devoted to serving your needs, as the 48th Codex I will advise and council our Emperor and his successors in every breath I take until I leave this existence and am returned to the flames."

The crowd were silent, Reira sunk back into herself, her hearts

began beating faster within her chest. The silence deafening until it was broken by a single clap. Reira looked out into the crowd, it wasn't there, she looked over to her right and was taken by surprise in what she saw, the single clap was then repeated, in slow succession. Reira was not surprised by the clapping but by who was clapping, Lord Arkin was clapping, an actual look of happiness flashed across his face.
Reira bowed gracefully and he nodded his head slowly. After this the clapping travelled across the crowd.

Reira looked ahead, and the crowd went wild. Overhead six ancient Impiri cloud skimmers blazed a trail of red smoke before travelling in six different directions, the smoke slowly dissipating.

Reira turned around and looked for Carila, once she saw her she smiled. She needed a familiar face to keep her grounded.

CHAPTER 24

23rd Hour of the 23rd Day of the 9th Month
IY (Imperial Year) 101

Imperial Library, Second Floor.

He lowered his gaze, slowly, and looked over the city, he squinted, rubbing his eyes with his right hand, now he could make out the glory of his city, his capital, his home, he could see the rooftops of residential buildings. The spires of the temples to the countless gods and goddesses, he could see she patches of darkness where the public parks were, only being faintly lit by street lights, which he couldn't make out due to the tops of trees blocking his view.

He turned around, looking back into the library, the walls of the library reached as far as the eye could see, this library had taken five thousand hands to create, and even here the Emperor felt humble.

He slowly staggered towards a table, on the surface of the table was a large book, move than a meter in length, and more than six inches thick, the boom was spread open in the middle, the emperor looked at the book, and coughed, covering his mouth with his hand, she stopped coughing, a surprise express flashed across his face as she looked at the back of his hand, a splatter or blood graced the back of his hand, he turned towards the door, and staggered forward again, coughing as he walked, spluttering blood onto the floor as he walked, he grabbed hold of his thoat as he coughed, with each successive cough he coughed up more blood, before falling onto the floor as he tried to grab hold of the handle on the library door.

Meanwhile across the citadel in the residential quarters.

Carila sat at the table, putting the fork down at the side plate.
"Rei, I don't know how you managed to get these ingredients this far from my home. But that was great. I'm Halaxian and I can't even get Geltret eggs this fresh, how did you manage it..." she beamed as she wiped her mouth with a cloth.
Reira sat across from her looking at her and smiled.
"A small gift from the Halaxian Ambassador, a selection of Halaxi delicacies, and I couldn't think of anyone better to share them with..."
Carila laughed openly, taking Reira by suprise,
"Whats so funny, what did I do now..." Reira exclaimed.
"Really Rei, normally a lover would cook Geltret eggs the way you did, is there something your not telling me..?." she mocked, causing Reira to sit up startled, blushing instantly.
"..no...no..., that wasn't my..." she nervously replied.
Carila stood up grabbing hold of Reira's hand and pulled her up, Carila stood in front of her,
"I'm not sure if it was the wine, the amazing first course or those Geltret eggs, more than likely the wine but..." she paused, now even more obviously intoxicated from the wine from earlier that night, her speech slightly slurred.
"I can't hide it any more...you know I did it don't you..."
"What do you mean Cari, I don't follow..."
"You got the news the same as I did, the news about Rako, you

know..." she gestured by dragging her outstretched thumb across her neck.

"I know about that, I can't even imagine that happening...but what do you mean you did it..., did what..."

"I did it, I ended his life...for you...I knew you couldn't do it, and I wasn't going to let him get away with it..." Carila replied, unable to hide it any longer.

Reira eyes opened wide at this revelation, she stepped back, shocked by the brazen way that Carila had just confessed.

"You can't have..., no of course not..." Reira stammered, she looked at Carila, who's demeanour changed, tears started to run down her cheeks.

"Rei, I'm not lying here, I did it, I did it for you..."

"Why...why did you do it..., why did you end his life..." Reira questioned, her voice concerned and laced with fear.

Carila turned around, not being able to face Reira's disappointed look which had appeared on her face.

"To protect you..." she murmured, Reira didn't catch all of this reply, grabbed Carila and turned her around so she could face her...

"I did it all to protect you..." she spoke again, trying to wipe the tears from her face.

"Why???" Reira screamed in shock.

Carila tried to turn away, but Reira stopped her this time,

She held Carila's face with both of her hands, causing Carila to close her eyes,

"Because I love, you...." she whispered, causing Reira to drop her hands to her side, taken aback by her response.

"Cari, what do you mean....you...you love me?." Reira's eyes wide with amazement, staring at Carila, who stretched out her arm, caressing Reira's cheek with the back of her hand. Reira pulled away, hesitantly, trying to make sense of why she had said those things.

They stood less than half a meter from each other, Carila looked at her, smiling nervously, trying not to cry. biting the right side of her bottom lip., with her other hand she ran her fingers through her hair, before stopping, she turned around walked the small distance between the kitchen and the bedroom, and sat on the side of Reira's bed, gesturing for Reira to sit next to her.

"Let me explain..." she whispered.

Reira stood there in shock, had she really heard those words from Carila.

Carila pulled her legs up crossing them, next to a spread-out blanket, covering the bed.

Reira stepped forward, slowly, unsure of herself.

"I wasn't going to tell you, you know that...?" Carila confessed, while nervously playing with her hair.

"Why not." Reira replied instantly, As soon as the words were out of her mouth, Reira regretted them.

"What do you mean, you weren't going to tell me...I mean you said, those words."

Carila looked at Reira, a concerned look flashed across her face, her shoulders sank.

"Rei, you can't even say it, can you..."

"Those words..." she murmured,

"I said, I love you, and your too embarrassed to say the words I said to you..." Carila snapped., taking Reira by surprise, causing her to stop walking towards the bed.

Reira stopped, squatted down and looked at Carila in the face, placing her hands on Carila's legs.

"I'm sorry, it's just...a bit of a surprise" Reira spoke, her voice shaking with nerves, a small smile appeared on her face as Carila looked at her, before nervously lowering her gaze.

"I never expected" she added.

"Well, I had noticed some things over the years, but I thought I just misread the situation." Reira questioned.

"Why did you think you misread it?," she replied.

"Be honest...." She added.

"Because it's me" Reira asked, dropping her gaze again, she couldn't see why someone would love her, she was too flawed in her own eyes, she never thought highly of herself, she felt the only thing she was respected for was her heritage and her position as a high priestess.

"Couldn't you tell, I've been like this around you for for years...," Carila replied.

"I'm afraid of my own feelings," Reira said shyly as she stood up, turning away from Carila, who immediately got up and followed her, Reira looked out of the window, the moon light illuminated the room, Carila stood behind her. Illuminated by the light from the moon.

"Rei, why are you afraid of your feelings. What do you have to fear?" Carila asked as she placed her hand on Reira's back, the sensation of someone touching her back, sent a tingle down her spine. She turned around, looked at Carila.

"I'm afraid of what I'll do if I let my feelings out..." Reira cried,

trying to restrain herself.
"Rei, it's me. You know you can tell me anything..." Carila exclaimed softly.
"I've known for years, the way you look at me, the way you've held me when I've had enough and wanted to end it all. I thought it was all in my head. My mind playing tricks on me." Reira proclaimed as she stood close to her.
"I didn't want to ruin the friendship we have, based on me reading into something too much, it's got me into trouble before" she lamented.

Carila grabbed Reira's hand, pulling it close to her own heart.
"You can feel that can't you. My heart is going crazy right now. Because I love you, I always have..."
"Rei, you didn't read it wrong, you read me so well, but why can't you let your own feelings out"
Reira looked at her, ashamed of the answer she was about to give.
"In case you rejected me, I couldn't say those words to you, if I lost you it would ruin me..." she looked down, ashamed of what she had said.

"Again with those words, what's wrong Rei, can't you even say those words." Carila snapped, dropping Reira's hand instantly, her own emotions were so close to the surface tears began to form.

Reira stepped forward, grabbing hold of Carila, by her face, cupping her face with both of her hands.

"I love you, is that what you want me to say...." Reira exclaimed, her breathing shallow and labored.

"I admit it, Cari, I love you..." her voice trailed off, a look of realisation flashed across her face as she listened to the words she had just spoken.

She turned around and made her way to quickly to the kitchen, Carila following behind her.

"What's wrong..." she spoke nervously,

Reira stood at a cupboard, opening its door and pulling out two small glasses, setting them on a table beside her.

"With all of this, I need a drink, won't you join me...?" Reira spoke, as she brought out an already opened bottle of wine, before slowly smiling at Carila.

"I'll have a small one..." Carila replied, noticing Reira's smile. Reira carefully opened the bottle, pouring its dark red contents into the two glasses.

Reira handed her a glass. Carila took a small sip, the wine would only stifle her senses, which were on fire, her mind full of thoughts and feels she wanted to express.

Reira distracted herself by looking at the label on the wine bottle.

"Rei, your not just saying that you love me because I forced you to say it."

Reira was silent, lost in thought staring and Carila.

"Rei...?" She called out, snapping Reira out of her thoughts.

She never considered that Carila might be thinking the same, for her to be someone's choice.

"No, I was just so afraid to say anything, I can't loose you" she spoke, her mind drifting again.

'Okay' she thought: 'Right here, right now, I am in my home away from home, with someone who has confessed a lot of things to me tonight, she saved me from Rako, by committing murder, I can't even bring myself to think that about Cari, but she did it for me, I mean she killed someone because she loves me. She wanted to protect me, save me from myself. Maybe I can forget about that, in time. I admit I had wanted to end his life myself, but she stopped me from loosing myself to the darkness, she chose to seek out that darkness herself, even now I'm still in awe of her. I mean she is so painfully beautiful, when she touches me it sends shivers down my spine, no one has ever made me fell this way before, I never let them, why was I hiding, who was I hiding from' she thought to herself.

'You were hiding from yourself, just admit it' a voice rang out in her mind, that voice from deep inside her mind reared it's head again.

'Do it, show her how you really feel...' it whispered.

Reira made her way back to the bedroom, standing at the window looking out into the citadel, Carila following behind, carrying the bottle of wine and her glass.

Reira stared out at the citadel, a thousand lights of various colours lit the citadel, The sprawl of the rest of the capital expended as far as the eyes could see. Reira was lost in thought, admiring the vast amounts of time and effort and imagination and ingenuity that created this city.

"Thank you for being here with me," Reira spoke, for the first time in ages she wasn't nervous.

Carila sat her glass down on the floor beside the bed and gestured for her to come over. It is a sign which, despite the decades since anyone had flirted with her, not since she was eighteen. Reira could still read them perfectly.
Her hearts racing, should she turn back towards the window, ignore the thoughts running through her mind, or should she finally let herself love someone, to be touched in that way, a way she had rejected for most of her life. Maybe because they were not the right person, they weren't Carila and she was in front of her, beckoning her to join her.

Then that's the way it will be, she decided, taking a nervous step towards her, watching as Carila's eyes lit up. This experience that was so out of character it was giving her a rush more thrilling than anything she had ever felt. Nothing in comparison made her feel this way, not even the hunts for the Xanti gave her the adrenaline rush that she was currently experiencing, the scales on her back tingled, the sensation driving her wild.

Reira took a large gulp of the remaining wine from her glass before setting it down on the next floor next to Carila's.
As she stood up from placing the glass on the floor she was met by Carila, standing in front of her, she grabbed at Reira's hips pulling her close, mere moments later
Carila's mouth met hers. Her lips were soft and strong, pressing hers open, pausing for a moment then pulling away, an invitation to her mouth to push back against hers. Instead, Reira draw back.

"Are you sure about this," Reira whispered

"Yes" she mouthed,

Carila kissed her again, her tongue reaching just the tip of hers, caressing her and then withdrawing, inviting her to follow to finish what had been started.

Reira's instincts followed with an ease she had never known she was capable of. The lead and the follow of their kissing was seamless. She felt their breath merge, the air flowing between them warmed by their bodies. Reira looked at her, catching Carila's gaze as they locked eyes with each other.

Carila's thumbs slowly and carefully stroked Reira's cheekbones, her fingers tangled in Reira's silvery hair, finding the edges of her ears, the tender spot where jaw met the neck, she carefully caressed it, causing Reira to close her eyes.

Reira had never felt anything like this before, the sensations traveling up and down her scales was driving her wild. She could feel Carila's hand work it way from her face down her shoulder and around to her back, slowly caressing the ridges around the scales through the thin cotton of her shirt. Reira reached her arm around Carila pulling her closer. She was having trouble concentrating, the sensations of being kissed by her best friend. Countless thoughts ran through her mind.

'What am I doing? she thought 'I am kissing her, this woman, and soon I will be...experiencing even more? She had never experienced anything like this before, she had never been with anyone, this was not her world. But now it would be, she cast aside her reservations at that moment As she felt Carila's hands are moving up under her shirt, searching for bare skin, slowly caressing the ridges again, the gentle strokes causing Reira to moan.

Reira couldn't control herself, she moved her own hand and carefully caressed Carila's chest, stopping at her heart, feeling it beat against her hand, the beats were rapid, the heat emanating from her body warmed Reira.

She began to slide to the side, Carila following her lead, now they were both lying on the bed, in a passionate embrace.

Reira stopped, "I don't know what I'm doing" she whispered.

"Just do what feels natural...don't worry" Carila replied.

Reira drew herself back, just far enough that she could admire Carila, she lay there looking at her. she looked at her emerald green eyes, mesmerised by their beauty, she adored her, her tousled dark hair, those beautiful lips, dark brows shadowing those awe inspiring green eyes like emeralds lit by rays of sun. She stared into Carila's eyes, smiling peacefully.

"Cari," Reira whispered, Calling her name now felt different, more personal, her name flowed from her mouth elegantly.

"Yes Rei, What is wrong..." Carila mouthed.

"Nothing, I'm just unsure, I don't even know what feels natural...." Reira replied, causing Carila to smirk,

"Then maybe I'll have to teach you a few things" before leaning over the small gap between them, planting a delicate kiss on Reira's lips. Taking her by surprise,

Carila let herself lay back, as Reira moved closer before straddling her waist.

Reira closed her eyes as she could feel Carila's hands move under her skirt, her delicate fingers tracing the lace edges of her underwear, before slowly moving downwards, then further down, further in. Reira moaned as she felt Carila's thumbs press on her, by now her scales were tingling, out of control, never had she experienced pleasure like this, this was what she had denied herself for all these years.

Reira opened her eyes slowly, staring down at her, Carila glancing up at her seeming to ask for permission, Reira nodded her head slowly, placing her hands on Carila's shoulder to allow her to lift her weight as Carila drew her underwear down, She closed her yes as she felt them slide off, manuvering herself until they were off.

Reira straightened up, opening her eyes again, seeing Carila looking at her mischievously. The feeling of her own smile which was slowly making its way across her face, made her think of running away from all of this, to spend all of eternity with Carila.

"You are beautiful," Reira gushed, admiring Carila.

"So are you."

"I'm naive and innocent," Reira replied, dismissing it. "Thats all."

"Not to me, I couldn't travel across the empire for anyone, I only did it so I could be closer to you." Carila replied before placing her hands under Reira's shirt again, placing her hand on her torso.

Reira leaded over, shortening the distance between them. Carila wraps one long arm around Reira's back, cradling her, and with the other hand began to stroke her inner thigh, caressing it open. Reira closed her eyes, savouring the sensation, feeling Carila touching her, touching her in ways she had never experienced, wanting to reciprocate those feelings with Carila growing stronger inside her, with every passing moment.

She felt Carila's fingers pressing gently against her most intimate areas, the sensations of pleasure travelling across her body, mixed with the sensations she could feel from the wine coursing through her body in conjunction with the heat radiating from Carila's body, she was in paradise.
These sensations went into overdrive when Carilas fingers on her other hand slowly caressed the bottom scales which ran down her spine. Her scales were the most sensitive now, her body began heating up, she could feel the burning deep inside her core, this was normal, but different this time. The voice inside her,which she had managed to suppress thins long was screaming.
"Finally, go with it, do those things that you've wanted to do, those things you try and hide from yourself..."the voice laughed, causing Reira to stop for a moment, smiling to herself, before thinking.
"Okay...lets do this...".

They embraced each other with a uncontrollable passion, Carila pulled her closer, kissing her passionately. She exhaled in pleasure as Carila lead, Reira becoming submissive. For the first time in ages, she was finally free Reira thought to herself, she felt liberated, finally releasing this part of her personality from its confinement deep within her subconscious.

Her breathing became shallow, sometimes unable to catch her breath. Carila's hands gliding effortlessly across Reira's toned body, she began arching her back as Carila's hands caressed her, her back arching as far as it would allow. Luckily the bedroom was far from the door, masking the noises which they were both making.

Reira's eyes rolled back, becoming white, startling Carila as she felt them both lift off the bed, and into the air, before her urges took control, pulling Reira closer to her, Reira's hands ran over Carila's hips before nervously pulling her closer before sliding her hands gently across her abdomen, up towards her breasts, pulling her nipple slowly towards her mouth before kissing it gently, ending waves of pleasure through out Carila's body, her hands moving down Carila's arms and grasping her hands tightly.

Some time later,

Carila lay naked on the bed, clutching hold of Reira in a passionate embrace, their breathing laboured and shallow as she disconnected their embrace, Reira slowly kissing Carila's neck, before resting her head on her chest, shuddering in her arms. Carila slowly running her finger up her spine., brushing against the scales on her back which were now dark blue, almost black in colour.

Eventually Reira opened her eyes, finds Carila looking at her.

"I didn't expect that!"
"What didn't you expect" Reira quizzed lightly.
"That, I didn't expect you to find that...so easily and quickly"
"I'm a quick learner, you know that" Reira smirked, before laughing. Her laugh infectious, causing Carila to laugh openly.

After a while Reira paused, sighed, and then started to speak,
"I...I?." She shuttered, her mind still going crazy with thoughts, she clenched her fists,
"I don't know what happened..?, what did we just do..." She stammered,
"I think I told you that I love you, and you said the same, then we spent the night together..." Carila joked, laughing slightly, before stopping, noticing the concerned look on Reira's face.
"That what I'm talking about, ...I'm not sure...I can...." she sheepishly replied.
Carila's face, expressed her concern, she knew what was going to come.
"I can't love you. I don't know how..." Reira cried, brushing her hair away from her face, looking at Carila
"But Rei..," Carila implored, her happiness broken, the moment they had shared together had now explicitly ended. As she spoke she tried to lift herself up from lying on the bed.
"I'm sorry..." Reira blubbered, tears running down her cheeks,
"If I knew how..." she added.
"You broke my heart, when you said that, and all you can say is sorry...?" Carila exclaimed, holding her hands up towards Reira, tears running down her cheeks.
"I've never told you that secret, it was too painful to express, I

don't know how to love anyone,...I couldn't risk losing you". Carila looked at Reira in surprise.

"Are you being serious?" Carila replied.

"It's unbelievable, you blame yourself for so much, you give yourself one moment of happiness, and you think that if you love me, you'll risk my life..."

"It's the only way to keep you safe..." Reira pleaded.

"How about I show you what it is really like to love someone, when you don't care about the consequences of loving someone...the fact that you would even kill..." she paused. Reira looked at her intensely, the memories from the confession earlier that night rushed back.

"...to keep them safe..." Carila added.

"Cari, I know what you did, I'm still trying to come to terms with that, maybe in time I'll forget that, but this."

"Just give me the chance to show you that this can work..." Carila implored, trying to force a smile.

Reira looked at her, trying to gauge her emotions, her own emotions were still in a state of flux, her own thoughts clashing with the other forty seven identities, and the dark voice inside her, tempting her.

"Go on, there is nothing to loose, next time, let me out and we can show her what fun really is...", Reira smiled devilishly as she looked at Carila.

"Okay...lets give it a shot..." she spoke, causing Carila to instantly smile, Carila leaned across and planted a delicate kiss on Reira's lips.

"We have some unfinished... things to attend to..." she whispered as she broke the kiss, just before she was about to kiss her again the intercom buzzer sounded, causing her to sigh. “You’re Eminance, I have a priority one message to give you, can you please come to the door.” The intercom relayed. It was the guard from outside her quarters, his voice sounding different than it usually did, this startling Reira.

Reira rolled over, reaching for the intercom,

“I’ll be out in a minute, just...” looking at Carila, who had already sat up and was dressing herself.

“Getting ready...give me a minute...” she added as she quickly grabbed at her clothes which were scattered on the floor beside the bed, quickly putting them on, while trying to fix her hair, which had become disheveled in the earlier activities.

Moments later,

Reira opened the door, the guard stood to attention, before speaking.

“Your Eminence…” the guard spoke, his voice trembling, he was having trouble speaking.

“Lieutenant…, whats wrong, whats with the disturbance at this hour?”

“At 01:01 Imperial Time this morning. Emperor Valnesh was found …” he stopped, coughed and tried to shake himself right before adding nervously.

“Ma’am, The Emperor is Dead…” causing Reira to instantly break composure, a tear quickly ran down her left cheek.

“has everyone been told…?” Reira replied harshly, trying to hide her emotions by being formal.

“..The Imperial Chamberlain and the Master of Imperial Arms were informed immediately.” He replied, choking back his own tears Reira turned around, looked at an illuminated clock on the wall, before replying.

"its been 3 hours, why the delay in informing his highness's Codex..I need to pay my condolences to his heir." Reira questioned, noticing Carila make her way closer to the door to hear the conversation.

"The Imperial Praetor was also informed, as is protocol, thats whats caused the delay."

"Has his heir been informed?" Reira quizzed, "of course they have" she thought to herself the moment she asked the question.

"The Emperor never decreed who was his heir after the death of the crown prince. Because of this, Imperial Lawyers and the office of the Imperial Praetor were consulted." As he spoke, two members of the Emperors guard walked down the corridor, there opulently decorated armour was easy to notice, there armour was emblazoned with the imperial crest. In front of them was Dolek Saminar, The Imperial Chamberlain, as he approached Reira could see that his eyes were red, remnants of tears still hung on his eye lashes. As he walked he carried a large bound book. The guard stopped speaking as the Chamberlain and the Emperors Guard approached., stepped back and to the left as the Chamberlain drew closer.

"Your Eminence, I'm guessing you have heard the news of the sad passing of our Emperor, 'May his Light Be Reborn Rejuvenated' the guards added, just as the Emperor was mentioned.

"As you may or may not be aware, the Emperor had not

completed his grieving for the crown prince and had not named his successor. This is why I am here."

"I had to consult with The Master of Imperial Arms, The Imperial Praetor, Minister Clabar Eenkar. They have all agreed that in this time of mourning we need tradition, a symbol of the Empire, someone the people will follow in mourning.

"As is precedent, in Imperial Canon Law, Article 246, Paragraph 01, Subsection 21B, and I quote "During times of a vacant throne (Death of an Emperor / Empress, with no named Crown Prince/Princess) a rite of ascension will be overseen. The Role of Imperial Arbiter and Protector of the Empire will be…" he stopped.

"You can see where I'm going your Eminence. , but to be clear. As of the death of the Emperor, you are as of now, Arbiter of the Crown." he proclaimed.

"Of of now 03:43 Imperial Time on the 24th Day of the 9th Month of IY 101." he paused.

"IY 0" he corrected himself nervously, trying quickly to recover from the error.

"And in accordance with such a precedent, you are to be hereby styled as Her Imperial Grace, Defender of the Empire and The Faith." His voice trailed off, trying to keep his emotions in check.

As this moment the guards stood to attention, and saluted. Reira was speechless. Carila stood behind her, she had been listening to everything.

"I, Nidiri Reira Abrasar, The Sacred 48th Commissioner of the

Codex hereby swear to uphold the honour of the Empire until the Rite of Arbitration and the Rite of Ascension has been completed." Reira spoke, her hand trembling on the top of the book, as she pulled back her hand the guards saluted again. Before turning around and standing to attention.

"What's going to happen Rei?" Carila spoke, her voice trembling, her breathing shallow, her eyes fixed on Reira. The situation overwhelming her.

This surprised Reira more than anything else, the effect of this on Carila shook her to the core, she was normally the rational one, the once whom nothing would shake, but now the tremble in her voice was more powerful than any word.

Reira sighed, a thousand thoughts going through her mind, from fear to pure dread.

'I told you that things were going to change, didn't I' the voice inside her head screamed out,

'I told you that you would have to listen to me if you wanted to survive, I'm sure you need me now' it added.

"I don't know…something is wrong here, I feel a darkness coming, I don't know how I know this, but this isn't going to be easy…" she said, the voice inside her head laughing before adding. 'Now it begins...'

To Be Continued…

The Twin Thrones
Book 2 of the Redemption Trilogy
Coming Soon

ABOUT THE AUTHOR

Thomas Rai can usually be found either reading a book, frantically writing down notes for an ' idea that must be kept', or travelling. If reading, that book will more likely be a gripping thriller or epic fantasy saga.

Writing a novel was always on his bucket list, and eventually, with The Darkness Within, it became a reality. The Darkness Within is the first book in his Redemption Trilogy. When not absorbed in the latest gripping page-turner, Thomas loves cooking, travelling, enjoys photography, history, and otherwise spends far too much time at the computer. He lives in The UK.

ACKNOWLEDGEMENTS

I would like to express my gratitude to the many people who saw me through this book; to all those who provided support, talked things over, read, offered comments, and assisted in the editing and proofreading.

I would like to thank my publishing platform for enabling me to publish this book.

Above all I want to thank my family, who supported and encouraged me in spite of all the time it took me away from them. It was a long and difficult journey for them. But I thank you for allowing me to express myself this way.

I would like to thank Alice Stocker, Rosie Jones, Arjun Chohan and Assad Chaudhry for helping me in the process of editing and for countless others for being beta readers.

Last and not least: I beg forgiveness of all those who have been with me over the course of the years and whose names I have failed to mention.

ACKNOWLEDGEMENTS

Did you enjoy this book? You can make a big difference...

A Review can be the most powerful thing for an author. Especially a new author like myself. It helps an author like me reach other readers like you.

An honest review of this book could help bring its attention to other likeminded readers.

If you've enjoyed this book I would be very grateful if you could spend just five minutes leaving a review (no matter how long or short) on the books Amazon page.

Just search for the books ISBN (located on the copyright page)

I would again like to thank you for reading this book and for allowing me to tell you this story.

And now a reward for finishing this book...

A sneak peak at the prequel...just turn the page and enjoy.

SNEAK PEAK AT THE PREQUEL WHITE HOUSE, RED HEARTS

Prologue

"Your home is a wreck, you could of at least cleaned the kitchen." She scowled, looking around at the mess around her.

"Had I known I was going to have unexpected visitors breaking down my door at three o'clock I would have." Suriema replied as she picked up the overturned chair, righting it before grabbing hold of a brush, wanting to brush the broken glass away. The floor was covered in broken glass, not a single part of the floor was safe.

"And where's the tea?, I can't find anything in here..." she retorted, Namit always trying to attempt to lighten the situation.

"So what were they after this time....?"

Old Kalsuur down the street suspected that I was hiding Makhara - Sandy Blood in here, really me, hiding those Makhara bastards. Not likely." Suriema retorted, her brown furrowed.

"How do you know it was her ?" Namit's voice desperately inquisitive.

"Said a concerned citizen had informed them, of course there could be someone else, but I doubt it, you know what she's like. She accused Mr Jasetu of being a Makhara, that he had lied about being unmarked and had his mark removed." She scowled.

"As I said, she's the only choice, I'll have words with her, if she dares show her face." She angrily replied after picking up a cup, its hand had been broken.

'That was my favourite cup.' She thought as she looked at it before throwing into the nearby trash.

Across Town

Kalidral turned shyly towards her father, her hands behind her back, clutching her hands together. He turned as he put his gloves away in his draw, before shutting the draw. He carefully glanced down at her, and smiled a nervous smile

"It's okay, I made sure they won't bother you again...", he patted her on the head, his hands large and dry, his knuckles were inflamed, the skin pink instead of its usual light tones, Just under the cuffs of his shirt a dark blue tattoo could be faintly made out.

Kalidrals breaths came as fast as she was walking, The existed the room, turning back towards her father, smiling a nervous smile before closing the door behind her. The sound of footsteps echoed across the hall.

"Who is that?." she thought to herself, she nervously walked towards the back of the house, towards the kitchen, her mother was in there cooking something, she could hear the laughing of her mother and sister talking, the clatter of knives chopping on the wooden counters.

As she entered the kitchen she turned around, looking down the corridor towards the room her father was in. A tall young gentleman was standing at the door talking to her father.

This made made a chill go down her spine, she couldn't

understand why, but she was afraid of this man. He spoke well, dressed immaculately, but something about his demeanour scared her, she stared at him for a second, before he noticed, causing her to turn sharply towards the kitchen and walk into the doorway. Her hearts pounding, she sighed.

Kalidral was still nervous, her hands trembled as she carried the drinks tray with two hands, to make sure she didn't drop it, why was she the one to have to take these drinks to her father and that man. Just the thought of seeing that man again sent chills down her back.

She reached the door, while holding the tray with one hand she struck the door with her other hand...

"Father..." she called out, but nothing...

"Father..." she cried out again. This time the door swinging open.

www.ingramcontent.com/pod-product-compliance
Lightning Source LLC
Chambersburg PA
CBHW020257030826
48979CB00026B/1331/J

* 9 7 8 1 9 1 6 1 1 7 1 2 9 *